Black Rock

Mary Alice Hawthorne

Book One

There's no place like home.

—*Judy Garland*, The Wizard of Oz

Chapter I

TOMMY SAT AT the girls' table fighting back tears, gritting his teeth. His mother had insisted that he wear a fuzzy pink bunny costume to the first birthday party he'd ever been invited to. The uncomfortable young boy kept pulling down long, fuzzy ears over his face so that no one from his school would recognize him. The girls at the table had tried to get him to talk and play games with them, but much to Tommy's relief, they eventually left him alone. Tommy hung his head in shame and prayed the party would soon be over.

He'd been the center of his family's universe until he started the first grade, but once he was there, the other kids singled him out, and he did not like it one bit. He was the pudgy little know-it-all nobody wanted to be friends with, and it hurt him that the other kids didn't like him. Recess at school was awful, and no one had invited him to any of their parties until now. Tommy was the new kid and didn't fit in with the other kids.

Tommy knew all too well that he was the outsider, the weirdo, and if the classmates who picked on him found out that his mother had made him wear a bunny suit, he would never live it down. Since he started school, Tommy had become a pariah, and he usually sat alone at the lunch table and watched the popular kids from across the cafeteria as they laughed and had fun, all the while wishing he was one of them. Tommy had tried to hide the invitation from his mother and Nana Harris and was mortified when Nana found it inside his spelling book. Since it was the week before Easter, brightly colorful eggs covered the party invitation, and when his mother realized one of his classmates had invited Tommy to a birthday party, she was overjoyed. In fact, his mother, Babe, was much more excited than Tommy was about the invite.

"Your first party! How exciting!" Babe cheered, and she could hardly contain her enthusiasm. "I'm so happy you are finally making friends."

Babe worried about him. Ever since her husband had hired Nana Harris, she didn't have much say about her son's upbringing. The only children Tommy had ever been around before he started school at St. Luke's were the ones he'd met in his Church of Christ Sunday school class.

"I don't want to go," he protested to his mother. Tommy was still wearing the gray pants and white shirt that were part of his school uniform as he yelled at his mother. "It's a girl's party. The other boys in my class aren't going. Why do I have to?" Tommy cried before stomping his feet. He'd overheard the other boys in his class joking about Emma's party at school, and if they found out he went, they would have even more ammunition to use to taunt him.

"Nonsense, you're just being silly," Babe insisted. "You'll have a wonderful time!" She brushed her dark brown hair out of her eyes as she shrugged him off.

Babe was a talented, imaginative artist who was especially skilled with a needle and thread, and since Emma's birthday fell right before Easter, Babe had the idea that she would make a bunny costume for Tommy to wear to the party. It was a pink suit with a white tummy; the hoody had long, pink ears, and there was a big fluffy tail on the back. Tommy felt physically ill when he saw it, and he frantically tried to talk them out of making him wearing it.

"I wish my dad was home," Tommy yelled the morning before the party when Babe insisted that he wear the bunny suit. "He would never let you make me wear that terrible thing or make me go to Emma's party, either."

The Colonel was away on one of his many extended business trips. He was in Washington, DC, and wouldn't be home for another two weeks. He had entrusted Tommy in Nana's care while he was away, believing he couldn't exactly trust his wife to take care of Tommy by herself, though he would never publicly admit his doubts to anyone outside the family.

On the day of the party, Tommy anxiously tried again to talk his mother out of making him wear the bunny suit. He threw a huge fit when reasoning with them didn't work, and when that failed, he pretended to be sick. Unfortunately, he got no sympathy from Nana Harris; Tommy had pretended to be sick so many times that Nana just gave him a disapproving glare.

"I'll inform your mother," she said coldly.

"My mother is too proud of the costume she made to be concerned with my feelings," he shouted as he slammed his bedroom door. Babe watched from down the hall and heard what Tommy had told Nana Harris.

"Tommy, you are going, and you are wearing the cute little bunny suit. I spent so much time making it, and I really don't care what you want," she scolded him through the door. "And don't try to lock yourself in your room, or I'll make Arnold take the door off the hinges."

Around lunchtime, Tommy's mother accompanied him to the party. Babe was excited to show off her son and her handiwork to the other parents. Tommy was so terrified and embarrassed that he could not speak. Ashamed and self-conscious, he sat with his head down and let the bunny ears fall in front of his face to hide his indignity.

When Emma's mother saw Tommy with the girls at the party and told him how cute "she" was, he became truly nauseated. "Oh God! She thinks I'm a girl," he whimpered to himself. He sat quietly at the girls' table staring down at the floor. He fought back the tears and hoped that the horrible bullies from school would never find out that his mother dressed him up like a pink bunny.

He glanced up for only a moment to see who else was at the party and was thankful that the few boys from his class who had come stayed away from the girls' table. No one had recognized him, and the girls snubbed him when he wouldn't talk. Tommy was relieved when heard one of the girls say to Emma, "She is being so rude! I hope you never invite that girl to another party." Eventually the girls at the table gave up and left to play party games, leaving Tommy alone in his misery.

"Your daughter doesn't seem to be having much fun," Tommy heard the hostess say to Babe. The young boy cringed, waiting for his mother's reply, and he was glad that she didn't correct Emma's mother, telling her that he was her son, not her daughter.

They stayed at the party for only a little over an hour, and by the time they got home, Tommy was seething. He went straight to his room and wouldn't come out for the rest of the evening. He already despised his mother, and on the ride home he swore silently that he would never forgive her for the humiliation she'd just put him through. Usually Tommy could depend Nana to protect him from his mother's antics, but this time was different. Not only did Babe betray him, but he felt like Nana didn't do anything to stop her. When she went to his room to check on him, she found that his door was locked.

"Come to dinner, Tommy. The cook made your favorite," Nana said through the locked door.

"Go away," Tommy replied curtly.

Tommy lay on his bed in his plaid pajamas reading *Treasure Island* by Robert Louis Stevenson. Tommy was reading at a level years ahead of his classmates. The other kids called him Tubby Tommy and Sissy Bookworm. Unfortunately, it was too late before he'd figured out that showing off how smart you were only made the other children dislike you more.

Nana knocked again, and this time she got no response. After a minute of silence, Tommy heard her walk away and went back to reading his book. He was hungry, but the sting of humiliation hurt much worse than hunger pains. Tommy preferred to bide his time until later that evening after Nana went bed and his mother retired to her room with her nightly gin and tonic. Tommy had been embarrassed by his mother's insensitive behavior before, but this time he felt like she crossed the line. He continued to read his book until the house became quiet and then snuck down to the kitchen to eat the fried chicken and mashed potatoes and gravy he found in the refrigerator.

Tommy didn't like being alone all of the time, but he didn't see how he could fix the problem. He dreaded going to school, and he didn't care for anyone in his family except his father, who was gone most of the time, leaving Tommy adrift in a house full of women. The only male besides the young boy in the house was their chauffeur, Arnold. Occasionally, Arnold would feel sorry for Tommy and play pool with him in the basement or stop at the drugstore to treat him to a milk shake. But it wasn't enough. It wasn't nearly enough.

Tommy had a half-sister Beverly. She was nine years older than him and kept her little brother at arm's length. She didn't care for Nana, thinking she was always poking her nose where it didn't belong—which was probably true. His sister was always blaming the nanny's constant interference for pushing her mother into one of her melancholy moods.

Although she was in high school, Beverly had heard that her little brother was the class weirdo and that he didn't have any friends. At home, she barely acknowledged her younger brother and would tell him, "Keep me out of your problems at school, and I won't tell Nana Harris that the other kids are teasing you." Tommy didn't tell anyone that he was being harassed, especially his mother or Nana. They would only meddle and make the situation worse. Just the thought of his mother or Nana getting involved made his stomach hurt.

Before bedtime each night, he'd lay in bed reading his books imagining what it would be like if was adored like the hero. Tom Sawyer was his favorite especially enjoying the freedoms he seemed to have just to be a boy and how loyal Huckleberry Finn was as a friend. He poured over his books believing maybe he'd find some morsel or clue that would help him fix what went wrong at school and if he was more like the characters in his books he'd be less of a target.

He'd drift off to sleep thinking that someday things would get better.

My life just couldn't possibly get any worse than it already is.

Chapter 2

TOMMY'S MOTHER GIVEN name was Beverly Louis, though she was called Babe by her closest friends and family. A former Dallas debutant, Babe was a lively, fun-loving woman who had been widowed too early in life. Her late husband had been a successful and handsome businessman named Whitaker Manning. She was very much in love with her dashing husband when they married, and though she was young when Tommy's sister was born, Babe's life was the American dream until Whit joined the air force after the attack on Pearl Harbor. He was stationed in the Aleutian Islands of Alaska when a squadron of Japanese planes attacked their remote outpost.

Babe was distraught when she heard her husband was presumed dead when his plane was shot down over the ocean. A young widow with a young daughter, she dabbled in modeling, making a meager living working for the department stores in Dallas. Tommy's grandmother, Miss Eddy, helped her daughter out financially and encouraged her to land another suitable husband to support herself and her child. Babe, devastated by her husband's death and left alone to care for their young daughter, secretly turned to drinking to numb the pain she felt from losing the love of her life. By the time she married the Colonel, Babe was a serious alcoholic.

Babe's mother had been deeply concerned about her daughter and put out her feelers among her old-money friends in the Dallas social network until a friend of a friend told her about an eligible divorced gentleman named Colonel Richard Ellison. He was a wealthy oil man and powerful political wheeler-dealer, and it was rumored that the Colonel was looking for a new wife.

"There's a political fund raiser next week, and I hear that Colonel Ellison will be there," one of Miss Eddy's friends told her. She soon finagled an invitation to the fund raiser. Miss Eddy's matchmaking efforts worked, and after just a few months, Babe and Colonel Ellison were married in a small civil ceremony. Initially, Babe married for convenience, believing that love with the Colonel would come with time. But she was taken aback when Miss Eddy started hearing rumors that Colonel Ellison had married purely for appearances, just because he wanted an heir.

Babe was in her early thirties when she married her second husband. The Colonel was much older—a tall, handsome man with a serious disposition. "You have to make it work," Miss Eddy told her daughter.

Babe, who had grown up in Dallas, didn't fit into the Houston social scene and felt like she was looked down upon in Houston, even though her cold, powerful husband was welcomed and even idealized in most social circles. After Babe became pregnant, the Colonel went back to his work as a Washington power broker, leaving her alone for months at a time while he was off saving the world or working behind the scenes for great and powerful men.

The year after they married Tommy was born at Memorial Hospital in Houston, Texas, on a dreary winter day in January 1949. There was nothing out of the ordinary about his birth. Babe had stopped drinking during her pregnancy but began to drink heavily again once her husband started leaving her alone for long stretches after their baby was born. Babe felt isolated in a new town where she didn't have any friends and had been left to raise her two children while her husband paid little attention to their family and routinely traveled for extended periods of time.

Babe and the Colonel lived in a modest house on the edge of River Oaks when they were first married, but by the time Tommy was two years old, the Colonel had leased a gracious mansion in a gated community near Rice University and Herman Park. This made Miss Eddy very happy. "I envisioned a different lifestyle for my daughter's new family," Miss Eddy would tell her friends at her country club. "At least the Colonel is taking care of her financially."

The mansion had ornate marble floors and columns that were imported from quarries in Italy. There were six fireplaces with intricately carved mantles, along with high ceilings and arched windows in all the main rooms on the first floor that opened to a well-manicured garden. Babe occupied herself by decorating the mansion and shopping for furnishings. "It's every woman's dream," she boasted to her mother.

The family hired a staff of maids, gardeners, a cook, and a chauffeur to tend the household, and Babe would throw large dinner parties for her husband's influential colleagues. Tommy's half-sister was soon enrolled in the best school in Houston, St. Luke's Episcopal School in River Oaks. But it wasn't long before Tommy's mother quietly began to comfort herself by drinking heavily and in secret, so as not to blemish the Colonel's impeccable reputation. He knew that his new young wife was drinking, yet the Colonel hated conflict and thus avoided confronting his wife's drinking by throwing himself into work. The Colonel was spending more and more time away from home, and at the urging of his sisters, he decided to hire a nanny, putting an ad in the newspaper for the position.

Jane Harris answered the Colonel's ad and was hired almost immediately. She was given a modest room on the third floor of their mansion and moved into to attend to Tommy full-time. Jane Harris was in her late forties; she was a petite woman who was plain in appearance, with thin graying hair that she wore pulled back in a bun. She had been married and left her husband for reasons she had never felt compelled to explain. Hopping a train from the East Coast, she rode it as far as her money could take her.

The Colonel was born in 1896 in an East Texas town called Black Rock. He had six sisters, along with two brothers who had died when he and sisters were young making him the only boy. The Colonel's sisters were devout church-going women and pillars of the community who idealized their brother. Black Rock was a small town in a dry county, and Aunt Annabelle liked to think that she was her brother's favorite and took a particular interest in her brother's new family. After his mother's death, the Colonel had inherited his mother's house in Black Rock. The Colonel was extremely proud of the home that he had built for his mother after he had made his fortune, and he insisted that his wife and children spend time in the country with his sisters and extended family.

The Colonel's father and uncle owned a mercantile store in Black Rock on the courthouse square, and his family had lived in Black Rock for several generations, immigrating to Texas from Alabama after the Civil War. The Colonel's sisters had lived in Black Rock their whole lives, and at least three of his sisters were convinced that if their father had not been orphaned in the Civil War, they would be able to trace their lineage back to the British crown.

"I am concerned about your wife's taste for liquor," Annabelle complained to her brother on many of their visits to their country home. "You must protect Tommy from the devil's drink if you want your son to grow up to be a suitable heir." Aunt Annabelle was a small, thin woman, stern in her beliefs, and she felt it was her place to ensure that her brother's son was well cared for in a manner she approved of.

"You must keep an eye on Babe," Aunt Annabelle said to the new nanny. "I fear that her taste for the demon drink will endanger the spiritual well-being of the boy."

Aunt Annabelle treated Babe with contempt and put on airs when it came to Beverly and Miss Eddy, too. She pretended like she accepted the poor little orphan girl that her brother had taken in, saying it was the Christian thing to do, but it was obvious that she did not approve.

After she was hired, Nana took her responsibilities very seriously and decided to dedicate every waking moment to caring for Tommy. Before long, she became overly attached to him. She felt as though both the Colonel and Aunt Annabelle had sanctioned her work, and in her mind, the boundaries between employer and employee became blurred. Once she was comfortable in her role as nanny, she started to interfere in the family's affairs by pitting Tommy's father and sisters against his mother, sister, and grandmother.

Nana could start a family feud with a whisper, a disapproving glance, or a gesture at a well-staged opportunity. Her well-placed traps were hard for Tommy's inebriated mother to avoid. Nana would not hesitate to give elaborate reports to Babe's unsympathetic husband after he returned from one of his business trips, magnifying the failings of his drunken wife, and to the impartial observer, it almost seemed as if she relished all the trouble she caused. Nana Harris used her advantage over Babe—and the other women in the house—by starting fights between them and then stepping back to watch the fur fly. Nana was slowly but surely undermining Babe's position in the household, and the Colonel had gradually lost faith in his wife's parenting skills.

"She has forgotten that she is the hired help," Babe would nag her husband, but her complaints fell on deaf ears. The Colonel was much more concerned about his son's legacy than his wife's opinions.

By the time Tommy started elementary school, he was a spoiled-rotten little brat who threw many a fit when he didn't get his way, which only added to his problems at school. But all that mattered to the Colonel was that his son was making good grades and that he was well behaved.

"As far as I can see, Tommy is turning into a fine young man, and Nana Harris is doing an excellent job," he said, rebutting his wife's arguments. The Colonel didn't pay attention to anything other than Tommy's education and never noticed how lonely and socially awkward Tommy had become.

"Don't you think the boy needs friends?" Babe would ask her husband when they were alone and Nana wasn't around.

"He will develop social skills soon enough." The Colonel patted his wife's hand dismissively. He seemingly believed that Tommy didn't need friends his age. "Playing around would only distract him from what is expected of him," he continued.

Babe shook her head in disbelief. "Your priorities are causing most of the conflict in this house," she said under her breath, knowing she was powerless when it came to raising her son. "Am I the only one who thinks that little boys need playmates their own age and socialization outside of the numerous crazy adults in our family?"

Sometimes Nana or Aunt Annabelle tried to exert their influences over Beverly, but Miss Eddy would put a stop to it. "Beverly is my only granddaughter, and she isn't going to be raised by a bunch of small-town, small-minded British royalty wannabes."

Miss Eddy was not intimidated by her son-in-law or his sisters. She'd watched as her grandson had been taken away from his mother and voiced her opinions regularly about her daughter's backwoods sister-in-law's interference in her grandchildren's lives.

"I can't stop them from meddling in Tommy's life, but my granddaughter is none of their business," Miss Eddy declared in no uncertain terms to her son-in-law. "Beverly will be raised in a way befitting someone who comes from Dallas and will be groomed to be a debutant like her mother, even if it's in Houston."

The Colonel hated the constant confrontation at home. He stayed out of the catfights as best he could and looked the other way when there was friction between the women in the family. He decided that it was easier to just allow Miss Eddy and Babe to raise Beverly as they thought best. Beverly was old enough to see that Nana's intentions were not always good, and as a result, she developed a healthy distrust for the woman.

"Nana is devious and causes a whole lot of problems in our family," she would tell her grandmother. "And she takes too much pleasure in causing those problems."

Beverly pulled away from the woman and watched helplessly as her mother slipped further into alcoholism and Nana turned her brother into Little Lord Fauntleroy.

Beverly, like her mother, had blossomed into a strikingly beautiful young lady, and when she was sixteen, her grandmother bought her a shiny red convertible. Suddenly, she was free from the insanity at home, and as long as she gave her little brother a ride every once in a while, nobody asked any questions about what she was doing when she wasn't home. Beverly reveled in her freedom. She was overjoyed that she was beyond Nana's scrutiny, which made her feel like she was like she was normal, like her friends from high school. She was having fun, hanging out after school at the drugstore across the street from St. Luke's with her friends and flirting with cute boys.

Highlands Drugstore was the local after-school hangout and had a food counter where all the kids from St. Luke's met after school. It was also where Beverly would meet Billy. Billy was a bus driver who hung out at the food counter about the time school let out. Billy was in his twenties, and he was tall with handsome features, black hair, and dark eyes. He was a smooth guy, and the high school girls giggled and swooned when he would laugh and joke with them.

Beverly thought nothing of her harmless flirtation with him, but when Billy would turn on the charm, she couldn't help being flattered by his attentions. The soda jerk and the drugstore manager were concerned that Billy was only looking for a rich-girl meal ticket and warned him repeatedly not to cause any problems. But Billy just laughed at them, saying, "It's only harmless fun," while disregarding the soda jerk's disapproving glares.

Beverly had lived a sheltered life until then and was tempted by the allure of forbidden fruit. "He looks like James Dean," she told her best friend, Abby. Soon the young woman had succumbed to Billy's charms and would steal away with the handsome bus driver when no one was watching. It was not long before Beverly turned up pregnant late in her senior year, and it was Billy the bus driver who was responsible.

William Louis Cane Jr. married Beverly in a civil ceremony, and a few months later, William Louis Cane III made his entrance into the world, followed two years later by Candice Elizabeth Cane. Now that they had two children, things weren't working out, and everyone knew it but no one was saying anything.

Babe had started to drink heavily again, and she tried very hard to hide it by staying in her room or her art studio most of the time. She had started keeping a bottle of gin in her closet, convincing herself that no one knew she was drinking. Even Tommy had started to feel sorry for his mother, as more than once he'd found her passed out on the floor outside her bedroom.

By the time he was in junior high school, the distance between Tommy's parents had grown into a great, impenetrable chasm, and the constant insults by Nana and Annabelle about how she was a drunk and failure as a mother only gave Babe more reason to feel worse about herself, pushing her further into the bottle.

The stress of the constant bickering in Babe's family took a toll on Miss Eddy's health. In her youth, she'd been a force to be reckoned with, but the once strong and vigorous woman was aging, and the constant turmoil of the family's dynamic was more than she could bear. Her grandson was eleven years old, and Nana Harris had overstepped with regards to the boy and ignored boundaries that would've gotten most nannies fired. Yet despite her best efforts, Miss Eddy's grandson had fallen under the control of the odd nanny.

"My husband loves me. I know he does. He isn't a demonstrative man." Babe shook wiping her eyes as she told her mother. "He's just one of those men who shows how much they care by the way he takes care of you. If Nana wasn't around our relationship would be so much better."

"She is not family, but Tommy has grown to think of her as such," Miss Eddy steamed anytime as she stroked her daughter's hand. "Your husband has allowed his staff's unprofessional behavior to go on for too long. There's something wrong with that woman."

One summer afternoon in 1958, Miss Eddy passed away. Babe was devastated; her mother had been her only ally and loved her unconditionally. As Babe and her husband sat alone in Miss Eddy's living room in Dallas before the funeral, she told the Colonel, "My mother left everything to me and to Beverly. I wish she had left something to Tommy, but apparently, she wrote her will long before Tommy was born. If you could help sort this out, I would be grateful for your help." She said as she put her head on the Colonel's shoulder.

"I'd be honored to help." He replied quietly with an uncharacteristic hug.

Just outside the door, Nana Harris happened to walk by and overheard Babe and her husband discussing Miss Eddy's estate. Without thinking, she took it upon herself to explain to her young charge about the terms of his grandmother's will. Nana Harris had always mistakenly treated Tommy as though he were much more mature than his age. In reality, he wasn't old enough to understand that the old bat had left him out of her will. Tommy had never liked the pushy old woman, but it wasn't until Nana told him that he had been disinherited that he began to believe that Miss Eddy really didn't care for him, either.

"I will never know why that woman didn't like me," he told Nana after the funeral. "Nobody likes me."

"Poo," Nana retorted. "You are a charming young man. You mustn't let the actions of a bitter old woman discourage you. You are the sole heir to your father's estate, and you will inherit far greater wealth than that old battle-ax could ever give you. You just have to be patient. It really doesn't matter what your mother's family thinks of you; your father's opinion is the one that counts."

Chapter 3

COLONEL ELLISON CLAIMED that he divorced his first wife because she couldn't have children, but in reality, his first wife dumped him for being an unaffectionate workaholic. "Life is too short to spend your life with someone who doesn't love you," she said tearfully as she handed her coldhearted husband divorce papers.

Richard Ellison was fifty-four years old when Tommy was born. He'd waited so long to have children that maybe he was a little too old for them. He'd had ideas about how he would raise his heir, which had little to do with the day-to-day actuality of parenting—never admitting to himself that he really didn't have a clue. As a result, he left much of the work to someone else. According to the Colonel, raising children was women's work; there were more vital things for men to attend to. Tensions between the United States and the Soviet Union were high, and Colonel Ellison's diplomatic expertise was needed in Washington.

But deep down he realized that parenting was not easy and, in fact, involved more of his time than he was willing to give. He didn't have any interest in the complexities of children's inner worlds, and baby talk was not his style. On top of it all, he was a little too old and set in his ways to play peekaboo or catch, or read bedtime stories. The Colonel's idea of Christmas presents for his son were books and stamp collections, and he would have been perfectly happy if Tommy had skipped childhood altogether and went straight to adulthood. Before Tommy was born, the Colonel had been at the top of his game, working for the chiefs of staff for Presidents Roosevelt and Truman. He'd amassed power and influence, as well as a fortune. Regrettably, parenthood was something that was low on his list of priorities.

When the Colonel hired Nana Harris to look after Tommy, he didn't consult his wife on his choice for nanny. He didn't think that he needed to. He was worried about Babe, and hoped a nanny would alleviate the strain his wife was under due to his constant absence, but by the time he saw the problems that Nana Harris's presence caused, it was too late.

"You have to let him have friends, or he'll grow up needy and awkward," Babe told Nana Harris repeatedly, but Nana Harris had her own agenda and, as a result, ignored Babe. She worked for the Colonel, and pleasing him was the only thing that mattered. Nana Harris began grooming Tommy for greatness early on by taking him to his father's office at a very young age, and the Colonel delighted in this, encouraging his son to visit his office anytime he was in town.

"I want the boy to have a solid work ethic," he'd said in a booming voice sitting behind his desk upon one of his young son's visits to the office. "The sooner he is exposed to work and the office, the greater the chance the boy will follow in my footsteps."

By the time Tommy was of school age, most of the people he saw in his daily life were adults. The only contact with other children his age was mostly through the Black Rock Church of Christ Sunday school. He tried to make friend with the kids at Sunday school but was always swept up after church and taken to dinner with the family at the home of one of his aunts. Sometimes he would play with his elderly aunts' grandchildren. But Tommy never really bonded with any of them, and just as with the kids at school, he didn't know how to act around his cousins. They weren't interested in his books or stamp collections, and they seemed standoffish around Tommy. They couldn't rough play with him the way they played with most kids their age. He didn't really climb trees or get dirty or catch snakes and frogs the ways they did. And if Tommy got hurt or didn't get his way when they played with him, there was hell to pay.

"I don't want to play with Tommy. He doesn't play fair, and he doesn't know the rules. And if you don't let him win, he cries," one of Aunt Mildred's grandsons blurted out dramatically after a Sunday afternoon playdate with Tommy.

"I know, sweetie. But we have to be nice to Tommy," his grandmother replied.

When Tommy started school, he was well prepared scholastically for success, but he was a social misfit. Tommy was not only unnerved and ill at ease; he was completely out of his element. He didn't know how to act when the other kids really didn't like him. Nobody wanted to play with him, and the teacher didn't force them if they didn't want to.

For the first few weeks of school, he came home crying. He wanted more than anything to be liked by the other kids, but he didn't know what to do to accomplish this. They didn't laugh at his jokes, no one wanted to sit by him, and he didn't know how to play the games they already knew how to play. Worst of all, Tommy was usually the last boy to be picked for the teams at recess…if he was picked at all. Tommy went from the center of the universe to just another kid in the classroom. Fortunately, he was smart and well behaved, so the teacher found him to be a wonderful student, but it wasn't long before the other kids started calling him Tubby Tommy, the teacher's pet, and made up a song about him, singing it at recess when the teacher wasn't around.

When Tommy was in Sunday school he learned that teasing and call people names was wrong. The Sunday school teacher taught the children something to say to bullies: "Sticks and stones will break my bones, but words will never hurt me."

Needless to say, Tommy was sorely unprepared when this didn't work. At recess the next week, someone called Tommy a sissy and said he threw a ball like a little girl. Tommy quoted the "sticks and stones" passage he'd learned in Sunday school and almost immediately realized what a horrible mistake it was.

Immediately he was surrounded by eight boys who ganged up on him, taunting him and calling him all sorts of horrible names. But the worst thing of all was the name that stuck—Tubby Tommy. Tommy started to cry when he heard the taunt Tubby Tommy, and once the bullies saw that he weaker than them, they kept coming back to torment Tommy again and again. After recess was over, Tommy made the mistake of telling on the bullies, and from that day forward, he had a target on his back.

Nana Harris had always encouraged Tommy to tattle, telling him that it was her job to protect him from others' bad behavior, but now it was backfiring on him. Tommy was labeled a tattletale, and it would never wash off while he was at St. Luke's. PE and recess were the worst times for Tommy, since the teachers weren't around to witness the ridicule. He wasn't good at any of the games, and the other boys laughed at him and told him he threw like a girl, calling him a sissy. He especially dreaded dodgeball. He didn't run as fast as the other boys, so he was usually easy prey. The other boys teased when he whined because someone hit him intentionally too hard and laughed at him because he was usually the first one out.

The other kids also made fun of Tommy when Nana Harris would pick him up in the limousine. Most of the other children were picked up by their mothers. His classmates laughed at him, telling him that only babies need a nanny. Tommy did his best to pretend their barbs didn't hurt him, but it was hard. Being picked up from school by the nanny was better than getting picked up by your lush of a mother.

Tommy was ashamed of his mother's drinking and didn't want her near the school. When the Colonel traveled, his mother would drink a lot, and she would drink during the day, not just evenings. Sometimes Tommy or his sister would wake up to get ready for school only to find his mother at the kitchen table, her hair a mess, the buttons on her silk pajama top misaligned, and the rancid smell of gin or scotch emanating from her pores. She had clearly stayed up all night and would stagger drunk through the house, knocking over furniture or holding on to the walls so she wouldn't fall down.

Babe made excuses for herself, like, "I had insomnia last night. I can't sleep when your father is out of town and had a drink to relax so that I could sleep." She then slurred her words, spilling what was left of her drink on the carpet as she stumbled down the hall to her bedroom.

But Tommy knew better. It enraged the boy that she cared so little about what she was doing to herself and the people around her. Inevitably, he would have to help her up and put her to bed. Tommy wasn't just ashamed of his mother's drinking; he hated his mother for what she put him through.

Once when he was in the fourth grade, Tommy received an award at a ceremony in the gymnasium in front of the entire school. He tried his best to hide the upcoming ceremony from his mother, but somehow, she found out about it. Nana Harris, who wouldn't miss the presentation of this academic award for the world, had showed up early and was seated in the back of the gym. Tommy thought he was OK, but when Babe showed up after the ceremony started, his heart sank.

Tommy could tell as soon as his mother walked in that she had been drinking. She was stumbling and swaying, and her clothes and hair were a mess. Tommy sank down in his chair and hoped nobody would notice. Since it was late, the only available seats were at the top of the bleachers. Babe stumbled about halfway up the stands and then fell, rolling two rows until she landed on top of one of the parents.

Tommy cowered when he saw the astonished and disapproving look on the woman's face when she realized that the woman who had just fallen on her had been drinking. Several other parents helped Babe up, but her fall disrupted the ceremony. Tommy felt frozen as if the events unfolded in slow motion and the whole world could see into his soul. He glanced around to see many of his classmates pointing and laughing as one of the teacher held on to his mother's elbow and escorted her from the gymnasium. He looked over to where Nana Harris was sitting to see her standing and shaking her head. By the disgusted look on her face, he could tell that Nana was quietly debating whether she should stay, but she eventually followed Babe and the teacher as they left the gym. Tommy was humiliated and mortified, and tried his best to control the rage he felt toward his inebriated mother so that his tormenters wouldn't know who she was when they laughed and pointed at her.

The weekends at their home in Black Rock were becoming more and more a welcome relief from the pressures of school and of constantly defending himself from kids who took great pleasure in causing him misery. When he was in the town of Black Rock, Tommy got to be around people who liked him and who treated him with respect, even reverence. Tommy loved their family home in Black Rock and considered it his domain and sanctuary.

Every Friday at 3:00 p.m., Arnold would pick Tommy up at school and drive north on Shepard Drive until they got to Conroe and then turned northwest toward Black Rock. There he was free just to be a kid. He spent much of his time playing outside with his dog, Spotty, and riding his bike around the neighborhood. Tommy's father had built a guesthouse behind the old family house, along with a swimming pool, and Tommy soon took it over, setting up his model train in the living room.

Even Babe began to appreciate their weekends in the small town of Black Rock. Babe loved to garden, but the well-manicured garden of their mansion didn't allow her much more satisfaction other than walking through the grounds. Babe was never as happy or as grounded as when she had dirt under her fingernails from the soil from their garden and the warmth of the East Texas sun on her face. Tommy watched the change in his mother in amazement and liked to believe that she saw the outdoor spaces around their house in Black Rock as a blank canvas where she could create her own beautiful landscape.

Over time, Tommy and his mother transplanted live oak trees around the pool, and the gardener put in a large vegetable garden patch just outside the fence. Sometimes Tommy would help his mother work in their garden. "I love to garden; it's so satisfying to plant something and watch it grow," Babe told her son. She didn't want to let on, but one of the reasons she loved gardening was because of the quality time that she spent with her son.

The gardener helped by taking care of the day-to-day upkeep. He planted garlic, onions, greens, okra, collard and mustard greens, lettuce, broccoli, beans, and peas in their vegetable patch, and in the spring and summer Babe and Tommy would pick vegetables together for the cook. Beside the garden, a grapevine grew up the trunk of a hackberry tree, and Tommy would use a ladder to climb the tree and pick the wild grapes so the housekeeper could make jelly. Alongside the hackberry grew a huge fig tree that Tommy's grandmother had planted, and each year the gardener would sit nearby with a slingshot, keeping the squirrels and birds from eating all the figs before they could pick them.

As Tommy grew older, he started spending a lot of time in the guesthouse, as he enjoyed the freedom it afforded him. It allowed him to get away from the screwed-up adults in the main house. Even Nana would allow him his space when he was in the guesthouse (she had a small room to the back of the main house with a clear view of the guesthouse from her window). Now that Tommy was getting older, he was beginning to get annoyed by Nana's constant hovering. He was happy he could get away from her, even if she could spy on him from the vantage of her bedroom window.

Tommy started to venture out into the surrounding neighborhood when Nana wasn't looking, sometimes with his bike, and tried to make friends with the neighborhood kids, who were a lot more receptive toward him than the boys at St. Luke's. One of the friends he met was the Methodist minister's son, and before long Nana reluctantly allowed Ronnie to come over to play at the guest-house on occasion mostly because his parents were good and upstanding people, but also because they lived down the street from them, and she could easily monitor their activities.

When Tommy was about ten, he was outside playing with his dog when the next-door neighbor walked over to the fence and started up a conversation. "My name is RRRRoy. I sssaw you ppppplaying with your dddddog and riding your bbbbbike in the sssstreet. What's your name?" he stuttered as he introduced himself.

Roy was a heavyset man with dirty blond hair who appeared to be in his twenties. He was dressed in overalls with a dark gray T-shirt underneath and dirty-brown work boots that were only laced halfway up.

Tommy noticed that he was a little slow, but he seemed nice enough. "His name is Spotty." Tommy smiled and laughed as he scratched Spotty behind the ear. "He lives here with Robby, the gardener, and I see him when I come home for the weekends. My name is Tommy."

Tommy knew who Roy was. After all, everyone knew everyone in Black Rock. Roy lived with his elderly parents across the street from the guesthouse and worked at one of the local grocery stores on the town square as a stock boy. He had a speech impediment and spit a little bit when he talked because of a lisp. Tommy made fun of him sometimes along with Ronnie, and the other boys he knew in town. However, it wasn't long before Tommy became friends with him. Tommy knew all too well how mean the other boys could be and felt sorry for Roy at first, but soon Tommy started to like his new friend and really was glad for the attention.

Tommy began see his friendly neighbor more and more whenever he was playing outside or riding his bike, and the young boy started inviting Roy over sometimes to show him the model train collection he'd set up in the guesthouse. The relationship became a little friendlier each time Roy came over. Roy would give Tommy a pat on the back, a discreet stroke of the arm, a disarming hug. Then one day, Tommy bent over to fix a loose piece of track and he felt Roy's hand slide down his butt. Tommy froze and didn't know what to do. He convinced himself that it must have been an accident, because after he regained his composure he turned around and, much to his relief, Roy had backed up and was standing a few feet away.

After that Tommy was a bit weary of inviting Roy over to the guesthouse again, but after a time or two when Roy came around and nothing happened, things went back to the way they'd been. But one day it happened again, and this time Roy's advances were more sexual. Tommy was again bending over to adjust something on the model when he felt Roy's hands around his waist, and before he could react, Roy had pulled the young boy's body against his groin and was unzipping the young boy's pants and fondling his penis and balls. Tommy was terrified. In an instant, Roy pulled Tommy's pants down around his ankles and threw him onto the green sofa, and like an animal, his face was in Tommy's crotch and the boy's penis and balls were in his mouth. Roy licked and sucked on the young boy's penis while he stroked himself to climax.

After he was through, Tommy lay shaking on the couch, curled up in a ball and fighting back the tears. Roy got up, walked into the kitchen, and cleaned himself up with a dish towel that was on the counter. Before he left, Roy turned to Tommy and said, "You kkkkeep your mouth ssssshut about what jjjjjust happened or I may have to use my dddddaddy's gggggun on that cute little dddddog you gggggot in the yard."

Tommy felt helpless to stop his neighbor and believed that Roy was watching from his parents' house for his next opportunity to molest him again. Tommy wanted to tell someone, but he was afraid of what Roy would do to him if he did. Roy had molested Tommy under the nose of the ever-vigilant Nana Harris (who never noticed what was going on), and he continued to molest the boy off and on over the next couple of years.

Luckily, the universe intervened when Tommy's half-sister became pregnant during her senior year at St. Luke's and his family turned their attentions to his sister's ill-fated circumstances. He was eleven years old when Roy's sexual attacks escalated and Tommy considered his sister's untimely pregnancy a distraction overshadowing his shame. Before long, his father decided that Houston wasn't the best place to raise children. He'd seen a disturbing change in his son's demeanor that he just couldn't put his finger on and decided that it was time for a change.

"I need to reevaluate whether Houston is the best place for our son to get the kind of education I expect for him," the Colonel told his wife gently as they ate dinner one evening. He took a bite of food and then took a sip of iced tea from the brown glass beside his plate. "The Episcopal school system as a whole is excellent, but I don't want to take any chance with our son's future. I realize that St. Luke's isn't responsible for what happens after classes let out, but you must admit there is a certain element that allows bad behavior among the students there, and Beverly has fallen under their influences."

It was evident that Colonel Ellison believed that the wealthy children at the school were not the kind of influence he wanted his son around and was determined to find a better school for his son.

Richard Ellison knew about an Episcopal boarding school that had recently opened in Austin, Texas, which had been founded with money he'd helped to raise. After seeing that Tommy needed a change, Colonel Ellison decided it was the best option for Tommy's education. St. Martin's was intended to be a place where parents living in the smaller towns in Texas could send their children to get the kind of outstanding education that was unavailable to them in their public school system. The Colonel enrolled Tommy in St. Martin's beginning in the fall of the next year.

St. Martin's Episcopal School was built on land on the far west side of Austin, in the limestone hills outside the city limits. The buildings of the school were fabricated from the native limestone readily available on the school property. The school was small, and the teaching staff lived on campus and served as both teachers and dorm parent, but the education the students received was world-class.

Colonel Ellison believed that he was saving his son from the unacceptable cultural impact at St. Luke's, never realizing that the real threat to his son's well-being was happening to his son when they were at their weekend retreat. Although he had seen the change in his son's personality of late, Tommy's father assumed that it was due to the bad influences of his classmates at St. Luke's.

"I don't want the same distractions that tripped up my stepdaughter in Houston to distract my son from the life that is ahead of him," the Colonel told Babe while she ate. "I have bigger plans for Tommy, and marriage to a gold digger or an unwanted pregnancy is not an option."

Babe bristled at her husband's remark about her daughter. She put her knife and fork down beside her plate, and turning to her husband, she said. "If Tommy goes to boarding school, then I guess we don't need Nana Harris anymore."

She studied her husband's face as he sat silently weighing the situation.

"I don't want that nasty woman under our roof anymore," Babe declared when she realized that this may finally be her chance to get rid of Nana.

Tommy's mother had lobbied to get rid of the meddlesome nanny for years, and boarding school would mean that Nana would not have any reason to be employed further. Even the Colonel was starting to believe that Tommy's unnatural attachment to Nana Harris was unhealthy, and he was admittedly becoming concerned about it.

"I think you've been correct in your assessment of Tommy's unhealthy attachment to the nanny." The Colonel rarely admitted he was wrong, and this would be one of those rare occasions when he did. "It's time for Tommy to grow up and learn to be a man; Nana Harris has babied and coddled our son for too long."

When he heard the news, Tommy begged his father to keep Nana on staff, even after he left for school in Austin, and the Colonel agreed to do so only under the condition that she would move out of the family's home and work only during summers when Tommy was home for school. Shortly before Tommy went off to St. Martin's, Nana Harris moved into a cottage behind Mrs. Willie Harper's house. Willie Harper was a family friend whose husband owned an oil field service company in Black Rock.

Mrs. Harper was a little apprehensive when Babe asked her for help finding Nana a place to stay, but figured if she didn't help Babe's marriage would implode due to Nana's interference. Willie Harper had known the Colonel all her life believing her old friend would never have married Babe if he didn't love her. "It's not my place to judge." She told Babe as her friend complained about the stories Nana had embellished about her drinking.

The house Nana moved into behind Mrs. Harper's was a little one-bedroom house clad with drab gray asbestos shingles. It had a tiny kitchen and living room that was quite adequate for a woman who had very few possessions. The Colonel agreed to pay her rent and a small stipend to appease his son. In turn, Nana Harris agreed that she would take care of Tommy when he came home from boarding school for the summer.

"Things are looking up," Babe gloated as workers helped Nana Harris pack her things for the move to her new home.

Things were looking up for Tommy, too. He'd struggled at St. Luke's Episcopal School and wanted a new start at a new school. By the time he'd figured out the ins and outs of the childhood social order at St. Luke's, Tommy had already become a pariah.

Tommy couldn't wait to start at St. Martin's, where he wouldn't be treated like the school outcast anymore. But most of all, Tommy grateful he was getting away from Roy. Tommy avoided Roy as much as he could, but he still felt like Roy was watching the guesthouse from across the street. His private sanctuary away from the family had become a place where Roy's attacks violated Tommy and robbed him of his childhood innocence.

Tommy was having nightmares about the horrors Roy had inflicted, and he had started walking in his sleep. Tommy was just a boy and was terrified that someone would find out and he would have to relive everything. He had to make Roy stop before someone found out and his private horror was turned into another screwed-up family drama.

Tommy stopped sleeping in the guesthouse and moved back into his room in the main house. He also started getting up early and going out to the Colonel's ranch whenever he was at their house in Black Rock. Tommy knew that Roy would never dare knock on the door looking for him and hoped that eventually he would leave him alone.

Peach Tree Ranch was mystical place where Tommy could get lost. Located about thirty miles from Black Rock, it was a beautiful property along the banks of the muddy Brazos River where an old ferry crossing had once been. Some of the locals claimed that Davy Crockett had taken the old ferry across the Brazos on the way to the Alamo. The Colonel had bought it twenty years earlier for the mineral rights beneath the property, but as Tommy's father had gotten older, he'd fallen in love with the place and fancied himself a gentleman rancher. The more fertile lands nearer the river had been cleared for farming before the Civil War, but the rest of the land was heavily wooded with a native hardwood forest that was slowly being cleared by a heard of goats who ate away at the thick underbrush and who were kept safe from the coyotes and wolves by five very protective donkeys named Mikey, Buck, Pearl, Willy, and Jonesy.

The Colonel owned a herd of registered Brahman cattle that were becoming world renowned for their bloodline. India had long banned the export of Brahman cattle because it was a sacred animal and the country didn't want them to be used for food. There were only a few breeders in the world who could trace the bloodline of their herd back to India, and the Colonel's herd was one of them. Colonel Ellison was ecstatic that his son was taking an interest in the ranch. Tommy's father was not getting any younger, and in the past, he'd tried hard not to show his disappointment in his son's lack of interest in the family business. But now he was hopeful that Tommy seemed to be losing interest in his toy trains and was finally growing up.

Late in the summer before Tommy left for boarding school, tragedy struck unexpectedly when a tree fell on the Colonel while he was supervising a dozer operator who was clearing land for a new hay meadow. The Colonel escaped with only a broken leg, but the whole family was terrified.

"Richard Ellison, you are no spring chicken," Babe scolded him when she picked him up at the hospital.

The Colonel was sixty-six years old when the accident occurred, and for the first time in his life, Tommy saw his father as a flesh-and-blood human being instead of an immortal. Nana Harris had always put his father on a pedestal, and Tommy had never seen his vulnerable side until he was injured.

When they arrived home, they assisted the Colonel out of the car, and he couldn't help but notice how uncomfortable he seemed. His father wasn't just in pain from his injury, but he could tell he was perturbed at the thought of being dependent on others until he recuperated. He grimaced and opened their trunk to retrieve his father's crutches while his mother steadied her husband holding one arm while he clutched the car doorframe with the other.

Seeing the look on her son's face as he opened the front door for the Colonel, Babe could tell Tommy was rattled.   She whispered in his ear as he held open the kitchen door for the Colonel as he hobbled inside. "Nana has done a great disservice by teaching you to worship your father like a hero. Even heroes aren't perfect all the time."

Chapter 4

In August of 1963, Tommy's parents loaded his belongings into the Colonel's Cadillac for the short drive to St. Martin's Episcopal School in Austin. The Colonel was on crutches with a cast, so Babe had to drive. Tommy was excited and full of hope, and was amazed that the Colonel would make the effort to take the trip, even with a cast on his leg. Tommy was leaving his troubles behind, and all he could see ahead of him was a new start. He was already the smart kid, but now he was going to be popular. He was sure of it.

The Ellison's checked their son into his dorm room at the eighth-grade-boarding-student orientation. His room was fifteen by twenty feet, with cinder-block walls that were painted stark white and gray asbestos tiles on the floors. One window divided the room, and on each side were a nondescript twin bed, a desk, and a chest of drawers.

At the orientation breakfast at the dining hall, Tommy hopes for a new start were dashed when he spotted one of the bullies who had unmercifully tormented him at St. Luke's. His name was Peter Taylor, and he was sitting with his parents on the other side of the dining hall. Tommy stared straight ahead, pretending not to see him, and Peter, in turn, pretended not to see Tommy. Tommy couldn't believe his rotten luck but still wasn't ready to give up on his new start until things went from bad to worse. When they went to his dorm room, he discovered that Peter, the bully from St. Luke's, was his new roommate.

Apparently, Peter wanted to start off at his new school on the right foot, and after their parents left, he said, "I don't want any problems, so can we let bygones be bygones?"

But Tommy couldn't forget the torture he endured because of Peter, and he wasn't going to back down if a problem came up. Soon after his parents left, Tommy went to the director of boarding. "Mr. Longstreet, is it possible for you to assign me a different roommate?" he asked sheepishly.

Mr. Longstreet looked at Tommy oddly and asked, "Why? Is there a reason we need to move you? We put you together because you came from the same school, and we assumed since you already knew each other, it would be easier for both of you to adjust."

Tommy, not wanting to sound like a whiner or a tattletale, simply replied, "I just don't like him. We don't get along, and I don't want him to be my roommate."

Mr. Longstreet was sympathetic but answered, "Our dorm space is limited this year, and it will be a problem to move you to a new room, so if you could try to settle your differences I would appreciate your help. If problems arise between you and Peter, we will revisit the issue."

Mr. Longstreet often got requests from the students to change roommates at the beginning of the semester, but he had found that if he left well enough alone, most of the time things worked themselves out. Space was limited at the small school, and he needed more reason than simply Tommy not liking his roommate in order to move him.

Tommy had learned long ago when not to argue, mostly from the strong-willed women who'd controlled his life up until that point. Feeling defeated, he Tommy went back to his room and expected the worst. He was upset that his dreams of a new start were defeated before he even a chance but he wasn't going to show it to Peter.

The rest of the semester were tense between Tommy and his roommate Peter, and even though there weren't any fights or arguments, neither boy seemed to be able to get past what had happened between them at St. Luke's. Peter tried to apologize, saying that he and the other boys were just joking around. But Tommy really didn't want to hear it.

"Look, I don't like you, and you don't like me," Tommy retorted after hearing Peter's halfhearted apology. "I'll leave you alone if you leave me alone."

When Peter didn't return to St. Martin's after the Christmas break, Tommy was given a new roommate. Peter's leaving meant that Tommy now had another chance to make friends and be popular. Most importantly, it meant that he could rewrite history the way *he* wanted. He finally had his new start.

St. Martin's was a small school and had been established less than ten years before Tommy got there. Consequently, to help offset their costs they had begun to admit day students from the local area. Austin was still a funky old eccentric town in those days and was only starting to feel the growing pains of being a haven for the rich and famous. St. Martin's was becoming one of the best college preparatory schools in Texas, and soon Tommy felt right at home. He enjoyed the diverse areas of study that St. Martin's offered and readily took advantage of the opportunities the school afforded him. He studied Greek, theology, and philosophy, and best of all, no one picked on him for being too smart or weird.

The year Tommy came to St. Martin's, a new chapel was constructed at the top of the tallest hill on campus. The Episcopal Archdiocese had built St. Martin's on a high limestone bluff overlooking Lake Austin, and just below the school were rugged cliffs that led to the lake's edge. The craggy landscape was covered with native live oaks, cedars, and Texas mountain laurels. Wildlife teamed around the school campus, and Tommy regularly saw deer, rabbits, raccoons, opossums, armadillos, coyotes, and bats flying around for their nightly feast of bugs swarming the only lights that illuminated the area for miles.

The school was far enough outside of Austin that at night the stars shown so brightly that they seem endless; on a clear night, the capitol building could be seen lighting up the downtown Austin night sky from the hill. At the time, the largest employer in the city was the University of Texas and the second largest was the State of Texas. Austin was still a small city built on the banks of the Colorado River and carved out of the wilderness, with a population of about 150,000 people. The wild landscape was peaceful, and its beauty was intoxicating, and it was easy for Tommy to grow attached to the school.

It wasn't long before Tommy found out that his family moved out of the mansion in Houston and into a small apartment in a downtown high-rise. He was sad when he heard that he staff was let go but he wasn't surprised.

Tommy knew that his mother was moving against her will, moved lock, stock, and barrel into the old family house in Black Rock. Most of Babe's antiques and belongings that couldn't fit into the house in Black Rock were put into storage in a large warehouse on the edge of town by the cemetery where the Colonel's grandparents were buried.

"If I am going to be stuck in a backwater town like Black Rock for the rest of my life, I want a new house," Babe protested to his father.

She started badgering the Colonel incessantly about tearing down the house he'd built for his mother. The Colonel thought she was acting crazy and just ignored his wife. He loved his mother's house and for the life of him could not understand why she didn't like it. Life in in the big city of Houston was over for Babe, and she now lived in a dry county in rural East Texas. Black Rock was fifty miles from the nearest liquor store, and the Colonel secretly hoped deep down that this would help his wife stay sober. But soon Babe joined the local country club, where there was a bar and booze and plenty of friends to share in her fun, and Tommy was grateful to be out of the melodrama of his mother's life, even if it was only for a few months at school.

When he came home for the summer vacation, he convinced his father to allow him to stay at the ranch until the fall. Tommy was now fourteen, and Nana Harris was all too happy to chaperone him so he would not be living out on the ranch alone. There were a lot of reasons not to go home—Roy and his mother were among the biggest. Tommy knew his father would agree to let him live at the ranch for the summer if he proposed the idea in the right way.

"It would give you a reason to get out of the house and visit the two things you love the most, your ranch and your son," Tommy joked when he asked for the Colonel's permission.

The Colonel had convalesced at home most of the year from his broken leg. He had long ago gotten his cast removed, but recovery from that kind of injury at his age was especially difficult. "It's time for you to slow down," Babe reminded her husband. "You need to start spending more time with your family."

This had been the longest period of time that Tommy's parents ever spent together since they married over sixteen years before, and Tommy wondered if they were driving each other crazy. The Colonel, not used to sitting still, wasn't exactly tolerant of people who violated his peaceful realm; he was cranky and irritable, and didn't care whose feelings he hurt. In return, Babe had little patience for his tantrums and even less sympathy for his plight. "A man your age should know not to stand too close when a dozer operator is pushing down trees," she said repeatedly, berating him for his foolishness.

But worst of all, Tommy's aunts all hovered over the Colonel, driving their little brother even crazier than his wife. His sisters would come to visit and would gossip about things that the Colonel deemed inconsequential, asking for his opinion on the color of hat someone wore to church on Sunday. He felt trapped, and he couldn't get away from any of them. He could ignore his wife, but he could not ignore his sisters and their incessant chatter and pillow fluffing.

At least Babe knew when to leave her husband alone to read, watch TV, or just to rest, but his sisters, who were not that perceptive, saw it as an opportunity to show him how much they cared. By the time the school year was over, his father was more than ready to get back to work. When the newly elected governor of Texas, who was a friend of the Colonel, appointed him to several boards, one of which was to the board of regents of the University of Texas, the Colonel jumped at the chance.

Meanwhile, Beverly's marriage was hitting the rocks. Beverly had quietly married Billy after she found out that she was with child. Tommy's sister had realized as soon as she married Billy that she'd made a mistake and was looking for a way out of the marriage. Billy was a handsome stud but was also very unrefined. Billy had plenty of ambition and lots of big ideas that never seemed to work out, but he didn't have a clue how to turn them into a money-making enterprise.

"Handsome will only get you so far in life if you don't have the skills to get anywhere," the Colonel would tell his stepdaughter when she asked for his advice.

Beverly did her best to raise her children by herself, as she didn't have the money to hire anyone to help her. She also suspected that Billy was unfaithful to her but didn't know for sure and dared not accuse him. She'd taken a job working for an antiques dealer part-time and had been paying the household bills from the money that she made, along with the money Miss Eddy had left her in her will. Babe tried to help her daughter out financially by taking her children on shopping sprees and buying them groceries, clothes, shoes, and toys, and by paying her mortgage and utility bills when she was short on cash. She tried to keep this on the q.t. so that her husband wouldn't find out how bad things were and explode into diatribe about his son-in-law.

Beverly had gone into marriage hoping for the best, but she was fearfully aware that the odds of her marriage lasting much longer were not good. Finally, after six years, Beverly had decided that enough was enough. But divorcing Billy was like trying to get a piece of chewing gum off the bottom of your shoe—it was a big sticky mess. Billy was politely asked to leave, which caught him by surprise. His meal ticket was kicking him out, and he was totally unprepared despite the fact he was the only one who was surprised by this turn of events.

After their divorce was final, Beverly moved into a small house off Wesleyan Street in Houston with her two small children. She soon started an interior design business on the side and was very good at it; shortly after, Beverly was in high demand. Even though the court had ordered Billy to pay child support, Beverly presumed she would never see a dime from her ex-husband. But she did hope that now that they weren't married anymore, Billy would at least try to be a good father.

Two of her friends from high school, Valerie and Cybil, made sure that Beverly was included on the guest list for all the biggest social events in town and planned to help her find a new husband.

"I feel as though I need to do something," Cybil told her at lunch one day.

"You spent too many years with a man who was uncivilized and didn't treat you the way you deserved. It's time that you met meet a man with a good head on his shoulders," Valerie said, patting her on the hand as they sat in parlor of her River Oaks home. "It's very the least I can do to help."

Within a year, Beverly had met an investment banker named Bob Andrews at a fund-raising gala for the Houston Ballet. At the gala, Beverly had looked stunning in a designer ball gown that Babe had bought for her. Beverly stood beside her friends when she asked, "Who's that handsome gentlemen talking to Herb?"

Beverly and her friends giggled like schoolgirls as Cybil discreetly pointed out Bob across the room. "That's Bob Andrews. He owns his own financial services company and is very well connected. He's wealthy and smart, and he looks fabulous in a tux."

"I can see that," Beverly replied in a whisper. "But is he single?"

"Oh yes, he's a friend of my husband's. Let me introduce you," Cybil said. Taking Beverly by the elbow, she led her across the room to where Bob and Herb were talking. Bob was holding a scotch and water in one hand as the two women walked up. "Excuse me, I hope I'm not interrupting an important conversation, but I would like to introduce you gentlemen to my lovely high school friend, Beverly."

"Very nice to meet you," Bob replied in a well-bred tenor. "I see that you don't have anything to drink yet—can I get you something?"

"Yes, please, I would love a glass of Chardonnay." Beverly tried her best to not to show her excitement.

Beverly became enamored with Bob immediately, and the couple fell in love after a whirlwind courtship. Bob was everything that Beverly wanted. He was ten years older and had never married, and he was successful, sophisticated, and cultured. She was relieved to finally meet the man of her dreams.

The couple married after a year and moved into a house in the River Oaks area. Before long, Beverly and her new husband were regulars at all the parties and galas, and were standouts in the social register. They were a handsome couple, and their pictures were often featured in the society columns of local newspapers. "I finally made my grandmother's hopes for me come true. I just wish Miss Eddy were still alive to see it. I'll never make a mistake like Billy again," Beverly vowed to her mother.

⊷⊷▣ ▣⊶⊶

Beverly's divorce created some drama but did little to affect Tommy's summer home from school. In fact, it was one of the best summers he'd ever had. He learned to drive in an old beat-up pickup truck on the dirt roads of the ranch and farm. He baled hay all summer long and learned to drive a tractor. The smell of the fresh-cut hay was heady, and he decided that to him it smelled like happiness. Tommy marveled at the birds that followed the tractor's path in order to feast on the bugs whose hiding places were freshly exposed. Tommy skin tanned darkly from the summer sun, and he would often eat the lunch that Nana packed under a water oak tree at the edge of the hay meadow. He loved the simple life he found at Peach Tree Ranch: no expectations and no pressure to perform. He wasn't the heir to the throne sitting under a tree in the hay meadow; he was just Tommy.

He had gone through puberty earlier that year while he was away at school, and he felt like that went easier because the other boys in his dorm had let him in on their jokes about girls and puberty. He was glad they had included him and thought that if it had not been for life in the dorm, it would've had taken a lot longer to figure out all this stuff on his own, especially if Nana was involved.

He also felt as though he was learning how to hide the shame of what Roy had done to him. If it weren't for the joking and laughter of his new friends in the dorm he wouldn't have known how to deal with the ugliness he felt. What Roy had done to him made Tommy feel dead inside, but now he was laughing again. Tommy knew that what happened between himself and Roy wasn't normal, and he wanted more than anything to move on and forget about that part of his life, pretending it never happened. He wanted desperately never to think about it again.

At night after dinner with Nana Harris, Tommy read books in bed. The nights were hot, and the air was thick and humid. There was no air conditioner— only an attic fan. They slept with the window open in old frame house through the night, and Tommy would light a citronella candle on the floor beside his bed before he went to sleep to combat the swarms of vicious mosquitos. Tommy had brought his dog, Spotty, out to the ranch to live with them, and he let the dog sleep with him at night. Tommy was forbidden to let the dog into his parents' house, but Nana Harris didn't see the harm and agreed as long as Tommy kept the dog bathed and there were no fleas or ticks in the house.

The ranch was far enough from the nearest town that thousands of stars dotted the summer night sky. The wildlife was plentiful in the Brazos River bottom, and he could hear the screech owls off in the distance as he drifted off to sleep. Tommy loved this simple, serene life. It was so therapeutic. It was light-years away from his mother's drinking and the constant fighting between Babe and Nana Harris.

Occasionally they had problems with skunks and armadillos under the pier-and-beam house. Nana put Tommy in charge of keeping mousetraps around because the field mice would make their way into the house and she didn't want a big rat snake to come into the house looking to eat the mice.

"I'm an animal lover but will not abide mice or snakes," she insisted to Tommy when she made him take care of the traps.

The only condition for his summer of freedom was that Tommy still had to attend services at the Church of Christ and have Sunday dinner with the family. Aunt Annabelle was getting old and was now sharing Sunday dinner duties with her younger sister, Sally. Sally had married a man who had worked his way up the Texas Prison System hierarchy to become a warden at a nearby prison. Their house was on the prison property, and Tommy thought it was cool to have Sunday lunch at Uncle Rueben and Aunt Sally's house. He couldn't wait to tell his friends when he went back to school that he got to spend time at a maximum-security prison.

"This is turning out to be the best summer ever," he said as he fell asleep in his bed one evening. "I don't think it could get any better than this." And as he drifted off to sleep, he wondered if his dad ever had this much fun as a boy.

Sometimes on Sundays Uncle Rueben would bring convicts who were in line to be released for good behavior over to his house to help cook Sunday dinner. They would be escorted by a guard past the front gate of the prison to his house, and after the meal had been cooked and the dishes washed, the guard would escort the convict-cooks back to the cell block. After church one Sunday, the Colonel commented to his brother-in-law that dinner was particularly tasty; they had feasted on southern fried chicken, fried okra, mashed potatoes and gravy, green beans, mustard greens, tossed salad, homemade biscuits, and apple pie for desert. The irresistible smells emanating from the kitchen made it hard to wait to eat, and when the food was served, it tasted as good as it smelled. It was a meal fit for a king—as long as the king was a southerner.

At the end of the meal, the Colonel remarked to Uncle Rueben, "I liked his cooking. I'd gladly give him a job if he were ever paroled."

The following week, there was a knock on the door. The Colonel answered to find huge black man in a new suit, holding a small suitcase. The man stuck out his hand to shake the Colonel's, saying, "I am Fredrick. Mr. Reuben told me that I was to come to you for the job as your cook." Tommy's father shook the enormous hand that Fredrick extended to him and promptly gave him the job. Fredrick moved into a tiny one-room house behind the family compound. As soon as he met Fredrick, Tommy took an immediate liking to the man, and he began to think of Fredrick as part of his extended family.

Fredrick was a gentle giant who'd caught his wife in bed with another man after he'd returned home from a night of drinking and killed her in an uncontrollable rage. He spent several years in prison, and during his time there, he prayed each and every night for forgiveness. After staring at the cold concrete walls of his cell, he decided that if he hadn't been drinking that night, his wife, Camellia, would still be alive and his children would still have their mother. He believed so strongly that alcohol had changed his life that Fredrick never touched another drop of the stuff again.

Of course, Babe was horrified when she heard the news that her husband had hired a convicted felon for a cook. "There's a murderer in my kitchen," she complained as he served the couple breakfast, and as usual, the Colonel ignored her.

Once Tommy overheard what his mother was saying about Fredrick as he walked into the kitchen and was appalled. Tommy would spend most of his time in the kitchen with the ex-con whenever he was home, and he had gotten very close to him. Tommy believed that he could tell Fredrick anything without worrying about any judgment.

He said to Fredrick, "Don't let my mother talk to you the way she does. You know my father rules the roost, and if my daddy likes you, you aren't going anywhere no matter what my mother says." Tommy leaned on his elbows on the kitchen counter as he complained.

Fredrick did his best to tolerate Babe's snide remarks. He had done his time for murdering his wife and knew that it would be a long time before he gained the respect of Miss Babe. "She don't mean no harm. I'm used to taking crap from rich white women, even though I don't like it," Fredrick told Tommy.

But one day when Babe was being particularly snooty, she commented, "These eggs are terrible. How did you feed crap like this to the inmates without getting mugged?"

Fredrick had enough. He turned to her and said, "You do know that I have already spent time in prison for killing a woman, right?"

Babe threw her head back and began to howl in laughter. She knew that Fredrick was tired of her mouth, and she got the message loud and clear. She gained a lot of respect for her cook that day, and eventually Babe and Fredrick began to tolerate each other—and after a while, they even liked each other. Fredrick started buying her beer to take with her when she went fishing so that no one she would know was still drinking. Even though he could not abide booze and had stopped drinking years ago, Fredrick didn't judge others for drinking—and especially not Babe.

As the end of the summer neared, Tommy was excited about going back to school, but his time working on ranch had changed his life. He was growing up and was starting to feel like a man. He knew that he really didn't need Nana, but Tommy but felt sorry for her and didn't have the heart to tell her no when she asked if she could help him pack. Nana was getting older, and she didn't have anything in her life outside of church and the people she lived with.

"She endured my mother's bitchiness and stayed to make sure I grew up with some semblance of a normal childhood—I think I owe her something," Tommy told Fredrick before he left for school.

He again asked his father not to let her go. He tried to reason with the Colonel. "She has forsaken everything for my sake, and she doesn't have any-thing but our family's generosity to help her." He didn't care what his mother said, Tommy was determined to show Nana the same loyalty that Nana had shown him his whole life. He would make sure she was always taken care of.

When it came time for Tommy to return to St. Martin's for his sophomore year, the farmers were just beginning the harvest. It had been a good summer, not just for Tommy, but for the farmers, too. They had planted grain sorghum, cotton, and corn. The weather wasn't too hot during the growing season, and they'd had just the right amount of rain. The farmers had started baling the cotton, and as he left the ranch for the summer, Tommy passed huge combines picking the cotton, as well as enormous bales of cotton sitting on the roadside, just waiting to be delivered to the gins. Tommy stared out the car window at the white cotton balls that dotted the landscape like snow in the summertime. Tommy felt sad to leave, even though he loved St Martin's.

"Harvest time will soon be over," the Colonel said to his son as they drove away.

The entire family had settled into a time of relative calm. *It must be the calm before the storm*, Tommy thought to himself. He couldn't help noticing that he felt a little uneasy as he watched the farmers out the window. *Nothing ever stays this peaceful for long around here.*

Chapter 5

OVER THE SUMMER, Tommy had grown a foot and gained thirty pounds, and as a result, the football coaches at St. Martin's noticed him right off the bat. He wasn't the whinny little kid the bullies beat the crap out of at dodgeball anymore. The coaches didn't care if he'd never, ever played before or even that he wasn't very athletic; in general, all they cared about was that he was big. They decided to put him on the offensive line between the defense and their quarterback.

Tommy was scared to death of playing any contact sport because he had a very low tolerance for pain. But, admittedly, the idea intrigued and flattered him, because for the first time in his life, he'd been asked to join a sports team. Secretly, he'd never put any stock in the game and never understood why football so revered as a sport—and once he joined the team, Tommy realized how little he knew about the game. Everything he knew about football he'd learned from watching television with his father every Sunday after dinner.

At first practice was kind of fun. Tommy went through the motions; he was learning the game and was pretty good at mimicking the others on the team. "Maybe this won't be so bad," he commented to a teammate while they practiced. At least that's what he thought until scrimmages came along. Here the team split up into offensive and defensive squads, and squared off against one another in the summer heat.

Tommy got beat up pretty badly. But when he complained, the coach told him, "Shake it off, and get back in the game."

After practice Tommy went to the nurse, who patched him up and told him, "You'll be fine."

Tommy spent the night thinking long and hard about playing football and while he decided that it really wasn't what he wanted to do, he thought that maybe he would give it another try. The next day Tommy tried again, but this time he hurt his knee and couldn't walk. He went back to the nurse and talked her in writing a medical excuse to get out of playing football. He quit that same afternoon.

His father had been elated when Tommy joined the football team. "I have dreamed of my son playing football for the University of Texas since the day he was born," the Colonel told his wife, trying not to show his excitement. So when he heard that his son had dropped out, he could barely conceal his disappointment. The Colonel was stern, even overbearing at times, and could never show any emotion to his son outside of ire. But Tommy felt the full impact of his father's disappointment, and it hurt worse than any punishment he could have received. Tommy wished that the Colonel would accept him for who he really was, but after dropping out of football he knew it wouldn't happen anytime soon.

Returning to his routine after his embarrassing attempt at football as fall progressed, no one really noticed that Tommy had returned to his books. The other boys in the dorm were spending more and more of their time with the girls on campus. Tommy tried to conceal that did not feel the same way as best he could. He had slowly been noticing that he was having other kinds of feelings—about boys. He found himself attracted to them as more than friends. These feelings he was having were powerful and a contradiction of everything he'd been taught in Sunday school. The last thing he wanted was for anyone to find out before he could reconcile them. The whole time he blamed Roy for what he was going through.

The dorms had several communal bathrooms located in each wing of the dorm, and the morning rush to the bathroom was often hectic. There were only a few shower stalls but they were in a separate area of each communal bathroom, which meant that the boys were often rushing around in towels trying to shower (and in some cases shave) before the breakfast head count. Tommy was finding that he was increasingly fighting the urge to watch the other boys during their morning routine. A sense of shame would grip him at times, especially when he remembered what had happened between him and Roy years earlier in the guesthouse.

The other boys spent much of their time talking about girls and boobs, which girls were desirable, and which girls were just coyote ugly. Tommy would join in most of the conversations so that no one would realize that he was sizing up the boys, not the girls. Tommy was a chameleon. His home life had made him an expert at masking his feelings and hiding anything that might expose him as weak or different or ungodly.

For whatever reason, the school priest had taken it as his own personal challenge to make sure Tommy grew up to be whoever God intended him to be. Father Michael had been with the school for long enough to know when someone was struggling with inner demons, and Tommy appreciated the special attention his school priest was giving him. The Episcopal Church had a much more liberal viewpoint about sexuality than the views of the Church of Christ that had been pounded into him. The priest spoke of understanding and acceptance of all people in chapel, and through these sermons Tommy slowly began to realize that he had to forgive himself for letting Roy touch him.

Maybe it really wasn't my fault.

Before long, Tommy, Jeff, and two friends started to sneak into Father Michael's house when he wasn't home to steal the old priest's booze. They would then slip out of the dorms on Saturday night after dorm check when the coast was clear and climb down the rocky trail on the side of the hill that led to the lake. There, he and his friends would drink the stolen booze and sneak back up the rugged trail to their dorm, climbing back into their rooms through an open window.

Tommy and the other boys thought themselves quite clever, but Father Michael discovered his missing booze and figured out what was going on. He was well aware of their trips to the "canyon," as the students at St. Martin's called it.

"It's harmless fun," Father Michael told his wife. "I would rather they steal our liquor than get it someplace else where they might get into trouble." Father Michael never reported the misdeeds to any of the other faculty, knowing that

Tommy and his friends would be sent before the disciplinary committee if this ever came to light.

As the spring semester began, his social life at school changed when he got invited to go home with his new best friend to spend the weekend with his parents. Tommy was ecstatic. He knew he couldn't ask his father to sign the permission form to leave campus for the weekend, so Tommy asked his mother to sign off on the visit with his friend. His friend's name was Jefferson, but everyone called him Jeff. Jeff's family were rice farmers from El Campo. Jeff and Tommy had bonded over their love of farming and ranching during their first year at St. Martin's.

It was decided that Jeff's parents would pick up the two boys from the school on a Friday afternoon in April when the weather was starting to warm up; they were planning to take the boys water-skiing. Tommy had met Jeff's parents several times over the past year and a half, but he was still nervous because he had never spent any extended time with anyone outside his own family, except for the hired help.

The following weekend the Burlesons picked the boys up from St. Martin's. As they drove the hour and a half southeast of Austin in Jeff's family's sedan toward the Burleson family farm in El Campo, Tommy started to relax. Jeff's parents were the salt of the earth; they were fun people who just wanted their guests to enjoy their hospitality. Jeff teased his mother about her messy hair and asked her when the last time she had brushed it was. Mrs. Burleson laughed and joked that she couldn't afford a hairbrush anymore now that she was paying for his boarding-school education. Tommy watched in amazement how easily Jeff could laugh and joke with his parents and that they would actually laugh along with him.

If I told my mother how messy her hair was, she would immediately pull out a mirror to fix it, and I don't think she would see it as a joke.

The boys blabbed on about their exploits at school. Tommy told the Burlesons about how he and Jeff had caught several tarantulas and turned them loose in one of the girls' dormitories. Jeff's parents listened intently and laughed so hard he thought they would have a wreck. Tommy was surprised that Jeff's parents enjoyed their stories and were truly interested in their son's happiness.

If I'd told that story to the Colonel, he probably would have been irate and started lecturing me on my juvenile behavior.

Tommy had never really been around anyone like that before. "You're lucky that your parents are genuinely interested in your life. The only thing the Colonel has ever been interested in is my grades," he told Jeff as they rode in the back seat.

They arrived in El Campo around suppertime, just before dark. Jeff gave Tommy a brief tour of the house. The house was a white wooden farmhouse at the end of a dirt road that was lined with trees on either side. There were three barns behind the house, with John Deere tractors and farming equipment parked nearby. The fields surrounding the house were flooded with knee-deep water for the rice, each separated by levees—making the house and barns seem like an island in the middle of an immense ocean of rice fields.

Proudly, Jeff showed his guest his room and then took Tommy to the barn to show him his horse. Jeff stroked the chestnut mare's mane with love. "Her name is Blaze." He petted the animal as he showed Tommy how to give the mare some carrots he'd brought with him from the kitchen. Then they were called to the house to eat.

Mrs. Burleson had set the kitchen table for dinner. This was the first time Tommy remembered eating in the kitchen with someone other than Fredrick or the household staff. She had made hamburgers and homemade steak fries, which Tommy thought were delicious.

Tommy smiled and told Mrs. Burleson, "Eating with my hands at the dinner table would have been frowned upon at home."

He was exaggerating, though. His mother loved to have formal dinners in the dining room with her beautiful place settings and fine china and crystal, but there had been plenty of times when they ate hamburgers, sandwiches, and fried chicken with their hands.

Jeff's mother chuckled, saying, "Well, we aren't that formal at our house. You'll have to get used to eating with your hands when you come to visit."

She figured he was probably exaggerating and didn't think anyone could be as stiff and stodgy as the boy was making his parents out to be. She offered him some vanilla ice cream with chocolate-fudge drizzle and crushed nuts for dessert.

After their meal was over, Jeff, Tommy, and Mr. Burleson watched TV while Mrs. Burleson and Jeff's little sister Julia did the dishes. Mr. Burleson let Tommy pick the TV show they watched, and this made Tommy feel very special because it was just another thing that had never happened before. He thought it fascinating and oddly comforting to know that there were families in the world that weren't as stuffy as his own. There were only three stations out of San Antonio and Houston that the TV could get. The Burlesons had an antennae mounted on a fifty-foot-tall tower, and periodically Tommy and Jeff would take turns going outside and moving the windblown antennae back into position until the television reception was good again.

As soon as the dishes were done, Mrs. Burleson and Julia joined them in watching TV until the adults retired to their bedroom, leaving the young men and Julia to watch *Project Terror*. The three kids then ate popcorn while they watched *Creature from the Black Lagoon*. Tommy and Jeff teased Jeff's little sister, startling Julia at the scariest part of the movie, which would make her scream, "Stop it!" She squealed when Jeff grabbed her just as the creature's hand reached out of the water to grab the heroine. "That's not funny," she declared as she punched her brother.

The three of them were loud and rowdy as they watched the movie, throwing pillows at each other and spilling the popcorn as they played. Tommy told Jeff later, "My mom and dad would have come out of their bedrooms to tell us to be quiet and go to bed." He was getting a taste of a regular family, and he was happy. This was the first time he had ever spent the night at a friend's house. At home, Tommy could only play in his room or in the guesthouse, and even then, Nana would never have allowed him to roughhouse or be loud and rowdy.

The three watched TV until the station signed off the air for the night. Tommy slept on the floor in Jeff's room (Jeff had offered the bed to Tommy, but he took the floor). The boys talked awhile before falling asleep.

"Wow, your mom and dad are so great," Tommy told his friend.

"They aren't always great, but we have a lot of fun most of the time," Jeff replied. "Besides, I've met your mom and dad, and I didn't think they were that bad. You need to give them a break. I'm sure things aren't as bad as you think."

Tommy was grateful that he had caught his mother alone gotten her to sign the permission form for his weekend visit the Burlesons' farm.

Maybe my mother wouldn't have a drinking problem if the Colonel hadn't been so old and set in his ways when they were married.

He'd never really wondered what went wrong in his mother's life before. Tommy had been told all his life that his father was perfect, and now that he was getting older, he was beginning to think that perhaps the Colonel wasn't so perfect after all—and he was starting to resent all those years the Colonel hadn't been around when he was younger.

The next morning, Mrs. Burleson woke the children up early for breakfast. Mr. Burleson was hooking up the ski boat to the family pickup truck because they would be driving to Lake McQueeny for a day of water-skiing.

"I've never water-skied before," Tommy said to Jeff. "But I've always wanted to try, and I'm excited that I'm finally going to get the chance to learn."

"Really?" Jeff replied as he patted his friend on the back and tried to sound surprised. "You'll have a lot of fun." Jeff had already realized that his friend probably hadn't ever water-skied before.

After breakfast, the family and their guest loaded into the pickup. Lake McQueeny was a short drive away, so the Burlesons and Julia rode in the cab while Tommy and Jeff rode in the bed of the truck. Tommy was amazed that Jeff's dad didn't mind them riding back there.

If my father knew I would be riding in the bed of a pickup truck, he would never have allowed me to come.

They reached Lake McQueeny, loaded the skis and picnic supplies into the boat, and launched the boat from a boat ramp just off the highway. Tommy had been to New York, DC, Chicago, St. Louis, Boston, and Los Angeles with his family or with Nana, but this was by far the most memorable trip he'd had in his young life. There were no itineraries or expectations for everyone except to have fun.

The Burleson family spent the whole day on the lake. Tommy learned how to ski on his first try. He felt like an Olympic athlete, and for the first time in his life, he forgot he was a gawky, awkward boy. He was actually good at something athletic and loved it! Before the day's end, Tommy learned how to slalom as well.

"Tommy, you are natural," Mr. Burleson said jokingly. "You clearly misled us when you said you never skied before."

Tommy beamed with pride.

Mrs. Burleson let the boys sleep in the next morning. It was afternoon by the time they woke up, and it suddenly dawned on Tommy that this was the first time he could recall that he had not gone to church on Sunday outside of being deathly ill. About three o'clock, the Burlesons loaded the two St. Martin's boys into their sedan to head back to the school. The weekend had gone by too fast. Tommy was sunburned and sore, but he didn't care and he didn't whine.

Tommy stared out the window as they drove back to school and couldn't help but wish his own parents were more like the Burlesons. Now that he thought about it, Tommy couldn't ever remember his parents taking him on a real vacation. Since he started going to St. Martin's, Tommy was finally able to step back and look at his dysfunctional family in a new light. Tommy's feelings about his mother and the effect that her heavy drinking had on his life were obvious. He had very little respect for Babe and felt like she was shallow and put far too much emphasis on appearances. But lately, he was beginning to resent his father also. Now that Tommy was older, he felt it was cowardly for the Colonel to leave them for months at a time (though he supposed that his father just didn't want to deal with his wife's alcoholism). Most of all, neither one had considered that maybe it was odd for an adult male to hang around a young boy without questioning what his intentions were.

If I ever get married, it will be for love, and if I have children, I will allow them the kind of freedom that I had this weekend. I will never make the same mistakes with my children that my parents made with me.

He sat quietly, not really wanting to talk yet hoping Mrs. Burleson would notice he was being quiet and ask if something was wrong. This was, in fact, the first time that he'd ever entertained the notion of marriage and children. He had noticed girls' boobs, like all the other boys, but the idea of girls being sexual was such a foreign concept, and his same sex attractions only complicated his feelings adding to his bewilderment. His parents had a sexless marriage, and between the aunts, Tommy's mother, and Nana Harris, Tommy had a screwed-up view of relationships.

⤙▦ ▦⤚

A few weeks after they got back to school, Tommy got invited back to the Burlesons again. In fact, he was invited back to Jeff's house three more times before the semester ended. When school was over, the first thing Tommy did when he got home was take his driving test. Tommy had been driving for a long time, and he drove himself to the highway department in one of the ranch trucks. Once he passed his driving test, he was one step closer to freedom.

"I can't wait to tell the other kids at school," he said excitedly to Fredrick.

Tommy was working at the ranch again for the summer, but since he'd gotten his driver's license, he didn't have to live with Nana on the ranch anymore. She was still living in her small house, paid for by the Colonel. Nana was getting older now; she was in her sixties, thin and frail.

Tommy worked all summer long, remarkably without the usual distractions that the freedom of a driver's license would tempt other boys his age. He saved up his pay, simply because he was the kid with everything and there was nothing he could think of that he wanted to spend his money on. Soon Tommy found out that the US Army Corps of Engineers was building a new reservoir on the Trinity River just outside of Livingston, Texas.

Learning to water-ski had made him feel like he was just another run-of-the-mill kid, and so Tommy decided that when he grew up, he wanted a house on a lake so that he could go water-skiing every day. The boundaries of where the new lake would be had been established, and developers were already buying up blocks of land around what would be the shoreline. When Tommy wasn't working, he would drive over to research the ultimate lake lot where he could build a house someday. Since Tommy had always been treated like he was a grown-up, even as a child, it never occurred to him that this was an odd thing for a teenager to fixate on.

Tommy gave the developers his home phone number, and it wasn't long before the Colonel figured out that his son was talking to real estate developers about buying property on what would someday be Lake Livingston. "Tommy, what are you thinking? Are you seriously looking into buying lakefront property on a lake that hasn't been built yet?" The Colonel had scolded and belittled his son before, but he had run out of patience, and his ire was evident in the tone of his voice.

"I learned how to water-ski this spring, and I decided that I would like to live on a lake someday so that I can water-ski whenever I want." Tommy faltered when he timidly confessed to his father. He'd just walked in from working on the ranch, and his father had caught him off guard.

"You are underage and can't own property without the consent of your parents." His father pursed his lips and spoke with a cool, even tone. "When were you planning on discussing this with me?" The Colonel's face was red; Tommy had never seen his father that angry.

"I don't know," Tommy admitted self-consciously as he stared at his feet, "I guess I didn't really think it through."

"I don't understand what you were thinking at all. This really is not like you to behave so compulsively." With that, the Colonel summarily dismissed Tommy and went back to reading his book.

The summer couldn't end soon enough for Tommy. He started packing up to go back to school weeks before it was actually time for him to leave. Tommy was going to be a junior this year, and school could not start soon enough for him.

Tommy never felt the kind of anger toward his father that he was feeling at that moment; he had been mad at the Colonel before, but this time it was different. Tommy wasn't a child anymore, and he didn't like being treated like one. His father had been disappointed when he dropped out of football, but this was different. The Colonel wasn't going to let Tommy have an independent thought. Tommy was only allowed to want the kind of future that the Colonel wanted for him.

When it was time to go back to school, Fredrick took his clean laundry to the guesthouse when Tommy told him what had happened. "All my life he has treated me like an adult instead of a child, and the one time I take some initiative and start acting like an adult, he treats me like a child." He was slamming his things around as he packed.

"Don't you think you're overreacting a little?" Fredrick retorted as he sat the laundry basket down on the couch. "My dad would have kicked my butt if I had done something like that. Besides, how on earth you going to pay for land?'

"I have a trust fund with plenty of money in it. Besides my mother would probably sign the deed if I asked her to." Tommy didn't like having to defend himself to Fredrick, too.

"You mean she'd sign it if you caught her when she'd been drinking," Fredrick quipped.

Tommy stopped and glared at his friend as he walked out the door. "I can't wait to get back to St. Martin's!"

Chapter 6

THE LATE AUGUST summer heat in Austin combined with a lack of air conditioning made the dorms swelter, and Tommy and the other boarding students either hung out in the recreation center or the library to bask in the air conditioning. It would be mid-October before the weather would finally start to cool off and the nights would drop down into the sixties. Tommy was a dorm proctor this year, assigned to the freshman dorm, so he had gone back to school a week earlier than his classmates to attend proctor training, which was perfectly fine with him.

As he was going through the training, Tommy came to the realization that his behavior would be under a microscope and antics like stealing liquor from the priest would not be tolerated. He would be expected to mentor the new freshman, helping them with their transition into the St. Martin's way of life.

Every morning the entire student body was expected to attend chapel; afterward, the students would disband and go to their classes. Neither the boarders nor day students were allowed to leave campus for lunch, so the dining hall was always full, buzzing with students trying to get their meal eaten quickly so that they would have some downtime before their afternoon classes.

St. Martin's was gaining an international reputation, and slowly more and more international students were being enrolled into the boarding program. A few of the freshman in Tommy's charge were young international boarders who had never been that far from home and who had not yet become fluent in the English language. These kids needed a little extra attention from the proctors, and Tommy was more mature than his classmates and very patient with his young charges. In each dorm, there were three faculty members acting as dorm parents who rotated their time on the weekend duty roster. But the proctors were expected to be on campus 24-7. Free weekends were few and far between, especially for the proctors, so Tommy couldn't go home on the weekends with Jeff like he did the year before, and that was a disappointment. He had grown attached to Jeff's family and was so looking forward to spending time with them again.

Jeff hadn't applied to be a proctor like Tommy and lived in the junior/senior boys' dorm because he wanted to enjoy his last couple of years of high school. Most of the other kids had always made fun of the proctors because they were stuffy and had too many responsibilities. The atmosphere in the junior/senior dorm was electric, and the upperclassmen's excitement about being at the heap could be felt as soon as you walked through the doors. The seniors were at the precipice of their high school experience and were determined to make it the best year on record. And the senior boys in the dorm were already planning how to best the last senior class with the senior prank. The junior and senior boys sized up the girls on campus, often arguing over who was going to get to invite which girl to homecoming and the prom and comparing notes about which one they believed would let you get to first base, second base, or even all the way.

The atmosphere of the freshman dorm was much different than the junior/senior dorm. The freshman boys were gawky, and for most of them this was the first time away from home. Although they tried to hide it, Tommy could tell that a lot of the new freshman boarders were homesick. Tommy had to show many of them simple things like how to do their laundry or sometimes even how to make their beds.

One morning, Tommy went to breakfast in the dining hall after rounding up his charges and herding them out the door, only to find Jeff eating at the table with a new transfer from McAllen named Casey. As he walked up with his tray, he heard them talking, "Yeah, the canyon is a cool place." Tommy assumed that Jeff must have been telling him about their adventures stealing booze from Father Michael and going to the canyon to get drunk.

The moment Tommy walked up, Casey started to shush Jeff. Jeff turned around, saw it was Tommy, and said, "Oh, he's cool. He may be a proctor, but he won't rat us out." But Tommy could tell by the concerned look on Casey's face that he really didn't know whose side Tommy was on.

Tommy was caught in the middle between the teachers and his classmates. No one came to his room to visit him in the freshman dorm. He felt lonely because he was left out of a lot of the conversations and jokes. These feelings were only exacerbated when occasionally he'd find his friends laughing and they would stop as soon as they saw him. He was starting to think that becoming a proctor was a mistake.

When Tommy had applied for the proctor position the year before, he'd told the school counselor that he was doing it to improve his chances for getting into college, but really, he'd done it for more selfish reasons. Until he went to boarding school, Tommy had never shared anything with anyone, and he'd discovered that he really didn't like sharing a room. After Peter, his first roommate, had moved out, Mr. Longstreet didn't assign him another roommate, and he'd finished out his freshmen year with a room to himself.

But the next year, Tommy was assigned another roommate that he had even less in common with. Truman was from Taiwan and was really nice and polite but didn't speak English very well. But that wasn't the real problem for Tommy. The problem was, Truman was a pig. Tommy had grown up with maids and didn't clean up after himself, either. He learned to live in his own mess but didn't especially like living in Truman's mess, too. So Tommy decided to apply to become a proctor so that he could get a room to himself to get some privacy.

However, the main reason he'd become a proctor ran even deeper. He was hiding some very powerful urges that he didn't want the other boys to see: he was still grappling with his sexual attraction to men. Tommy would wake up with an erection and would jack off as he fantasized about the captain of the football team taking a shower just down the hall. He was determined not to let the other boys in the dorm know that he was attracted to them. Tommy liked having friends and didn't think they'd still want to be his friend if the other boys found out. The sexual revolution was underway in places...but those places were far away from Texas, where homosexuality was still taboo.

During his childhood, Aunt Annabelle had preached that it was a sickness, a sin against God and humankind, and even though in his heart he knew that wasn't really true, it was always in the back of his mind. Tommy had witnessed homophobia all his life. He couldn't tell anyone how he felt—he just couldn't risk being discovered and excommunicated from the social order again because of these new confusing feelings. As a proctor, Tommy knew he would have a room to himself and was less likely to have to confront those feelings that he was trying to repress and figure out.

When Tommy was asked who he was inviting to homecoming or prom, he simply said, "I don't know." Tommy didn't want to think about asking girls on dates.

"What about her?" his friends would say, pointing out some girl in the lunch line.

Tommy would come up with some character flaw that was repulsive or make fun of the girl's looks, saying, "I can't help it if I'm picky. I guess I'm just saving myself for that special girl."

His friends would groan in response and eventually gave up trying.

Volunteering was another clever strategy Tommy used to avoid those awkward moments. He began setting up events with the audio and lighting systems; he would volunteer to be the DJ and would be indispensable behind the scenes so that he would be unavailable for dates. Tommy discovered, with no small sense of relief, that he could use his chameleon-like skills to help avoid the dreaded dance.

Before he'd come to St. Martin's, his mother had decided he needed to take ballroom dancing classes. For three years, every Tuesday and Thursday Nana Harris picked up Tommy after school and took him to dance lessons. It wasn't long before Tommy became a pretty good ballroom dancer, but when he attempted a fast dance like the kids on *American Bandstand*, he looked a little like a chicken scratching for feed in the barnyard. So, dancing in front anyone was out of the question.

⊷▬◍ ◐▬◖

At the end of the school year, Tommy was ready to go back home, but the sting he felt over his father treating him like a child the previous summer was still fresh in his mind, smoldering beneath the surface. Tommy planned on again working at the ranch for the summer, living in the same little house where he and Nana stayed when he was younger.

That summer, he would visit home to check in with Fredrick or his mother, but he put on a polite, cool act whenever the Colonel was around. Unfortunately, for Tommy, working on the ranch had lost its luster. He would wake up early and drive a tractor in the hay meadows most of the day. It was hot, and this summer it just seemed like driving a tractor was becoming more of a job than any kind of fun—as it had been when he'd first started a few years earlier.

Nana still lived in the small one-bedroom house behind Mrs. Harper, and every once in a while, Tommy would go by to visit her. Mrs. Harper lived next door to her three sisters, each having their own house, one next to the other. Nana was always welcome for meals and was invited to the ongoing domino and card games that were held by the sisters almost daily. There would always be lots of food, friends, gossip, and laughter at the games, but Nana rarely stayed to participate, mostly because Mrs. Harper and her guests would indulge in alcoholic libations during their games and, oftentimes, Babe would be invited.

Nana Harris found that it was uncomfortable watching Tommy's mother drink, so she sat quietly and nervously watched their games, knowing that now she was dependent on Babe's goodwill for her survival. Once Babe was at the Harpers' domino game drinking vodka and orange juice in the middle of the afternoon. Nana later told Tommy about his mother's undignified behavior, saying, "She was loud and acted very unladylike."

Tommy became incensed, not at his mother but at Nana, saying, "I've gotten past my mother's problems with drinking. If she wants to drink herself to death, I'm not going to lift a finger to stop her." Tommy's voice was shaking, and he was obviously overwrought. Nana Harris was taken aback, because Tommy had never spoken to her in such a disrespectful tone.

Babe didn't know what had happened between her son and Nana Harris, and didn't care. All she really knew was that Nana's judgmental opinions were no longer an issue. "Nana Harris can't look down her nose at her at me anymore because she knows that she is beholden to my generosity," Babe chortled to Mrs. Harper in their kitchen after a few cocktails.

As for the Colonel, the older he got, the more emotionally detached he seemed. Tommy's parents lived in the same house, but that was about it. The only time they spent together was at meals or when they had company. More and more, the people who come to visit the Colonel were only there seeking favors or political contributions, and the Colonel found it déclassé for someone to come all the way to Black Rock to ask for something from him. He only welcomed longtime friends who would come to visit simply because they were friends.

One Sunday afternoon, Tommy was sitting in the kitchen while Fredrick cleaned up after lunch when the Colonel and his friend got into a heated debate in the living room over the Gulf of Tonkin incident. At one point the debate turned into an argument, and through the kitchen door Tommy heard his father say loudly, "Just because Robert McNamara yells communist doesn't mean we should send American boys to their deaths in the rice fields of some insignificant Southeast Asian country."

"It isn't often that someone will stand up to my father and tell him that he is wrong," Tommy said to Fredrick, remembering what had happened when he himself had stood up to his father over the lakefront property on Lake Livingston.

Fredrick laughed and said, "Your daddy's right more often than he's wrong."

"I hate how he still treats me like a child. I'm nearly seventeen, and he still treats me like a baby in short pants. Even if I stood up to him, things wouldn't ever change," Tommy confessed as he took a bite of apple. "Look at the way he treats my mother—like she doesn't exist."

Tommy paused to see what Fredrick's reaction would be. "I will never understand how my parents can be so charming to outsiders but so cold to each other."

"You're probably right—your daddy may never change," Fredrick agreed. "He's bullheaded and set in his ways. But there is more good than bad in him. And you're going to have to learn that he don't mean no harm and is doing the best he can. He's an old man, and he just don't remember what it was like to be your age."

⇢⟞⊙ ⊙⟝⇠

Tommy left home for St. Martin's for the last time at the end of the summer. It was his senior year, and college testing would take place in the fall.

The previous spring, Tommy and his parents had toured prospective colleges in the Northeast. They visited Harvard, Princeton, and Yale, but Tommy ultimately settled on Amherst. He couldn't put into words why he chose Amherst. "That's just where I want to go," he explained when his father asked why.

Tommy liked the small-town atmosphere of the town of Amherst. It was a picturesque township in the foothills of the rugged granite Berkshire Mountains in a rural part of western Massachusetts. And despite the University of Massachusetts being in Hadley, the next town over, Amherst still had the old Ivy League character of brick and stone structures, classical architecture, and tree-lined streets that seemed untouched by time.

Tommy had planned out his senior year with every intention of taking it easy. All was quiet during most of his senior year. He'd managed to make it through all four years of high school without any problems or fights...that is, until after spring break when "senioritis" kicked in. Senior prank was too much temptation for Tommy and the other boys, who were quietly surveying the weakness of the school campus to see what they could get away with. The school faculty and staff had announced at the beginning of the year that there would be little tolerance for the senior prank and that anyone caught in the act would go before the headmaster for disciplinary action.

Tommy, Jeff, and two other boys decided on a plan of action. One night in mid-May, just before final exams, the four boys broke into the library and proceeded to stack a few hundred books in front of the entrances so that none of the doors could open, leaving the same way they came in. The next morning, after the library staff discovered that they couldn't get into the building, the headmaster announced that any senior involved would not graduate. The four boys, fearing the repercussions, never told anyone of their involvement until after the graduation ceremony when they announced it to the whole class. Everyone was incredibly impressed that the four were able to get away with the prank.

In reality, the headmaster already knew who the culprits were. In fact, he had pulled Tommy aside the week before graduation and said, "You must not think that you are so clever as to outsmart us. St. Martin's is a small community. I simply changed my mind about the punishment when I found out who was involved."

Tommy winced and said nothing.

"I am letting you graduate so that your father won't be disappointed in his son," the headmaster continued.

Tommy felt the stab in the chest, just as sure as if the headmaster had used a real knife. He hung his head and stared at his feet. He'd spent his whole life trying not to disappoint his father.

Chapter 7

ANTICIPATION FILLED THE air on the day Tommy graduated from high school. Tommy had grown up into a handsome young man and was ready to step out into the world. Graduation ceremonies at St. Martin's were held on Memorial Day weekend. It was already hot at the end of May in Austin, and tents were provided as shelter from the hot sun.

The ceremony was held at the St. Martin's chapel on the beautiful hilltop over Lake Austin and the rugged Texas hill country. It was a still day, and there was very little breeze circulating in the tiny chapel. The sliding glass doors were opened and the ceiling fans on full blast to combat the oppressive heat. The few clouds in the sky did not yield much shade from the intense sunshine. When the procession of seniors entered, Tommy's white shirt was soaked with sweat underneath his dark blue blazer. The excitement of the day was electric, and the pride of the seniors' accomplishment shown bright in their radiant faces.

The chapel was crowded with parents and graduating seniors. Onlookers were asked to stand outside and watch through the opened sliding glass doors. Nana Harris among them. Nana had asked Mrs. Harper to drive her to Austin to the graduation ceremony, saying, "Tommy is as close to a son as I will ever have."

He'd grown into a good-looking young man with both the best and worst attributes of his parents. He'd grown a mustache his senior year that the teachers made him shave off for graduation. Tommy's hair was dark brown like his mother's—gone was the blond hair he'd had in childhood.

"Tommy got his mother's good looks and looks nothing like his father," Mrs. Harper articulated to Nana as the two women watched the procession. The Colonel was tall and thin man with piercing blue eyes; Babe's dark brown eyes and an olive-colored skin tone were exactly like her son's, even though she was beginning to show her age and routinely lied about it. Still, anyone with eyes could see that Tommy looked more like his mother than his father.

"Tommy inherited his father's intelligence," Nana grumbled, as she didn't like admitting that Babe contributed at all to Tommy's upbringing.

As Tommy walked down the aisle of the chapel for the last time as a high school student, a toothy grin was on his face and his thoughts were a whirl. Although he'd inherited his father's book smarts, he'd also inherited his mother's irrational and compulsive behavior. On top of that, Tommy had a chip on his shoulder. Although he was born into privilege, Tommy believed with all his heart that he'd been forced to suffer through a tragic childhood and deserved special treatment for everything he'd had to endure.

Since he'd been thinking about his future for most of his senior year and had decided most certainly that he wanted to be rich, Tommy planned to take over the company and turn it back into a money-making venture again. The Colonel was older now and was spending too much time on his philanthropic endeavors. All he had to do was be patient. After all, his father couldn't live forever, and once Tommy could do what he wanted with the company, then the world would be his oyster.

Graduation seemed like it took forever. After the ceremony, the seniors were expected to clean out their dorms. Suddenly, a deep sadness came over Tommy as he packed to go home. St. Martin's had been his safe haven.

This place saved me from Roy, he thought as he packed. *I don't know what would have happened if I hadn't come here.*

St. Martin's had become more like home to Tommy than his own home, and his classmates and the faculty seemed more like a family to him than his own parents and sister. The St. Martin's experience was the best time he'd had in his life, and he was apprehensive and insecure about the future.

Even though he'd never told anyone what happened with Roy, his resentment toward the adults who failed to protect him from the neighbor kept growing, and Tommy was developing some distasteful defense mechanisms to protect himself from emotional distress. At the time, he'd made a conscious decision to hide from his family the pain he'd gone through, but now that he was older, the resentment he felt was almost unpalatable. He relived it in his mind over and over, and he'd started to hate his family—all of them—for not knowing, not seeing what he had been through.

And now that he'd graduated, he was going back to that crazy place, and it made him very anxious.

No one cut him any slack. The adults in his life had always placed such unreasonable expectations on him, and so he'd decided that now that he was an adult, he was going to push back and earn some respect. Tommy decided to rewrite history by changing reality.

His parents had disappointed him sorely. Tommy was quick to judgment and to blame others for his misfortunes.

My father has planned out my life for me, but I want something more than what he wants for me. I want to be my own man instead of just someone who follows in my father's footsteps!

As he left the dorm, Tommy turned one last time to soak it all before he headed home, knowing that he wouldn't be home for long. But that was little comfort to the young man as he put the last box into the trunk of the Colonel's Cadillac.

Tommy felt like he'd left home as soon he went to St. Martin's—that he'd grown up the moment Roy pulled his pants down and molested him. Tommy lost his innocence that day and didn't know how to get it back. He was polite and well spoken, but down deep he had a hole in his heart that he didn't know how to fix.

Tommy had been invited to plenty of parties that night, but his father had annoyingly decided that they were a frivolous waste of time, telling Tommy he wasn't allowed to go, so the family headed home instead. Besides, Tommy's sister, her new husband Bob, and her children William and Candy had attended his graduation, and the family was going to meet at the County Line BBQ restaurant for a celebration first.

After his celebratory dinner with his family was over, Tommy and his parents headed back to Black Rock. He sat quietly in the back seat of the car, deep in thought as they drove down the highway, east toward home. Tommy's mother chattered incessantly while the Colonel nodded sometimes, saying, "Uh-huh." Tommy wanted to listen to music so he didn't have to listen to his mother, because her small talk was irritating beyond belief, but he knew better than to ask his father if he would turn on the radio. Tommy's father was a pragmatic man who was raised in the Black Rock Church of Christ. The Colonel thought music was a foolish indulgence and didn't listen to it.

Tommy's thoughts went to the guesthouse and his summer off before he went off to college. Once more Tommy would stay there while his parents lived in the big house, and he would only go into it for meals or to use the telephone. Roy, the pedophile, still lived across the street from the guesthouse but had long since stopped paying attention to Tommy now that he was a grown man. Tommy knew his fear was irrational. He was a grownup now and could protect himself from Roy, or anyone else for that matter, but the fear still lingered.

I wonder who Roy's latest victim is?

Just the thought of Roy sent a cold chill down his back. Tommy tried not to show it, but he still had a strong visceral reaction anytime he saw the man.

Tommy was still struggling with his attraction to men and blamed Roy for those homosexual feelings. He would lay awake at night wondering if his experience with Roy caused it or if he was born this way.

Was it that obvious even when I was young that I was attracted to men? Did Roy's see it and exploit it? How could he have possibly known? Would I be normal if Roy had left me alone?

Questions like these haunted Tommy, and he desperately yearned to make peace with his past. The gloom and dread Tommy felt increased with each passing mile. The ride home from St. Martin's felt like it was taking an unusually long time—or so it seemed, despite the fact that his father was a lead foot and would pass several cars at a time. Babe sat next to him in the front seat complaining about her husband's driving while the Colonel ignored her the best he could.

He could see that his mother was in a bad mood. Tommy figured that for the sake of appearances she had refrained from drinking over the weekend of his graduation, and he reckoned that it was harder than she thought it would be. He figured that his mother probably wanted a drink right about now. She was getting wound up, and he could tell that she couldn't wait to get home and have a snort from the bottle of gin that she hid in the drawer of the dresser in her closet.

Mother has had about all the nice little family she can stand for a while.

Babe was perturbed and complaining that Nana Harris had nerve to show up at Tommy's graduation, even though it really wasn't a surprise. "Nana Harris always acted like she was Tommy's mother instead of the hired help the whole time that she worked for us," she groused, even though no one was listening.

Tommy's father still gave Nana financial support, and it annoyed her that it was just another fight she was never going to win. "Even though the woman is gone, she still lives nearby and is getting money for what? She made my life miserable for years. She's a freeloader, and we are never going to be free of that woman!"

It stuck in Babe's craw, and she was going to make sure that her husband and son knew exactly how she felt about the woman. Babe had always had a sneaking suspicion that Nana Harris wanted her out of the way so she could take over, and she also suspected that Nana Harris didn't just want her son but her husband, too.

Tommy closed his eyes and pretended to go to sleep. He understood all too well what was coming—he had seen it a thousand times. Babe was whipping herself up for a bender, and he wanted out of the car in a bad way.

I'm going to be in purgatory for the next few months until I can go to college.

Tommy shook his head and sunk down in the back seat. Now that he'd spent so much time away from home at boarding school, he was even less tolerant of his mother's emotional drama. Finally, the Colonel pulled into the driveway of the family's house, Tommy's parents went inside, leaving him to unpack the car and move into the guesthouse.

Fredrick came out, greeted Tommy, and offered to help.

"I think Mom is heading for her stash of hooch," Tommy declared as he opened the trunk and lifted a box out. "She's pissed that Nana showed up for my graduation."

Fredrick laughed and went back to his cooking, leaving Tommy to unpack.

Tommy took his things back to the guesthouse, wishing that at least his father would have had the consideration to park closer so that he didn't have to carry everything so far. When he opened the door, it looked like no one had been there since the last time he was home. There were dead roaches on the floor, dust on the furniture, and spider webs in the corners, and the sheets on his bed needed changing.

This is a fine welcome home from your parents.

Tommy stacked the boxes he was carrying on the floor just inside the door and went back for the rest. Fortunately, the evening sun was getting low, and the long shadows of the live oaks around the yard helped to cool the day off.

Everything changed when one day the Colonel told Tommy to go down to the dealership and pick out a car. "I don't want you hitchhiking like those flower children on the news," his father told him.

Tommy had never had a car of his own, and he was elated. He had been driving since he was fourteen but always drove a beat-up ranch truck or his mother's Buick.

The next day, Tommy walked around the only car lot in Black Rock, trying to decide what kind of car he would like. Eventually, the salesman, Mr. Johnny Whitehead, found him and brought him into the showroom.

And there it was, every young man's dream car: a 1968 Pontiac GTO. It was green, with a black vinyl roof. Tommy fell in love while running his hands over the smooth curving lines of the fenders—it was the most beautiful car he had ever seen. Once Johnny saw how much Tommy loved the car, he told Tommy he would take care of everything.

"Drive it home to show to your father. If he says no, then you can bring it back and we'll pick out another one," Johnny smoothly declared as he handed Tommy the keys. He knew by the look on the young man's face that he'd just made a sale and that once Tommy drove that GTO, he'd be hooked.

Tommy drove it straight home, and when he got there, he showed it to his father. And when his father said he could keep it, Tommy tried to hide his excitement...at least until his father went back in the house. But as the Colonel shut the door, Tommy did a dance out in the yard. Fredrick and Babe watched through the kitchen window as Tommy lay on the hood of his new car as if he were hugging it.

"It looks like my husband told him he could keep it." Babe smiled at Fredrick as she sipped her evening toddy. She was relieved that her husband had finally allowed his son an indulgence, even if he didn't realize it.

As Tommy admired his new GTO in the driveway, all he could think about was that he didn't have to drive a beat-up ranch truck or borrow his mother's car anymore. Now he was free from his parents, and he could come and go as he pleased.

A few weeks later, Tommy began to pack up for Amherst. He was starting to get excited about his second new start in life. He would soon be saying good-bye to the guesthouse and going to college. And now that it was really starting to feel like it was going to happen, Tommy could hardly contain his excitement.

When Tommy's father had gone off to the University of Texas, it had been before the start of World War I. The Colonel had ridden a horse back to North Zulch, where he boarded a train to Waco and then changed trains to go to Austin, the trip taking him two long days. Now it was Tommy's turn to go off to college—not just college but an Ivy League college. And even though they didn't show it, both of Tommy's parents couldn't be prouder of their son.

--->===◯ ◯===<---

It was the dog days of summer. The August heat was almost unbearable the morning that Tommy headed for New England. At that time of year, the nights didn't cool off much; the temperature was still eighty degrees as the sun came up over the horizon. The air was still and humid, and a thick layer of morning dew covered his new car.

Tommy had packed his car in the twilight hours the night before, when the evening air was full of the sounds of cicadas singing their evening song. It was impossible to swat mosquitos with his arms full, so Tommy got several bites on his arms and legs as he packed up the trunk of his car. Fredrick had baked him a pie and packed a lunch of fried chicken for his long drive. Tommy plotted his course on a map that he folded carefully into square sections that could be easily read on his drive. He had promised his mother that he would spend the night somewhere in Tennessee, but he'd lied to get her off his back. He had no intention of stopping once he hit the road to the Northeast. Excitedly, he said his good-byes to his family and waved good-bye to Fredrick as he pulled out of the driveway of the family home.

It had been daylight for about an hour and was already getting hot when he pulled out of the drive. As he started down the caliche roads that were the short-cut out of Black Rock, a cloud of dust followed just behind him. He headed north toward the highway that led to Texarkana and the Arkansas boarder. Tommy planned to drive through Arkansas, crossing the Mississippi River at Memphis and traveling the length of Tennessee, then continuing along the spin of the Blue Ridge Mountains in western Virginia into Maryland, Pennsylvania, and upstate New York, finally arriving in western Massachusetts. Tommy would get to Amherst the next afternoon; he planned to stop at a rest area in Tennessee that evening and sleep for four hours in his car before continuing on to western Massachusetts.

Tommy arrived in Massachusetts on a crisp, cool day with temperatures that were mild; it was a far cry from the summer heat he'd left behind in Texas. The New England late summer sky was brilliant blue and dotted with wispy clouds. The majestic old elm trees lining the streets of Amherst would soon change from brilliant green to browns and reds before the leaves fell from the tree branches. Fall in Texas fall only lasted about two weeks, with the trees seemingly dropping their leaves from exhaustion due to the heat of the long, dry summers, and Tommy was looking forward to the change.

His excitement was hard to contain as he turned off his radio and parked the GTO in the first spot he could find in front of the college admissions building. Incoming students had been instructed to go the admissions office, sign in for freshman orientation, and pick up their dorm assignment. Using the map of the college that the lady at the admissions office gave him, Tommy found his way to the Alpha Chi where his dorm assignment was located.

The college campus was mostly deserted. There were only a few students on campus this early, but he greeted and introduced himself to everyone he met. He was starting a new life, and he was going to make as many friends as he could at college. After unpacking his car and settling into his room, Tommy showered, changed into a new pair of blue jeans and a clean shirt, and went to explore the campus on foot.

Tommy people-watched as he strolled, happy to see that most of the students on campus walked or rode bikes. He figured that when he toured the campus with his parents, the college only showed them what they wanted his parents to see; now he could see the stuff they didn't show on the campus tour. All his tours had been scheduled during the college's spring break, when almost the entire student body was gone and tours were routinely guided by select students who understood that the impression the parents walked away with determined whether Amherst College was chosen or not.

Tommy was getting his first real glimpse of what college life was honestly like, and he soaked it in as he sat eating a burger and drinking a beer at a sidewalk café on the town square that was walking distance from campus, taking in the glorious late summer sunshine. "It's pretty groovy drinking a beer at a restaurant," he told the waiter, realizing as soon as he said it that he probably sounded juvenile. Nevertheless, he thought himself quite clever for getting away with ordering a beer since the legal drinking age in Massachusetts was 21 years old and he was only 18. In any case, the waiter had neglected to check his I.D.

Tommy had grown his mustache back during the summer, and it made him look older and more mature. He'd gotten a haircut before he left for college at his mother's insistence, and as he looked around at the other college students milling around, he was already regretting it. Everyone he saw had long hair, and he looked like a hillbilly redneck from Texas.

Almost immediately he'd become aware that he spoke with a thick Texas accent. As he sat by himself, he listened to the other young men and women, trying to pick up some hip phrases so that he wouldn't sound like a hick from the South. On the way back to campus, Tommy stopped at a shop and bought some T-shirts, and he thought he might cut off a pair of blue jeans into a pair of shorts when he got back to his room.

When he returned from his walk, the dorm was abuzz with activity. Tommy opened his dorm-room door to find his new roommate and his parents unpacking. Tommy introduced himself politely and took a moment to size up his new roommate. His roommate was a tall, thin young man with dark brown eyes, dark hair, and wire-rimmed glasses. His name was Nathan Goldberg, and he was a premed major from Long Island, New York. He and his parents seemed very nice, and Tommy was relieved. He knew from his boarding-school experience that if you didn't get along with your roommate, it would only make the semester drag by.

At orientation, Tommy enrolled in his classes, which were scheduled to begin the following Monday. It wasn't long before met the only other Texan at orientation, Robert Martin, who was from Fort Worth. Robert was premed like Nathan but was planning on becoming a psychiatrist.

Tommy had decided when he was in high school that he would major in economics, and so he registered for classes that his counselor believed would be most beneficial to him. His course load appeared to be no problem for him to handle, so he bought his books at the campus bookstore and settled in for the semester. While he was at the bookstore he introduced himself to a young named, Brandon Wycliffe who was buying the same books for his classes. "Looks like we'll be seeing each other around," he quipped as they stood in line to pay.

After returning to his dorm room, he was happy to see that he wasn't going to be in class all day every day. "We'll have time off during the day to study or goof-off," he commented to Nathan after Nathan's parents left.

As the semester progressed, football season began and, with it, party season. Tommy went to lots of parties and found that he could outdrink most of his classmates. Also, he was amazed to see how prevalent drugs were at the parties—everything from marijuana to LSD circulated around. It was the late 1960s, and the drug culture was in full swing, especially in the Ivy League colleges of the Northeast.

But Tommy didn't feel comfortable indulging in drugs the way many of his classmates did. Marijuana was the drug of choice of the hip and cool on college campuses at that time. A lot of Tommy's friends used it regularly. Tommy tried it a few times but found he didn't like it. Unlike alcohol, which numbed the senses and loosened up your inhibitions, Tommy found that smoking pot made him emotional and paranoid. Tommy had spent most of his life bottling up his emotions, so he decided that pot wasn't the drug for him. Also, he thought that maybe that he was allergic to pot, because smoking it would clog up his sinuses so badly that he couldn't breathe.

As a result, when someone was passing around a joint, Tommy would simply say, "I'm allergic to pot. Maybe when my roommate becomes a doctor, he can test me for my pot allergy?" Tommy would laugh and hand it off to someone else.

As Tommy settled into college life and became acquainted with more of his peers, overwhelming insecurities began to take hold of him. Tommy remembered back to Miss Eddy, his maternal grandmother, who used to talk about old money and how he was being raised like new money in Houston. Tommy was clearly too young to understand what she meant when she called them "new rich," but now he was starting to get the picture.

In grade school, he was always one of the richest kids in school. But as Tommy became better friends with his fellow classmates at Amherst, what his grandmother meant by "old money" hit home. He was in college with several young men who came from third- or fourth-generation East Coast old money, and Tommy found it quiet intimidating.

Even as he tried to exude confidence, Tommy was plagued by self-doubt. Whenever he'd introduce himself to someone new, all they wanted to know was what it was like growing up in Texas.

"Wow! You grew up on a ranch in Texas. How cool! Did you ride a horse on cattle roundups?" Spencer, one of his new Amherst acquaintances, asked him shortly after they met.

"Sure, I worked cattle on horseback with the other ranch hands most every summer." Tommy embellished his story without thinking. He didn't think of it as a lie but thought it was better than telling them he drove a tractor and baled hay all summer.

If making new friends was difficult, meeting girls at college was a lot more stressful. Girls from the surrounding colleges would come to parties and local bars to mingle with the Amherst men. Tommy was astounded at how much more sexually permissive the girls in college were compared to high school. His roommate, Nathan, was getting laid regularly, and all he usually had to do to get a girl interested was to tell her he was premed.

"Premed is like an aphrodisiac to the college girls," Nathan said and laughed as he came in late one evening after being with his latest conquest.

Occasionally, Tommy and a group of friends would venture into Springfield and go to bars, pool halls, and restaurants for some local atmosphere. The bars usually were full of girls going to the University of Massachusetts in Springfield, and Tommy would watch as his friends would troll for the UMass coeds they called "townies."

"It is a lot easier to get into the pants off a townie than the preppy girls from Wellesley or Smith. They're usually looking for a husband when I'm just looking to get laid," Nathan professed while give his roommate tips on the conquest of the fairer sex. Tommy watched in amazement as his roommate made picking up a townie at the local beer joint look so easy.

Eventually, Tommy's luck would change. On one trip into town, Tommy was drinking beer and got loud at the local pub they always hit on Tuesday night. Tommy was playing pool and was winning as usual, using the skills that Arnold, the chauffer, had taught him when he was a kid, when a townie named Julia Russo came up to him and introduced herself. "I've seen you here before. You're a pretty good pool player. Where'd you learn to play?" she asked him as she sat down on an empty stool next to him.

"I learned how to play in high school at the school rec hall," he lied, thinking it sounded cooler than "the chauffer taught me in the basement of my parents' house" and not wanting to tell a townie about Arnold and his childhood. Julia was a dark-haired girl with ivory skin and piercing blue eyes, and she smiled as Tommy offered to buy her a beer. After her second beer, Julia leaned in to kiss Tommy.

Tommy tried not to let on that hadn't kissed a girl before, and he hoped that it wasn't obvious to her or his friends. After the kiss, Julia turned her back to Tommy and leaned back between his legs as he sat on the wooden stool, pressing herself against his crotch. She leaned her back against his chest, and Tommy could smell the scent of her perfume. He instinctively started to kiss the back of her neck and found that he was becoming aroused.

It wasn't long before Tommy led Julia outside to the side street where he'd parked his GTO. Without a word, he unlocked the door and the couple climbed into the back seat of his car. It was a cold night in mid-November, and before long the windows of his car were fogged up so that no one other than his friends in the bar knew what was happening in the back seat.

Tommy lost his virginity to Julia. She was the first girl he'd been with. Julia was an exciting and patient lover, and obviously had a lot more experience with sex than he had. As soon as they got into the car, she pulled his pants down around his ankles after pulling her own pants off and straddled Tommy, sliding his hard member inside of him. After a few minutes, Tommy ejaculated inside her and the couple lay in each other's arm.

"So, what part of Massachusetts do you come from?" Tommy asked.

Julia chuckled and asked, "How did you know I'm from Massachusetts?"

"It was the way you talk that gave you away," he responded as he stroked her hair.

"Well, I'm from Hadley, just down the road from here. My parents have a farm on the Connecticut River where they grew vegetables that we sell at the farmer's market in Springfield during the summer. My dad and brothers are electricians and have a shop in Hadley."

After a few minutes of pillow talk, Julia put her hand on Tommy's cock and began stroking it gently, and before long Tommy's member was once again at attention. Julia climbed back on top of Tommy, and they had sex again. Tommy had finally had sex, and it was with a woman.

After a couple of hours together, he drove Julia back to her dorm at UMass. On the short drive back to Amherst, Tommy didn't think about anything except how really good it was to finally have sex with a woman. And for the first time since he'd been molested in the guesthouse, he didn't think about Roy when he thought about sex.

I could get used to having sex with women. Maybe I'm not really homosexual after all.

When Tommy got back to his room later that night, his roommate was already there, sitting on his bed with a book open on his lap, studying. Nathan knew the rules of picking up chicks—if your ride leaves with a girl, find your own way home.

"Well? I want details." Nathan said annoyingly.

"None of your business, man," Tommy responded as he pulled off his boots and started to undress. "I don't kiss and tell."

Chapter 8

As THE FALL semester moved on toward Christmas break, Tommy and his roommate were studying hard as finals closed in. Everyone in the dorm was cramming for exams as the first snow of the winter left a light dusting of powdery white snow on the ground. There was enough fallen snow that a group of people brought the plastic trays from the dining hall out to the big hill above the football practice field and used them to slide down the hill. The crowd grew as the morning went on, and Tommy watched as mostly freshmen rode the cafeteria trays like they hadn't seen a whole lot of snow before.

Tommy's grades from the fall semester were good. However, mostly this was because he didn't find his classes too challenging. Unfortunately, his grades were average compared to most of the other guys in college. Until Tommy went to Amherst, he'd been one of the brightest and most talented students in school. Now he found himself surrounded by the best of the best, and it was quite intimidating. Tommy didn't know how to react to being an average, run-of-the-mill student and soon found himself less and less interested in being the best student and more interested in having friends and partying.

There was no doubt that Tommy was the life of the party. "I don't know how he does it," Spencer marveled to Nathan. "I can't believe how much Tommy can drink and still function in classes the next day."

Spencer was a thin young man who was maybe five foot nine inches tall from Buffalo, New York. And though he loved to go drinking with Tommy, he was no match when it came to holding his liquor.

His friends all noticed that Tommy could drink better than some of the lightweights in college, which made him a pretty popular person to go out with to clubs or parties at night. "I don't think Tommy is taking a very heavy class load like some of the rest of us." Nathan tried not to sound too judgmental, but he also knew that Tommy was drinking an awful lot and the future doctor tried not to show that he was overly concerned.

After he'd lost his virginity to Julia the semester before, Tommy didn't see her again for several months. Julia had written her number on the inside of a matchbook, giving it to Tommy as they kissed good-bye in front of her dorm. As she went inside, she looked back at Tommy and blew him a kiss, saying, "Call me sometime."

But Tommy callously never called her, claiming he'd lost her number. It was in mid-November when they'd had their encounter, and the next week Tommy went home for Thanksgiving, only returning to Amherst for final exams. After finals were over, Tommy and his fellow Texan, Robert, had loaded up the GTO and driven to Texas for the Christmas break.

In the new semester, Tommy had stopped going with his friends to the pub in Springfield on Tuesday nights, mostly because he was afraid he would see Julia again. Like his father, he didn't like confrontations with women. But when Nathan invited him to go with him and Robert one Tuesday in February, Tommy figured that she'd forgotten about him and moved on.

"I'd like to go, but I don't want to see that townie chick I screwed last fall," he explained. Mostly this was because Julia had seemed like a nice girl and Tommy felt like a jerk for blowing her off, though he'd never admit it.

"She'll get over it," Nathan lamented. "They always do."

Later that evening, the trio went to their favorite pub in Springfield to play pool. The three found an open pool table, and immediately Tommy spotted Julia laughing with one of her girlfriends at the bar. Nathan saw Julia too and yelled, "Hey, Tommy, you go get us some beers, and I'll set up the pool table."

Tommy swallowed hard but agreed, knowing full well that his roommate may have just tossed him into the lion's den. "Sure, I'll buy the first round if you get the next," he said as he casually walked up to the bar near where Julia was seated. Tommy slid up to the bar between Julia and another patron just as she turned to see Tommy.

"Hi, babe. How's it going?" Tommy tried to sound cool but could tell by the unhappy look on her face that she wasn't glad to see him.

"Screw you, Ivy League trust-fund baby!" she shouted, throwing her beer in Tommy's face she gathered her purse and tossing a ten-dollar bill on the bar. She and her friend stormed out the door.

The bartender roared with laughter as he handed Tommy the beers he'd ordered, saying, "You messed with the wrong townie, Ivy League."

With Julia's drink dripping down his face, Tommy paid for the beers and walked across the bar, painfully aware that everyone in the pub was laughing and pointing at him. He set the beers on the table next to his companions and wiped the beer off his face with the bar napkins the bartender had given him.

"Man, you're just lucky that she didn't have a full beer!" Robert teased, laughing so hard his eyes teared up.

"I don't think I will ever understand women," Tommy confessed as he cleaned his face.

Clueless about women, even though he'd grown up in a house full of them, Tommy continued to try to get dates. His friends would fix him up, and he had sex with a few of them, but the second date rarely ever happened. Now that the pressure of losing his virginity was over, he found that he liked having sex with woman, blaming his sexual attraction to men on the unnatural acts the monster next door had done to him.

Maybe if I can figure out how women tick I can have a normal relationship with a woman someday.

Girls would hit on Tommy, but he never picked up on their signals. And he'd get even more frustrated when friends would laugh at him whenever he bombed out with a girl.

"I don't think you guys are such great role models when it comes to women, either," Tommy grumbled as he picked up a pool cue and broke the rack Nathan had set up on the table. In reality, Tommy wasn't ready for any kind of relationship yet.

⤖ ⤔

Later that spring, before the semester was over, Tommy and a group of his friends went into Springfield to eat and to find a bar to hang out at after dinner.

Tommy pointed a bar out and suggested they go there. Brandon was there and had a very visceral reaction, saying, "That's a gay bar, man. We're looking for chicks, not fudge packers!"

Caught off guard, Tommy defended himself, saying, "Don't get upset. I had no clue that was a gay bar."

The whole deal was pretty awkward. Even though his friends had joked around, calling each other homos and fags, this was the first time he'd witnessed, not just homophobia, but a real hatred of homosexuals.

Later he decided that maybe he'd go into a gay bar just to check it out someday—without his friends—but he was terrified that someone he knew from college would spot him going in or out. So, he decided that he'd maybe someday go someplace like New York or Boston where he could explore all the feelings he was suppressing away from prying (or judging) eyes.

I want to see what happens, but I just don't know if I have the courage to do it. I am just a horny twenty-year-old who wants to screw anything and everything that walks.

Only a few of his open-minded friends seemed to have figured out that he might be gay and struggling with his sexual identity, including his room-mate, Nathan. Nathan was secure enough with his own sexuality that the idea didn't bother him. When Tommy got back to their room that evening, he found Nathan studying and told him what had happened.

Tommy wanted more than anything to confess everything to Nathan, but the words just wouldn't come out. He explained, "Where I grew up, the only gay man I knew about was a creepy pedophile who was looking to fondle innocent, unsuspecting young boys."

Tommy tried his best not to let on that he was talking about himself and that he was one of that pedophile's victims. Just the thought of what Roy did to him make him feel like he was "unclean," like he needed to take a shower. Now that he was an adult, he wondered what was wrong with him because he had let Roy touch him.

"Pedophiles aren't homosexual. Pedophiles are mentally disturbed individuals who get sexual gratification from overpowering and victimizing helpless children. Pedophiles are sick people who need to be locked up. Gay people are consenting adults who like having sex with their own gender. It's not the same thing at all." Nathan raised his voice as he excitedly explained this, shaking his head.

Nathan had only known his roommate for a short time, but he'd noticed that when Tommy talked about home, he would mostly talk about growing up on their ranch or going to boarding school. Tommy left a lot of things out and seemed like he had no intentions of filling in the blanks.

Tommy was a little agitated by the whole conversation. He paced around the room, fidgeting with the change in his pocket as they talked.

Openness and acceptance was one of the benefits of a liberal education and a sign of the times, but Tommy had grown up believing that his sexuality was something he should hide. As a child, he'd gone to the Black Rock Church of Christ every Sunday (Aunt Annabelle made sure he was there), where the Minister preached that sin of the flesh sent you straight to hell, especially homosexuality. He'd been living a lie most of his life, and he was becoming better and better at it, but conversely, he was becoming worse and worse at hiding the truth.

After the most awkward five minutes of his life, Tommy finally walked over to the door and turned to Nathan, saying flippantly, "Maybe someday I'll figure this sex stuff out. There are too many rules for something that should be so natural! Right now, I need to take a leak."

-->==◎ ◎==<--

The next semester, Tommy was invited to move into a house off campus that three of his classmates had leased earlier. "One of their roommates moved out and they offered me the room," Tommy explained to Nathan as he packed up his things to move.

He liked Nathan, but he'd lived in a dorm most of his life, and Tommy need a change. "I'll see you around," Tommy said as he carried the last of his boxes to his GTO. Things between the roommates had been uncomfortable to say the least after their discussion about homosexuality. Tommy didn't want to leave on an uncomfortable note, but Nathan had gotten a little too deep into his psyche and he didn't like facing those touchy, feely emotions that he'd spent years burying in the depth of his soul.

How could Nathan think I'm gay when I don't even know myself? I know he means well, but he doesn't have a clue what I've been through, and I have no intention of reliving it again. It was like ripping the bandage off a scraped knee. All he did was jerk the scab off and make it bleed again.

That afternoon, he moved in with his new roommates, Mike, Doug, and Paul. The house they leased was on the outskirts of town, a two-hundred-year-old farmhouse built shortly before the Revolutionary War. It was at the end of a long drive, with old elms and evergreens around the property—a huge place, white with peeling paint, four fireplaces, and as many bedrooms. Tommy's new college home was drafty and cold, but it was built soundly from sturdy construction that had obviously been completed with pride and care, and built to last. The hardwood floors were uneven and wavy, and one corner of his bedroom was a good two inches higher than the rest of the room.

"In Texas, old houses like this one are rare," he marveled to his new roommate Doug as Doug showed him around. Tommy's bedroom was an addition that had probably been added on a hundred years after the rest of the house. His room was the smallest and at the back of the house. The bathroom he shared with Doug was constructed out of what was originally part of the back porch and had been subsequently turned into a bathroom with the advent of indoor plumbing.

"I hope this is OK," Doug said. "You know the roommate rules: first one there gets to pick."

"Are you kidding? It's great!" Tommy replied as he put his suitcase on the bed. "I'm just glad to have my own room. This is perfect." As he spoke, he began to unpack and settle in, pulling out shirts from his suitcase and stuffing them into a worn chest of drawers in the corner.

⊷═◉ ◉═⊶

Fall turned to winter, and winter turned to spring. Tommy decided that the term "spring semester" was a misnomer. Spring in western Massachusetts was downright cold that year because the snowfall lasted late into March. He had never been in that cold of a climate before, and he needed to adapt. He bought a real winter coat because the coat he'd brought with him from Texas was really just a jacket. He also bought some waterproof boots because it wasn't long before he discovered that his cowboy boots weren't suitable for trudging through snow banks.

Tommy continued his studies in economics, although his course of study was not that challenging for someone of his intellect. He took accounting and math classes, and had a 4.0 average. Doug was majoring in engineering and spent a lot of time studying. Tommy and Doug would get into heated debates about engineering and science.

"Engineering isn't that hard. It's just a lot of math," Tommy would taunt Doug.

"OK. If you think it's that easy, then next semester you should take an engineering course," Doug challenged Tommy, just to shut him up.

"Not a problem," Tommy replied with a snort. Since Tommy's third year of college was going to be scholastically uneventful, he elected to accept his roommate's challenge. The overconfident Tommy thought he could do anything, so that spring he signed up for a course in thermodynamics. It wasn't long before he realized that he did not have a clue about what in the world enthalpy and entropy meant, or what this had to do with the theory of converting heat and energy into work.

But Tommy's pride had gotten the better of him, and he stuck it out, thinking that sooner or later he would catch on. But all of his hubris only resulted in earning him his one and only "D" in his entire education. Much to his surprise, the Colonel didn't belittle him for this, saying only, "It's good that you are challenging yourself, Tommy."

Tommy went home to visit between semesters, but then he enrolled in the summer semester to bring his grades up to make up for that bad grade in thermodynamics. Tommy fully expected that, once he was home, his father would make sure Tommy knew how disappointed he was with his first bad grade, but the Colonel didn't say anything. "Wow, I don't know if he even noticed," Tommy told Fredrick as he snacked on an apple.

"Oh, he noticed," Fredrick said as he put away the dishes he'd just washed. "He just didn't say nothing. Your daddy is probably grateful you ain't one of those idiots running off to California." The summer of love was in full swing in San Francisco; young adults were rebelling and running away from their parents to find themselves, living on the streets in the Haight-Ashbury district, where they usually wound up strung out on heroin, selling drugs or prostituting themselves just for food. Many of them died in the streets, their grieving parents never knowing what happened to them—the utopia promised to them by other flower children having turned into a hell on earth. Tommy thought about some of the kids he'd heard about at college who freely experimented with drugs and had messed up their lives saying as he dropped his apple core in the trash, "People are just stupid sometimes."

"Well, you just can't fix stupid, can you?" Fredrick smiled as Tommy burst into laughter, nodding his head in agreement.

->=() ()=<-

In the fall of 1969, Tommy finally worked up the courage to go into the gay bar in Springfield, Massachusetts. It was the same gay bar that had been the target of Brandon's homophobic rant two years earlier. He drove the GTO over one fall evening, parking a few blocks away so that if any of his friends recognized his car and asked what he was doing there, he could concoct a cover story. He walked the few blocks to the Ball Park Bar, looking over his shoulder to make sure no one he knew was around. The Ball Park was a dark little dive with the windows painted dark purple. There were two bars at each end and a raised dance floor in the back that was routinely elbow to elbow with men paired up and dancing together to loud rock and roll.

As Tommy walked through the door, he paused and took a deep breath. He then timidly made his way over to one of the bars and ordered a beer. It wasn't long before someone struck up a conversation with him and asked him to dance. "I haven't danced since my mother made me take ballroom dancing in grade school," he joked as he set his beer down on the bar.

"Oh, sweetie, there are no judgments here. This isn't *American Bandstand*."

Tommy roared with laughter, and in an instant, he was out on the dance floor, dancing his heart out. Tommy was really having fun, and it was such a relief to be someplace where he could let his guard down.

That evening Tommy met several very colorful and interesting guys he liked a lot. After a few hours, he left by himself—not that he didn't get any offers, but Tommy just wasn't ready for that step. His thoughts were racing with "what if" and his feelings were a mixed-up cyclone of emotions as he headed home.

I just wanted to see for myself what all the hubbub was about. The guys I met tonight were fun, but I still can't imagine myself having sex with a man. I just want to be normal. How can I ever be normal if I'm gay?

After he left the bar that evening, he decided that he was proud of himself for taking the first big step but terrified of his homosexuality. That lifestyle was far from being accepted into mainstream culture, and homophobia was still prevalent, especially back home in Texas.

He was a young man who already had issues about being liked, and he was scared to death of anyone finding out that he had spent the evening dancing with men who were kissing and doing the bump and grind on the dance floor. He'd felt like a voyeur as he'd watched the men pair off and stick their tongues down each other's throats, and he was aroused. When he got home, his roommate, Mike, was still up studying; he was making a sandwich, digging through the refrigerator.

"Where'd you go tonight? You didn't stay out very late," Mike asked as he buried his head deep in the fridge, digging for some cheese.

"Nowhere special," Tommy replied as he reached into the refrigerator to grab a beer on the top shelf as Mike continued to rummage.

Tommy had a hard time falling asleep. He had a boner and jerked off, thinking he could go to sleep if he relieved himself. But instead he played the night over and over in his head as he lay in bed. Tommy had been struggling through a dry spell when it came to women and was seriously considering going back again.

I've only done this once, but it sure seems like it would be a lot easier to pick up a guy for sex than a woman. But I still can't imagine having anything more than friendship with a man.

With that thought, he nodded off to sleep.

Chapter 9

IN THE FALL of 1970, Tommy started his last year in college. The years had gone by so fast that it wasn't until Tommy took the LSAT in preparation for his application to law school that the reality of graduating from college really hit him. All his friends were either applying for graduate schools or internships with companies, and some of his friends had already gotten married and started families.

He'd known since high school that he was probably going to law school after he graduated. His first choice was the University of Texas College of Law. He had other choices, but he decided that he wouldn't even apply. He was confident that he was a shoo-in.

"They have to admit me," Tommy claimed arrogantly. "How many of their law school applicants will have an undergraduate degree from Amherst?" he joked as he and his roommates drank beer.

He was a little too confident, believing that it would be his grades at an Ivy League college and his LSAT test scores would impress the UT Law School selection committee. But the UT admissions office was impressed with the size of Tommy's father's wallet and the fact that his father was once on their Board of Regents; the admissions counselor would have let Tommy in no matter what his grades were.

In any case, he was excited when he received his acceptance letter in February of 1971. Tommy believed wholeheartedly that he'd gained admission to UT Law solely on his own merits.

Tommy graduated from Amherst in May of 1971, and his parents came to Massachusetts for his graduation. They had not visited since they took him to tour the campus spring break of Tommy's senior year of high school. Amherst was his own little world that didn't include his parents, and now they were there to watch him graduate with his classmates.

Tommy's father was now in his late seventies. No one knew exactly how old his mother was, but it didn't matter anyway, as she routinely lied about her age. "I am fifty-nine," she swore if anyone asked.

The Colonel was still tall and still stood straight as an arrow, even though he'd put on a few pounds from years of eating Fredrick's cooking. Unfortunately, the years had not been as kind to the one-time beauty from Dallas. Her hair had turned white many years ago, the rosiness was gone from her checks, and the deep lines on her face had grown ever deeper as time crept on. She'd started wearing too much makeup, which only accentuated the lines and flaws of her sagging skin. It was very hard for her to grow old. Babe had put so such stock in her beauty in her youth, and now she was even more lost than before. Tommy noticed that the sadness was really starting to show on her face, like she regretted wasting her life and she had just given up. For the first time in years, Tommy actually felt pity for his mother instead of rage.

After the commencement ceremony was over, Tommy and his parents went to dinner at the Lord Jeffery Inn where his parents were staying. The Inn was always sold out for graduations, reunions, and football games. Tommy's parents retired after dinner and drinks, as they were leaving early in the morning. Tommy wondered if his parents were actually sharing a bed at the Lord Jeff.; He joked to his roommates when he introduced them to his parents, "They got stuck in a room with two double beds and I bet were uncomfortable even sharing the same bathroom for one day." Tom always figured that it was a miracle that he had ever been born.

Tommy said goodnight to his parents and headed out for the last round of parties before everyone left for the summer. Tommy partied late into the evening and woke up the next afternoon butt naked on the floor of his room wondering how in the world he got home that night and what he had done. He lost track of time after he and his friends started downing tequila shots. The last thing Tommy remembered was polishing off one bottle and helping his friend Dudley, who was barfing in the bushes in front of his house, and had fallen in his own puke. After that the night was a blank.

The next morning, Tommy awoke and put on a pair of shorts, heading into the kitchen for a glass of water. His mouth was dry and his head was pounding. He opened the cabinet where the clean glasses should have been to discover it empty. Molly, his roommate, Doug's girlfriend, had long stopped doing dishes for everybody but herself and her boyfriend. So, Tommy went to the sink and dug around in the pile of dirty dishes to find the cleanest dirty glass there was. After rinsing it out, he filled it to the rim with water from the tap and chugged it, refilling the glass and emptying it again. The last time he filled it, Tommy walked back to his bathroom to find some aspirin for his splitting headache. After finishing the last glass of water, he began packing up, as he knew he had to be gone by the end of the week. After graduation, the landlord had given them notice to vacate the old New England farmhouse that they had called home for the last few years.

A few days later Tommy loaded his GTO for the last drive home from Amherst. He stalled as long as he could, but regrettably he knew that he had to go back to Texas and the uncertainty of his messed-up family. "I am going to miss this place," he told his friends as he said good-bye.

Over the four years he spent at college, Tommy had put over ninety thousand miles on the car driving everywhere when he and his friends went. Spring in New England was late in coming the year that he graduated and had only just begun in the Northeast when he pulled out of the drive of the old farmhouse for the last time. The apple and cherry trees were in bloom, and the fragrance of lilacs and rhododendrons filled the air as Tommy drove the winding back roads of the Berkshire Mountains one last time on his way to Troy, New York, where he would turn south toward Pennsylvania.

He'd grown to love New England but had never really developed a taste for Northern food. Soon he'd be south of the Mason-Dixon line; he was ready for some southern cooking. "The only thing I really miss about Texas is Fredrick's cooking," he'd say when his friends goaded him to tell them stories about life on a Texas ranch.

The first stop he made on his trip home was in West Virginia at a roadside dinner, where there were several cars in the parking lot. Tommy and his friends had a saying: "A full parking lot means good grub." Tommy went inside and ordered fried chicken, mashed potatoes and gravy, green beans, corn bread, and iced tea. He ate well up North, and Tommy never missed a meal, but it was mostly Italian and deli food with some burgers mixed in. He was looking forward to some good old Texas BBQ and Mexican food.

It was late when Tommy got to the outskirts of Memphis, so he decided to stop at a motel for the night to get some sleep. Four years earlier, he'd have pulled over to the side of the road and caught forty winks, but this time he wasn't in any hurry to get home. He decided he would get a fresh start in the morning.

There was something psychological about crossing the Mississippi River this time that made Tommy a little melancholy. As long as he was still on the eastern side of the Mississippi, the reality of being a college graduate on his way home to the crazy family he left behind was not yet tangible; once he crossed the river bridge into Arkansas, it would be an undeniable reality. And he wasn't ready to make it real yet.

His anxiety about going home kept him awake most of the night. He lay awake thinking seriously about his future for the first time since he graduated. He tossed and turned in his cheesy hotel room for hours. He tried reading a book and watching television, but nothing could distract him from his fretting.

The taste of freedom he'd enjoyed over the past few years was not just freedom from the rules of his parents—they didn't really have that many rules. Rather, it was freedom from the expectations of being heir to the throne and especially following in the Colonel's footsteps. Everyone always assumed that he was going to take over after his father passed away, and he'd never realized how much pressure that was until he went away to college. Tommy didn't just want to take over; he wanted to make his mark in the world. He wanted to be somebody besides the Colonel's son, but his father's legacy loomed large, and even though he believed in himself, he was always afraid of the harsh judgments from others if he didn't live up to the Colonel's lofty expectations.

Tommy slept late after a fitful, restless sleep, getting up around ten in the morning. He dressed, packed up his things, and checked out. He ate bacon and eggs, with grits, toast, and a glass of orange juice at the diner before he left. Soon after he'd paid his bill, Tommy decided that he'd stalled as long as he could and finally got on the road after gassing up.

As he crossed the river at West Memphis on the old cantilevered and truss bridge, Tommy drove slowly, marveling at the construction as he drove across and thinking that engineering was played up to be harder than it really was. "Engineers are just full of themselves. Anyone could build a bridge like this if they had enough money," Tommy muttered arrogantly. He was still licking his wounds over making the worst grade in his life in thermodynamics. But marveling over the construction methods used on the Mississippi River bridge momentarily distracted Tommy from the fact that he was going home.

The farmlands of Arkansas lay on the opposite side of the great levee that held back the powerful Mississippi and its massive floods. Farmers tended the crops they planted in the ancient fertile floodplains created from thousands of years of the river meandering its way to the sea.

Like magic, the turmoil of the night suddenly subsided. Tommy drove with the windows down, and the smell of the newly plowed dust filled the GTO as he reached down to plug in his Janis Joplin eight-track tape for the ride through Arkansas. Texas was only hours away.

Before long, after two days of driving he was home once again. But this time he was home for good instead of just for a visit. It was late in the evening when he pulled into the driveway behind the guesthouse. The lights of his car shined on the back of the house, and he hoped the didn't wake anyone up. As he opened the door and turned on the lights, he noticed that the guesthouse was clean.

My mother must have hired someone to clean up knowing I was on my way home.

Tommy was tired from his drive and went directly to bed.

⇥▬◉ ◉▬⇤

The next morning Tommy woke up about nine thirty, and after taking a long, hot shower, he reached into the linen cabinet to dig through the tattered towels that had been in his bathroom since he was a little boy, but to his amazement he found the cabinet full of a new set of clean towels.

Wow! I'll have to thank someone for making me feel so welcome.

After he shaved, he opened the bathroom door and suddenly realized that the sheets he'd slept on last night were not just clean but new also. He looked around the rest of the guesthouse and was sure grateful to come home to something besides spider webs, dead roaches, and dust.

I've been living here since boarding school, and this is the first time I've come home from school to a clean house. I'm getting the five-star treatment; I'll have to ask Fredrick whose idea this was.

Tommy got dressed and cut through the backyard past the vegetable garden on his way to the kitchen, noticing that no one had planted yet for the summer. Then he walked passed the pool and noticed it wasn't clean, and wondered why Fredrick hadn't cleaned it in a while. Thinking it odd, Tommy stopped and looked around, wondering if he was just imagining things or were things really different. He rounded the corner of the house to find a strange woman sitting in a chair by the back door, humming a tune.

Tommy was puzzled. She was tall, with dark skin, and she hummed the same tune over. He guessed she was in her sixties but did not look a day over forty. As she stood up from her chair, he noticed scars on left hand and both arm from burns.

"Oh my gosh. That's a pretty nasty scar." Tom blurted out trying not to be rude.

"I got that from a fire set by an overturned kerosene lantern when I was a young girl," the woman said as she looked at her hand. "It don't bother me now. But when I was a little girl my daddy was a share cropper and I couldn't help pick cotton in the fields so I started cleaning houses instead."

"You must be Tommy." The woman put out the cigarette that she was smoking when she saw him. "You look just like your picture. My name is Etta Mae. We've been expecting you. Breakfast is ready if you're hungry." She smiled sweetly, acting as though she was genuinely happy to meet Tommy as she turned to go inside.

Tommy seemed confused and looked around for his mother or Fredrick.

"You must be the one who's responsible for cleaning up the guesthouse. I sure appreciate what you've done for me. I've been after Fredrick for years to clean up down there, but he always claims that he cooks and he don't clean." Tommy laughed, half expecting Fredrick to stick his head out the door. Then he asked, "Where is Fredrick?"

Etta heaved a heavy sigh. "I'm so sorry to tell you this, but Fredrick passed away suddenly three months ago. He went to the doctor to have a routine surgery to remove cataracts, but he had a terrible reaction to the anesthesia and passed away on the operating table."

Etta saw the shocked look on Tommy's face and realized that no one had told him about Fredrick's passing and that it obviously upset him. "I worked for Mrs. Harper's sister, Lucy, for many years, and after Miss Lucy had a stroke, Mrs. Harper moved her sister into her own house, so I came to work for your family."

Tommy stood just wordless as Etta Mae continued to talk. "I've nine children, twenty-seven grandchildren, and eight great-grandchildren. Most of them lived on the north side of town with me or nearby, but most of my family is close enough that I see them every day."

Etta Mae paused for a moment to see if Tommy would speak. "My family and my church are the most important things in my life."

Tommy felt like he'd been punched in the stomach. He had considered Fredrick more than the family cook; he thought of him as part of the family. Etta was obviously concerned about Tommy, even though they had only just met. "My cooking isn't as good as Fredrick's, but I clean better." She softened her tone, hoping that once Tommy got over the shock of losing Fredrick, maybe he'd warm up to her.

Tommy was quiet for a minute, staring at the ground in front of his feet as though he was deep in thought. Looking up, Etta could tell that his mood had gone from grief to anger. "Is my mother home?" he asked as he pushed past Etta.

"She's in the sunroom having her morning coffee." Etta was sorely afraid of what the young man was going to say to his mother.

Tommy charged into the sun porch on the back of the house, slamming the door behind him. His mother was sitting in a rocking chair next to one of the windows overlooking the backyard and working on her needlepoint. Her coffee sat on a table by the chair, and a floor lamp shined downward on her, illuminating the intricate needlework. She looked up over the glasses she wore, so that she could see the tiny patterns she was sewing, with an expression of shock and surprise on her face.

"Why didn't you call me?" Tommy yelled at his mother. "Fredrick was my friend." Tommy had raised his voice to his mother before but never like this.

Babe stared in disbelief at her angry son. "What on earth are you yelling about?" she asked as she lowered her needlepoint down to her lap.

"Fredrick died three months ago, and nobody bothered to tell me!" He picked up a pillow off the couch and threw it at her. "I saw you and dad at graduation! You've had plenty of opportunities to tell me he's dead, but you are too selfish and inconsiderate to think about anyone but yourself!"

Tommy whirled around, threw open the door to the backyard, and stormed off to the guesthouse, yelling, "I'm leaving just as soon as I find somewhere else to live!"

Chapter 10

NOT LONG AFTER his return to Texas, Tommy moved to Austin. Fredrick's untimely death had not only caught him totally off guard, but the knowledge that his mother didn't even let him know that Fredrick had passed away way was the icing on the cake. Tommy didn't stay in Black Rock long enough to unpack. Something like that was typical behavior from his father but not his mother. Babe didn't fit into the Jim Crow–era of the South where black men where not property but indentured servants.

And for the life of him he couldn't understand what on earth his mother was thinking when she neglected to tell him about Fredrick's death. No matter how thick the protective layers Tommy built around him, it was like his mother had the one armor-piercing arrow that could penetrate it and hit him right in the heart.

Soon after his rocky return home, Tommy rented a 1930s East Austin bungalow on Rosewood Avenue; he knew he could live there while attending law school at the University of Texas. In fact, the funky little limestone rock house where he was going to spend the next couple of years was just a few miles from the university. Tommy decided to buy a ten-speed bicycle to ride to school. Parking was at a premium around campus, but he had also racked up almost a hundred thousand miles on his car, and it was beginning to show the high mileage from four years of college in New England. The house he rented was just on the other side of the interstate from the university and would have been a pleasant walk if the route hadn't been divided by Interstate 35.

The little rock house in East Austin had two bedrooms and was cheap enough that Tommy didn't need to have a roommate. "I am done with roommates," he told one of his high school friends upon moving back to Austin. The house had a window air conditioner that Tommy used at night when it was stifling hot and he couldn't sleep. The limestone exterior insulated the house, keeping it cool enough in the long, hot Austin summers—except for July and August when it got ungodly hot and he ran the air conditioning all the time.

Tommy set up the other bedroom with a desk for studying. He'd decided to specialize in oil-and-gas law at law school, since that was what he would use the most if he took over the family business. He believed that his father would have to depend on him more if he were a lawyer and that this would pretty much cinch up his position as the heir apparent.

Still stinging from the rage he felt toward his mother, he'd calmed down enough to go to the kitchen to apologize to Etta for his outburst before he left. "I feel pretty badly about throwing a screaming fit in front of you on my first day home," he said sheepishly to Etta, who was sweeping the kitchen.

Etta stopped and cocked her head to one side as if she were sizing Tommy up. "Your momma didn't mean you no harm. She's just regular people, just like you or me. It's your momma you should be apologizing to, not me," she said and went back to her sweeping and humming.

That sounds just like something Fredrick would say.

He never apologized to his mother, but after a few days, the tension between his them seemed to ease. Soon after, Tommy raided his mother's antiques in her warehouse to furnish his rent house in Austin. He brought along a bed and dresser, a couch and a couple of chairs, a table, and a sideboard that he put his TV and stereo system on. He didn't want anything too fancy, and so he'd picked out some things that he thought he could live with comfortably. "I would love to help you decorate," Babe had told him when he'd asked for the key to the warehouse.

"Thanks for the offer, but I'll be just fine."

Tommy bristled at the idea of his mother coming to Austin to help him decorate; after all, they were barely on speaking terms again and there were still plenty of unresolved problems between them. When it came down to it, he wasn't really interested in her reasons for not telling him about Fredrick.

⇥⊜ ⊜⇤

When Fredrick passed away, Babe felt like she'd lost her best friend. But in the days of the Jim Crow South, it wasn't respectable for a white woman to grieve the loss of her black cook, so Babe had slid back into the throws of heavy drinking in the privacy of the sun porch. Babe didn't tell Tommy about Fredrick's death out of malice; she simply couldn't bring herself to say the words without falling apart.

Unbeknown to Tommy—or anyone else for that matter—Babe had started going to AA meetings at the Episcopal Church in Bryan on the days when she said she was going shopping. She didn't want anyone to know because she didn't want to disappoint anyone if she fell off the wagon again. She was desperately trying to get sober but was finding that after almost fifty years of heavy drinking, it was incredibly hard to quit.

She'd found that she could go only a few weeks, sometimes only a few days, before life would throw her a curve ball and she would find an excuse to drink again, especially after Fredrick passed away. Babe knew that, while her son didn't want to hurt her feelings, he had given up on his mother a long time ago.

⋆⊷⊷ ⊶⊶⋆

After living in his new house in Austin for a few weeks, Tommy discovered that he was sharing it with a nest of scorpions. Scorpions were common in that part of Texas, but they were particularly attracted to limestone structures like his funky little rental house. "There are more scorpions in Austin than people," he had often kidded. Tommy had learned to live with scorpions when he went to boarding school at St. Martin's, and they didn't really bother him.

"All you need to do is call an exterminator," his mother nagged.

"Nah. I always shake my shoes out before I put them on, and if I leave any dirty clothes on the floor, all I have to do is shake them hard when I pick them up."

Tommy would very carefully sort his clothes when he did laundry, and he always hung his wet towels up and shook the towels out when he pulled them out of the cabinet in the bathroom. The "occasional" scorpion sighting was so common that he would just stomp on the creature and go back to what he was doing.

Moving back to Austin was more like moving home than moving back to Black Rock had been. This was his real home, not the crazy home he had shared with his parents. Tommy felt relaxed and at ease in Austin. The Austin of his childhood had not changed much. The weird old funky part of the city was still the same as it had been when Tommy first went to boarding school a few years before.

Unexpectedly, though, the Austin that he loved was in the throes of a population explosion, the yuppie influx spurred by several land developers being elected to city council. Their election was threatening to ruin the small-town atmosphere as they implemented their plans to turn Austin into a big city.

Austin was a creative mecca for many artist and musicians, and now that he was back in town, it didn't take long before he discovered all the vibrant culture Austin had to offer, as well as some new and exciting restaurants, bars, and music venues.

As soon as Tommy got settled, he began to reconnect with old friends. He'd already begun reaching out to some of his high school buddies as soon as he decided to apply to law school in Austin. The first people that he went to dinner with were Bobby and Joan Billingsley. Bobby was in his law school class and had also been one of the day students from St. Martin's. Joan was a year younger and had been a boarder like Tommy. Bobby and Joan had gotten married not long after Joan graduated, and they lived in an apartment on the south side of Austin. Bobby worked part-time waiting tables while he and his young wife were attending the university.

They laughed and joked about the good old days at St. Martin's while they talked about how to get in touch with a few of their mutual friends. Tommy was looking forward to finding more of his high school friends, but the hair on his neck bristled when Joan asked, "Have you been dating anyone since you got back into town? I have a lot of nice friends if you want to meet anyone."

"Thanks, sugar, but I don't think I'll be needing any help finding a date."

Tommy Smiled at his old friend saying, "I appreciate the thought, but I think I can find my own dates."

"Have you been to St. Martin's since you got back to town?" Bobby asked as he sipped his margarita.

Tommy had gone out to St. Martin's a few days after he moved back, just to see who was still around at his old school. He'd driven around campus and was relieved that to find it had changed very little.

"Yeah, I drove up there just to check things out," Tommy replied after taking a swallow of beer. "The school has a new entrance off West Lake Hills. I guess they needed a way into the school besides that bumpy old dirt road. Now that they have a new entrance, they can attract more day students."

Tommy remembered how much trouble the boarding students had had with the day students. The day students always acted as if the boarding students got special treatment and resented the boarders because they could go back to their dorm rooms during the day while the day students could not enter into the dorms without special permission. However, Tommy didn't want to get into it any further with his friends and quickly changed the subject.

"I heard Father Michael left. There was a rumor going around Austin that he *had* to leave." Joan looked around to see who would be listening. "I heard that some of the boys on campus were complaining that he'd been a little too friendly, if you know what I mean."

"That is such bullshit." Tommy complained as he leaned back in his chair, shaking his head. "He would never do anything like that. Don't believe everything you hear."

In fact, Tommy knew that Father Michael had been assigned to a new church right after Tommy's class graduated. Apparently, the headmaster had found out that Father Michael was letting the boarding students drink and asked him to leave. Tommy desperately wanted the magical world that St. Martin's had been to him to stay magical, so he changed the subject, latching on to the banal subject of the weather, more out of desperation than anything else.

July had been especially hot for some reason. The nights just didn't seem to cool down, and morning lows were averaging seventy-eight degrees Fahrenheit, reaching eighty-five degrees by 8:00 a.m. Tommy had been in the Northeast for a few years and was finding it hard to get reacclimated to the Texas Hill Country weather, though this was surprising to him.

When he had been in college up north, he'd always bragged to his friends, "I'm a tough Texan, and I love hot summers." But this summer seemed particularly hot to Tommy. He'd bought his new bike at a shop on North Lamar Street and started out with small rides around the neighborhood, just to acclimate to the summer heat. He rode in the mornings, usually before it got too hot, determined to get used to the Austin heat before his classes started in August.

"I hear that finding parking at UT is hard," Tommy said, wiping the sweat from his face with the bandana he carried in his pocket.

"We usually park under the interstate and walk. The parking is free, and it isn't that far of a walk, unless it is raining," Bobby replied. "There's also a pretty good bus system that will take you almost anywhere you want to go."

⇥▶● ●◀⇤

Law school began in mid-August, so Tommy decided he would ride his bike on a daily basis until school started. There was no real reason for this decision, other than he enjoyed riding. Tommy was one of those people who had to stay busy or the demons would creep in; he needed to turn his brain off and not think of anything. Another reason Tommy decided to start riding was because he'd become even more self-conscious ever since his weight ballooned in college (when he started drinking daily) and thought that riding his bike would help him slim down.

Law school started in August. As soon as school began, Tommy realized he was unprepared for what it had in store for him. He expected things to go much like they had during his undergrad years at Amherst and was fully prepared to skate by, doing as little as possible and partying as much as he could with his old friends and the ones he would make at UT.

Much to his surprise, a couple of days into the semester he figured out that if he wanted to stay and graduate, he was going to have to work as hard as everybody else. In one of his first classes, the professor passed out a syllabus on the first day and on the next dove immediately into the curriculum. It caught Tommy completely off guard when Professor Dryden asked him a question. "Well, I really don't know," Tommy replied, anxiously flipping through his notes.

"Mr. Ellison, you obviously did not prepare for this class. If you want to pass my course, you had best come prepared every day. No one can pass this course by simply cramming for the exams. Class participation is a major portion of your grade, as I stated on the first day of class."

Professor Dryden had made an example of Tommy. Tommy didn't like being chastised in front of the class for being unprepared.

Soon he figured out that law school at UT would be no picnic. All the students there were very serious about what they were there to do. Tommy showed up for class in cut-off jean shorts as he had at Amherst, only to see other students in dress shirts and ties. Most of the students there were men. There were a few women in the classes, but all of them were there for one thing: to pass the bar and become an attorney.

These people weren't just serious, they were downright competitive. "The best grades and law review will catapult you into the big time," one of his professors lectured them on the first day of class.

The level of competition he was facing was obvious and downright intimidating. Tommy had skated through most of his life, and for the first time he was really going to have to dig deep and work for his Doctor of Jurisprudence degree.

About halfway through the semester, Tommy found himself resentful, even jealous of those classmates who were getting better grades than him. He was starting to look at his competitors as objects to defeat instead of classmates or friends. Tommy began to feel an overwhelming need to use ruthless or destructive behavior with his classmates. UT Law was infamous for developing the "win at all costs" attitude of an attorney, and Tommy got caught up in this. He had been left to his own devices, which only fueled the competitive flames.

By the end of the semester, Tommy actually found himself actually wanting to go home to Black Rock. Christmas somehow had always been the time Tommy actually liked to be around his mother. The holidays brought out the best in her. She was in a happy, festive mood when Tommy got home, and she helped Etta Mae cook lavish family meals.

Babe loved to decorate the house with the beautiful Christmas decorations she'd collected over the years, and Tommy loved to help her. Tommy would go all out putting up the Christmas tree and lights on the outside of their house. In fact, one of the few things he agreed upon with his mother was the *more* lights the better. Christmas was the only time of the year when the family would call a truce and genuinely enjoy one another's company.

Even better, the locals would come from miles around to see their Christmas lights, which made Tommy feel like a kid again. Tommy had planted two red cedars in his parents' front yard when he was a teen just so they could put Christmas lights on them. Over the years, they'd grown strong and perfect for their outdoor light display.

Early one morning, Tommy climbed up into the attic of the old wooden house to dig through the boxes and boxes of lights and decorations that were stored up in the crawl space. He brought down box after box, using the creaky fold-up ladder that led to the attic, and brought them down to the sun-room, where he and his mother and Candy sorted through the treasures. Candy was on Christmas break and had come to stay with her grandmother for a few days.

"Can I help you untangle the light strings?" she asked her uncle as she danced around excitedly.

When the lights were ready, they ceremoniously took them outside and hung them in the trees. The weather was mild for a December day. It was early afternoon, the sun was shining brightly, and the sky was a crisp winter blue. Using a twenty-foot ladder and a plastic pole with a hook on it, Tommy, Candy, and Babe strung the lights in each tree.

It was late in the afternoon when they finished with both trees, and there was a chill in the air as the long shadows of the winter dusk engulfed the yard. Candy and Babe went into the house to put sweaters on, just as Tommy plugged in the first tree. When they came back outside to admire the fruits of the day's labor, they brought Etta Mae out to enjoy the beautiful trees with them. They clapped and cheered as Tommy plugged in the second tree, and then the four of them stood silently admiring their beauty. Tommy felt at peace for the first time in a long time, and everything was right in the world.

That evening, Tommy put on Christmas music as they sat down to eat the dinner that Etta Mae had prepared for them while they worked outside. Etta had watched out the window, humming her usual song, as she cooked fried chicken, mashed potatoes and gravy, mustard greens, and corn bread. As usual, the Colonel wasn't home. He was gone on a business trip, and Etta was glad that Tommy and Candy were there to keep Babe in good spirits. Etta was concerned about Babe. She knew that Babe was trying to quit drinking, and days like today made it easier for her to control her yearnings.

After dinner, Candy decorated Christmas cookies in the kitchen with Etta Mae. The smells of cinnamon and allspice filled the kitchen each time Etta opened the oven door. Candy dusted the cookies with Christmas-colored sugar sprinkles while they were still warm and was eating them just as fast as she decorated them when she looked at Etta and asked out of the blue, "Why does Tommy hate my grandmother?"

"Your Uncle Tommy don't hate your grandmother." Etta stopped what she was doing and looked intently at the girl, her brow furled. She'd only been there for a little while but long enough to notice that no one openly discussed the subject of Babe's drinking. "He's just mad at her all the time because he thinks she's weak." Etta took a deep cleansing breath, deciding that she needed to be honest with the girl.

"Miss Babe's drinking is a sickness, and it's hard, hard to quit that demon liquor all by herself." Etta knew that it wasn't just a character weakness like the white folks believed. "I am sure grateful to see that you and Tommy are being kind to her today," she said, and she patted Candy on the shoulder and went back to her baking.

Chapter 11

CHRISTMAS FELL ON a Friday that year, and the Colonel came home from his travels a couple of days before Christmas Eve. Etta Mae baked pies, cakes, and cookies all week long. The house was decorated with a cedar tree, and the unmistakable fragrance of the freshly cut tree filled the house with the Christmas spirit. Tommy had cut it down on the ranch and brought it home for Babe and Candy to decorate in the living room by the fireplace. Candy was staying all week until her mother, Bob, and her brother, William, drove up from Houston on Christmas Eve day to pick her up and exchange gifts before heading back to Houston for their own Christmas celebration.

William was now fourteen and a freshman in high school. He was turning into a handsome young man, and the girls at school swooned over him. He was tall and played all the sports the family had hoped Tommy would play. But William was turning out to be a bit of a rebel. He was drinking, smoking pot, and constantly getting in trouble at school. In fact, the school was threatening to throw him out, even though he was a star athlete.

Like any boy his age, it was obvious that William didn't want to be at his grandparents' house on Christmas Eve. In fact, he walked in with an attitude. William had developed a comedic way of being a smartass by making fun of people and laughing jokingly while he insulted them. Tommy was amused by young William's humor most of the time but had little patience with his nephew when he got too cocky.

Beverly's family arrived just before lunchtime on Christmas Eve. Etta Mae had cooked a big lunch, setting the table with the best china and setting up the buffet with all the dishes that would be served for the main course and the desserts that would follow. Etta had pulled out all the stops, cooking a huge roast beef and stuffed quail, stuffing and mashed potatoes with gravy, green beans, asparagus, steamed broccoli, fruit salad, and green salad, along with fresh dinner rolls. The smells of the Christmas Eve luncheon filled the house with the savory aroma of the delicacies that she'd worked all morning to prepare.

Aunt Annabelle made her appearance just before lunch. She and Aunt Sally were the last of the Colonel's sisters and were now getting old. Most of his sisters had passed away over the past few years while Tommy was in college. Along with Aunt Annabelle's husband, Uncle Jerome, who had died a few years earlier. Nana Harris was also gone. She'd died in October of that year after a long battle with cancer, and this would be Tommy's first Christmas without her.

Tommy had not seen Aunt Annabelle for some time and was shocked at how tiny and frail-looking she had become. It was quite a change from the strong, domineering woman who had scared him to death when he was young. His aunt's live-in caregiver, Lillian, joined Etta in the kitchen as she prepared the feast.

The family sat down for lunch, and it went surprisingly well. Etta and Lillian stayed in the kitchen listening to the hum of the small talk and laughter. Etta had put a bell at the end of the table by Tommy's parents and knew they would ring it if they needed anything. She emerged from the kitchen periodically with a pitcher of iced tea to refill everyone's glasses and to check to see how the lunch was progressing.

"Let me know when it's time to put on a pot of coffee and clear the table for the dessert service," she said and then disappeared back into the kitchen, humming her usual song.

Tommy was overjoyed at the pleasant conversation and jovial atmosphere that surrounded their Christmas Eve lunch. His mother, sister, and Aunt Annabelle were not just getting along but acting like they cared about one another. It seemed that Aunt Annabelle had finally mellowed and no longer enjoyed picking fights with other family members since the passing of her husband and sisters.

"It is really nice to have a quiet Christmas," Tommy said as he cut into the pecan pie. "Even little William is behaving himself."

"He can be very charming when he wants to be," Beverly replied. Beverly was always very well-mannered and tried to teach her children to behave at the dinner table.

After lunch was over, the weather suddenly changed. The winds were howling as a blue northern raced through the area, bringing clouds and a misty rain that chilled down to the bone. Tommy put on his jacket and went outside for firewood.

"I think I prefer the snow up north to the cold, wet winters of Texas," he muttered to himself. The winters in Texas seldom got below forty degrees, but when it was windy and rainy, the cold somehow just felt colder than the dry snow up north. Tommy built a fire in the fireplace to take the chill out of the old house. He then mixed a drink from the bar and sat down on the couch to watch the college bowl games on TV with his father.

Not long after lunch was over, Lillian took Aunt Annabelle home to get some rest. After they left, Bob decided to pop the cork on one of the bottles of wine they had brought. After a little while, Etta Mae brought a punch bowl of eggnog with some bourbon whiskey and set it on the buffet in the dining room.

After she cleaned up and put away the leftovers, Etta announced that she was going home for the evening. "I'll be taking Christmas Day off. The leftovers are in the refrigerator in the kitchen. I figure you all can get by without me for at least one day." Etta wished everyone a Merry Christmas and went home to her own family.

Shortly after the football game was over, Beverly and her family left to drive back to Houston. It was late in the afternoon when they said their good-byes, packing their presents into their car.

It was starting to get dark, so Tommy went outside to plug in the Christmas lights and get some more firewood. The lights from the trees outside shown through the windows as Tommy and his parents drank some more eggnog and watched Christmas programs on TV.

Tommy's parents went to bed, each to their separate rooms, and Tommy stayed up to watch some more television. After a little while, Tommy raided the icebox for some leftovers, realizing that they didn't eat dinner. When he finished eating, Tommy put on his shoes to make the wet, cold walk down to the guesthouse.

Tommy had been so involved in the Christmas festivities that he'd neglected to light the heater in guesthouse, so the first thing that he did was to turn the old gas wall heater on. Tommy couldn't remember the last time anyone used the heater; luckily, the electric pilot light was working, and it wasn't long before it warmed up. In the meantime, he pulled out an extra blanket from the top of the closet for a little extra warmth. The blanket was old and made of wool, and it had holes in it where the bugs had eaten it. Tommy shook it out, hoping that a good hard shake would ensure that none of those bugs would be in bed with him that night. He opened the book he was reading and turned on the lamp on the table by his bed. He read until he fell asleep.

I can't believe that things went so well today. It's so weird when my family is nice to one another.

The next morning, Tommy woke up about seven thirty with a strong urge to piss. The guesthouse wasn't exactly warm, so he jumped back in bed for a little while longer. When he was a kid, he would wake up as early as he could on Christmas morning to see all the presents under the tree, but the excitement of presents had long since been replaced with the anxious anticipation of some nerdy gift like a stamp collection that the Colonel would give him.

Who in the world gives their kid a stamp collection for Christmas?

For a long time, Tommy had suspected his father sent his secretary out at the ninth hour to get something for his wife and son.

After he got dressed, Tommy went up to the main house to see who was up. Hopefully, Babe hadn't drunk that much eggnog yet. If that were the case, then Tommy was pretty confident that things would be quiet. He opened the back door to the kitchen; surprisingly, he found his mother up, cooking and cleaning. The Colonel sat at the kitchen table reading the paper. She offered them both some coffee before she realized that neither Tommy nor his father drank it. It was strange to see his parents in the kitchen, but they both acted like it was a normal occurrence.

Maybe I've been gone so long that I don't know my parents the way I thought I did.

It wasn't a typical Christmas morning. After breakfast, the family sat around the Christmas tree, playing Christmas music while they opened presents, Tommy acted like he was thrilled with what he was given, which was mostly clothes. He was excited by one present: a black leather motorcycle jacket. "I bet you picked this out," he said to his mother while holding the sleek leather up to his torso. "I can't imagine my straight-arrow father buying something like this."

After Tommy was done, Babe opened her present from her husband: a tasteful ruby necklace. The Colonel always gave his wife jewelry. She knew it was most likely picked out by the secretary, but she didn't care. It was beautiful, and she loved it.

After the presents were all opened, Babe cleaned up the mess under the tree and Tommy took the half-empty punch bowl into the kitchen and poured what was left of the eggnog into the kitchen sink. For the rest of the day, the Colonel ignored everyone while he watched Christmas Day football on TV.

⊷▬◉ ◉▬◌⊷

Tommy didn't have to go back for his second semester until the second week of the new year. He'd planned to go back to Austin for New Year's Eve until his old friend Ronnie, who was home from the seminary, asked what he was doing for New Year's when he saw him at the grocery store. "We should have party at Alligator Lake to ring in the New Year," Ronnie suggested.

"Wow! That's a great idea. I was planning on going back to Austin, but I really didn't have anything in particular to do there." Tommy was almost shouting; he was so excited.

Alligator Lake was an old oxbow lake left behind when the Brazos River changed its course as it meandered through the ages toward the Gulf of Mexico. Tommy hadn't spent much time there since he and his friends used to go water-skiing at the lake in the summers before college. There was a camp house there where Tommy had spent lots of time as a kid with Uncle Jerome, who would take him fishing when the feminine energies around their houses raged with estrogen-fueled aggression. Tommy missed his uncle Jerome.

Alligator Lake was the perfect place for a party.

The plan was for everyone to camp out there overnight so that the partygoers wouldn't get snagged by the cops on the way home. Tommy started collecting firewood for a bonfire and agreed to provide the beer, food, and fireworks for the evening.

"If anyone wants something stronger or wants to bring one of those left-handed roll-your-own cigarettes, they'll have to bring their own." Tommy and Ronnie howled with laughter.

Tommy had not seen Ronnie in quite a long time. Ronnie was the son of the Methodist minister in Black Rock; his parents still lived down the street from Tommy's own parents. Ronnie was in the seminary somewhere in California, so he rarely ever saw his childhood friend. Tommy thought Ronnie would make the perfect East Texas preacher, telling him, "You have all the qualities a good preacher needs, like the ability to misbehave when no one's looking."

Word soon spread around town, and before long, Tommy heard that between thirty or forty people were going to show up. In his excitement, Tommy went all out. It was his first real party since his time at Amherst, and he was going to make it the best New Year's Eve party the county had ever seen.

New Year's Eve fell on a Friday night, and the Colonel was scheduled to return to Washington, DC, on the Wednesday before, so the likelihood of his father getting wind of the party was slim to none. All week long, Tommy's excitement was building.

As soon as the Colonel pulled out of the driveway for his trip to Washington, Tommy started working on setting up for the party. He took some of the Christmas lights they hadn't used out to the Alligator Lake camp house and strung them from tree to tree in a circle around where they were building the bonfire.

Tommy also borrowed a barbeque pit from one of the ranch hands to cook hot dogs and hamburgers at the party. The pit was rusty and had a flat tire when he went to pick it up, so he drove into town for a can of "Fix-a-Flat" to air up the tire so he could haul it the mile or so to the camp house.

There was an outhouse behind the camp house with a toilet that didn't always work. When Tommy checked on the condition of the toilet, he found that it was nasty and that a nest of some kind of rodents was living there. They had used the toilet paper left there from the summer as a nest. It took a little more effort than Tommy had planned to get the toilet cleaned up and working for the party, but he did it.

"I've had enough experiences with parties at college to know that if the toilet doesn't work, the women won't stay. And if there aren't any women, the guys won't stay very long either, no matter how much beer you have," Tommy said to Ronnie, laughing.

Tommy tried to hide his party preparations from Etta Mae and his mother, but Etta figured out that something was going on when she found Tommy's beer stash. Once the cat was out of the bag, Tommy asked her to help him with the food. "I want New Year's Eve off," she insisted, crossing her arms over her ample chest. "If you're out of the house, then I can get away early."

Etta Mae relented and agreed to make up the hamburger patties so that all Tommy had to do was put them on the grill. She also bought some condiments, chips, and buns, which they stashed with the beer in the guesthouse.

She didn't worry about Tommy, but Etta felt some trepidation about leaving his mother alone for New Year's Eve—but not enough to cancel her plans. Her church was having services, and that was where she planned to spend her evening.

After Tommy left for the party, she told Babe that she was leaving for the evening. Etta Mae knew that Babe was spending the night alone and was worried, as being alone on New Year's Eve would test anyone's resolve to sobriety.

"Thank you, Etta, for your concern, but I will be all right. This is not the first time I have been alone on New Year's Eve," Babe assured Etta, gently patting her hand and smiling.

"You know you can call me if you need anything."

Etta was proud of Babe; she knew the struggle she went through every day facing down the demons. Etta said good-bye and glanced back at her employer one more time with concern and sympathy as she walked out the kitchen door. Babe waved at Etta, saying, "Go and enjoy your family; I will be all right."

Babe watched through the kitchen window as Etta pulled out of the driveway. She then pulled out the beer that she'd taken from Tommy's not-so-clever hiding place in the guesthouse. She put a couple in an ice bucket to cool them.

As she popped the top on her first beer, she thought about how many times her husband had had something more important to do than spend New Year's Eve with her. She fought back the tears as she raised the beer to her lips and slowly took a swallow. "Happy New Year's to me!"

⊷⊷▐⊙ ⊙▌⊶⊶

Alligator Lake was a mile-long lake on Peach Tree Ranch that was several miles down one of the ranch roads. Tommy'd marked the blue gate to the lake with a sign with an arrow so the party goers could find their way down the winding dirt road to the lake.

It was a beautiful, clear sunny day at the lake. The sun was high in the sky, and a gentle breeze came across the lake from the northwest. It was a warm day for late December, but the news predicted that the temperatures would fall into the upper forties after sunset. Tommy had brought along his new leather jacket that his mother had given him for Christmas in case he needed it later.

As he pulled up to the lake, Tommy noticed that there were some cattle in the pasture and fresh cow patties all over the camp house. "Crap!" he cried as he got out of his car. "Maybe the cow dung will dry out by the end of the day. The cattle will move out once people start showing up."

Tommy hoped the cow poop wouldn't put a damper on their party, but this was East Texas and most everyone had dealt with cow manure before. The ranch hands had put out some hay for the cattle earlier in the week, but the cattle apparently wanted the green buds on the grass at the camp house instead and had pooped all over the camp.

The two unloaded the groceries and beer. Tommy had bought a few bags of ice at the fireworks stand, and he set up ice chests in the camp house to ice down the beer. Tommy and Ronnie then started the fire. It was about four o'clock, and the winter sun was low in the sky and the long shadows of the trees cooled the camp house. Tommy began cleaning the grill so that he could start cooking when the guest started to show up. They could see the dust cloud of the cars on the long dirty road before they got there. The sunset over Alligator Lake was spectacular that evening, and Tommy took it as a good omen.

The sky was filled with reds, oranges, and purples that were reflecting off the wispy high winter clouds. The flames of the bonfire took hold just as the last light of the day faded from the sky. Tommy was busily cooking as more and more guests started to arrive. The guys outnumbered the girls, and most of the girls who were there had brought dates, but it didn't matter. Laughter and music filled the air.

Tommy very still happy that everything had come together so easily, considering he'd only had a few days to pull the party together. About an hour into the party, Tommy finally sat down and started to enjoy the evening's festivities. He had popped open a beer when everyone arrived, but it was finally time to relax and enjoy the night.

Shortly after dark, the guests started popping firecrackers. Apparently, Tommy wasn't the only one who'd brought fireworks, and it wasn't long before the party revelers were blowing up cow patties with black cats and a bottle-rocket war started.

As the night cooled off, a circle of chairs surrounded the campfire, shifting now and again as the smoke from the fire changed directions. Periodically, a few people would disappear into the darkness of the tree line to smoke a joint. Marijuana was still not as accepted in the Bible belt of East Texas, and most people who smoked were discreet about it.

The crescent moon had risen early before sunset that evening and was directly overhead as the smoke from the bonfire drifted skyward. A multitude of stars shown in the dark night sky, and the partygoers could clearly see the constellation Orion on the horizon. Ronnie and Tommy were setting off pyrotechnics when they saw headlights bouncing along the road at a distance. Tommy and Ronnie guessed that it was a late-coming party guest but warned some of the pot smokers that maybe they should put away their stash.

It was a little after eleven o'clock when the car pulled up to the camp house, sliding to a stop. A dust cloud enveloped the partygoers sitting around the campfire. The door to the white Ford pickup flung open, and Dale Colby, a local grocer and one of Tommy's neighbors, jumped out of the truck and frantically started calling for Tommy. Tommy handed the punk he was using to light fireworks to Ronnie and quickly walked over to the out-of-breath Dale.

As soon as Tommy reached him, Dale grabbed Tommy by the shoulders. "Your house is on fire, and your mother has been burned. It's bad—they're taking her to the hospital."

Without thinking, Tommy jumped into the truck with Dale, who madly drove down the bumpy road toward the highways. The truck hit the cattle guard to the Alligator Lake pasture so fast that the truck caught some air, landing with a hard jolt on the other side.

Book Two

The first thing we do, let's kill all the lawyers.

—*William Shakespeare*, Henry VI, Part 1

Chapter 12

NEITHER DALE NOR Tommy spoke much on the ride into town. After a long silence, Tommy asked Dale, "I forgot to turn off the Christmas lights. Was that what started the fire?"

"I don't know. The firemen didn't say," Dale answered.

Tommy mind raced and Dale's answer didn't help.

Did I put up too many lights? Did I overload the circuits? Maybe I should have checked them better before I put them up. Maybe they'd been up in the attic so long that they weren't fit to use.

Guilt and worry set in. As they neared Black Rock, the lights of the town seemed brighter than usual, and Tommy realized that the blaze of the house fire could be seen from the outskirts of town.

As they neared the house, Dale drove around to the back, knowing that the streets were blocked off by Black Rock's two fire trucks. Dale pulled into the driveway of the guesthouse, and Tommy flew out of the truck and ran toward the house. His heart sank as he saw the house fully enveloped, the flames rising from the roof, embers drifting into the air. The fire department was doing its best, but it was shorthanded due to the holiday. The firefighters' hoses were trained on the roof of the house.

Without thinking, Tommy ran toward the burning house, but one of the firefighters grabbed him before he got too close. The shock was evident on his face, and it took a moment for Tommy to compose himself enough to ask, "What happened? Where is my mother?"

"We believe the fire was an accident." The firefighter paused and looked around at the chaos. "Your mother was in the house sleeping when the fire started, and she had to run through the flames to escape. Her nightgown caught fire, and she jumped in the swimming pool to put out the flames. That was probably what saved her life," he said, pointing toward the ambulance.

Tommy frantically zigzagged his way through the chaos of first responders to reach the ambulance. When he finally found his mother, she was laying on the ambulance's gurney wrapped in a white sheet with an oxygen mask on her face. Her face and pajamas were charred and covered with soot, and he saw blistering burns on her arms and legs. Next to her stood Dottie Westbrook, one of her bridge buddies from the country club, was standing beside her, and he could see Dottie was trying her best to keep Babe calm while the paramedic attended her wounds.

Tommy was terrified and began to tremble when he saw his mother; he suddenly felt as though he were about to throw up. Dottie stepped away when Tommy walked up, saying she would give them some privacy. Tommy asked his mother what had happened, and as soon as she opened her mouth to answer, Tommy knew that his mother was drunk.

"I need you to go into the house and get my jewelry," she begged her son as she lay on the gurney. Babe could barely hold her head up as she slurred her words.

"Is that the only thing you can say?" Suddenly, a rage boiled up in Tommy. "I am not going into a burning house and risking my life for your stinking jewelry!" he shouted. Tommy was tired of his mother getting drunk and doing stupid things.

Tommy had never been so angry at his mother. Babe never accepted any responsibility for any of the damage she caused while she was drinking. And to know she'd burned the house down—it was almost too much for Tommy to bear. The firefighters were calling it an accident, but how could this an accident when she was drunk and started a fire? The firefighter had told him the fire probably started in her bedroom, and Tommy knew in his heart of hearts that his mother had been smoking in bed and passed out with a lit cigarette.

He turned without saying another word and walked away. Miss Dottie tried to grab his arm as he walked by her, but when she saw the look in his eyes and the black hatred on his face, she let go without saying a word and went back to the ambulance to be with her friend.

Tommy stood in the street and watched as his home, the house his father had built for his grandmother, burned to the ground. He felt like he was having an out-of-body experience. All the while he could hear his mother behind him shouting her drunken slurs, begging him to run into their burning home to save her jewelry. He stood there for what seemed like an eternity, numb, not even noticing when the ambulance drove off with his mother.

It was in the early morning hours when Ronnie found Tommy sitting on the steps of a house down the street from what used to be his home. The fire was almost out when Ronnie drove up on the scene; the fire crews were cleaning up their equipment, and there was nothing left of Tommy's house except a pile of smoldering debris.

Tommy was sitting quietly with his head in his hands. It had taken less than an hour and a half for the wooden structure to burn to the ground. The volunteer fire crew was ill-equipped to save the house; they were shorthanded, and the fire was just too intense.

The news of the house fire put a damper on the festivities, and Ronnie had driven Tommy's car into town after the party broke up. Tommy had left in such a hurry that no one realized what happened. When Tommy didn't come back, Ronnie decided to come looking for him. "Lucky for you, my friend, you left your keys in the ignition," Ronnie said as he handed him the keys. The swimming pool was full of rubble that had fallen from the house as the walls collapsed, but surprisingly, the guesthouse was still standing as though nothing had happened.

Tommy felt like he'd just woken up from a nightmare when Ronnie put his hand on Tommy's shoulder and asked if he was all right. Lifting his head, Tommy took a deep breath. His voice shook as he told his friend, "I need to call Beverly and the Colonel."

Ronnie asked, "Is your mother OK?" It took all the strength he could muster to tell his friend that she'd survived and was in the hospital.

Tommy had a blank, lifeless look on his face. "I found her. She was still drunk as they were loading her into the ambulance. She most likely passed out and started the fire." Shaking his head as he spoke, he said, "I knew that bitch would do something like this someday."

Ronnie was the only friend Tommy felt like he could talk about Babe's alcoholism to. Ronnie had spent enough time at Tommy's house when they were kids to know how bad her drinking was and how rough things were for his friend growing up with an alcoholic. Tommy was ashamed that his mother was a drunk and before that night had never spoken openly about her issues with booze.

They both sat silently on the steps of the neighbor's house for what seemed like an hour, but really it was only a few minutes. Ronnie patted his friend on the back and said, "You can call the Colonel and Beverly from my parents' house. They probably already know what happened. After all, news travels fast in a small town."

Ronnie's parents were either asleep or in bed trying to sleep when they snuck into the house. "Try to get some sleep before you start making phone calls to anyone," Ronnie said. "It's been a long night, and there is nothing anyone can do before morning anyway."

He let Tommy have his bed, and Ronnie went to sleep on the couch in the living room. Tommy slept fitfully, but he did sleep; the experience of watching his house burn to the ground was exhausting beyond description, and he felt like the flames had sucked the life out of him.

The next morning Tommy woke up at almost nine and sat straight up in the bed as if someone had flipped a switch. Everything flooded into his consciousness at once. The dread of having to call Beverly and the Colonel was almost paralyzing, but he surrendered to it. Tommy got up and got dressed. He found Ronnie and his parents at their kitchen table; Ronnie's mother offered Tommy some breakfast.

"Thank you," he said politely, "but I have too much to do. I have to call Beverly and the Colonel."

"You know you can use our phone," Ronnie's mother offered considerately, standing to pour more coffee for herself and her husband.

Tommy declined and walked to the front door. "This is something I have to do on my own." He sighed, his shoulders sagging; he looked like he was fighting back tears as he turned the doorknob.

Ronnie had given Tommy his car keys on the walk home last night; he felt so incredibly sorry for his friend. Ronnie knew from his years in the seminary in

California that you can only offer to help; you can't make someone take it. "Call me if you think of anything I can do."

"I will," Tommy said politely and left.

He walked slowly up the street to the guesthouse.

How ironic. The guesthouse was untouched by the fire. It looks just like it always did.

Tommy went into the guesthouse and looked out the windows across the garbage-filled pool to the still-smoldering pile of rubble that had once been his home. He flipped on the light switch, but the lights didn't come on. Realizing that the firemen had probably turned off the electricity, he went outside and flipped on the main breaker to the guesthouse, praying that nothing else would go wrong. Beyond the rubble, he could see the two cedar trees that he, his mother, and Candy had decorated just a few days before Christmas. In that moment, he felt a lot like those trees; he was scorched but still standing.

He picked up the telephone and dialed Beverly. She'd already gotten a call the night before from Dottie at the hospital. She was clearly shaken and told her brother that they would be there before lunch. Tommy didn't say much about what happened, just telling her that they would talk more when she arrived, and then he hung up. Beverly would not be very sympathetic to the rage he'd felt over the condition he'd found their mother in when they were loading her into the ambulance. He decided that the less he said, the better.

"Now comes the hard part," Tommy said under his breath as he dialed the number to the hotel in Washington where his father was staying. Someone at the front desk answered, and Tommy asked to be connected to his father's room. Tommy figured that Miss Dottie had also called, beating him to the punch, and that the Colonel was expecting Tommy's call.

His father answered on the first ring; Tommy told him what happened, again omitting the fact that his mother had been drunk and probably started the fire. The Colonel listened intently and then told Tommy, "I have a lot of important work to finish before I can come home. You will have to handle the cleanup. I will be home when I'm done with my business." He then hung up the phone.

It never ceased to amaze him that the Colonel could be so cold and callous at times. They'd just lost their home—the home that the Colonel himself had built for his own mother as a gift—and his wife was in the hospital. However, Tommy figured that his father probably felt the same way about Babe as Tommy did at that moment and probably didn't want to talk about it.

Tommy took a shower and shaved, and after he put on some clean clothes, he sat somberly staring out the window for what seemed like an eternity. He was well aware that other people would expect him to be a good son and go to the hospital to check on his mother. He dreaded the idea of sitting in the same room with her, but he begrudgingly worked up the strength to do what he had done his whole life—pretend like he loved his mother.

By the time Tommy drove over to the hospital, it was almost noon. He was hoping Beverly would already be there so that he wouldn't have to be alone in the room with Babe. He'd resented the Colonel ever since childhood for never being around; it wasn't enough just to have Nana Harris there to be a buffer between him and his mother. Maybe having Nana around did help a little, as Tommy was clean, fed, and always got to school on time. But no one protected him when it really counted.

The Colonel hated confrontations, especially with his wife, and his business trips were obviously a way to avoid dealing with Babe and her issues with alcohol. Tommy always understood why his father left but held a grudge because the bad stuff always seemed to happen when he wasn't around.

And now that the Colonel was hiding out in some Washington hotel, leaving Tommy to clean up the mess. He was almost as angry with his father as he was with his mother. "What a coward," Tommy whispered as he stood outside the doorway to Babe's room.

He heard the sound of his mother's laughter—laughter, for God's sake—and it made him bristle.

She almost died in a house fire and only by the grace of God is she still alive! Our house burned down and all our possession have been destroyed! Now she is laughing like nothing happened.

Tommy felt sick, and he considered turning around and leaving.

I spent the morning staring out the guesthouse window at a smoldering pile of shit. All because my lush of a mother was feeling sorry for herself for being alone on New Year's Eve and chose to get drunk.

Tommy stood out in the hall for a few minutes, debating whether or not he should go in. Finally, the rage subsided, and he decided to get it over with. After all, the quicker he got this over with, the sooner he could return to Austin.

When he went into her room, he found his mother lying in bed with bandages on both of her arms and legs. Tommy walked over and kissed on the forehead like a dutiful son. Candy was sitting at the end of his mother's bed, and Beverly was in a chair over against the wall. There was an empty chair on the other side of the room, and Tommy quickly sat down in it and started reading the book he'd brought with him.

The family said polite hellos to one another, and a tense, eerie quiet fell over the room, like everyone was holding their breath to see how Tommy would react. After a few minutes of silence, Tommy asked his mother, "When are you going to be released?"

"Oh, the doctor said the burns was minor," Babe answered gaily, waving one small bandaged hand. "I have some second-degree burns, but Dr. Mattingly said I should heal quickly if I take it easy and do what I'm supposed to, I should be released in a few days." She smiled at her son. Evidently, she had no idea what had happened the night before.

"Have you spoken with your father?" she asked, changing the subject. "Did he say when he's coming home?"

"Yes, I spoke with him before I came up here, "Tommy replied coldly. "He said that he would be home after he was done taking care of his business in Washington."

His mother's joyous mood suddenly grew dark; sadness came over her, which was evident to everyone in the room. She was being punished for her lapse in judgment.

Did she expect that her husband would drop everything and rush home to be with his injured wife?

Tommy didn't know whether to be pissed off or to feel sorry for her. The four of them sat in silence once again for several minutes. This was one of those profound silences that was more revealing than anything that could be said. After a while, Candy began her mindlessly chatter about school and her friends, while Tommy went back to reading his book. It wasn't at all interesting, but it occupied the time and he could tune out the chatter. After about thirty minutes, the conversation caught his interest and pulled him out of his reading.

Tommy overheard the two of them discussing architects. Babe was talking about her grand plans to build a palatial manor. "I have always loved Spanish or Mediterranean architecture. Maybe something like a house in Tuscany."

Tommy glared at his mother over the top of the book. He knew she always hated living in their house and that she'd begged his dad for years to let her build the house of her dreams.

Couldn't she at least wait until she gets out of the hospital before bringing it up?

Tommy could feel the fever of his face flushing, as if the rage inside of him was causing his blood pressure to increase. The ruins of the fire were still fresh in his mind, and she was already talking about the mansion that she was going to build. He sat for a few moments staring at the pages in the book, unable to focus, reading the same page three times before he could speak again.

"Dad asked me to arrange for a crew to show up on Monday with a front-end loader to start the cleanup. Maybe someone should arrange for a crew to sift through the debris to see if there's anything worth saving," Tommy interrupted as he looked straight at Beverly when he spoke. "I have to go back to Austin. The spring semester starts next week."

Beverly's lips tightened, and her eyes narrowed. She stood fuming, glaring at her brother without saying a word. He wasn't going to be around to take care of it; it was her problem, not his, and he really didn't care how pissed off Beverly got.

Tommy stayed at the hospital for another hour and then headed back to the guesthouse to make the calls and arrangements for the cleanup crews, as he promised the Colonel he would. But he had already decided that he would do the bare minimum to fix this mess, and he damn sure wasn't going to stick around to supervise the cleanup. If his mother could burn a house down, she could figure out how to fix it.

Tommy packed his things and called the ranch manager, Rick. Rick had already heard about the fire and arranged to have a crew bring a front-end loader over to where their house once stood to clean up the debris. "I have to go back to Austin today, so I'm counting on you to take care of this before the Colonel gets back," he instructed Rick and hung up.

Tommy quickly packed and left as soon as he could. On his way back to Austin, he stopped by Alligator Lake. The night before it had been the site of a joyous celebration meant to ring in the new year. To his amazement, someone had cleaned up campsite already. The only traces that were left of the party were paper on the ground from the fireworks and the ashes from the bonfire. The trash was gone, the generator was gone, and the barbeque pit, the ice chests, and the Christmas lights were all gone. It was almost like the party never happened. Tommy stood staring across Alligator Lake, wishing he could erase the memory of the fire as easily. Feeling completely numb, Tommy got into his GTO and headed back to law school.

Chapter 13

WHEN ETTA MAE heard about the fire, she called the hospital to check on her employer. Beverly answered the phone, and after she eased her mind that Babe was OK, Etta Mae asked, "What can I do to help?"

"Could you please go over there and see what, if anything, survived the fire? If there is anything that can be saved?" Beverly spoke softly, her voice a whisper, as her mother was sleeping.

Before she hung up, Beverly told Etta, "I am very grateful for all the care you have given my mother over the years." Beverly knew that her mother didn't have many friends, and right now she needed all the friends she had to help her get over her injuries.

Etta arrived in time to see Tommy pulling out of the driveway behind the guesthouse. Although Etta Mae was disappointed by Tommy's leaving, it was not unexpected. Etta closed her eyes and thanked her lucky stars that none of her children were as self-absorbed as Tommy. When she opened her eyes, she was overwhelmed by the shear enormity of the devastation to the once lovely old house. Etta could never understand why Miss Babe hated that house so much. "That house was nicer than anything me or my family have ever lived in. For the life of me, why can't white folks be happy with what the good Lord gives them?" She got out of her car, shaking her head.

After standing there staring for what seemed an eternity, wondering where to start, she put on a pair of coveralls that she had borrowed from one of her sons. She thought to herself, *I will probably have to buy him a new pair of coveralls because these won't ever wash clean after digging around in this mess.* She then put on a pair of rubber boots that she used during the winter months to keep her feet dry and some gloves that she used for gardening.

Etta started in on what used to be the kitchen where the charred remains of the two refrigerators were. One was still standing, and the other was on its side beside what used to be the washer and dryer. Stepping carefully over burned and charred rubble, she picked up a pot here and a plate there. She started a pile in the yard of the treasures she found so that they could to be cleaned up. She found the kitchen table and chairs, and decided that with a little cleaning, they could be saved. If her employers didn't want them, Etta was sure she could find someone in need around town who would be more than happy to have them.

As the day progressed, Dottie Westbrook showed up with her daughter, Lynn Ann, and a couple of hours later, Beverly and Candy came, too. Beverly cried when she saw what was left of what used to be her mother's house, telling Etta Mae, "We feel so blessed that nothing more happened to Mother than her burns."

The women worked for hours until it was almost too dark to see. By late in the evening, it was becoming more and more evident that the household items were not a total loss. They found books, dishes, pots and pans, chairs, tables, desks, and all kind of other furnishings and knickknacks that could be salvaged—even a silver music box and the clock that had sat on the mantel above the fireplace.

The worst of the damage had occurred in the area around Babe's room where the fire started. Beverly had been hopeful before she pulled up to the house that the fire had spared the closet dresser where her mother kept her jewelry. Her heart sank as she surveyed the damage. "I always told Mother to put her jewelry in the Colonel's office safe, but she didn't think it was necessary." Beverly choked on her words as told Etta.

She didn't just want to find her mother's jewelry because of how valuable it was. She wanted to find her mother's jewelry because it represented something more to her mother—it symbolized the idea that her husband really did love her.

Beverly began to tremble as the sun grew lower and lower in the sky. The shock was setting in as she began to grasp how much they had lost, and she wondered if anything would ever be the same. A feeling of sadness shook her to the core. It was increasing evident just how close they had come to losing Babe. If the swimming pool had not been just outside the back door, Babe might not have made it.

But once the shock subsided, Beverly was overcome with rage. She was incensed that neither her brother nor her stepfather seemed to care that they had almost lost her mother. "All they care about is that stupid house," she told Candy when no one else was within earshot. "That spoiled little brother of mine is a selfish jerk!"

As the day faded to night, Beverly called to everyone who had helped out and thanked them warmly for the kindness they'd shown. Beverly kissed Mrs. Westbrook on the cheek as she was leaving. She caught Etta taking her son's filthy coveralls off at her car and asked if she could arrange for a few men to be there in the morning to help finish up before the heavy equipment came to shovel the remains of their home into the Dumpster.

Candy, who had stopped working hours ago, was sitting with her chin resting on her bent knees by a stack of books, staring at what used to be her grandmother's bedroom. Beverly took her daughter's dirty hand and walked back to the guesthouse to spend the night. The guesthouse always had been Tommy's domain, but Tommy was gone, and after the way he'd behaved over the past twenty-four hours, Beverly really did not give a crap if he was offended.

Candy had never spent the night in the guesthouse; she wasn't allowed inside without Tommy's consent. She was proud of her mother. Candy thought that her uncle was a spoiled snob who treated her mother and grandmother badly.

The guesthouse had two bedrooms that were mirror images of each other. Tommy always stayed in the west bedroom, the "yellow" side, so Candy and Beverly made themselves at home in the east bedroom. Candy took the first shower while her mother ordered a takeout pizza.

After her shower, Candy and Beverly went to pick up their dinner and took it to the hospital to eat. Black Rock's hospital only a few blocks away. It was small, and the medical care was limited, and most of the patients that needed urgent care were transferred to the hospital in Brian-College Station. Beverly was relieved that her mother was spending the night in Black Rock, which probably meant her mother's injuries were not too serious.

It was almost eight o'clock that evening when Candy and Beverly arrived. Candy's grandmother was up watching TV and in obvious pain. "When was the last time you had any pain medication?" Beverly asked her mother and was dismayed when Babe answered that they had just given her some.

Beverly excused herself and went to the nurses' station to ask about her mother's medication. "The dosage should be ample to give your mother relief from any pain," the nurse replied. "Dr. Mattingly will be back in the morning for rounds. You should talk to him then if you have any concerns."

"What time do you think the doctor will make his rounds tomorrow?" Beverly asked the nurse impatiently. The nurse has simply shrugged her shoulders and went back to her work.

Frustrated, she went back to the room to sit and watch TV with Babe and daughter. It was Saturday night—she couldn't imagine that the doctor would be in early on a Sunday. Beverly couldn't focus on the TV. Candy sat on the end of her grandmother's bed, chattering to Babe about the things they'd found in the rubble. After a while, Babe started to settle down and enjoy the company of her daughter and granddaughter. She listened as Candy told her about staying in the guesthouse. After an hour and a half, they said their good-byes and went back to the guesthouse to try and get some rest, maybe even sleep.

"The worst is over," Beverly told mother as she kissed her good-bye. "Get some rest, and don't worry about anything."

⇥═◉ ◉═⇤

The next morning Candy and Beverly arrived at the hospital about eight thirty. Candy didn't really want to spend all day there, but given the choice of the hospital versus the cleanup, the hospital won. She also suspected that if she tried to stay at the guesthouse, she would have to hide from Etta Mae, who would most likely snatch her out of bed and put her to work. Watching TV with her grandmother was much more appealing than rolling around in a sloppy mess looking for things that might or might not be salvageable.

Beverly stopped to grab coffee by the nurse's station before going into her mother's room. Babe was finishing up her breakfast and asked her daughter, "How did you sleep last night?"

Babe lied and told her, "I slept like a rock." In reality, she'd had a crappy night, tossing and turning.

"The guesthouse is cold and dirty." Candy chortled as she climbed onto her grandmother's hospital bed and turned on the television. "I can't believe Tommy likes it there."

Before long Babe fell asleep, and Beverly and Cindy decided to let leave. As soon as she woke up, Babe began to feel terrible and asked the nurses for more pain medication. The nurse had checked her chart hanging on the wall by her bed, saying "Your blood-alcohol level was pretty high when the ambulance brought you in. You need to detox from the alcohol. I can give you a little something for the pain, but we don't want you to have a bad reaction to any medication that I give you."

At first Babe was angry at the nurse, but she decided not to argue. The quicker she got out of the hospital, the easier it would be to downplay how much she'd had to drink when the fire started.

Babe couldn't remember much from that night. She remembered feeling sorry for herself because she was all alone on New Year's Eve again. She remembered starting out with beer and progressing to gin once the beer was gone. She didn't remember going to bed that night, and she certainly didn't remember how the fire started. She just remembered waking up in a panic to flames and a burning sensation on her arms and legs. She remembered looking down and seeing that her bed was on fire, and running and jumping in the swimming pool. After that, things were a blur. She didn't know who called the fire department and didn't remember the ride in the ambulance. No one asked her about it, and she wasn't going to volunteer any information if she didn't have to. She was scared and worried what would happen to her if the Colonel found out.

When the doctor showed up later that afternoon, Beverly and Candy were already gone. They'd waited around as long as they could, but Babe was relieved that they'd left. She didn't want her daughter talking to the doctor. Dr. Mattingly had warned her for years that her drinking was going to kill her someday and that she needed to cut back or, better yet, stop entirely. Babe had started attending AA meetings in Bryan for the past year; she'd fallen off the wagon a few times before, but nothing as bad as what had just happened.

After examining Babe for what seemed like a long time, Dr. Mattingly insisted on writing her a prescription for Antabuse, a drug used for detoxing from alcohol. The doctor explained that when given in lower dosages it could curb the craving for alcohol. "I believe this will help you. The next time you may not be so lucky," Dr. Mattingly gently explained.

"I am worried your husband is going to react badly to the house fire and add even more stress to your life," he said, his brow wrinkling in concern. He knew that the Colonel hadn't exactly been supportive of his wife's efforts to stay sober. "You backslid on New Year's Eve, but you're alive and you still need to lay off the booze."

Babe's body was showing signs and symptoms of liver disease and cirrhosis of the liver from the years of uncontrolled alcohol consumption. Dr. Mattingly told her that she wouldn't last long if she didn't stop drinking.

Dr. Mattingly left, but not before making Babe promise him that she would call her sponsor and go back her AA meetings again. "You're going to be released in a couple of days, and Beverly will eventually be going home. That will be the time that you'll need the most help."

Maybe it was because her medication had worn off, or because reality was sinking in, but until that moment, Babe had been oblivious the extent of the damage the fire caused, but suddenly it hit her that this time it was bad. The fire was accidental, but if she hadn't been drinking it probably wouldn't have happened. Babe had burned down the house that her husband built for his mother. It was more than just his family home; it was a gift to his mother, and symbol of his success.

Dr. Mattingly left the room, and her blood ran cold. Babe began to cry. "What have I done?" she said as she lay back on her bed and sobbed. "My husband will never forgive me for burning down his mother's house."

Chapter 14

TOMMY DROVE STRAIGHT to Austin after he left the hospital, gritting his teeth the whole way. The only stop he made was at a liquor store to buy a bottle of whiskey and a couple of cokes for mixers. Tommy didn't wait to leave the parking lot before his mixed a drink in a plastic cup for the road. He knew better than to drink and drive; he just didn't care anymore about anything.

No one seems to care if my mother is a drunk. Why should I care if it's dangerous?

The rage he felt was the kind of anger that could make a person physically sick. His mother was talking about building her dream house with his sister before the cinders of their home had even stopped smoldering. The resentment he'd felt all his life had just transcended into hatred.

Tommy slammed back his first drink and poured another before peeling out of the liquor store parking lot. It was a two-and-a-half-hour drive to Austin, and Tommy seethed and obsessed about his mother the entire way, drinking one mixed drink, then two, then three while he drove.

She doesn't have a clue about the consequences of her actions. She's never taken responsibility for the problems her drinking has caused for our family or the problems she caused for me.

Tommy was on his fourth drink when he pulled into his driveway in Austin. He was pretty boozed up, but he'd stopped caring after his first drink. He was in the middle of his own private pity party, and that was all that mattered to him.

He'd been gone for almost two weeks, and as he unlocked the front door, he threw his bag and backpack on the floor. His funky Austin house was cold. As he flipped on the light switch and looked around the room, he was glad to be away from the nightmare. He was tired of thinking. Tommy walked into the bungalow, hoping that when he closed the door behind him, the nightmare could be forgotten—at least for a little while.

It was late in the afternoon, and it was cold inside. Tommy lit the wall heater, hoping it would take the chill out of the air. Next, he lit the space heater in the bathroom and sat down on his couch. As he turned on the TV for some noise, an overwhelming feeling of utter aloneness came over him. It was the kind of loneliness that he hadn't felt since he was a little boy, a blackness the light could not penetrate. It was something he hated more than he hated his mother. He was alone with monster that was his anger and thoughts.

Tommy was exhausted and wanted to punch a wall, but instead he decided to go to the Matt's El Rancho and get something to eat. There was nothing in the house; he had cleaned out the fridge and taken out the trash before he left for Christmas.

Tommy got in his GTO and drove downtown, where Matt's El Rancho was located on East 1st Street. Usually there wait on Saturday nights, and it probably wouldn't be too crowded since classes at UT weren't starting up for another week. Matt's El Rancho was small family owned restaurant a hole in the wall that seated only about 40 people, but it was reputedly the best Tex-Mex food in town so with any luck he wouldn't have to wait long for a table.

He parked on the street in front, and went inside, surveying the small crowd, and not recognizing anyone. Tommy was a little disappointed because he'd hoped someone he knew would be there so he could vent. He found an empty table close to the window, and the server showed up within seconds of him sitting down. She was short with brown hair tied up in a bandana and wore a red skirt and white shirt with ruffles around her neckline. She brought a glass of water and a menu. Setting them down on the table in front of Tommy, she smiled, asking, "What'll it be?"

Tommy looked up at the server, and without opening the menu, he ordered the beef Chile Rellenos, and a double bourbon and coke. Tommy was hungry; as his stomach started growling, he suddenly realized that he hadn't eaten since the night before at the party.

"Sir, the Chile Rellenos takes between 30 and 45 minutes to prepare." She said without looking up as she wrote down his order.

"That's fine," Tommy responded while he leaned on the table.

When the server came back with his drink, a basket chips and some salsa, Tommy slammed it down ordering another one before she left. He was on his third drink when she brought his food to the table; the server saw his empty glass, and asked if he needed anything else. He started eating and ordered another double before she walked away.

The server told the bartender, "I'm beginning to think I should cut him off. It's a slow night and I need to make some tips, but I really didn't want that guy behind the wheel of a car." She brought Tommy the check with his drink, hoping he would take the hint and leave after he paid.

Taking the hint, Tommy finished his food and left, and as he pulled out of the parking lot, he decided to go to Ziggy's Cabaret. Ziggy's was one of the classier gay bars in Austin. It was on a dimly lit street, and it didn't have a sign out front of the red brick building. The main entrance was in the back, where a rather large bouncer stood guard to ensure there wasn't any trouble from any redneck homophobes looking to beat up a queer.

Tommy had avoided the gay scene since he left Massachusetts. He knew too many people in Austin and was reluctant to explain or make excuses for any of his lifestyle choices. Besides, he'd been too busy with law school and was walking the straight and narrow. But that night, Tommy just didn't care about being straight, much less walking the straight and narrow. In fact, he didn't care about much of anything.

Tommy parked down the street and walked around back to the entrance. The bouncer nodded to Tommy as he opened the door. The music was loud, and he could feel the thump of the bass from the speaker as soon as he entered.

The bar was dimly lit, and there were mirrors behind it with elaborate gold gilded frames. A mirrored disco ball rotated over a parquet dance floor, and intermittent laser lights refracted off the mirrored globe as couples danced to the music. The bar was relatively empty; the big event had been the night before on New Year's Eve.

Tommy was already tipsy from drinking all day, but he walked up to the bar and ordered yet another drink. Before long a man came up to the bar and sat down beside him; he could see the man in the ornately gilded mirror behind the bartender, and the two made eye contact. He was a tall man, dressed very sharply, with jet-black hair and a well-groomed goatee.

Immediately the man offered to buy Tommy a drink and introduced himself. His name was Lucas Damon. After a few minutes and another drink, he said something that shook Tommy to the core. "I am very sorry that your family lost their home."

Stunned, Tommy asked the stranger how he could possibly know about his parents' house burning down. Lucas replied, "I know a lot about you. I'm a friend of your family. I'm an attorney from Houston—I've done some oil-and-gas legal work for the Colonel off and on for the past several years."

At first Tommy was nervous that a friend of the family had found him in a gay bar, but Lucas assured him that his secret was safe, and the two men began to talk. Tommy opened up to Lucas, telling him things about his family that he'd never told anyone. He told him about how his mother was a drunk and how angry he was at her; he told him how his father neglected him and treated him like a piece of furniture.

Locus responded as he took a sip from his glass, "Surely that doesn't surprise you."

"I guess not," Tommy replied.

After their third or fourth drink together, Lucas announced that it was time for him to leave, but before he left, he stated frankly, "There will come a time when you may want my help." Lucas gave him his business card and extended his hand. The two men shook hands, and Lucas was gone.

Tommy thought, *How odd*, and finished his drink.

⊷▬◉ ◉▬⊷

The next morning Tommy found himself naked and face down in a strange bed with a naked stranger next to him. Tommy didn't remember how he got there, or who the man was beside him, or if he'd had sex with the man. Tommy tried to get up without disturbing him but didn't succeed.

The next thing he knew, the man rolled over and started stroking Tommy's penis, which stood erect to the man's touch. Immediately, the strange man rolled him over and started licking Tommy's hard member, sliding his mouth down his cock. As the man started giving Tommy a blow job, his erection exploded in the man's mouth.

After he was done, the naked man got up and went to the restroom. Tommy leaped from the bed and frantically started dressing himself. He needed to take a piss in a bad way but was so desperate to leave that he decided to piss outside. Tommy dressed quickly, calling out his good-bye as he walked out the door.

Once outside, he relieved himself in some hedges on the side of the house. When he turned toward the street, Tommy saw his car parked in front. Happy that he could make a painless exit, he jumped in the car and sped off without knowing which direction to go. He finally got his bearings when he found Expedition Street in the Tarrytown section of Austin; he knew how to get home from there.

Tommy didn't think too much about what had happened. He was just relieved that the two of them had gone to the other guy's house, so he wouldn't know where Tommy lived. His home was still his sanctuary, and Tommy was not in a place emotionally to violate that inner sanctum—the only place left that was safe. The guesthouse had been his sanctuary as a child, and he remembered how Roy would drop in whenever he felt like it and how he'd always felt helpless to stop him. Tommy was older now, but still he didn't want that to happen again.

When Tommy got home and opened the front door, he found that it was roasting hot inside. He'd left the heater on when he left for dinner the night before, thinking that he would be coming right back after dinner.

I could have burned this house down like my mother.

After turning down the heater in the hallway and laughing at himself for being so careless, he went into the kitchen. He pulled a glass out of the cupboard, filled it with tap water from the sink, and drank the whole glass. Standing and staring out the window over the sink, he realized that he was dehydrated from drinking so much the day before.

As he filled the glass for a second time, Tommy became aware the he felt dirty and he smelled his musky scent, much like the smell of dirty gym clothes. He smelled like he'd had raunchy, sweaty sex with a man, and all he wanted, needed, was to take a long, hot shower.

Tommy finished his water and went into the bathroom, turning on the water as hot as he could stand it.

Chapter 15

THE SPRING SEMESTER of law school started in mid-January, and after a couple of weeks of classes, Tommy was able to put all his problems out of his mind. He was glad to get back into the law school scene. Some of the people he'd taken classes with in the fall were enrolled in his new courses in the spring semester, and now that everyone was more comfortable about the expectations of school, they were starting to warm up to Tommy. He threw himself into his studies, mostly to distract himself from the house fire and the fallout between his parents. He found that he was actually starting to enjoy his coursework.

Much to Tommy's annoyance, Etta Mae took it upon herself to call him regularly to keep him apprised of what was happening between his parents since his departure from Black Rock. As soon as Babe was released from the hospital a few days after the fire, she moved into in the guesthouse. After the shock of the devastation set in, Babe decided to take Dr. Mattingly's advice. She filled her prescription for Antabuse and started going to AA meetings again every Tuesday and Thursday.

The Colonel didn't come home from Washington until several weeks after the fire. And when he came home, he showed no sympathy or support for his wife. In fact, he'd come home to Black Rock to find a vacant lot where his family home once stood. He left after an hour and stayed in his apartment in the high-rise in downtown Houston when he wasn't traveling.

Nothing Etta told him was a surprise to him, and Tommy was relieved that he was in law school. It gave him an excuse not to get involved in the cleanup and the reconstruction of the new house. "If I weren't in law school, the Colonel would try to pawn it off on me. It's time my father took care of his own dirty laundry," he told his old friend Ronnie one evening. "I have all planned it out. I'm taking a full class load and won't have any time to help out."

Ronnie was on his way back to California for his last semester in the seminary and stopped off in Austin to check on his old friend before he left.

"Your father's has been evading the issue of your mother's drinking for a long time," Ronnie said sympathetically. "They both have swept it under the rug all these years, and now they can't do it anymore."

Tommy had heard from Etta and Beverly that his parents were disagreeing about everything these days, especially concerning the reconstruction of the house. Babe had hired an architect from Conroe named Jamison Hollingsworth and commissioned him to draw up plans for a grandiose Spanish-style hacienda. When the Colonel saw the preliminary plans, he hated them and threatened not to pay the man. Babe was devastated that she wasn't getting the house she always dreamed of and started talking about building two houses next to each other—one for her and one for him. The Colonel thought that idea was ludicrous, and they fought about the two houses for a few months until Babe finally gave up, realizing her husband would never pay for it.

The second set of preliminary plans took another three months to draw up, and when the Colonel saw them, he believed the new plans were almost as ridiculous as the first set of house plans. But even though he hated the house the architect proposed, he yielded under the pressure. The Colonel finally conceded, telling the architect, "My wife has never built a house before, and you're taking advantage of her inexperience by indulging her fantasies just to make a buck."

Tommy's father was too old to fight over house plans with his wife, so he just stayed away and refused to pay the architect whenever he didn't do what he was told. Tommy's father had no problem using money as very effective weapon against people who didn't do what he wanted. After what seemed like an eternity, the house plans were completed and construction started on the new house in October of the next year.

It had been a struggle, but Babe managed to stay sober the whole time. "I couldn't have done it without the Antabuse the doctor prescribed," she admitted at one of her meetings. She had been living in the guesthouse all by herself the since the house fire.

Tommy didn't go home the whole time she was residing there. Etta Mae saw him around town a time or two, but he asked her not to tell his mother that he was in town when she asked him if he'd gone to see Babe. Etta Mae only shook her head disapprovingly, saying, "I'm just the maid. I'm not getting in the middle of your family business."

Babe suspected that her son had washed his hands of her and didn't know what to do except to seek help and guidance from her support group at AA.

In the meantime, Tommy was buried in his law school studies and was glad to be busy with his classwork. He studied at the UT Law library with his law school friends until about midnight on the weeknights, and sometimes when he was in the mood, he would sneak off to Ziggy's or one of the other gay bars in town after he'd finished studying.

Tommy wasn't sure if he was getting braver or more accepting of his sexuality, or if he'd just stopped caring if anyone found out. "Once I woke up next to a strange naked man, I threw caution to the wind and started enjoying myself," he told one of his new gay friends. But Tommy was drinking pretty heavily, and that made it easier for him to go home with whoever he met.

The thrill of hiding his sexuality from his friends and family gave Tommy a sense of power over them. It made him feel quite clever and superior to be able to fool people. The lies he told made him feel untouchable and impervious to the inadequacies he was really covering up. "Relationships with women are fraught with problems. Women are like a minefield you have to tiptoe through, and every once in a while, if you stepped in the wrong place, you could get a leg blown off," Tommy joked on a night out with his new friends at Ziggy's.

-→-▪◉ ◉▪◄-

When Christmas rolled around, Tommy went skiing in Aspen, Colorado, with a group of his new friends. He drove to Black Rock and dropped off some presents with Etta Mae for his family, and then left for his ski vacation. He told Etta that he was planning to stay gone until the new semester started in January.

They had rented a house just outside Snowmass. Tommy and his friends skied their pants off by day, hitting the Aspen hot spots by night. They were like most young gay men in Texas at the time and made every effort to keep their sexuality under wraps, but in Aspen, they could let go and go wild partying.

One of Tommy's friends, Rusty, had a connection in Aspen who could set them up with as much cocaine as they wanted, "We are going to have a white Christmas!" Rusty excitedly exclaimed.

So, Tommy's Christmas in Aspen was a blur. Tommy did more cocaine than he'd done in his entire life. He'd tried some coke earlier that year when he was having sex with someone he'd met at a gay nightclub and found that he liked coke a lot. In fact, it was probably the only drug he enjoyed doing. He found that the high made him feel invincible—unlike pot, which made him feel paranoid and sick. By the time he got home from Aspen, he had been awake for several days. Tommy promptly crashed, sleeping it off for three days.

⊷⊷ ⊶⊶

Summer school started in June, and the construction of Tommy's parents' house had slowed to a crawl, just one step above a standstill. The relationship between the Colonel and Babe had turned quite petty. For the most part, Tommy's parents weren't speaking to each other, but when they did, a ferocious fight would ensue. They fought mostly about the house, the architect, and the contractor. Babe would tell the contractor to do something, and it seemed that the Colonel would tell the contractor to rip it out and do it his way a few days later. Then as soon as the Colonel left, Babe would tell the contractor to rip it back out and redo it her way.

Tommy watched from a distance in horror as his parents made asses of themselves. Etta Mae and his sister kept him apprised of the fighting, and Tommy began to find the ruckus entertaining. Tommy would laugh that the contractor was making a fortune off his parents' fighting. "He's getting paid by the hour. I figure he's going to retire on that house build."

Etta Mae still came to work through all the fussing and fighting; her work was now keeping the guesthouse clean. The guesthouse was small, and since Babe was alone most of the time, Etta was usually done by lunchtime. "I stay around until three or four o'clock just to keep Miss Babe company," she told Tommy, knowing he'd never ask about how his mother was doing.

Etta Mae heard others had seen him around town, but when she asked Babe if she'd seen her son lately the answer would always be "no." Etta saw Tommy pulling out of the parking lot at the lumberyard one afternoon. When see asked the cashier what he was doing; he responded that Tommy was buying rat poison to kill some of rodents in the hay barns. He'd before he'd seen Etta. She if he'd be home for supper he'd call, but he never did, and Etta never brought it up.

"I'm sorely disappointed in Tommy's behavior towards his mother," she told her daughter when she got home that evening. "It's none of my business, and all I can do is pray for him."

Etta saw loneliness come over Babe and was concerned. The stress of the house and fighting with the Colonel was taking its toll. Most of Babe's friends were her drinking companions from the country club, and Babe tried to stay away from those friends as she took her Antabuse and struggled to stay sober. Babe and Etta would sit and watch soap operas together, and watch the contractor and the workman building her house. Etta was usually the only person Babe would talk to during the day, except on the days when she went to her meetings.

One day Etta and Babe were talking over coffee as they watched the workmen through the windows. "I have stopped going to my AA meetings," Babe admitted to Etta Mae. "The twelve steps just aren't working out for me."

Babe didn't especially want to make amends for all the wrongs she caused people in her years of drinking.

"My husband and son are assholes and deserved every bit of the crap they have gotten over the years. I'm working every day to stay sober for myself and for my grandchildren," she claimed. Etta could hear the angry tone of her voice.

Babe had sobered up long enough to come to the stark realization that she was old and that she'd missed out on so much of her life. And now that her health was starting to suffer from all the years of heavy drinking, she'd given up. Her hands shook most of the time, and her joints hurt from gout. The olive complexion of her youth was now yellow and jaundiced from cirrhosis of the liver.

A few weeks later, Etta came to work as usual on a beautiful sunny morning in late July. She showed up at the usual time and found the door locked. The door was never locked, and Etta didn't have a key. She knocked on the door, thinking it odd because Miss Babe usually would tell her if she was going out. Babe didn't respond as she banged loudly on the door, thinking that Miss Babe was in the bathroom and had locked the door so that one of the workman wouldn't let himself in while she showered. When she got no response, Etta decided to walk around the outside of the guesthouse to see if there was a window that was unlocked.

Etta Mae gasped in horror as she looked through the window and saw Babe lying on the floor in a pool of vomit. She was frantic by the time she found an open window and climbed in; her hands shook as she reached down to touched Babe's lifeless body. Miss Babe was in her nightgown, cold to the touch. Her lips were blue, and she was lying in a pool of vomit.

On the floor beside her was an empty bottle of Antabuse and a half-empty bottle of gin. Babe must have taken a handful of Antabuse, washed it down with gin, and passed out on the floor.

"Poor woman choked on her own vomit," Etta Mae said, tears welling up in her eyes. She stood quietly for a moment and said, "Rest now, Miss Babe; your suffering in this life is over."

Chapter 16

TOMMY HAD BEEN out drinking with his friends the night before and was still in bed trying to get up for his first class. When he heard the phone ring, he let the answering machine catch the message. It was Etta Mae calling. He couldn't make out what she was saying and only wanted to sleep only a few more minutes.

It wasn't out of the ordinary for Etta to call. She would call to relay messages from his parents all the time. But this time, her voice was different. Tommy only had one phone in the house, in the living room, and he kept the volume down on the answering machine so that it wouldn't wake him up.

Tommy would graduate from UT in mid-August; he'd submitted his application for graduation in mid-July, and even though the university only held their commencement ceremony once a year in the spring, he would be receiving his diploma, and soon he'd be studying for the bar exam. He was feeling guilty because he didn't study the night before as long as he should have. He definitely didn't study as long as the more ambitious law students who made law review. The hard part of law school was over, and all he had to do was to graduate and pass the bar, and the world would be his oyster.

Unlike most of his classmates, he already had a job lined up for him in the family business. The Colonel had offered him a position in the leasing department, and Tommy had big plans for turning their outdated dinosaur of an oil company into a major enterprise.

"I expect you to go through the oil-and-gas leases and get them in order," the Colonel had instructed his son when he'd offered him the job.

Tommy wasn't exactly thrilled with his father's offer but told himself that he had to start somewhere. Passing the bar exam was the first step in the process.

He knew that if he didn't pass the bar right away, his father would lose respect for him, and he couldn't let that happen. Besides, he felt pretty confident about passing the bar, and suffering the shame of disappointing his father was not an option—especially now that the Colonel was on the outs with his mother and he was the golden boy.

Tommy opened his eyes and looked at the clock; it was a quarter after eight. He'd hoped to sleep a little longer, but he was awake now and the urge to piss had kicked in. Tommy got up and went to the bathroom and then into the kitchen, filling a glass with water and drinking it while gazing out the window over the sink into the backyard.

Damn it, Etta Mae! Why do you have to call so early when I'm hungover?

He filled the glass from the tap a second time and looked for some aspirin in the bathroom. It was Tuesday, and Tommy first class on Tuesdays and Thursdays wasn't until eleven. After taking a couple of aspirin, Tommy opened the refrigerator and pulled out the last piece of cold pizza he'd had delivered last weekend. "Nothing cures a hangover like cold pizza," he said as he finished off the last bite.

Feeling better, Tommy took a shower and got dressed. He then sat down on the couch to listen to his messages on the answering machine. After filtering through several messages, he got to the end. The message from Etta sounded hysterical. Etta didn't say what it was about but told him to call her back at the guesthouse number immediately.

The panic in Etta's voice both startled and concerned him. His first thought was that maybe something had happened to the Colonel. Tommy's father was well into his eighties now, and even though he was really fit and his mind was sharp, Tommy knew that his father had lived a long life and wouldn't be surprised if something had happened.

Tommy took a deep breath and dialed; the phone rang a few times before Etta answered. Her voice was still shaking, and she was in obvious shock.

Tommy could tell that Etta was grateful to hear his voice. "What in the world is the matter?" He questioned. "You act like you've seen a ghost."

He'd been the first person she'd called when she found his mother's body. Etta was hysterical but also terrified. She was a good Christian woman, and finding a dead person did not sit well with her.

"I found your mother this morning. She passed away during the night." That was all Etta could choke out.

This wasn't at all what Tommy was expecting. "Did you call anyone else?" It was rare for Tommy to be at a loss for words, but at this moment he didn't know what else to say.

The second call she'd made was to Daily Funeral Home. "I called you first, and I called Budgy down at the funeral home to come get Miss Babe before I called anyone else. I've been waiting outside for Budgy Daily to leave with the hearse when the phone rang."

The Daily Funeral Home was just down the street.

"Budgy was here in less than fifteen minutes. A sheriff's deputy showed up a few minutes later. But he left after Budgy told him that Miss Babe died naturally and he suspected no foul play."

They both knew that naturally probably meant that her liver had finally given out.

After she hung up, Etta Mae went back outside. She was a religious woman and believed firmly in God and Jesus, but she also believed very deeply in the devil, demons, and ghosts. So she was praying as Budgy and his helper loaded Miss Babe into the back of the hearse.

She didn't go back in until the hearse pulled out of the drive. Now that Miss Babe's body was gone, Etta prayed that her soul had gone to the other side and wasn't hanging around the guesthouse.

When she went back inside she saw that the vomit Babe's body had been lying in was still on the floor. Etta stopped short of walking through it and was perturbed because Budgy and his helper had spread it around as they collected Babe's remains onto the stretcher and had left it for her to clean up.

After she finished cleaning, she opened the windows to air out the house. It still smelled like death. She knew she needed to call Beverly, suspecting that Tommy had no intentions of doing so.

"Thank you for taking care of my mother. I'll call my stepfather and brother, and make the arrangements for my mother," Beverly said before hanging up, still in shock.

"I should have asked Etta if she knew how my mother died," she told her husband, Bob, after she hung up.

After speaking with Etta Mae, Tommy sat quietly numb for a few moments as he gathered his thoughts. He felt nothing. He felt no pain, no sympathy, not even loss. The only thing he could feel was guilt because all the feelings he was supposed to have about his mother's death were not there. "I always thought that Mother would outlive the Colonel," he said aloud, since his father was at least ten years older than Babe.

After a few minutes, Tommy called his father's office and gave him the news. Tommy's father was silent, as if contemplating what his reaction should be. The Colonel was a man of few words, but the silence on the other end of the phone unnerved Tommy. The Colonel finally broke the awkward silence by stating in a very matter-of-fact tone of voice, "I will give Etta a call and drive back home this afternoon," as if he had some important business to complete before he went home.

But when the Colonel asked Tommy to handle the funeral arrangements, Tommy did something rare; he told his father no. It was three weeks before law school graduation, and he was in the midst of taking his finals. "I'll call Beverly and ask her to take care of the funeral and interment arrangements," he offered.

"That is acceptable" was all the Colonel said to his son, and then he hung up without another word.

What a prick. You can't even show any emotion after your wife died!

Stunned was the only word to describe how Tommy felt. Weird, morbid, and guilty came to mind also. He had wished his mother dead so many times, and now she really was dead. He dreaded calling his sister more than calling the Colonel. He really knew she'd be distraught about losing their mother, and no matter what he said, Beverly would probably take it the wrong way.

He hesitated for a few minutes, hoping to give Etta enough time to call her first. Finally, he worked up the courage to call. His hands shook as he dialed his sister's phone number.

He didn't know what to say, but he'd think of something.

Chapter 17

THE NEXT COUPLE of years were chaotic for Tommy. Gone was his illusion that the world was his oyster. Reality had smacked him right between the eyes when his mother passed away. When'd he called his sister the morning she died, things went as well as could be expected until he'd asked Beverly to take care of the funeral arrangements.

"I can't really help very much. I am taking finals and studying for the bar exam," he'd explained, hoping she'd let him off the hook without an argument.

"Surely you're kidding? Don't you think you should help?" she'd asked curtly. "You used the same bullshit excuse when the house burned down."

Before she hung up, Beverly had agreed to take care of everything, but Tommy knew that he'd pissed his sister off and that someday there would be hell to pay.

Babe's funeral was a few days later, and Tommy went home to Black Rock for it. It was a lovely, dignified funeral, and he thought his sister had done a bang-up job. Tommy's mother was buried in the cemetery outside of town where the rest of the Colonel's family were interred.

After the funeral, everyone went back to the guesthouse for coffee and desserts. It was a small gathering, mostly of family and friends. Everyone was polite, and the Colonel was a perfect gentleman, stoically greeting all the well-wishers as only a statesman of his caliber could. But you could cut the tension with a knife—Tommy and his sister barely spoke but that was fine with him. He had important things to take care of and she'd get over it soon enough.

That afternoon after all the guests left Tommy decided to take a tour of his father's new house under construction. It was the first time Tommy had walked through the new house, and he was instantly perturbed. It was over six thousand square feet with ten rooms, only two bedrooms, and six bathrooms. Apparently, Babe had told the architect not to bother to include a bedroom for Tommy in the house plans, and that only pissed him off more.

The house was split down the middle, with two parallel hallways adjoining each other. There were two separate living areas, one in the front of the house and one in the back. The kitchen was huge, which was the only part of the design that Tommy liked. There was also a giant dining room between the formal living room and the kitchen for the Colonel to hold court and entertain his guest and dignitaries.

The house was disjointed and made even more odd with its flat roof. All Tommy could see was all the changes he'd have to make after he passed the bar, including adding another bedroom and bathroom upstairs above the garage so that he'd have a room in his own father's house.

⊷►═◉ ◉═◄⊶

Three weeks after his mother's funeral, Tommy graduated from law school to somewhat less fanfare than he'd received when he'd graduated from Amherst. Tommy took the bar examination a week after his law school graduation. He'd studied hard and thought the was ready but had a stroke of bad luck when he woke up the morning of the exam running a fever. He'd contracted the flu and was sick as a dog when he took the exam. Tommy held one eye open during the exam so he could focus on the test and believed that it was a miracle he'd still managed to pass.

After graduation, Tommy moved out of his house in Austin and bought a house in Houston in the Montrose area just a few blocks south of Westheimer. It was close to their downtown office, and he bought it at an estate sale from a little old lady who'd lived in the house since it was built in 1929. Tommy had lived away from home for over ten years and was excited that he was finally putting down roots. The house was structurally sound, but the interior had long been neglected. The kitchen was badly in need of updating, but he fell in love with it as soon as he walked into it.

It reminds me of our old house in Black Rock before the fire destroyed it.

Tommy bought the house thinking that he would take it on as a project, remodeling it while he lived there. But shortly after he bought it, the Colonel ordered him to oversee the completion of construction on the Black Rock house. Tommy's own plans for rebuilding his house got put on hold, and he moved temporarily back into the guesthouse.

Tommy worked hard and managed to get the house finished up a year after the expected completion date. He implemented all the changes he'd come up with on his first walk-through on the day of his mother's funeral. Much to his surprise, Beverly joined in to help, decorating the house with furnishings out of the warehouse that their mother had been collecting for years.

The architect had pissed Tommy off as soon as took over the construction, and he fired him on the spot. "He took advantage of our parents' dysfunctional relationship to make a quick buck," he told Beverly as they worked together to finish the house.

But the truce between the siblings was short-lived, and lasted only until the house was finished. As soon as Babe's estate was probated, tensions between brother and sister flared again but in a weirdly polite manner that only people with too much money can understand.

Texas was a community property state, and over the twenty-five years Tommy's parents had been married, half of everything that his father earned belonged his to mother's estate. And his mother's will bequeathed everything to Beverly and her two children. Tommy had only been left a few things in her will; most of the most valuable items went to Beverly. And much to his surprise, Beverly and her children got half the ranch and half the oil-and-gas interests.

Tommy was livid. As soon as he found out, he went out and found some cocaine. "I've been promised my whole life that everything was going to be mine someday, and now I've found out that half of everything goes to my sister and her two rotten kids," Tommy said to his friend after snorting a line. "All she gave me was the job of taking care of my sister's money. She couldn't even leave me alone after she died."

Tommy hated his mother more and more every day, and the Colonel, who'd shown very little emotion or grief from the loss of his wife at her funeral, was visibly upset when he came to the realization that he would have to cough up half of everything he worked for over the past twenty-seven years and give it to his stepdaughter and her children.

Immediately, the Colonel called in his team of lawyers from Fulbright and Jaworski to try and stop it from happening, only to be told there was nothing he could do. "Texas is a community property state, and your late wife could give her property to anyone she wanted to as long as your half of the community property was untouched."

Everything the Colonel had had prior to the marriage would come to be considered separate property, and Fulbright and Jaworski brought in a team of forensic accounts to ensure that Babe's estate wasn't traced back to earnings from before their marriage. The arduous task of sorting out Babe's estate would take over two years and would leave many scars and hard feelings between brother and sister, further straining their relationship.

Tommy never imagined that Babe would have a competent estate attorney write her will, but her estate attorney was brilliant and had written an iron-clad will for his client. And after her will had been signed and notarized, it sat in the office safe, never to be thought of until Babe's passing. His mother's wishes brought up a deep-seated resentment that Tommy had to relive from his child-hood, and he fought long and hard to keep it from becoming legally binding.

But even Tommy's best efforts were for naught, and his father eventually conceded to the rule of law and begrudgingly set up his late wife's estate in ac-cordance to her will. The oil-and-gas business would manage the trusts set up by his late wife's will.

Before long Tommy realized what an incredible brilliant man his father was. "This is a way to keep control of the assets without violating the intention of the trust agreements," the Colonel told his son in confidence. "We'll simple use your sister's money to limit our liability as we invest in an aggressive drilling program." The old fox had figured out a way around the law.

Tommy put aside whatever feelings he had about his sister and her kids and conducted himself accordingly. He'd worked for the family business most of his life, but now it was different. It was supposed to be just Tommy and the Colonel; instead, it was all five of them. He wasn't the boss's kid driving tractors for the summer anymore. Tommy had paid his dues, and his sister had had it handed to her on a silver platter. He was an oil-and-gas attorney, the trustee of his mother's estate, with a fiduciary responsibility to take care of them in a professional manner—no matter how he felt about it.

All his life, Tommy expected to walk in the front door and take over, and life had just pulled the rug out from under him again. His first few years of work were fraught with cold, hard rude awakenings to truths he'd never had to face before.

The only exceptionally good thing that came from the forensic accounting was that Tommy was the only who really understood where the money went and who got what. Beverly had barely graduated from high school, and Tommy had a degree in economics from an Ivy League college. "I can baffle my sister with bullshit, and she'll just do whatever I advise her," he informed the Colonel, smiling.

"Now you're catching on!" the Colonel said as he sat behind his desk in his new office at the new house in Black Rock.

Regrettably, the Ellison family was splintered and would stay that way over the next few years.

⊷═◉ ◉═⊷

After the dust settled, Tommy finally began to remodel his house. After he'd spent so much time working on his father's new house, he decided it would be best just to hire a contractor and oversee the work. He was going to live in his urban cabin, as he called it, while the work went on around him.

Life was finally looking up as work on his house was completed and he was adjusting to his new world order. Work and home both started to synchronize into a peaceful rhythm. Three years after he purchased his first house, Tommy had finally finished rebuilding it and could live comfortably in the house he loved.

But Tommy couldn't sit still for very long, and now that things had slowed down at work and home, he was looking for things to keep him busy so that he wouldn't get lost in his thoughts. His life had not gone the way it was supposed to, and he blamed most of it on his mother. Tommy was almost twenty-seven years old, and most of his friends and acquaintances were married with children. Tommy had been fixed up on dates with friends of friends, but nothing had panned out. As usual, he told his friends that he was just too picky and that he hadn't met the right girl yet.

But in reality, Tommy really wasn't looking for a girlfriend, though he hadn't given up hope on marriage and having a family yet. Not only did he have big mommy issues that he'd never resolve, no matter how hard he tried, but he didn't like any of the woman he dated well enough to marry them. He had a hard time figuring out the qualities he would like in a prospective wife.

Most of Tommy's sexual escapades were with men, but he couldn't see those relationships going anywhere, either. They always started out hot and heavy, but eventually the attraction would wane, and Tommy would move on to the next conquest. And Tommy really didn't like the way some of his gay friends acted so nonchalantly toward VD—like it was just part of the gay lifestyle, something you had to learn to live with. Tommy had to visit the Montrose area VD clinic more than a couple of times, and that didn't sit well with the young man who'd been indoctrinated at a young age to the Black Rock Church of Christ. The first time he went, he found out he'd contracted gonorrhea and was prescribed a course of antibiotics, which thankfully got rid of the problem.

One night when he was doing coke with his friend Oswald, Tommy asked him about living the lifestyle. He wanted to know what had motivated Oswald to come out and if he had any regrets. Down deep, Tommy really wanted to be in a loving relationship. He wanted a woman more like Nana Harris than his mother or his sister if he were to marry. Nana Harris had always thought the best of him, and even when Tommy told her a bold-faced lie, she believed him. "Nana Harris dedicated her life to my happiness. That's the kind of woman that I want to marry," he confessed to Oswald.

"Isn't that a little odd to have a fantasy about your nanny?" Oswald rolled his eyes. "Give it up, sweetie. You're gay!"

"I'm not really gay," Tommy protested. "I really do want to get married and have children someday. Your opinions are clouded because *you're* gay. I see lots of my friends happily married to wonderful women, and I want that, too. I just think that all the good ones are already married." Tommy paused, then asked, "When did you realize you were gay?"

"I've known it all my life. My parents did this to me. How can you be anything but gay with a name like Oswald?" Oswald was joking, but Tommy really wanted to know. "They used to call me Wally, thinking that would make me less of a target in school. It didn't work; I still got beat up on the playground."

Tommy laughed. He knew his friend was joking, but he was being serious.

Oswald continued. "Why in the world would you want children? You'll just mess them up. All parents mess up their kids, even if they're good parents. If that wasn't true, there wouldn't be so many therapists in the world."

Oswald made a good point, but Tommy wasn't buying it. Oswald had wonderful parents who loved and supported him for who he was.

"I just like having sex with men. It's so much easier than women," Tommy explained.

He still didn't consider himself to be gay; he was just experimenting until he found a woman that ideal for marriage. He had convinced himself that he was waiting for the right opportunity and figured if it were meant to be, God would provide him with the ideal mate.

"I want children, and I have no doubt that I could be a much better parent than either of my parents," Tommy argued. "The Colonel was disappointed when I quit football; I don't want to think about what he'd do if he found out that I was having sex with men."

Tommy changed the subject after that.

The Colonel was now almost ninety years old, still sharp as a tack, and had decided to focus on more altruistic endeavors. He'd always been a righteous man, and now that he saw how well Tommy had learned the business, the Colonel gave him more and more to handle. He spent less time traveling and more time in his new house entertaining his altruistic colleagues or at Peach Tree Ranch admiring what some called "the finest ranch in that part of Texas."

The Colonel would hold court in his living room, which was filled with the books he'd spent a lifetime collecting. Anyone who came to do business with him was expected to come early enough to take a ride out to the ranch to inspect his registered herd of Brahman cattle. His Brahman bulls were not like the rodeo bulls that struck terror in the hearts of the rodeo cowboy. The Colonel's bulls were gentle giants, strikingly beautiful animals, and he enjoyed watching the looks on the faces of his guests as he walked up to the magnificent animals and pet his prized bulls.

The Colonel was only going into the Houston office one day a week; he would hold court there with the loyal employees who'd dedicated their lives to him. Tommy and the Colonel were in full swing in the midst of an aggressive drilling program and had included Beverly and her children's trusts in the program—"spreading the risk," the Colonel called it.

. "If we make a good well, then all of us get rich, and if we drill a dry hole, then the losses are spread out among the family. It's a good deal for us all," the Colonel told his son.

-⟶▮▢ ▢▮◂-

After they'd drilled a few oil wells, Beverly decided that she wanted her husband to join the company to help take care of her interests. The Colonel and Tommy both understood what this meant. They didn't want Beverly or her children to sue them. If Bob were involved in their decisions, then their liability would be decreased significantly.

When Tommy's brother-in-law, Bob, joined the business, Bob and Tommy were able to work well together, but the Colonel's secretary, Minerva, did not trust Bob, not even a little bit. She would keep the Colonel's door locked when he wasn't in the office, keeping an ever-vigilant eye on the happenings around the office to ensure everything was on the up-and-up.

As far as Bob was concerned, his feelings about Minerva were mutual. He had no respect for the woman, either. Bob's job was to keep the peace in his family, and even if Minerva poisoned the rest of office staff against him, slowly undermining any authority that Bob possessed, he was taking care of his wife's best interests.

Tommy, however, ignored Minerva. He'd known women like her his whole life and wrote her off as a paper tiger. The Colonel never cared about office politics, and now that he was spending his time as a gentleman rancher, he cared even less. The only reason Minerva left Tommy alone was because he was the only son of her employer. "Even a man-hating harpy like Minerva isn't going to mess with me as long as the Colonel has his wits about him," Tommy said as he laughed with Bob.

Tommy liked having Bob around, and he had no reason not to trust him. After all, Bob was only doing what he would do in the same situation. Having Bob as a partner freed Tommy to do the things he preferred to do—hanging around the office dealing with paperwork was not his cup of tea. Tommy liked going out in the field and checking on the farmers, ranch hands, and oil-field hands, and he started traveling more and more on company business.

Tommy would also attend antinuclear symposiums and political venues for the Colonel. He was also expected to take care of his father's charitable interests. He loved stepping into the Colonel's shoes; he relished the respect that being his father's only heir commanded.

But it really wasn't until Tommy had stepped into his father's shoes that he began to realize what a tremendous man the Colonel was. Tommy had always resented all the sacrifices the family had made throughout the years in service of his father's glory, but when he took over the Colonel's duties as a statesman, it all changed. All Tommy's life he'd seen his father as selfish and narcissistic, and suddenly, as if lightning had struck, Tommy saw things differently.

My father really is man who effected huge change for the greater good of all humankind.

Tommy remembered the judge who swore him in after he'd passed the bar exam saying to him, "It is difficult being the son of a great man." Now Tommy finally understood what he'd meant and felt small compared to his father. The Colonel really was incredible man. A giant among men.

He didn't know how he'd ever fill his father's shoes. It was like he was seeing his father for the very first time.

Chapter 18

THE CANADAIZATION MOVEMENT was in full swing in the mid-1970s, and several laws had been passed to ensure that Canadian interests were being preserved by making it mandatory that any company doing business in Canada was required to be at least 51 percent Canadian owned and operated. Canadians were all too aware that Canada was becoming too Americanized, and most Canadians felt like their country was essentially becoming another American province when American companies were allowed to have 100 percent ownership of companies in Canada.

The Cattleman's Oil Company was one of those companies. It was fully owned by the Colonel, as it had been part of his separate property; he owned some oil-and-gas interests in Saskatchewan and Alberta that he operated from his Houston office. Once the sweeping reforms were passed by the Canadian Parliament, it became more and more evident that Cattleman's Canadian assets would fall under this new provision of Canadian law.

The Colonel was well aware of the implications and limitations that Canadianization laws would put on his company, and he wanted to sell out in Canada. He had likewise owned a sulfur mine in the State of Tampico, Mexico, during the 1950s and was force to sell the mine at a severely discounted price when the Mexican government nationalized it. Inadvertently, the Colonel had comingled the money he got from the sale of the mine with communal assets, making all the money he made with regard to the sulfur mine community property.

This was a difficult pill for him to swallow. He was a highly intelligent man, and the only thing that had shaken him up when his wife passed away was having to give up half his wealth to his stepdaughter and her two reprobate children.

In the latter part of 1976, Tommy was dispatched to Calgary to negotiate the sale of Cattleman's Oil Company's Canadian interests. This was one of his father's most valuable assets, and Tommy knew that what money came from the sale of Cattleman's Oil would eventually trickle down to him.

Tommy traveled back and forth from Houston to Calgary numerous times, staying weeks at a time in Calgary. While he was in western Canada, he criss-crossed the Canadian Rockies, visiting Jasper and Jasper National Park and Banff National Park. He stayed at the historic Banff Spring Hotel and Chateau Lake Louise. Tommy also explored the Northwest Territories as far north as Yellowknife on the Great Slave Lake. He fell in love with Canada and was astounded by the picturesque beauty of the rugged mountain landscapes and vast open wilderness of the Canadian west, hiking through the vast expanses of wilderness during warmer weather and snow skiing and cross-country skiing in the winter.

"It is like being on vacation but the company is picking up the tab," Tommy kidded with his brother-in-law, Bob, whom he left in charge of the office while he was away.

Tommy rode the train from Jasper to the west coast of British Columbia and was awestruck by the marvels of engineering as the train crossed the mountain switchbacks. He grew especially excited as the train went through the great spiral tunnel over the Continental Divide. When Tommy got to the west coast, he took a ferry across the Strait of Juan de Fuca to Vancouver Island and the outlying islands along the Northwest Passage, sailing as far north as Prince Rupert.

Calgary was an impressive city with wide vistas, a healthy standard of living, and a highly cultured and educated population. It was a quaint metropolitan city that held on to its frontier charm. Calgary was a fairly new city as cities its size go; its beginnings were only about a hundred years old, when it was founded as a trading post for the fur trade.

The residents of Calgary were friendly, very polite, and courteous people, and Tommy fell in love with the city, but try as he may, he found it hard to fit in. The loud and larger-than-life Texan stuck out like a sore thumb, and some of the Canadians he met were put off by Tommy's loud, arrogant, and bombastic personality—and didn't mind letting him know their opinion of loud, pushy Americans (politely, of course).

Tommy hired an attorney named Kevin Mulroney in Calgary to negotiate the sale of the Cattleman's Canadian properties. Kevin was a tall, lanky man with ice-blue eyes, red hair, and a thick red handlebar mustache. He was a brilliant and sincere Canadian barrister and also a prankster with a warped sense of humor and a boisterously loud laugh. Tommy took an immediate liking to him.

Tommy was impressed with Kevin's integrity and work ethic and was confident in his abilities to help find a buyer for the properties Cattleman's was selling. Kevin's law office was located in a high-rise building in downtown Calgary, so Tommy made it a habit of staying at the downtown hotel nearby during his trips to the north.

Tommy spent most nights dining alone, finding himself in the hotel bar making pleasant conversation with the other patrons. He would fill the days by reading or touring the city. Sometimes when Tommy was reading one of the locally published tabloids during his morning tea, he would read through the personal ads. He found it rather entertaining reading them when he was bored and especially found it funny that there were ads for male escorts in the personal section.

"This must be the polite Canadian way of advertising male prostitutes." Tommy chuckled as he read.

Since Tommy was on important family crusade and could not risk being seen hanging around a gay bar, the personal ads were intriguing as well as entertaining. Tommy had never paid for sex before and was starting to think that hiring a male prostitute might not be so bad. He had gone without sex for a long time, and he was horny and tired of beating off in the morning. So, Tommy took a hard look at the risks and decided to call one of the numbers.

It was awkward at first, but he arranged to have an escort meet him in his hotel room that evening and negotiated a price of 150 Canadian dollars for the evening. When he got off the phone, he was almost giddy. There was something appealing about being a bad boy that Tommy enjoyed way too much.

That wasn't so hard to do. The hardest part is getting past the stigma of paying for sex. Most of the married men I've seen out at the gay bars do it, so it shouldn't be that bad.

The rest of the day dragged by. Tommy spent it reading and editing the contract for sale. He was also on the phone with the Colonel several times that day discussing the terms of the sale. Since Tommy's father had been born in a time before electric lights and telephones, the fax machine was a concept that the Colonel could barely wrap his head around. "I'll messenger a copy of the documents to you to read when I'm done reviewing them," he finally told his father, and before the close of business, he arranged for Kevin's legal assistant to hire a courier to deliver the sales contract to the Colonel at home.

While reading the tedious legal prose of the contract, Tommy's mind wandered from time to time to his date for the evening. He found himself fantasizing about the escort he was meeting later at his hotel. He had a hard time concentrating. Instead, Tommy found himself sitting in the conference room in the twelfth-floor law offices staring out the window overlooking Calgary with a great big woody that wouldn't go away. He tried to concentrate on the documents, but he was distracted.

About three o'clock that afternoon, Tommy finally finished reading the contracts and met with Kevin in his office briefly. Tommy gave him a marked-up copy with the changes and asked Kevin to review them and give him his thoughts.

Kevin eyed it and said, "We'll revise the contract and present the revisions to the buyers. You do know that just because you want these changes it does not necessarily mean the buyers will accept them, right?"

"I understand, and so does my father," Tommy replied. In truth, he saw no point in calling the Colonel every time a little detail changed.

"Any more changes to the document will only prolong the negotiating process," Kevin explained, even though he already knew that Tommy understood the process. "I'll probably know by week's end if the revisions were accepted. If they accept the changes, we will go out to celebrate." The two shook hands.

"You've accomplished a lot today. I am certain that changes that my father and I asked for are not beyond reason." Tommy thanked Kevin for his help and input as he got up to leave.

As he walked along the streets of downtown Calgary, Tommy couldn't imagine why the buyer would reject any of the concessions he and the Colonel were asking for. He stepped into the downtown branch of the Royal Bank of Canada, where he opened a personal account and withdrew enough cash to pay the escort later that night.

"Escort." I like that better than "prostitute." It just sounds a lot less seedy. The Canadians really are a more cultured class of people.

After stopping by the bank, Tommy was ready for the evening and briskly walked to his hotel. It was late September, and a chill was in the air. The afternoon shadows from the sun's low proximity in the sky added to the chill. It was the end of the day, and workers from the high-rise buildings in downtown Calgary were emptying out into the streets. Tommy watched as they lined up at the bus stops to ride the public transit home to their families, and for a moment, he forgot he was alone.

It wasn't long after Tommy arrived at his hotel room before there was a knock on the door. Tommy nervously opened it. In the hall was a small man with bleached-blond hair. It was cut short on the sides, and the long hair on top was swept to the left, covering his left eye. He had a pencil-thin mustache and he wore tight blue jeans and a green-and-blue paisley shirt that was unbuttoned to show the hair on his chest and the gold chain around his neck. Stepping into the hall and glancing from side to side to make sure they were alone, Tommy introduce himself. "I'm Tommy." He extending his hand out to shake his guest's hand.

"My name is Charles, and there is no need for you to be so formal, sweetie. We are about to become close friends." Charles laughed loudly and swept past Tommy and into the room.

⇥▚▞ ▚▞⇤

The next morning, Tommy called his secretary and asked her to book an airline ticket back to Houston on the next available flight. Until they got a response back from the interested buyers, there was nothing else for him to do, he told her. But in reality, he wanted to get home to make sure that Minerva didn't gum up the works. Minerva was a sneaky old broad, and he didn't trust her any more than she trusted him.

Tommy arrived in Houston late in the evening and took a taxi home to his house in Montrose. The office had been running smoothly in his absence, except for the occasional fly in the ointment carefully place there by Meddlesome Minerva. Ten days passed before he got a call from Kevin.

On the day he got the call from Kevin that the buyers had agreed to the terms of the sale, the Colonel just happened to be in the Houston office. Tommy went into his father's office and shut the door behind him to make sure that nosy Minerva wasn't eavesdropping. He told his father about the details of deal he'd struck with the help of Kevin Mulroney.

The Colonel nodded off to sleep a time or two while Tommy talked. But occasionally the Colonel would open his eyes and ask him very pointed questions. Tommy didn't know what to think or how to react. His father was getting up there in age, but until that conversation, Tommy had never seen him acting like an old man. Even so, Tommy tried very hard to have patience, taking his time in his presentation so that his father could get all the facts and pertinent information to make a decision regarding the deal. After he was done presenting the details of the sale, he expected at least a "good job" or a pat on the back.

Instead, the Colonel instructed, "Get back to me as soon as you hear from the attorney." And Tommy was then summarily dismissed.

Tommy wasn't exactly sure how to get his father to sign a limited power of attorney without hurting his feelings or offending him. He called his secretary, Angelica, into his office, asking her to close the door.

Angelica was the opposite of Minerva. She was devoutly religious and highly professional, and believed that Tommy's family business was none of her business. After he laid out everything that needed to be done, he told Angelica that his main concern was Minerva's interference. He'd never discussed Minerva until then, and Angelica generally avoided getting dragged into the office politics that Minerva enjoyed stirring up. Tommy didn't have to get too far into his concerns before Angelica stopped him and took control.

"You need me to put together a limited power of attorney without anyone in the office, especially Minerva, finding out about it or else the deal is done?"

Tommy nodded.

Angelica knew that Minerva would relish the chance to telling the Colonel that his son was trying to steal everything and put him in a home. "Minerva means well, but sometimes she has a vivid imagination and crosses the line when it comes to protecting your father."

After some maneuvering, Tommy managed to get his father's signature on the power of attorney, and he put it in his briefcase before leaving the office. Tommy was more than a little pissed off at his father's secretary.

I shouldn't have to sneak around like a thief just to get my own father's signatures on legal documents. I am going to clean house when my father is gone, and Minerva will be the first to go!

Angelica made a flight reservation for Tommy for the next morning and called Kevin's office and asked him to set up the closing as soon as he could. Tommy flew to Calgary the next day, and the closing for the sale of Cattleman's Oil Company's Canadian properties happened within forty-eight hours of his arrival. Tommy was relieved when everything was signed, and the deal was done and dusted.

After they finalized the sale and the buyers had left, Kevin and Tommy stayed at the office while the legal assistant was finalizing the documentation and making copies that would be delivered by courier to Angelica in the Houston office. Kevin asked Tommy how long he would be in Calgary. "You agreed to a celebratory dinner with me and my wife," he reminded Tommy. They made plans for that night to meet at one of the best steak houses in Calgary.

He left Kevin's office with a new attitude. He was meeting Kevin and his wife, Michelle, for a celebratory dinner at the Stockman's Restaurant that evening. He didn't really have any plans before seven o'clock except for checking in with the Colonel regarding the closing. Tommy walked back to his hotel and was really unconcerned at this point about anything other than his business triumph.

That evening, Tommy dressed in a pair of jeans with cowboy boots and a tweed blazer. He had dined at Stockman's before and knew that the food there was outstanding. The restaurant boasted the largest porterhouse steak east of the Canadian Rockies. Tommy went downstairs and ordered a drink in the bar before taking a taxi to the restaurant.

When Tommy got to the restaurant, Kevin and Michelle were already there. The hostess showed Tommy to the table, and the first thing he noticed was that there were three people at the table: Kevin, his wife, and a brown-haired lady he hadn't met before. Michelle introduced the woman as a friend of hers, Marie Staples. Marie was tall and a little heavyset; she wasn't overweight, though in the South she would have been referred to as big-boned. Marie wasn't a bad-looking woman; she had strong British features with an olive complexion, dark brown eyes, and ample breasts that Tommy deliberately tried not to stare at.

"Marie is a nurse here in Calgary, and she spent a couple of years working for the government-run hospital in Tuktoyaktuk in the Inuvik Region of the Northwest Territories north of the Arctic Circle," Michelle elaborated.

Dinner went surprisingly well, considering that Tommy usually hated being fixed up on blind dates. Their conversation was light and cheerful, and Tommy was impressed with Marie. He was fascinated by her stories about growing up in the Pacific Northwest, of the Inuvik people who lived north of the Arctic Circle, and of what it was like living so far north. He was struck with how different that she was from the other woman he'd associated with throughout his lifetime. Marie had grown up on the west coast of British Columbia in Prince Rupert, and her father was a lumberjack who worked the treacherous mountain slopes along the Northwest Passage. She had lived with her stepmother while her father worked months at a time away from home in the wilderness of the British Columbia forests.

Tommy was so engrossed in the stories Marie told about her experiences up north that he sat quietly listening to her, only speaking up when he thought of a question. It was odd for Tommy to listen so intently to a woman; Tommy usually dominated any conversation with his bombastic, overly embellished stories, but this time he was quiet. He was captivated by this woman, Marie.

After dinner and drinks, the foursome enjoyed dessert and coffee. Tommy ordered a Grand Marnier with chocolate cake. Marie and Michelle chattered endlessly and Tommy did not interject his opinion once, and Kevin teased Tommy for being so quiet.

Tommy asked the waiter to call him a cab for a ride home when dinner was over, and when his cab arrived, Tommy pulled out one of his business cards and wrote down his home phone number and address in Houston.

"It was very nice to meet you. I had a really wonderful time this evening. You have lived an interesting life, and I enjoyed hearing all about it." He handed his card to Marie, saying, "If you ever come to Houston, you should drop by and we'll go out for dinner and drinks."

Marie was flattered by the charming Texas oil man's attentions and blushed. "I might just take you up on your invitation."

Chapter 19

SPRING CAME EARLY in 1977. The azaleas and red-bud trees started blooming in late February, along with the pear trees in the Colonel's yard. The winter was mild that year, with gentle misting rains, and the blooms burst out as soon as the winter rains warmed up and the south winds began to blow. It had been a rainy, wet winter; the kind of slow-soaking rains that the land drank up like a sponge. Wild flowers, blue bonnets, and Indian paintbrushes covered the ground like a carpet over the rolling hills in Texas. The blackberry and dewberry brambles along the barbed-wire fence lines were in full bloom, while the bees tended their fragment white buds, extracting the pollen to replenish their hives from winter dormancy.

Brilliant sunlight cascaded through the kitchen window as Tommy gazed at the yellow cedar pollen that coated his navy blue Blazer parked in the driveway of his father's house. He was allergic to cedar pollen and dreaded going outside, even though it was a beautiful morning. Tommy was spending a lot of time at the Colonel's house lately. His life had seemed to slow down after he got back from Calgary in October the year before.

Christmas had been uneventful, as it had been since his mother's death. The Colonel wasn't really interested in the pomp and pageantry that his wife had concocted at Christmastime. The drama of his mother's chaotic life was replaced by a sense of boredom that Tommy had a hard time dealing with. Tommy would go out to the ranch and cut down a small red cedar to decorate as a Christmas tree at his father's house, and his sister's family would usually come up from Houston Christmas afternoon for dinner. Then they would promptly go home that evening, leaving Tommy and the Colonel to watch the college football bowl games on television.

Tommy wasn't very interested in collegiate football, but the thought of leaving the Colonel alone on Christmas night seemed selfish.

If I got up and left, I wonder if he'd even notice I was gone.

Tommy's heart was beginning to soften toward his mother now that she had been dead for a few years. He was starting to remember the good things about her instead of resenting her and being angry all the time. Tommy still needed to resolve a lot of issues, but there was a glimmer of hope that someday, whether consciously or unconsciously, he would make peace with his mother. He hadn't quite forgiven her for burning the house down on New Year's Eve; it was an open wound and the main reason Tommy couldn't bring himself to decorate the house the way they used to before the fire. People would stop Tommy in the grocery store to reminisce and say, "Are ya'll gonna put the lights up this year? I sure miss the beautiful way your mother would decorate for Christmas."

Tommy would always lie and tell them, "Maybe this year." But when the time came to decorate, he just couldn't bring himself to do it.

Working for his father was getting harder and harder all the time. Everyone worshiped the Colonel, and Tommy did too, but he was getting senile and wished that the Colonel would retire instead of just pretending that he still had a clear understanding of what was going on.

It seemed that the older the Colonel got, the more people revered him. The Colonel had neglected and ignored Tommy his whole life, but it had gotten a whole lot worse since he went to work for his father. But however much he was mistreated, Tommy liked having access to the company's money to play with.

Tommy had woken up early that spring morning with a new project that was kicking off. The Cattleman's Oil Company was staking out the location to drill the Cattleman's # 1. The Cattleman's #1 was going to be the first oil well to be drilled on the Colonel's ranch in several years, and this was also going to be the first drill that Tommy was going to be completely in charge of. Tommy had done all the work; he'd obtained all the permits with the Texas Railroad Commission, hired the drilling company, and ensured all the geological studies were prepared to pinpoint the best location for drilling.

Tommy sipped some hot tea as he stared out of Etta's kitchen window over the sink at the pollen on his truck and contemplated everything he had to do.

It had been many years since he'd been this excited, and he couldn't wait to get started.

The fine layer of yellow cedar pollen on the hood of his truck was why he'd woken up with a runny nose and a scratchy throat. Etta offered to cook breakfast for him, but Tommy was meeting the surveyor at the location and said, "Sorry, Etta, I can't lounge around all morning at the breakfast table."

The Colonel was already at the table drinking his morning cup of tea and was starting on the oatmeal that Etta had put in front of him while reading the *New York Times*. Tommy's father hardly noticed when Tommy walked out the back door.

Tommy stopped at the garden hose to wash the yellow dust off his truck before he got into it and drove away. Tommy knew it wouldn't make any difference, but he decided to wash it off anyway. Excited about the new adventure, Tommy backed out of the drive and headed toward the ranch. He had driven the same route to the ranch his whole life, but on that particular morning, it just seemed like everything was cleaner. Even the trashy old trailer house with the beat-up old cars in the yard didn't seem so bad.

He had worked at the family oil business for several years now but mostly only did legal stuff. Tommy was drilling his first oil well without the Colonel, and he was excited, but he was trying to contain his enthusiasm as best he could. Tommy didn't want all the old hands at drilling to look down on him and call him a greenhorn, and he certainly didn't want them to think that his daddy was just sending his boy out because he was in semiretirement. Tommy wanted them to respect his skills as much as they respected his father.

This wasn't the first time Tommy had staked out a location; he'd done it a hundred times with the Colonel when he was growing up. When he was a boy, he'd imagined how he would act, even rehearsing in the mirror so that he would be ready when it came to be his turn to run things, when everything was his. But things just didn't turn out liked he'd imagined, and now Tommy had begrudgingly adjusted to his new reality. He didn't have to like it, but he accepted it.

After Tommy crossed the river bridge, he turned on his blinker to turn left off the highway. Tommy pulled up to the locked gate and got out of the truck with a huge key ring. Tommy kept every key he had ever been given by anyone his whole life on a key ring in the console of his truck; it must have had at least fifty keys on it.

I probably have every master lock key for every master lock ever made.

The gate had a series of locks interlooped with one another that kept unauthorized people from trespassing through the gate: one lock was for the farmers, one lock was for the ranch hands, and another for the oil-field crew and the pipeliners. Tommy swung the gate open and drove through it, stopping for a moment to close it behind him. He looped the chain around and didn't lock it so that the surveyor crew could get in. The geologist, Mike Hicks, was meeting them out there, too. Tommy wasn't worried about Mr. Hicks; he'd been his dad's geologist for forty years and knew how to get back to the location of the Cattleman's number one.

Tommy got back into his Blazer and drove down the dirt road through the field. The farmer was out early plowing. He would be planting corn soon and would be working dawn to dusk getting the fields ready to plant. After a mile and a half, Tommy came to a fork in the road, and he took the left fork, which went over the levee. On the other side, the road followed the toe of the levee around to the river bottom. He passed the old pecan tree where the eagle's nest was. A pair of eagles had started nesting there a few years earlier and had returned every year since. Tommy loved the majestic bird and threatened to fire anyone who bothered them.

The land outside of the levee was strictly used for ranching, and periodically, when the river came over of its banks, the ranch hands would have to move the cattle into pastures behind the levee for their protection. Tommy drove past Bone Ridge, where the cattle would go when the river was out. It was called that because animals that got caught there when the water was high would starve to death if the river stayed off its banks too long. These days, the rancher would either feed them by boat or swim them in high water out to safety.

About a quarter mile past Bone Ridge, Tommy turned off the dirt road into the pasture toward the tree line. The trees were a mix of oak, pecan, and yaupon, and the location for Cattleman's number one was just in front of one of those windbreaks near an old slough. Tommy drove slowly through the pasture because it was pretty rutted up because of the wild hogs that lived along the river.

A mist hung over the pasture as Tommy bounced along. The cattle were grazing on the other side of the pasture. Tommy was a little early, and he pulled his binoculars out of his glove box as he got out of the truck. He hadn't see the eagles when he drove past their nest, and he thought he would kill a little time looking for them while he waited for the others. It wasn't long before Tommy spotted Mike Hicks and his son, Greg, cresting the top of the levee, with the survey crew truck following along behind.

It only took a few minutes to stake the location, and when Tommy returned to the house, Etta had lunch ready for them. She'd made a pot roast with potatoes and gravy; Tommy still didn't think Etta Mae was as good a cook as Fredrick, but he would never dream of telling her so. Mike and Greg, were already there and Tommy could hear his father holding court in the living room.

They moved into the dining room when Etta Mae served lunch. As they ate, Tommy listened to his father laughing with Mike and Greg; the Colonel laughed a lot more since his wife died, and Tommy knew that he only laughed with people he considered his equal.

Mike Hicks was one of those people the Colonel respected and held in highest regard. He was one of the best geologists there was and had worked with his father since the beginning. Mr. Hicks was bald and overweight, and the yellowed tinge to his to his complexion was most likely due to the amount of scotch he'd consumed over his life. But he was an old-school geologist who could look at the lay of the land and point to the right spot to drill, and he rarely ever missed. He had been doing it for so long that Tommy used to think Mike Hicks could smell the oil in the ground.

When they were done, Tommy helped Etta clear the table, and when he walked through the swinging door that led into the dining room, through the doorway he could see Mike Hicks sitting on couch and his dad sitting in the old wooden rocking chair that was once his mother's. The rocker was one of the things that had survived the fire. Tommy had found it in the warehouse years later and restored it for his father because he knew how much it meant to the Colonel. Now that the Colonel was older, the old rocker had become a throne of sorts from which he held court.

After another half hour, Mr. Hicks announced it was time to leave and got up to shake hands good-bye. It was almost two o'clock when Mike and Greg left, and when Tommy came back into the room after seeing them out, his father was still in his rocker reading a book. Tommy sat back down on the couch and read the latest oil-and-gas journal.

Thirty minutes later, Tommy noticed that his father had fallen asleep in his chair; his book was in his lap and was open to the page where he dozed off. Tommy quietly got up and let his father sleep. Going upstairs, he packed his things to go back to Houston. It was time for him to get back to work in the office. There was a lot to do before they moved the rig in, and he needed Angelica's help.

-->=◉ ◉=<--

At the office, Tommy was working on the installation of a new state-of-the-art computer system. He didn't discuss it with the Colonel because he believed it was beyond his father's abilities to understand at this point in his life. Tommy's father was old-school, especially when it came to business, and all the accounting was still done by hand in ledger books. Computer systems technologies for businesses were now getting cheaper and cheaper, and Tommy was determined to be at the cutting edge.

Tommy hired a young man named Shawn Pendleton to run the new computer system. Shawn had recently graduated from Trinity College and had impressed Tommy immediately. He seemed to understand what Tommy was looking for and entertained good ideas on how to make things work—especially the new accounting software.

After the untimely death of his mother, it seemed like Tommy had had to postpone the dreams he'd when he was younger of bringing the oil business into the twenty-first century. Shawn would be an infusion of young blood and fresh ideas, and Tommy was excited about the different and forward-thinking prospective that he brought to the table. Shawn would bring the company into the computer age.

"The whole company has to become computer proficient if we want to be competitive with companies like Exxon or Shell. The big oil companies are starting to eat up the small independent oil producers like us," Tommy explained to Shawn. "I believe this is the best chance we have at staying competitive."

Tommy couldn't help but feel proud. "I wish I could make my father understand. The Colonel is too old to comprehend the benefits that computerizing the office will have on office efficiency." Angelica just nodded. Tommy forgot how uncomfortable she was talking about personal things regarding his father.

Tommy was smart enough to know that his father was at the age where any kind of change was considered bad, and he hoped that by the time that the Colonel realized what was happening, it would be too late to go back. When it came to the Colonel, Tommy knew that sometimes it was better to ask for forgiveness than permission.

Chapter 20

IT WAS A windy spring day when the drilling company spudded the Cattleman's number one. The day before, a fast-moving cold front had blown through the area and a torrential downpour came through, along with tornado warnings and hail the night before. The drilling company had set up the rig a few days before the storm, and fortunately it wasn't damaged, but the crew had been putting the finishing touches on the mud pits and pumps and were still hooking up diesel motors and the blow-out preventers when the storm went through the area.

It had almost been two months since Tommy had staked out the location with Mike Hicks. The logistics of getting the road to the location built up so that the trucks could carry the rig into the ranch was a bigger endeavor than Tommy had anticipated. Several loads of rock were brought in to build up the road to be able to carry the weight of the trucks, and it was necessary to reroute the road so that the heavy trucks could go over the levee without damaging it.

The levee that protected the ranch and surrounding area was maintained by the US Army Corps of Engineers, and Tommy had applied for a permit for the new road, which needed to be approved by the USACE Fort Worth Division. Since it was an existing road, the permit only required that soil core samples of the levee toe be analyzed to determine if the levee could withstand the weight of the trucks without damage, and that took time.

Tommy was losing his patience with the whole ordeal; he felt like the permit from the Corps was senseless and unnecessary. But his father insisted that he get the USACE permit; Tommy probably wouldn't have done it if his father hadn't made him.

The Colonel lectured Tommy about it one morning at the breakfast table like he was a little boy. "I want you to make sure that we are in good standing with the Corps of Engineers. If something happens to the levee, it will be on us to repair it, which will not only be costly, but if we have a falling out with them, it will be almost impossible to repair the damage to that relationship."

Tommy stood quietly as the Colonel talked. It wasn't as much what he said that stung; it was the tone of his voice. Anytime the Colonel criticized him or questioned his judgment it always perturbed him. Tommy was in his thirties and hadn't like lectures when he was a boy; now that he was a man, he hated them even more.

It was Aubrey, the driller, who finally expressed his concerns to the Colonel about the road over the levee. Aubrey had been with the Colonel for almost as long as Mike Hicks. Aubrey was the best driller in that part of the world, and the Colonel listened to everything he said.

Tommy didn't like being overruled, but he needed Aubrey's expertise. Aubrey set up his trailer out at the location and would live there for the next month or two until the well reached total depth and was tested and completed. Until then, the drilling location was his home.

Tommy's enthusiasm waned as he jumped through more and more hoops. "I'm just the Colonel's flunky again," he told Bob as he worked through the details of the USACE permit. His excitement about running with the big dogs had ended when he had to deal with the Corps of Engineers.

Tommy initially thought that since he put the initial deal together, that meant he was going to be the boss, but it was becoming abundantly clear that as long as his daddy was alive, the old guard would always defer to the Colonel instead of Tommy.

The next few weeks would be slow-going anyway, kind of like watching paint dry, so Tommy stayed in Houston when they started drilling. Angelica knew how to reach him if he was needed. Tommy was hanging around his house more and more, doing cocaine. He'd found a local drug dealer who was keeping him supplied and was snorting a couple of eight balls, doing busywork in between lines. He wasn't answering the door, and he was screening his calls.

Tommy had started out doing coke just every once in a while when it was offered to him; he didn't buy it because he was terrified of getting arrested like a common criminal. Drug dealers were scary thugs, and he didn't want them in his life…and the idea of getting arrested and the Colonel finding out was even scarier to Tommy than the dealers.

One time when he was doing coke with Oswald, they had run out early in the evening. Oswald called his drug dealer, who would deliver, and lo and behold, Tommy met his dealer, Javier. After he found a drug dealer he could trust, he started buying for himself.

Tommy had started slowly but now was using coke every two to three weeks. Sometimes he would invite a trusted friend or two over to party with him, but lately he was mostly hiding in his house alone. Unbeknown to Tommy, he'd started to become addicted to the drug and had convinced himself that if he hid at home, no one would notice how much coke he was doing.

No one in the office had a clue that their boss had developed a taste for cocaine and that his life was beginning to spiral out of control. Tommy spent a day or two recuperating after his binges, and no one was any the wiser.

⊷▪▮◉ ◉▮▪⊶

When Tommy got back into the office the following Monday, he was glad to see that things were running smoothly. He felt clean and refreshed, with a better attitude, and was ready to get back to work. The well reports were good; the rig crew had set the surface casing to a depth of fifteen hundred feet and were back to drilling. The drilling was going as scheduled, and they were a little over a mile down to the bottom.

The geologist was shooting for the Woodbine formation, a pretty prolific oil sand that was well known for its production longevity. They would only know what they had when they logged the well and set casing, unless they got some kind of show in the mud returns or a gas kick on the way down. Tommy was excited. It wouldn't be long before they made a well. All he had to do was sit tight and watch it happen.

Tommy spent the morning opening mail and returning phone calls. About midmorning, Bob stuck his head in the door of his office and asked him if he had a minute. Bob sat down in a blue leather wing-back chair opposite Tommy; in his hand, he had the business section of the *Houston Chronicle*. On the front page was an article about the recently created Department of Energy.

"Things are about to change in the natural gas business," Bob said as he handed Tommy the article.

Tommy was a little ambivalent about the article. "Natural gas is cheap. The Colonel says there's no money to be made in natural gas." Gas was usually flared off in oil wells, and gas wells were plugged because it wasn't cost effective to produce them. But Tommy listened to his brother-in-law, whose opinion he respected.

"It's my opinion that the new Department of Energy will be a positive change for the natural gas business, and the price of gas will slowly go up and will be more competitive in the future," Bob said holding a binder. He had obviously researched the numbers. "I've done the math and determined that it's our fiduciary responsibility to the royalty holder to capture the gas in a pipeline gathering system and sell it." He was mostly meaning his own family, but Tommy continued to listen now that his interest was piqued.

"This is the business plan I've been working on," Bob said, handing the smartly bound book to Tommy across his desk.

Bob knew he had to sell his idea to Tommy; the Colonel would never go for any idea that Bob brought to the table. He didn't trust Bob even a little bit, and Bob couldn't help but notice it. The only way to get his plan off the ground was to get Tommy to present it to his father.

"We can both make a lot of money if we put in a pipeline gathering system to start shipping natural gas to one of the major gas utilities," Bob added.

Tommy read through the plan, stopping only momentarily to ask questions and to discuss options. Bob could tell by the tone of his voice and the excited glint in his eye that Tommy was interested.

"This deal hinges on two things. The first is selling the deal to Lone Star, which I don't think is any problem at all. The second is the hard part—convincing the Colonel that doing so is in his best interests."

Tommy had heard about the legislated changes afoot and believed that Bob's idea was a chance to get in on the ground floor. He and Bob had discussed this idea before in passing, but this was the first time Bob had put the numbers down on paper, and Tommy liked what he saw. There was something for everyone, and if the numbers were correct, all three parties—Bob, Tommy, and the Colonel—stood to make money.

After a while Tommy stood up from the chair where'd he sat for the better part of an hour and said, "I'm going to take it home tonight and read it in greater detail."

Bob stood, extending his hand. "I believe this is an excellent plan, so take your time. Your input is appreciated. Let me know if there's anything else we need to consider."

Tommy left the office and got home about four thirty. He had ridden his bike to work that day since it was such a nice day. The weather wasn't hot yet, but the high temperature had been up into the eighties. Tommy was sweating profusely, so he took a shower and changed into a clean pair of shorts and his favorite T-shirt before making himself a drink and sitting down on the couch to study the business plan for the pipeline gathering system.

Tommy made himself another drink and sat back down on the couch to read the business plan. He was impressed with the detail Bob had put into it. The business plan showed that if they borrowed the money to construct the pipeline and charged a transportation fee, the system would be paid off in three to four years. Tommy got out his calculator and began crunching numbers, realizing that Bob was right. Tommy and Bob would make enough money that he could be independent from his father. With Bob's help, he could be his own man.

Is it possible that I could make enough money that I wouldn't have to be daddy's errand boy anymore?

Despite getting along with him at work, Tommy had kept Bob at arm's length for most of his life, and he really didn't know why. Maybe it was because his sister's first husband was such a disappointment.

On the other hand, Bob had never gone out of his way to have a relationship with Tommy. The two were cordial to each other, but that was it. There was just something about Bob that made you feel like you couldn't really turn your back on him, and Tommy just couldn't put his finger on it.

Maybe it was because the relationship between Bob and Beverly was more like a business deal than a love affair. Bob had always seemed icy with a dry personality, but he looked darn good in a tux, which seemed to be important to his sister.

In the end, Tommy decided to go into business with his brother-in-law. Tommy considered himself a savvy businessman and couldn't find anything in the business plan to make him think that it wasn't on the up-and-up. He decided he'd tell Bob in the morning.

As he took another sip from his glass, his future became clear. He was ecstatic. Tommy really was going to be his own man, and thanks to William, it was going to happen sooner rather than later.

Suddenly, there was a knock on the door that shook him back to reality. Tommy wasn't expecting anyone. Setting his drink down and glancing at the clock, he realized that it was six thirty. He'd lost two hours going over the business plan.

When Tommy opened the front door, he was his surprised to see Marie Staples from Calgary standing on his front porch. Marie was the last person he'd expected to see at his door that evening. "Well, hello. What brings you to Houston?" Tommy exclaimed in astonishment.

Marie smiled and said, "I was in the neighborhood and wanted to know if your offer for dinner was still good?"

"Well, you caught me at a good time because I have something to celebrate. Come in! If you give me a few minutes to change, we'll go get dinner and catch up."

He let Marie inside and offered her a drink while he went upstairs to change.

Chapter 21

IN HONOR OF his first real money-making deal, Tommy decided to take Marie to Tony Mandola's Seafood Restaurant. He showered and changed into a freshly starched pair of blue jeans and plaid shirt. Putting on his cowboy boats, Tommy went downstairs, saying, "I hope you like seafood. I know this great place, and you'll love it."

"I hope it's not too formal. I'm dressed pretty casual for a formal restaurant." Marie was wearing jeans and a floral blouse that was tucked into the waist. "Can I at least borrow your bathroom to fix my hair?"

Tommy laughed and directed his guest to the bathroom at the top of the stairs. Marie took her purse and was in the bathroom for about fifteen minutes. "This is a pretty simple house for a high-powered oil man," she commented as she returned.

Usually a comment like that would have insulted Tommy's sense of pride, but it rolled off his back as he flippantly remarked as he escorted his new Canadian friend out the door, "Well, I expect things will be changing for the better soon."

When they arrived, the restaurant wasn't very busy and the hostess seated them immediately, handing Tommy a wine list as they sat down. "I thought you weren't taking me to a formal restaurant. I feel very underdressed."

Marie fidgeted with her blouse as she surveyed the other patrons and saw that some of the men were dressed in suits and ties.

"Don't worry. This is Houston." He saw the same men that Marie was looking at and said. "Those guys are probably at a business dinner. You look perfectly fine."

"Well, I hope so." Marie quietly laughed. "My suitcase is in my motel on the north side of town, and it is too far away to go change. Houston is a lot bigger than I expected; I think I will have to move closer in, I think."

"Indeed, it is," Tommy replied politely. "So what brings you to Houston?"

Marie had come to Houston because she'd applied for the master's program in nursing and mental health at Texas Woman's University in the Houston Medical Center. She'd loaded up her car with everything she owned and moved to Houston before she even knew whether or not she'd been accepted into the program.

"Do you have any suggestions about where to stay? I have to budget myself until I get a job, and I can't stay in the Ritz-Carlton. I'm planning to find a job to support myself while I'm in school." She explained her plans to Tommy over dinner.

"I'm impressed with your faith in your abilities. Not many people would take the kind of chance that you have." After that night in Calgary, Tommy hadn't given the woman a second thought until she'd knocked on his door. But in a moment of generosity, Tommy impulsively said, "Why don't you save your money and stay with me in my guest room for a few days until you get situated."

He realized that he'd only met Marie one time. But Kevin and Michelle were good people, and Marie was a friend of Michelle's.

What could possibly go wrong?

"Oh no, I couldn't possibly impose on you like that." Marie sipped her wine, shaking her head. "That's far too generous for you to offer. I'm grateful, but we've only met the one time in Calgary, and I don't want to be a bother."

"Don't be silly. I insist," Tommy asserted as the waiter brought their dinner. "Besides, I'll be out of town for the next few weeks and you can have the house to yourself. I have work to do in the country, and I'll be staying at my father's house."

⊷▰▱◌▰◌▱▰⊷

After their dinner at the Stockman's in Calgary the evening they met, Marie was quite enamored with the handsome oil man that her friends, Kevin and Michelle, had introduced her too. Marie started researching Houston's job market and schools, and found out that there was a thriving medical community there with world-class schools and opportunities for nurses and medical technicians. During her research, she came across the master's program at Texas Woman's University and applied to the program, thinking that if things didn't work out between her and Tommy, then she would have an education and a job to fall back on.

She applied for a visa at the American consulate, and soon Marie quit her job, sold her furniture, packed up her brown Honda Civic, and left for Houston. It took her four days to drive to Houston. The first day Marie stopped in Great Falls, Montana, and spent the night at a dingy little off-brand motel on the outskirts of town. The second day she made it to Cheyenne, Wyoming, and stayed in a crappy little motel there, too. Marie was on a budget and taking a big gamble moving to Houston, and she knew she could ill afford to be extravagant. On the third day, Marie made it to Texas, where she spent the night in Amarillo at a motel next door to a stockyard (which she only found out the next morning when the wind shifted).

On the fourth day of hard driving, Marie arrived in Houston. It was late at night when she got to the north side, and Marie stopped at several motels along I-45 before she found one she could afford. She was exhausted when she finally got to her room; it was grimy, with orange shag carpeting and green-and-orange plaid curtains. The bathroom was barely acceptable, but Marie decided it would suffice for a few days until she found out where Tommy lived.

Marie rested at the grimy hotel on the North Freeway for a day, getting her clothes situated and relaxing after her marathon road trip from Calgary. She watched the local news as she studied the map of Houston that she'd paid for at the gas station next door. She found Tommy's home address from the phone book in the motel room.

Marie was shocked by the magnitude of the size of the Houston phone book. She was also pleasantly surprised when the map revealed that Tommy's house was relatively close to the medical center where she'd applied for college courses. Marie couldn't believe her luck. She was certain she was truly meant to find Tommy in Houston, and since he lived so close to where she submitted her application for college, she decided that he would be more likely let her stay at his house till she got established and got a job if it was nearby.

The next day, Marie headed into Houston to explore. She toured the Houston Medical Center and spent the day at Texas Woman's University, where she spoke with an admissions counselor. After her day at the university, she found Tommy's street without any problem, and when she got to his house she saw a car in the driveway, so she decided to knock on the door.

⇥▬◗ ◖▬⇤

Tommy admired Marie for taking a leap of faith in moving to Texas, not knowing if she'd been accepted into the graduate program that she applied for. "It took a lot of guts to blindly follow your dreams, and I respect you for your unwavering belief in your own abilities. The least I can do is give you a little bit of help getting started."

"I appreciate the help more than you know," she said meekly. "Once I get a job, I'll be out of your hair."

Marie was accepted into the Texas Woman's University program two weeks later and was interviewing for part-time nursing positions at the hospitals in the Houston Medical Center.

Tommy stayed at his daddy's house in Black Rock for the next couple of weeks. By the time Aubrey finished drilling the Cattleman's number one in early May and the well was logged, everyone realized they had caught a tiger by its tail. The well came in like gangbusters, and after they set pipe casing and the surface equipment, it was flowing over one hundred barrels a day. Tommy and Mike Hicks quickly put in another location, and the rig moved a quarter mile away and started drilling the Cattleman's number two. Aubrey's crew had broken down the rig and moved in record time, and were ready to spud the new well in mid-May.

Tommy and Bob submitted the articles of incorporation for his new pipeline venture and called the new company Summit Pipeline Company. Shortly afterward, Bob set up the financing to buy the pipe and pay for the construction of the new venture.

When he returned home, Tommy found that Marie was still there. "I apologize. I really don't mean to wear out my welcome, but I really have been trying." Marie had her things strewn out across the floor in the guest room, including applications that she was filling out for various jobs she was applying for. "I've had to go to the public library to use their copy machines because I really don't have access to office supplies," she confessed.

Things had been going so well that Tommy really didn't give it a second thought. "I hope that you find something soon," he replied, trying not to show his impatience with his new roommate. Patience was not Tommy's long suit, and he had not been able to do any drugs since Marie came to stay at his house.

One night when Tommy came home from his office downtown, he stopped by his drug dealer's house and picked up his usual couple of eight balls of cocaine. After a few drinks, he offered some coke to Marie. "I have some cocaine that I scored from a friend of mine. Are you into coke?" He didn't want to offend the woman who was beginning to overstay her welcome, but Tommy figured he'd offer. If she said yes, then he'd share, and if she said no, then he'd snort it upstairs in his room by himself.

"I've never done cocaine before, but I've had friends tell me that it's really cool," she replied.

The two stayed up snorting coke and talking about their lives and their plans and dreams. Getting choked up, he started to talk about his childhood issues. "My mother was an alcoholic. It was horrible being raised by a hopeless alcoholic who cared more about the booze than her own son. When I was in law school, she got drunk and burned the house down."

Tommy didn't usually talk about this to anyone and probably would never have told her about it if they weren't on drugs.

"That's awful! I know how you feel. My mother and I haven't spoken in years." Marie told Tommy about how her parents were divorced when she was young and how she was shuffled between relatives and foster homes until she finally moved in with her father and his second wife, Nancy, when she was twelve.

Tommy started to feel sorry for Marie. "It's a relief to finally meet someone who understands what it was like to grow up with a crazy parent," he said, believing that he'd finally met a woman with a kindred spirit. "I've always felt like I was alone, even in my own family."

The two talked for what seemed like hours, sitting beside each other on the couch. Soon Marie put her hand on the inside of Tommy's thigh and began to rub his leg. Tommy started to get aroused and leaned over and kissed Marie, sliding his hand inside her shirt he started to massage her ample breasts. Marie moaned as he pulled her shirt off and began to suck her nipples. Before long, Tommy led Marie upstairs and to his bedroom.

In the morning, Tommy woke up with Marie in his bed. Their clothes were strewn on the floor leading down the hall to the stairs.

⊷═◉ ◉═⊷

Much to Tommy's dismay It wasn't long before Marie wore out her welcome, and he noticed that Marie stopped looking for a job or another place to live.

"It looks like Marie has moved in and isn't moving out," he told Oswald. "I've been dropping hints, trying not to be rude, but she either isn't taking the hints or is just ignoring me. In any case, I don't think she wants to hear it."

"Well, that doesn't sound like you. Why don't you just tell her to get the hell out of your house?" Oswald smirked as he laughed at his friend's cowardice.

"Man, she's had a pretty hard life, and she moved here from Canada. I'm pretty sure she's spent all her cash and is broke," Tommy confessed.

"Well, tell her to get a job waiting tables or working at McDonald's. The longer you let her stay, the harder she's going to be to get rid of." Oswald was pushy but right.

Tommy and Marie had only had sex that one time, but since then she had moved out of the guest room and was now sleeping in his bed with him, and he didn't know what to do. Tommy had finally worked up the courage to tell Marie that she had to go when she announced that she was pregnant and wasn't going anywhere.

Tommy was stunned. He sat down on one of the dining room chairs and stared quietly into space for what seemed like an eternity. He'd always wanted children and always thought that he'd be a better parent than his were to him, but he'd also always believed that he would get to choose the time and the place and, most of all, who would be the mother of those children. Tommy slowly lowered his head into his hands.

Holy cow! What have I done? I've made mistakes before, but this one is a doozy!

For years, he'd looked down his nose at his sister for getting knocked up by accident, and now he'd gone and done the same damn thing. "I only had sex with you a once—how could this possibly happen? I like you as a friend, but I don't love you by any measure of the imagination." He clumsily tried to find some words so as not to offend Marie to terribly.

He'd always believed that he would be in love with the mother of his children and was trying to figure out what to do when he suddenly realized that Marie had been talking the whole time and he hadn't heard a word she said. Tommy finally looked up at Marie and asked her, "Are you sur—maybe you're mistaken?"

Marie was enraged by his insensitive question and started screaming, "I am quite sure! I'm a nurse, after all. I'm absolutely certain." Then out of nowhere, Marie picked up the book that Tommy was reading and threw it directly at his head.

Tommy looked up in time to miss the flying object. "Hey, you need to calm down," he said as he dodged the book.

"I'm not going to calm down, you jerk," she screamed as she threw another book.

After a half hour of screaming and flying books, Tommy managed to calm Marie down, saying, "I don't know what's going to happen, but it's not going to be decided tonight."

The next morning Tommy got up before Marie and packed a few things in his bag for an extended stay at his father's. He was determined to figure out some things, and he needed some space to think—or more likely, he needed a distraction to keep him from thinking. He couldn't decide which, and it didn't matter much.

Like his father, Tommy did what he always did when things were problematic with women—he left.

⋆►⬤ ⬤◄⋆

When Tommy arrived at the Colonel's house, Etta Mae was in the kitchen waiting for him. As soon as he walked through the door, he knew something was amiss because of the look on her face. Etta put her hand on his arm and led Tommy back outside.

As they stood in the driveway, she told Tommy, "The phone has been ringing off the hook this morning, and some woman named Marie who claims to be your girlfriend wants you to call her back." Etta was obviously irritated. "When I told that Marie person that you weren't here, she called me a liar." Etta stared at Tommy quietly for a minute. "I don't know what was going on with that woman, but I've taken care of you and your family for many years like you was my own blood, and I do not appreciate some scat of a woman who thinks she is your girlfriend calling me a liar! I unplugged all the phones in the house to keep her from talking to your daddy the way she talked to me."

"I am very sorry, Etta. Please don't hold this against her."

Tommy stared at his shoes; he was ashamed. Etta was more than the old black maid to him and his family. She'd stepped in when Fredrick died and found his mother when she died. Etta had helped clean up after the fire and took care of his mother when she tried her best to stop drinking. Marie's treatment of Etta only hammered home what a terrible mistake he had made.

Tommy went out to the office to call Marie. When she answered, he reassured her that he was only at his father's house on business and that he'd be home as soon as he could.

But deep down in his heart, he knew what the next step would be. Marie had already made it quite clear that an abortion was out of the question.

Once again, Tommy's fate had been decided by someone else, which didn't endear him to the new mother of his child. He could walk away, but he couldn't live with himself knowing that he had a bastard child somewhere, and Marie had made it very clear in her raging rant the night before that if he didn't want to marry her, that she would move back to Canada and he would never see his child.

Tommy had spent years avoiding women who would trap him into marriage, and the one time he'd lowered his guard in a drug-induced euphoria, it had happened. Tommy was going to have to marry Marie.

Tommy spent the day in the field. He went to the rig and checked on the farmers who had been planting for the past few months, getting ready to start irrigating the fields during the hot summer months ahead. He met with George Hammond again later that day and planned out the route for the first leg of their new pipeline gathering system, and then he went to lunch at the Orange Cup Café, which was a hole in the wall were the locals went to eat and gossip. Tommy stayed busy, and the distraction from Marie was just what he needed.

He didn't know how he'd explain Marie to anyone. He could lie, but he'd have to make up a whopper and the likelihood of anyone believing it would be slim to none.

I'm just going to have to make the best of a bad situation.

Chapter 22

THE BIRTH ANNOUNCEMENTS welcoming Thomas Richard Ellison, Jr. into the world were sent out in mid-February. Marie had delivered a ten pound, eight ounce boy they decided to call Ricky at the Woman's Hospital of Texas, on Old Spanish Trail, a week before.

Tommy had already told so many lies about the circumstances of his son's conception to his friends and family in order to hide the truth about Marie that he had to memorize his stories to keep from getting them mixed up. He would repeat them verbatim to each person so that he could keep them straight.

But most of his family and friends had already figured out that little baby Ricky was unintentional. It didn't stop Tommy from trying to rewrite history anyway by embellishing the truth and peppering it with some convenient white lies. No one Tommy knew liked Marie, and were probably aware of all the excuses Tommy was making to cover up his mistake of getting her pregnant in the first place.

Worst of all, Marie had changed so drastically as soon as they got married. And as soon as her son was born, she stepped into the role of queen mother with great fanfare almost immediately. Tommy didn't know if she realized how she was acting, but money changed Marie right off the bat.

Marie was only a few weeks along when the couple married in a civil ceremony at the Harris County Courthouse. Once Tommy got over the initial shock of the pregnancy, he decided to move quickly in order to protect his interests as a father. He'd always thought he'd be a good daddy and knew firsthand that Marie was perfectly capable of disappearing back to Canada with his son.

Early in the summer, Marie and Tommy had a real wedding, with Tommy's preacher friend, Ronnie, presiding. It was a huge catered affair out on the ranch, with a band and a dance floor under a large tent that Tommy had borrowed from

Budgy Daily from the funeral home. Marie arrived in a horse-drawn carriage, and they were remarried in the eyes of God, family, and friends. But by this time, the cat was already out of the bag and everyone already knew.

Tommy tried to defend his wife as best he could. He understood that before he'd met her, she'd had a pretty difficult life, and he wrote off her bad behavior as her just not knowing any better.

Marie's father was a World War II veteran who met Marie's mother when he got off the train transporting the victorious Canadian troops home from the war. She was part of the crowd, and they both were swept up in the euphoria of the war heroes home coming. Her parents had only known each other a few days when they married and would have five children before their divorce. Marie and her siblings stayed home for months at a time with their mother, while her father traveled from logging camp to logging camp, working under dangerous conditions to provide for his young family.

Tragically, Marie's mother was one of those women had no business having children and didn't want the children she had. "She was cruel and neglectful, and didn't really care if we lived or died. She would beat us and lock us in closets while she would be gone for hours at a time," Marie confessed to Tommy.

After her parents' divorce, Marie went into foster care as a ward of the government, and she and her siblings were split up. Eventually, one of Marie's aunts found out where she was and brought her home to live in Prince George, a small town at the confluence of the Fraser and the Nechako Rivers in northern British Columbia. Marie's father had remarried and had three new children, and eventually Marie moved in with her father, stepmother, and half siblings in Prince Rupert when she was thirteen, where she stayed until she graduated from high school and moved out to live on her own.

After he'd found out that Marie was pregnant, Tommy arranged for his sister and Bob to go to his father's house for Sunday dinner, so he could announce their engagement to the family. Tommy took her to Black Rock for Sunday lunch with the Colonel, Beverly, and Bob. But Marie was so intimidated by his family that she locked herself in the bathroom and wouldn't come out until after Bob and Beverly left.

"Please, never mention this to Tommy, but it's pretty evident that the woman Tommy is marrying has a screw loose. There must be more going on," Beverly told Bob in the car on the way home.

Much to his dismay, Marie tried to take over the Colonel's household almost immediately. Etta had kept things running after the house burned down and cared for Tommy's father after his wife passed away. "Now some uppity, Yankee white trash who got herself knocked up and trapped Tommy into marriage is acting like the lady of the manor," Etta bristled to her oldest daughter after Tommy left with his new wife.

Tommy did his best to smooth things over. "Could you please to be patient with Marie?" he asked Etta. "She really doesn't mean to come off so condescending." Tommy tried to explain to her that some people in Canada just treated people differently than they did in the South. "Marie doesn't understand just how much you mean to our family."

Tommy also tried to enlighten Marie, telling her that, because of the history of slavery and the Jim Crow Old South, she couldn't talk to Etta tersely or harshly. "Please try not to come off so bossy with her," he pleaded with his new wife.

But Marie would only stare at him and say, "How you dare speak to me that way! She's incompetent and lazy, and she steals. She needs to be fired so that we can get proper help."

After a while, Tommy did his best just to stay out of it. He knew the issue was just a powder keg waiting to explode, and he really didn't want to be in the crossfire when it happened. Now that he was married, he envied the Colonel for the way he could tune it all out.

Tommy understood logically what was expected of a good husband and father, but now he realized that it was going to be harder than it looked. He'd always assumed there were a few really important things that made a good marriage. The first was that the husband had to be a good provider; he had that one under control. The next thing was to be loyal, honorable, and faithful, and that was proving to be a little more difficult than Tommy had imagined. Before

Marie came along, he'd a pretty active social life. He didn't date per se and didn't consider himself to be gay, but he had his regular partners that he could call up when he was horny. Now he had to give that all up.

After Tommy got married, he'd told all his regular sex partners that he didn't need them anymore and asked that they respect his marriage by making themselves invisible. Then in the first few months of pregnancy, Marie cut Tommy off; she just wasn't in the mood anymore.

At first Tommy had been attracted to his pregnant wife and actually liked having regular sex. Marie was a large-breasted woman to begin with, and after she got pregnant, her breasts grew even larger and Tommy couldn't keep his hands off them when they were alone. Tommy was beginning to think that having a wife wasn't so bad. But then Marie cut him off, and worse yet, she was starting to look pregnant and act pregnant. She gained a lot of weight, and her emotions raged out of control.

After he got cut off from sex, Tommy had to beat off in the shower in the morning. He hadn't beat off this much since high school, but he was convinced that the lack of sex was only temporary and that once the baby was born, they would start having sex again. But then jacking off in the shower wasn't enough, and after a couple of months, Tommy started getting erections in the worst places. Once he'd gotten an erection in the bank when he saw a cute guy. He was also having fantasies about people—mostly men, but some of his fantasies were about big-breasted women.

Eventually he gave up and started sneaking around behind her back. It wasn't often enough to make him feel guilty, but all the same, in the eyes of the Black Rock Church of Christ he was cheating and it was a sin.

After a few months, Tommy bought his wife a new car and a new house in Old Braeswood, over by the medical center. It was in an expensive neighborhood, just a few blocks away from Texas Woman's where Marie was working on her master's degree. Then Marie opened up credit accounts at several stores without telling her husband and started buying furniture, clothes, and baby toys, just sending the bills to Tommy's office.

Before long, Tommy had to put his wife on a budget, which she didn't like in the least. "You're making lots of money. I'm not buying anything we don't need for our new house and baby."

Tommy tried reasoning with his wife about money, but there was nothing he could say to make her understand that she couldn't blow through money just because his family owned an oil company.

A few days after they closed on the new house, Tommy informed Marie that he needed to go to New York City on business for a couple of days. Marie was so excited about her new house that she couldn't have cared less and didn't even ask why he was going. But instead of going to New York, Tommy rented a room at the Hyatt Regency downtown and called up one of his old lovers, who also brought along a pile of cocaine. They hung the Do Not Disturb sign on the door and proceeded have sex and snort coke until it was all gone. Afterward, Tommy kicked his old lover out and slept it off for a couple of days.

When he finally woke, he slowly rolled out of bed feeling like he'd been hit by a bus. Standing in the hotel bathroom, he leaned on the vanity, looking at himself in the mirror. His eyes were bloodshot, and his hair was a mess. The bathroom light was bright and unforgiving, and he noticed that he was starting to get gray hair. His mother's hair had begun to turn gray when she was in her thirties, and Tommy shook his head at the thought of being like his mother. He unwrapped a plastic glass from beside the bathroom sink, filled it with water from the tap, and drank it down.

After he drank sufficient water to rehydrate, Tommy sat on the edge of the bed and called room service to order a big breakfast. He was hungry since he hadn't eaten in a full day. He ordered a three-egg omelet with a side of bacon, toast, and orange juice, as well as some hot tea. Tommy didn't drink coffee, but hot tea sounded like a helpful pick-me-up. After breakfast, he took a long, hot shower. He felt sticky from drug sweat and smelled pretty ripe. After he cleaned himself up, Tommy felt like a new man, and about midmorning he checked out and took a taxi home, acting like he just got back from the airport.

Tommy was amazed at how easily Marie accepted his lies. She was so wrapped up in her new house and making arrangements for the birth of their son that she didn't even have a clue. Tommy didn't feel bad that he had cheated on her.

After all, he felt liked she'd lied to him. The person she was now was not anything like the person he'd met in Calgary the year before. Tommy had dumped a lot nicer girls than Marie in high school and college, and now he regretted it.

He'd waited to get married, thinking that the storybook love of his life would come along, but instead he'd been seduced by one of the worst gold diggers he'd ever seen and who paled in comparison to the bus driver who had seduced his sister.

He was trapped in a bad marriage, and there was no way out. All he could hope for was that maybe, just maybe, things would change after the baby was born.

Chapter 23

FROM THE FIRST time Tommy held his son, he understood what real love was. He'd searched for it his whole life, and he'd finally found it the moment he looked into the eyes of his newborn son. He looked into Ricky's eyes, and Ricky looked back, and it was magical.

At first, Tommy wasn't thrilled to be in the room during the delivery, but he was glad he was there afterward and got to hold Ricky as soon as they cut the umbilical cord and cleaned him up. Ricky was a happy little guy. He didn't even really cry. In fact, the entire process was nothing like what Tommy had expected. He forgot about all the problems he and his wife had been having.

"It all will be over soon, and everything will get back to normal, I promise," Tommy said to Ricky as he rocked him in his arms.

Marie watched as her husband held their son for the first time. She didn't know what to feel; she was overwhelmed with a swirl of emotions. She felt anxiety, guilt, anger, possessiveness, protectiveness, joy, gratitude, and elation all at once. Her doctors were monitoring her closely because they were very concerned about the stress of childbirth bringing on a psychotic break. The doctor administered a shot of Demerol in her IV to knock her out for a while. Shortly after, the nurses took their baby to the nursery.

"She needs the rest," the OB told Tommy. Marie's doctor motioned for Tommy to follow her into the hall. "Now that the baby has come, you need to make sure that your wife gets back on her medication as soon as possible. But if Marie chooses to breast-feed, then there is a high probability that her meds can show up in the breast milk, so I encourage you both to discuss your options. Marie shouldn't breast-feed more than a few months so that she can continue her treatment."

Tommy stood silently, trying to pretend that he knew what in the world his wife's doctor was talking about. The OB saw the perplexed look on his face and suddenly realized that Marie hadn't discussed her mental-health issues with her husband at all.

"Treatment? What treatment?" He was confused.

"Talk to your wife," the doctor said patiently. "Marie can live a normal, productive life, but she needs to take her medication as prescribed. She also needs your help and encouragement to continue her treatment." With that, the doctor walked away.

Tommy was exhausted and felt like a walking zombie, but what the doctor had just said was not only little shocking but also plenty confusing. This was the first he'd heard of Marie being on any kind of medication for some kind of medical condition.

Tommy was suddenly deeply concerned for his wife's well-being, wondering what in the world he would do. What if this mystery medical condition was life threatening? A cold chill went down his back, and Tommy really started feeling like a jerk for being so selfish. The whole time Marie was pregnant, he'd only been thinking of himself. He'd resented his wife and blamed her for trapping him into marriage.

Tommy was exhausted and a little stunned by what his wife's doctor had just told him. And in a flash, he decided to go home.

I can't think clearly. I need to go home and get some rest.

Their new house in Old Braeswood wasn't but a few minutes' drive away from the hospital. When he got home, he went upstairs to their bedroom and fell across the bed without even taking off his shoes. Within moments, he was sound asleep.

-»‒■◦ ◦■‒«-

Marie was keeping a pretty big secret from everyone, especially her husband. She never intended to be dishonest; she just didn't think the truth was anyone's business, not even her husband's, and she wasn't ready to confess the truth.

The mood swings Tommy had witnessed during her pregnancy were not exactly what he'd thought them to be. Years before she came to Texas, Marie had been diagnosed with bipolar disorder. Accordingly, Marie had been on some pretty powerful mood-altering drugs to control her illness. And she'd stopped taking them as soon as she found out that she was pregnant.

She didn't like to take her medication regularly. "My medication makes me lethargic," she used to tell her psychiatrist in Calgary.

"I strongly advise you to find a psychiatrist in Houston to ensure that your progress in your therapy will continue," he'd urged her when she announced that she was moving to Texas. Before she left his office that day, he'd asked his assistant to research the Houston-area medical community and gave her a list of well-respected psychiatrists.

Marie came to Texas with enough of her medication to last a couple of months and made an appointment with a new doctor before she left Canada. Marie started skipping her meds when she realized she was pregnant because she was fearful that the powerful drugs she was taking would affect the health of child. She had also decided to breast-feed and so didn't intend to start back on her medication until well after the baby was born.

When Marie was young, she'd lived with her Aunt Tilly in Prince George while she received nurse's training and certification classes at the University of Northern British Columbia, offsetting the cost of her education by signing up for a government program that guaranteed to pay for her education if she would serve at least two years working in government-provided health care in a remote outpost north of the Arctic Circle.

After she graduated, her assignment was in Tuktoyaktuck. It was while she was on assignment in Tuktoyaktuck that her mental health became an issue. The isolation and harsh living conditions proved more difficult for Marie than she had expected, and after a year and a half in Tuk, as the locals called it, Marie attempted suicide by taking an overdose of pills she stole from the clinic.

One of the doctors she worked for found Marie and saved her life. She spent some time recovering discreetly under his care, and when she started feeling better, her doctor friend told her, "I am not going report your suicide attempt to the government administrators. I have sympathy for what you're going through. The suicide rate in this part of the world is epidemic, and if you promise not to do it again and if you can finish the last six months of your internship, I'll report this incident as a bad flu."

After her assignment in Tuktoyaktuck was over, Marie moved to Calgary and got a job at a hospital in the emergency room as a trauma-care nurse on the night shift. Eventually she was assigned as a ward nurse in the psychiatric wing, taking care of low-risk patients. Marie started going to therapy while she was in Calgary, and she found her work in the psych ward incredibly beneficial in helping her recognize her own symptoms early so that she could get help dealing with the onset of depression.

About the time she was introduced to Tommy by her friend Michelle. Marie had been in therapy for long enough that she believed her issues were under control, and she was a fairly normal and well-balanced person living a productive life.

She'd already saved up money to go back to college for her master's degree when she met Tommy at the Stockman's Restaurant. It was Marie's friend, Michelle, who'd encouraged her to apply to a master's program in Texas. Michelle was French Canadian and was a hopeless romantic who was hoping that good things would come Marie's way if she just gave her friend a gentle push in the right direction.

A change in scenery was what Marie decided that she wanted. She really wasn't ready to jump into another relationship, but she was already applying to graduate schools, "A new boyfriend isn't in the cards. But a fresh start sounds wonderful," she told Michelle. "Moving to Texas might be just the adventure I need."

Except for her time in Calgary, Marie had been in survival mode most of her life. Now she was married and had given birth. And even though her master's degree was on hold for the next few months, Marie felt like she was on top of the world.

Marie had discussed her condition with her OB-GYN, who'd helped her manage her symptoms during her pregnancy. The doctor agreed that there was a slight possibility that her mood-altering medications could cause birth defects and so didn't press Marie on the subject.

"I am doing this for my son," she told her doctor when she got off her meds.

"You also should continue therapy with the psychiatrist. Between the two of us, we can help you manage your way through your pregnancy safely. Your psychiatrist can help you with coping skills to alleviate any stress that you encounter until you start back on your meds." The doctor looked Marie squarely in the eye.

But Marie still hadn't told her husband about her mental-health issues when Ricky was born, even though her OB-GYN insisted she should.

Chapter 24

THE DAY TOMMY brought his wife and newborn son home from the hospital was filled with joy and celebration. Marie's best friend, Brenda who'd lived around the corner from them when she first moved to Texas and two of Marie's friends from graduate school came over to meet baby Ricky. Marie beamed with joy and pride as she showed off her son to her friends. Both Tommy and Marie had good intentions for how to raise their son, but if the old adage "The road to hell is paved with good intentions" brought to bear, then they were paving an interstate highway straight to hell.

Tommy patiently waited until Marie's friends left so that he could ask his wife about her medication. He'd imagined all kinds of things, from cancer to diabetes, and he was worried about her.

She must want to spare me the worry about her medical condition. It must be pretty bad or she'd have told me.

Tommy was feeling pretty crappy about all the ugly things he'd done to her behind her back while she was pregnant. He contemplated coming clean with Marie and begging her for forgiveness, but he decided that was a bad idea, especially if she was terminally ill. It took Tommy a few days to work up the courage to ask his wife about the medication. And that afternoon, after all Marie's friends were gone, he finally saw his opportunity.

"Your doctor told me to make sure you got back on your medication as soon as possible. She acted like it was really important. What was she talking about?" Tommy asked his wife in the upstairs hallway just outside Ricky's nursery.

She'd just put Ricky down for his nap, and Tommy's inquiry caught Marie completely off guard and she flew into a rage. "My doctor had no right to disclose any of my private medical records to you!" she shouted and stormed into their bedroom, locking the door behind her.

Marie's fit woke the baby, and Tommy went into the nursery to care for the boy until she settled down. Tommy changed the boy's diaper and rocked him back to sleep with a bottle of formula from the refrigerator.

Tommy attributed his wife's explosive episode to being tired. "She hasn't slept much since we came home from the hospital, and your mom has been pumping milk and putting into the refrigerator," he whispered to Ricky as he rocked him. "You have been waking up every few hours for feedings, and your mom is the one getting up to feed you because she insists on breast-feeding you. Personally, I couldn't care less because I like our time together."

Even though the baby was still too young to smile, Tommy was convinced that Ricky smiled when his daddy talked. After about thirty minutes, his young son went back to sleep. Tommy put his son down and went downstairs. It hadn't quite been a year that he'd lived with his wife, but Tommy had figured out that the only way to calm his wife down when she went into one of her rages was to walk away.

Over the last year, he'd learned how to tune out his wife, and decided not to make a big deal of her mood. Tommy mixed a drink and turned on the television to watch the evening news. After about an hour, Tommy heard his wife come downstairs. He found her sitting in a chair in the sunroom; she was staring out the window.

Marie took a deep breath and said, "The medication my doctor was talking about was Lithium. It's a mood stabilizer. I was diagnosed with bipolar depression after a suicide attempt when I was in Tuktoyaktuk," Marie said stoically, never moving her gaze from the window.

After she'd confessed the whole sorted story, Marie assured her husband that she had started going to a psychiatrist in Houston again and had only been off her medications while she was pregnant in order to make sure there wouldn't be any ill effects to their son.

Marie half expected that Tommy would be grateful for the sacrifice she made by giving up her medication to ensure the health of their child. But this time, Tommy was the one who flew off into a rage. He paced back and forth, straining to keep his voice down so he wouldn't wake his newborn son.

"I've been worried sick about you. I've been afraid that you were going to die and leave our son without a mother!" He gnashed his teeth and growled.

He continued to pace frantically. All he could think about was that she had lied to him. Tommy had grown up believing that mental-health issues were a character flaw, like his mother's alcoholism.

"This is just a bunch of bullshit you're making up to cover up for the fact that you're a greedy bitch with a bad temper and no social skills!" Tommy could see that his angry words had wounded Marie, but he didn't really care. In that moment, Tommy wanted to leave Marie, but that's what the Colonel's reaction had been when he didn't want to deal with his mother and he'd always felt abandoned by his father.

I'm not going to abandon my son to a crazy woman like my father did to me.

He closed his eyes and took a deep breath. Then he calmly stood up and walked into the kitchen, grabbing his bottle of Jack Daniels by the neck. He headed outside to his workshop, where he had just started working on some building blocks that he was making for his new son. He locked the door behind him in case his "crazy" wife decided to come out there with him and talk some more.

-+≡⊙ ⊙≡+-

Their new baby wasn't home long when Ricky developed colic. Marie, who had started out as a gung-ho breast-feeding mother, couldn't keep up with the feedings every three hours. One ample breast was engorged with milk, making it so painful to breast-feed.

It wasn't long before the pediatrician recommended that she wean her son and start him on formula. The change to formula didn't help fix the little boy's digestive system as Marie hoped it would. The constant crying was too much for Marie, pushing her over the edge, and she started hitting the boy when she thought no one was looking.

But Tommy suspected as much and confronted her. "All the talk about doing everything the natural way is just a load of junk that you read in a book," he told her. "This crap is going to end now. You are going to the doctor, and you're going to start taking your medication, or I'm going do something you won't like." Tommy was ready to commit her to the psych ward, and she knew it.

Shortly afterward, Tommy hired someone to help out around the house. He told everyone that she was there to help his wife, but really, he needed someone to keep an eye on Marie so she wouldn't hurt his son. Rose came highly recommended, not only as a nanny, but she helped out around the house, too. Rose was a highly skilled black lady in her forties. She had an impressive résumé, and Tommy took an immediate liking to her.

Unfortunately, Marie did not. Marie was intimidated by Rose and complained to her husband that everything the woman did was wrong. And Rose only lasted a few months before Marie fired her, saying, "I can't stand that woman; she's judgmental and nosy."

They interviewed several other nannies, but Marie kept running them off. None of them stayed more than a week or two. Tommy was at his wit's end and knew that he needed to keep someone around to help with Ricky, mostly to protect him from his mother. Eventually, Tommy hired Rose back at a significantly higher salary and instructed his wife, "You are not allowed to fire Rose again."

Eventually, Marie started going to therapy again, and things around the house quieted down. But feeling betrayed by her doctors after Ricky was born, Marie changed doctors, going to the Houston version of the psychiatrist to the rich and famous. Her new psychiatrist's fees were almost double, but Tommy didn't really care just as long as his wife took her medication, saying, "That's what insurance is for."

Soon after they rehired Rose, Marie went back to graduate school and threw herself back into her studies. She only had another year to go to graduate, and when she wasn't in class or studying, Marie volunteered at a local crisis center's suicide hotline. Marie tried to make life appear to the outside world like it was great, but it was an act. Marie and Tommy's storybook romance and marriage was just that—a work of fiction.

On the other hand, Tommy was a mess and didn't care who knew it. He was drinking and doing cocaine almost daily, and was caught up in a drug-induced fog. He was even snorting coke at his office, where everyone could see plainly that he had drug issues. Bob had quietly taken over the day-to-day operations and only talked to Tommy when he needed a signature.

"Tommy is having problems at home. I sincerely hope things work themselves out before he hits the rocks," Bob told Beverly discreetly cluing her in about her brother's addiction. "If things go on like this for long, we may have to take action to protect your interests."

It was a blessing that the Colonel was too old and senile to understand that Tommy had an issue with drugs. Marie worked diligently to get on his good side, taking his grandson to visit him regularly. "I know how important your bloodline and legacy is to you," she would say.

It was obvious that she enjoyed torturing her strung-out husband by playing up the fact that his father didn't need him around, now that there was a new heir to the throne. Tommy felt helpless, as his crazy wife had found his biggest insecurity and used it like a club to punish him.

⋆⊶⟨⬤⟩ ⟨⬤⟩⊷⋆

Soon it was quite evident to everyone but Tommy that he was on a downward spiral and his life was out of control. He'd hated his mother his whole life because the alcohol was more important to her that he was, and now he was doing the same thing to his own son. For the first time in his life, he understood the enormous struggle that his mother had dealt with. He wanted to quit, but every time he tried, Marie would start a fight and that would give him an excuse to get drunk or high again.

Marie was living from one crisis to another, creating drama after drama so that she could feel the exhilaration when the crisis was averted. "Addictions are built on illusions and dishonesty. Denial is the building block of his addiction," her psychiatrist would tell Marie during their sessions. "Tommy's illusion is that he is in control of his life."

Thriving off the attention she was getting over Tommy addictions, Marie loved to complain about her husband and the adverse effects his drug use was having on their family. Not only did this give her something to complain about to her therapist, but his addiction problems made her feel less like a freak.

Their marriage was an out-of-control drama that was getting worse by the day. Watching Marie and Tommy's marriage was like watching a slow-motion train wreck heading for the precipice. Outsiders watched with amazement, wondering who would fall over the cliff first.

Eventually, Tommy could no longer deny he had a problem, waking him up from his drug-induced dream world.

First, Tommy's dealer disappeared. He'd arranged to score some coke, and when he went to pick it up, he found his dealer gone and a big hole blown in the door by shotgun blast. When he saw the hole in dealer's door, Tommy froze, then slowly turned around and walked calmly to his car, hoping the Houston police weren't watching. He was shaking so badly that he could barely put the keys in the ignition, and he started to cry as he drove away. Tommy took a roundabout way home so that he could tell if someone was following him. When he got there, he pretended to read a book while his wife studied and his young son played and watched cartoons at his feet in the living room. He periodically peeked out the window to make sure no one saw him or followed him home.

A few days later, Tommy started running a high fever and every joint in his body ached. He became jaundiced, and even the whites of his eyes turned a sickly yellow. Marie promptly sent him to the family doctor, who ran blood work and determined it was hepatitis B.

Dr. Barrett had long suspected that Tommy had been living life on the edge and had discussed the risks associated with unprotected sex on numerous occasions, but his lectures had fallen on deaf ears. "Hepatitis B is chronic, and you might eventually suffer from liver damage or even liver cancer," Dr. Barrett told him. "You really have to stop drinking, and you have to tell your wife about your alternative lifestyle."

"Me and my wife barely speak, and we haven't had sex in a very long time. If I tell her that I'm cheating on her with men, it will only cause more problems," Tommy replied, almost begging the doctor to keep his secret.

But a dark cloud came over Dr. Barrett, and he emphatically told him, "If you do not tell your wife, I will."

Seeing the look in the man's eyes, Tommy realized that he couldn't laugh this off; he could no longer pretend that he hadn't been living too close to the edge for so long. This time it was serious. Tommy dreaded telling his wife more than he did living with a disease like hepatitis B.

As soon as he got home, he mixed himself a Jack Daniels and Coke for a little courage. It was four thirty in the afternoon, and his wife hadn't returned from school or wherever she'd been that day. Rose was there taking care of Ricky, who was now almost three years old.

Ricky had grown like a weed into a rambunctious young toddler, and Tommy looked at his son like it was for the first time and sighed. It was hard to admit, but Tommy knew that sex, like alcohol and cocaine, had become an addiction that he had to get under control or he was going to die.

Tommy sent Rose home before his wife got back. He'd already had to give her another raise to get her to keep working for them, and he didn't want her to quit, especially now. Tommy didn't want to fight in front of Rose. The last time they'd gotten into a fight in front of Rose, she'd left and took Ricky with her. "It might get ugly again tonight when I tell her what Dr. Barrett said," he warned Ricky as if he could understand, and then he took a sip of courage.

When his wife got home about an hour later, and by then, Tommy had already slammed back three drinks. He took a deep breath and laid everything out on the table, confessing to everything from the drugs to cheating. Marie was quiet at first, which Tommy mistook as a sign of understanding, and so he continued to talk when he really should have shut up. After confessing, Tommy was actually relieved to have it off his chest.

Suddenly, as if someone had stabbed a balloon with a pin, Marie started yelling and throwing things. She even grabbed a large kitchen knife and threatened to kill her husband. Terrified not only for his own life but for Ricky's, Tommy calmly talked her out of using the knife on him by pointing out, "Ricky is watching."

Abruptly, Marie dropped the knife and ran out of the house, grabbing her purse. She jumped in her car and drove away.

"Well, that went well," he told Ricky, as if the child was old enough to comprehend what had just happened. Tommy continued to drink until he passed out on the couch and Ricky had fallen asleep on the rug in front of the television, and when Rose arrived the next morning, she could tell that something bad had happened the night before.

Tommy was still asleep on the couch, and there were two empty Jack Daniels bottles in the trash can and bunch of empty Coke cans scattered all over the kitchen.

The house was a mess. There were chairs knocked over, and broken dishes on the floor of the kitchen. Ricky was up already and had pulled a chair from the kitchen table over to the pantry and dug out a box of cereal. He was eating it out of the box in front of the television, where he was watching a He-Man cartoon.

Marie was gone and nowhere to be found. Rose took Ricky upstairs to bathe him and get him dressed. When they came back downstairs, Rose found Tommy awake and sitting up on the couch.

Rose simply shook her head, saying, "Uhm, uhm, uhm," before walking out the back door with Ricky to go to the park.

Chapter 25

When Ricky turned five in 1984, Marie planned a huge birthday party to celebrate the occasion. December and January had been one of the coldest and wettest in recent memory, and Marie was rolling the dice when she planned an outdoor birthday party in February. The day of the party started out gloomy; there was a chill in the air, as the temperature was fifty-seven degrees. Marie had hoped the sun would come out to warm the day up into the sixties, but it didn't.

Marie expected that the birthday party would be the event of the season. There was going to be a clown and a petting zoo in the backyard. But when the party started, only a few family and friends showed up with their kids, though the kids who had come were having a blast. She'd invited all of Ricky's preschool classmates, but no one had come from his school, even though Marie had called their parents the night before to remind them.

Their backyard looked bleak, despite Marie's efforts to get the gardener to trim up the tropical foliage in the flower beds to make it look less haggard from the winter frosts. The Mexican palm trees were ratty, mostly from the wind.

"The streamers, the balloons, and the splash of color in the tablecloths make things less winter-like and more springlike," Marie rambled to one of the parents at the part—as if when she said it out loud, everyone would forget it was still February.

Now that Ricky attended preschool at a small Montessori school on Kelvin Street in the Rice Village area, she hoped that Ricky would have lots of friends that would come to his party. She'd put him in the Montessori school, saying, "Ricky will get a lot more personal attention there."

But in reality, the other school's that she'd applied to wouldn't take him. Marie had tried to enroll Ricky at St. Luke's Episcopal School, but when they went for their interview with the head master, the rowdy little boy destroyed the man's office, breaking a lamp and the glass door on a trophy case. Needless to say, an invitation to join the school wasn't extended to Ricky, and Tommy was secretly relieved.

Next, Marie applied at St. Thomas in Meyerland, where Ricky was admitted for a while until the school kicked the boy out. "Ricky has disciplinary issues. He is unruly, aggressive, and disruptive to the other children," the headmaster explained as he broke the news to Marie.

Poor Ricky had behavior problems, but at least the teachers at the Montessori school were working with him and really trying to help. But the other parents didn't want their kids around Ricky, and it was obvious to everyone but Marie. When Marie first put Ricky into the Montessori school, she'd set up playdates with a few of the boys in his class, but it wasn't long before the parents always had other plans whenever she tried to arrange playdates.

Luckily, Ricky was having fun at his birthday party and didn't even notice that his mother was unhappy that there weren't as many kids as she'd invited.

Ricky was a towhead like his father had been when he was a boy. He was tall for his age and full of energy, running around the yard yelling and screaming and playing with the other kids at the party. Marie had tried to create an orderly, controlled party agenda, with games and entertainment scheduled one right after the other, but it was more than obvious that it wasn't working.

The only thing that worked out the way Marie wanted was when they cut the cake, but then things went downhill again. After the children ate their cake, the clown did his show. Marie had expected the nice little children to sit quietly while the clown performed. But soon she got flustered and frazzled that the kids wiggled and squirmed, and didn't pay any attention to the clown at all.

Tommy watched the whole fiasco from a lawn chair beside the door of his shop. "Quit being so anal and let the poor kids just have fun," he told her. But he could tell by the hateful glare she shot him that Marie didn't take his criticism very well.

He blamed Marie for his son's behavior and scoffed whenever Marie blamed him for Ricky's issues. In actuality, both were to blame and neither would take any responsibility for disciplining the boy.

Tommy had become an absentee parent like his father, staying gone most of the time. And when he was around, he spoiled and overindulged Ricky's every whim—that is, when Tommy wasn't drunk or on drugs.

Earlier that year, Marie had started dragging Ricky to a child psychiatrist to help with the boy's behavior problems, and he was quickly diagnosed with attention deficit hyperactivity disorder. Marie put the boy on Ritalin.

"He is only five, for the love of God. There isn't a five-year-old boy on this planet who can sit still for more than five minutes." Tommy hated the idea of his son being medicated at such a young age, but his protests fell on deaf ears.

⊸⊨⊙ ⊙⊨⊷

After his diagnosis of hepatitis, Tommy had really tried to stop drinking and doing drugs, and short of going to AA, he was pretty successful. But it always seemed that his wife would go out of her way to push him back over the edge.

"It's happened so many times that I'm beginning to think Marie doesn't want me to quit drinking and doing drugs. I think she's creating drama on purpose to stress me out just so I'll fall off the wagon," Tommy would rant to his old friend Ronnie when he called to check on him. "I suspect that she doesn't want me to fix my life, because if I did, then who would she blame her crappy life on in group therapy?"

In an attempt to try to get healthy again, he'd go to the YMCA to work out. If he ran into someone he knew from his other life who might would tempt him back into misbehaving, he had to tell him, "Sorry, I just can't live like that anymore." Most of the time, his friends respected his marriage. It was hard to resist backsliding, but Tommy was determined to change—if not for himself, then for Ricky.

While Tommy struggled to help himself, Marie was going to therapy three, sometimes four times a week and was going to group therapy twice a week. She was spending tons of money a month just on therapy. Tommy's health insurance didn't cover the entire amount, and what insurance didn't cover came out of his pocket.

"I wouldn't mind, except for after all the years she's been in therapy, her doctor still hasn't fixed her!" he lamented to Ronnie.

Once again, Tommy was battling loneliness. Most of Tommy's longtime friends couldn't see any redeeming qualities in his wife and really didn't want to get in the middle of their marital issues or Tommy's addiction problems. When Tommy had first gotten married, his friends had accepted her into their lives, but after six years of marriage, most of Tommy's old friends made excuses not to come over whenever they were invited. Only a few other friends stuck it out and remained friends with Tommy and Marie.

By the time Ricky's fifth birthday had rolled around, Tommy and Marie were simply going through the motions for the sake of their son. The writing was on the wall: Tommy wanted a divorce and was holding on as long as he could. He was staying married only because he was terrified that if they divorced, Marie would make good on her threats and take his son to Canada. If she left with his son, he'd only see him every blue moon.

Tommy's father had just turned eighty-eight, and although his health was OK for a man his age, if Marie took his grandson away, he was afraid it would break his father's heart. Having a grandson had melted the old man's heart, and sometimes Tommy thought it was worth putting up with Marie's crap just to see the sparkle in the Colonel's eyes when he watched his grandson run and play. Tommy's father had just had a hip replacement and a heart valve replaced. Most disturbing of all, Marie was manipulative, and Tommy suspected that it wasn't beneath her to use his grandson like he was a pile of poker chips to be cashed in at a Vegas casino—using their son as a hostage just to get more money if they divorced.

Even more disturbing was that Minerva had formed a very unholy alliance with Marie. Minerva saw the writing on the wall, too; she knew that their marriage had been on the rocks for a while. Tommy just didn't trust the woman and was paranoid that Minerva would talk his father into changing his will, giving everything to Marie to hold in trust until Ricky was old enough to take care of himself.

If that happened, it would be nothing short of catastrophic!

Not knowing what was in the Colonel's will, Tommy was frankly a little nervous that his father might have a dream or something and change the will, leaving everything to a bunch of cats. "A lot of great men have made a mess of their family's lives because of a messed-up will. I can't let that happen to the Colonel," Tommy confided in his brother-in-law one afternoon.

Tommy had cleaned up his life enough to see how low he'd sunk since he married Marie, and he was disgusted. Even though he'd been messing up long before his marriage, it was easier for him to blame Marie when he should have been taking responsibility for his own bad behavior. Tommy was in denial and was hoping that no one noticed he'd been doing drugs and cheating on his wife. Seeing the disappointed looks from his secretary, Angelica—who had started leaving the office if Tommy came into the office coked up—it was hard to pretend others didn't know. He saw a lot of disappointed looks from everyone he knew. He just hoped that his father was too old to understand what he had been doing with his life since he married the Wicked Witch of the West.

After Tommy was diagnosed with hepatitis B, Dr. Barrett had made sure his family was vaccinated against the disease. Tommy went for a checkup every few months. During one of his regularly scheduled visits, his doctor announced that he'd found a drug trial program for a new type of interferon the FDA was testing that showed promise against the hepatitis B virus.

Apparently, the drug trial was just what Tommy needed to live a long and healthy life. After discussing the details with Tommy, Dr. Barrett announced that he'd only enroll him in the interferon trial under one condition—Tommy had to tell his wife. Tommy groaned and fidgeted while he sat on the end of the examination table; the absolutely last thing he wanted was to evolve Marie and he told Dr. Barrett exactly that.

"This is not negotiable," he said emphatically.

The doctor was well aware that Tommy's marriage was strained, but still he insisted. "There are ethical issues involved with this trial, and I firmly believe she needs to know, especially since there are risks involved in any FDA drug trial."

Before Tommy left, Dr. Barrett wrote out an order for Tommy to go to the lab down the hall to draw blood so that he could run tests to ensure that Tommy was, in fact, a viable candidate for the drug trial.

At that time, the medical community was becoming disturbingly aware of a new disease that was devastating and that generally affected people who were gay or IV drug users. A new test had been recently developed to detect the retrovirus HTLV-III, and Dr. Barrett suspected that beneath the jokes and despite his stern warnings, Tommy was still putting himself at a high risk for AIDS. When he got Tommy's test results back, Dr. Barrett breathed a sigh of relief when Tommy's blood test came back negative for the virus.

When Tommy got home that afternoon, he reluctantly told Marie about the drug trial. Her reaction was strange; she was oddly ecstatic about Tommy joining the drug trial. Tommy thought, for a fleeting moment, that he'd misjudged his wife and that maybe she really did love him and wanted him to get better...that is, up until he heard her on the phone telling anyone and everyone about his drug trial. Tommy's heart sank like a lead sinker on a fish hook.

My treatment is just another way of getting sympathy and attention for her from anyone who will listen.

Feeling very much alone, Tommy was crushed by his wife's reaction and wondered why she didn't care if she alienated her own husband. Even though she was manipulative, mean, and self-absorbed, down deep he'd always hoped that she loved him, even if it was just a little—the same way he'd always hoped that his mother loved him more than the booze.

As Marie made a third phone call to one of her friends, Tommy mixed himself a scotch and water, and sat down on the couch to watch the news. The lead story was about a new disease that was ravaging the gay community and how the Center of Disease Control was issuing grave warnings about the rapid spread of this new disease called AIDS. The news report was grim. He'd already heard horror stories from some of his friends about the deadly disease, and the news report terrified Tommy.

Oh my God! I can't watch this right now!

Tommy's heart sank, and the sudden dread he felt was overwhelming. Pointing the remote control at the television, he asked Ricky what he wanted to watch.

Chapter 26

AFTER A FEW months in the interferon clinical trial, Tommy wasn't any showing progress. He'd gone to a clinic at the University of Texas Medical Branch, in the Houston Medical Center, every two weeks for most of the past six months, and he was beginning to become impatient for the trial to be over. Along with several other participants in the trial, Tommy was hooked up to an IV to administer the drug, and afterward, technicians drew his blood for testing.

Most of the other patients, like Tommy, had been exposed to hepatitis B through homosexual transmission. Usually only one or two other patients would be there while he was hooked up to the IV, and he'd entertain and regale the other patients with stories to cut the tension, telling tales of his antics from his younger days, mostly from college. Afterward, he would drive himself the fifteen blocks home before the side effects kicked in.

The side effects didn't hit him right away but only after a few hours. Tommy would feel tired and nauseous and would go straight to bed. At first Marie was pretty understanding and helpful in taking care of him, just as she would have tended to one of her patients in the hospital where she used to work: getting him water, fluffing his pillow, finding the remote control or the book he'd been reading. But it wasn't long before Marie lost interest and would begin to disappear after he got home from the clinic or wouldn't be home at all, so that Tommy would be on his own.

The nausea would usually only last for a day, but sometimes it would last much longer, and Tommy was grateful that he only had to go through the treatment every two weeks. Tommy lost his appetite, and his energy levels were so low that he spent a lot of time at home and he'd only go into the office occasionally.

Since he spent all that time at home, he'd taken over as Ricky's main care-giver, and he loved every minute of his time with his son. Tommy was reliving the childhood he'd never had with the Colonel. Ricky was in the second grade, attending a public school that was walking distance from their house. On the days when he wasn't suffering from the side effects of the interferon, he'd get Ricky up, get him dressed for school, and take his son to the neighborhood elementary.

Tommy and Ricky would walk to school together, or if Tommy felt good enough, they would ride their bikes. Tommy became a room parent and helped plan and decorate the classroom for parties; he chaperoned field trips and par-ticipated in fund-raising events even selling candy bars door-to-door with Ricky. When Ricky joined the Cub Scouts, Tommy became a den leader.

Tommy was living a dream he'd had most of his life. He was finally the kind of parent he'd always wanted to be. He was helping Ricky with his homework, playing games with him like Transformers and He-Man, and taking him to soc-cer practices and going to games, even secretly weaning Ricky off the ADHD medicine that Marie had put him on when he was a preschooler.

His wife had finally graduated from Texas Woman's University, and he was glad she finally had her degree. She'd been working on the master's degree off and on for the past seven years and could no longer use it as an excuse not to get a job. She'd ended up getting a master's degree in family counseling and by the way she talked couldn't wait to save the world.

He tried to be supportive, but Marie applied for jobs at the most prestigious counseling practices but never received a call back or an interview. She was about to give up and go back to school when she was referred to an up-and-coming family practice in the Sharpestown Medical Center by a friend of a friend. Marie begrudgingly applied for the position and was offered a job one week after her interview.

Once Marie started her new job, she threw everything into establishing her practice. "I am so excited to finally be able to help people," she told her husband on her first day as she was walking out to her car.

However, it was only a couple of months until Marie's enthusiasm for her new position as a family counselor waned. A few months after she started, Dr.

Ross, her supervisor, started observing Marie's patients, and some of them did not fit the profile that she had stressed repeatedly to Marie. "In my professional opinion, at least two of your patients should be referred to a psychiatrist for the kind of treatment that you cannot ethically give."

Marie did not like her practices and ethics being questioned, and became confrontational, resigning immediately.

That night, Marie came home and told Tommy that she'd resigned due to a minor conflict with her supervisor. "I want to open my own practice. I've got as much experience as a family counselor as many of the professionals in the Houston area."

Marie laid out her plans to Tommy, and he listened, trying hard not to interrupt and sound condescending.

"Are you sure this is what you want?" Tommy quizzed his wife. "I think you might be oversimplifying this."

But Marie was determined, and Tommy soon relented. He suspected she was hiding something, but he was having the best time of his life being a house husband, and he agreed to back her new practice temporarily on a trial basis, just to keep her out of his hair.

Apprehensively, he tried to discuss the financing with her as they ate their dinner. His wife really didn't have a clue about money and finances, and it made him very nervous. If it were anyone else who'd asked him to back a business venture, he'd ask them for their business plan. It was useless to ask Marie for one because it was way beyond her ability to grasp.

Finally, he said, "I'll invest in your new family counseling venture if and only if you agree to a budget."

Marie agreed, but Tommy suspect that she had no intention of doing so.

Within a week, Marie had rented a small office space in a shopping center on Holcombe Street and opened her own practice. Now she was gone most of the day, and Tommy loved not having his wife around. He had the whole day to do what he wanted without her interference.

First thing in the morning, Tommy would take Ricky to school, and then he'd meet his friends at the YMCA to work out before he went to the office. Before long, Tommy noticed that one of his longtime friends, James, hadn't shown up at the Y since he'd started back into his workout routine. He asked another friend, Doyle, if he seen James lately.

Doyle heaved a sigh. "James is in the hospital, deathly ill with AIDS," he said.

Tommy felt the color drain out of his face. This was news that no gay man wanted to hear. Tommy ran in a small circle of gay men, all who had been sexual partners with one another, as well as many others, off and on over the past several years. AIDS had been a topic of conversation among those in the gay community recently. Tommy was terrified; AIDS was considered a death sentence. Worse than that, anyone diagnosed with the virus suffered horribly before his death while being ostracized from society like a leper, victims of terrible prejudice.

The usually chatty Tommy sat quietly in shock, trying to think of the last time he'd been with James or someone else who had been with James. "Poor James, that's terrible!" Tommy mumbled halfheartedly. "When did this happen? I just saw him a few months ago, and he was fine."

"I know. It happened so suddenly. The poor thing went down so fast. I hear he hasn't got very long to live." Doyle kept his voice down as they spoke, looking around to make sure no one was listening. "There's only one funeral home in Houston that will accept the remains of someone with AIDS for burial. I think that is such an atrocity!"

Staring off into space as Doyle gossiped on, Tommy tried not to show his fear as he realized that it wasn't that long ago that he'd had sex with James.

This can't be happening! There's no way I could be in this kind of trouble!

After he was done with his routine, Tommy went home, and started looking for another place to work out.

I have to get away from those guys before one of them gives me AIDS.

Chapter 27

By the spring, more and more of Tommy's friends were developing AIDS. Tommy was scared and was withdrawing from his gay friends. He tried to be supportive, but it was difficult to watch his once-vibrant friends waste away to nothing in a matter of weeks, covered with sores and gasping for each breath because they'd developed some rare form of pneumonia. Tommy wasn't trying to be unsympathetic, but every time he heard that someone else had died of AIDS, he couldn't help but think that he could be next.

All the years he'd misbehaved...never mind that he'd just been through a drug trial for hepatitis B. He was ignoring that silent killer, hoping that the interferon from the clinical trials had done what it was intended to do. For the first time in twenty years, Tommy really was trying to walk the straight and narrow. He'd stopped picking up male prostitutes and "running errands," and was staying away from the downtown YMCA where all his gay friends worked out together.

Tommy had laid off the coke while he was part of the interferon trial, but now that it was over he'd fallen off the wagon and was back to doing cocaine once or twice a week. The stress of watching his close friends get sick had pushed him over the edge, and he wanted to numb the pain and fear he was facing.

The more he watched AIDS ravage the lives of people he knew, the less control Tommy had over his own. It was all he could do to hold it together when he went to Dr. Barrett and had his blood drawn. Yet for once in his life, he was actually celibate.

Luckily, Marie spent most of her time at symposiums and continuing education courses and was oblivious to her husband's neurotic fears. Marie was doing everything she could to get her message out about her new and exciting theories about family counseling. She'd written several papers for publication in various journals, which had all been rejected...surprising only Marie.

She had a hard time keeping patients coming back for more than a few sessions. The only patients she ever kept were poor innocent fools she'd talked out of killing themselves at the suicide hotline where she volunteered. Talking patients into counseling instead of suicide wouldn't be so shady if it weren't her own practice she was pushing. But because she was genuinely trying to help, Marie never really got in too much trouble for unethical behavior—or at least, she never got turned in to the state licensing board. Marie was close to throwing in the towel, but she was too proud and ambitious to quit.

⊶⊷ ⊷⊶

In an effort to take his mind off his past, Tommy was putting a lot of time into mending fences with Marie. Sometimes Marie insisted on date night with her married friends, and they went out to dinner or to the movies. Depending on which of Marie's girlfriends it was, Tommy was usually OK with going out. Arthur and Brenda were good; they had a longtime friendship with their old next-door neighbors. There were several other couples they would go out with, but most of them were strictly Marie's friends. However, they'd recently started having dinner with another couple, Jennifer and Steve Winters.

Jennifer was one of Marie's best friends; they'd met while in college at Texas Woman's. Tommy was fond of Jennifer, but he secretly had a crush on her husband, Steven was a tall, good-looking man with blond hair, blue eyes, and a smile that would melt ice. Steve Winters was an insurance agent whose office was in a shopping center on Wertheimer Road between Chimney Rock and Fountain View.

The first few times he'd met the Winterses, they'd had fun together, and it wasn't long before Tommy started thinking up ways that the two couples could spend more time together. Steve and Jennifer had a little boy named Ryan who was in the same grade as Ricky. The boys got along well and had playdates and sleepovers. The couples would often pair up for an evening out, and the two women would get together, ignoring their husbands while they chatted.

It was awkward at first because Tommy didn't know what to talk about. Steve would ask, "Did you see the game last night?"

"No, I didn't catch it."

Tommy wasn't much of a sports fan, so he would immediately go off into one of his liberal Republican-bashing rants. Steve didn't know how to react. "I really don't pay much attention to politics." Steve had learned as a salesman that you never talk about politics.

One day, though, Steve asked Tommy if he knew where he could score some coke; he'd heard his wife talking about Tommy's habit and figured he could get some from Tommy, and so Tommy started scoring cocaine for Steve every now and again, and eventually it became more and more regular.

"Why don't we get a hotel room to do drugs sometime so our wives won't know what we're doing," Tommy suggested.

Steve agreed, and Tommy set it up.

A few days later, Tommy scored some cocaine from one of his sources and let his new friend know. "I've got a hotel room for tomorrow night. I told Marie that I'd be out of town for the day, so you need to make up a story to cover your ass," he told him when he called.

So, Steve made up story about going to a baseball game in Dallas with a client, and they met at the Hyatt Regency downtown.

Tommy was already in the room when Steve got there. He'd already done a couple of lines when he heard a knock on the door. Tommy spied through the peephole before he answered. "There's a line for you on the mirror in the bathroom," he said quietly as he peered both ways down the hall, then hung the white plastic Do Not Disturb sign on the doorknob and locked the door behind them.

As the night progressed, the conversation turned from polite banter to topics that were more and more personal. "Have you every cheated on your wife?" Tommy queried at one point, peeking through the curtains as if someone could see what they were doing in their tenth-floor hotel room.

"Just between me and you, I do have a girlfriend on the side." Steve began to brag about how easy it was to fool his unsuspecting wife. "In fact, I've had several girlfriends over the years. Some I've only screwed once or twice, but the one I have right now is a long, cool drink of water. I've been screwing her a couple of times a week for months."

As Steve boasted about his sexual encounters with his mistress, Tommy found himself getting an erection. "Man, you are going to have to stop talking about sex because I am getting a woody that won't go away." Tommy laughed. "I am going to have to beat off!"

Steve was shocked as Tommy undressed and started playing with himself on the bed next to him. Awkwardly, Steve became aroused, and as soon as Tommy noticed, the bulge in Steve's pants began to grow.

Tommy reached over and started to rub Steve crotch, asking, "Have you ever been with a man? I'd sure love to suck your cock right now."

For the next year and a half, the two men continued their affair beneath the noses of their unsuspecting wives. Tommy would even arrange for them to go on family vacations with the Winters family. The two families went skiing in Colorado and rented a beach house in Galveston together. The two husbands would sneak off and have sex while their wives and kids were playing on the beach or shopping, and no one was any the wiser.

The jealousy over Steve's girlfriend was getting the better of him, and Tommy started trying to come between Steve and his mistress. What had started out as a fun little game soon became an obsession, and it started to give Steve the willies.

For the first time in in his life, Tommy was falling in love with a man, with Steve. Tommy thought about him all the time and hung on his every word, doing everything he could just to be around him. But Steve was just having fun. As soon as he saw that Tommy was getting a little too attached, Steve made excuses not to be around him. It wasn't long before Steve realized that he had to tell Tommy to back off.

After Tommy and Steve had "the talk," Tommy was embarrassed and lost. He'd never been dumped by anyone before—Tommy had always done the dumping. Feeling incredibly foolish, Tommy went to stay with the Colonel for a little while. He felt like he needed to get away so that no one would see he was heartbroken. Tommy had lied so many times to Marie that she didn't ever care where he was anymore.

"Since the Colonel turned ninety, I've been concerned that people have been trying to steal from him," Tommy told Marie, knowing that Marie hated the thought of people stealing from her father-in-law. "I need to stay with him for a little while until I sort it out."

Tommy's lie played into his wife's delusions; Marie had adamantly accused Etta of stealing from the moment they were married, and he knew that she'd end up letting him stay with his father.

Tommy stayed with the Colonel for the next six weeks, and Marie and Ricky would come on the weekends. Marie wanted to invite Jennifer and Steve, but Tommy told her, "I think it would be too much for the Colonel to have people around he doesn't know.

After a couple of months, Tommy snapped out of his self-imposed isolation and slowly returned to his life in Houston. Tommy had let too many things slide. Bob had been running most of the day-to-day operations at the office for many years, and Tommy was sorely pissed off at himself.

He'd allowed himself to get addicted to cocaine the same way his mother had become addicted to alcohol. He'd been walking to close to the edge and didn't care about the consequences. He'd stopped caring what happened since his mother died feeling as though he'd lost control of his destiny. His father was living longer than anyone expected, and until he passed away, he'd always be daddy's errand boy.

He was thirty-seven years old and his life was a mess.

I've never let myself get so emotionally attached to a man before. This is not the kind of life I'd envisioned. It's time to get over myself and get control of my life again.

He decided he needed to go back to work while he still had a job and started easing his way back into the office a little at a time and he hoped that his obsession with Steve and all the coke they were doing didn't affect his job. His brother-in-law was running things in his absence, and even though everything was running smoothly with Bob in charge, Tommy truly hoped that he hadn't lost Bob's respect since hitting rock bottom.

Once again, Tommy had cleaned up his act, and he was determined this time to walk the straight and narrow. No one had said anything to his face, but Tommy sensed that he'd lost the confidence of his office staff and business partner since his marriage to Marie and his downward spiral into drugs and alcohol.

When Tommy returned to the office, he did his best to act as though he'd been out due to an extended illness. Bob was the consummate professional and never complained or showed any judgment, but Tommy noticed that things had changed between him and his brother-in-law.

The damage has been done, and I don't know if I'll ever regain Bob's trust.

But Bob wasn't the only problem he had at the office. While Tommy had been out of commission of late, Minerva had started to undermine his position. It started out with Minerva complaining and watching his every move, and then spilled over to Angelica and the accounting staff not trusting him, either. Minerva's constant complaining was like a poison, and the uncertainty about their boss's addiction problems complicated everything. Several people quit, and others just quit caring about their work. Tommy was overwhelmed. He'd neglected his work for so long that he didn't know what to do to fix the problem.

And it didn't help that Marie continued to include her best friend, Jennifer, in every part of their lives. Tommy tried to put his foot down, saying that he was tired of having them around all the time. This worked for a little while until he came home from work one evening to find that Jennifer and Steve had come over to their house for dinner. It was pretty awkward between Tommy and Steve, but fortunately, Marie and Jennifer did most of the talking.

After dinner, the boys were playing in the den, and as usual, Marie and Jennifer were in the kitchen drinking wine while they cleaned up the dinner dishes. Steve lured Tommy upstairs, where he asked, "Hey, I was wondering if you still had your connections. I haven't done any bump in a while."

"Well, I've been staying away from coke and trying to live a cleaner life," Tommy said quietly.

They were standing at the top of the stairs, and Steve motioned for Tommy to follow him into the master bedroom.

"Come on, Tommy, you can do this one thing for me," Steve said as he closed the door and moved in closer to Tommy. He put his hand around Tommy's waist and pulled him closer. "I've missed you, and I want you again." Steve put his hand between Tommy's legs as he pulled him in and kissed him passionately.

Moments later, they both had their pants down and Tommy was on his knees with Steve's dick in his mouth. Unfortunately, they were so enthralled in passion that they didn't hear their wives come upstairs. Marie and Jennifer barged into the room.

"What the fuck is going on?" screamed Marie while poor Jennifer stood by quietly, mouth gaping in disbelief.

Book Three

If you drink much from a bottle marked "poison" it is certain to disagree with you sooner or later.

—*Lewis Carroll*, Alice in Wonderland

Chapter 28

BOB WAS A patient man, but his patience with his brother-in-law and business partner was wearing thin. He was tired of Tommy's behavior, and the only reason he hadn't dissolve their business arrangements was because everything was so interwoven and intertwined that it would take a forensic accountant to sort it out. Besides, the Colonel was old and wouldn't live forever, and they would have to perform one when the old man's estate was probated anyway.

While Tommy was out of the office Bob had hired a part-time college student to organize the production records for all the oil wells. She was attending graduate school at the University of Houston for engineering, and her name was Sarah McCullough. Bob had assigned her the task of organizing and computerizing the production records of the oil and gas wells, and Sarah had been doing a bang-up job. Computerizing their production records would go a long way toward helping them with the forensic accounting when the time came.

When Tommy announced his impending divorce to Angelica and the office staff, he was a little disappointed that nobody seemed surprised. Minerva had already told them all the gory details about the melee. In fact, everyone but Bob knew all about the sorted details. Tommy went straight into Bob's office after the announcement; he hoped that he could tell him what had happened before Bob heard it from someone else. That was the least he could do for his business partner, since Bob was the one taking care of the daily operations.

When he went into Bob's office. he found him at his desk behind a pile of paperwork, reviewing invoices.

"Do you mind if we talk a minute?" Tommy cleared his throat and shut the door behind him, before sitting down in the wing-back chair across from his desk. Tommy told him that he was divorcing Marie, leaving out as much of the story from the night before as he could.

Sitting stoically behind his desk, Bob said, "I'd be lying if I told you I'm surprised." Bob paused a moment before he continued. "I must say that I am very disappointed in how low you have sunk. I've tried very hard to stay out of your marital issues as well as your other problems."

Both men sat uncomfortably silent for several minutes until Bob spoke again.

"I truly hope things work out for the best for both you and Ricky." Bob looked Tommy in the eyes as he spoke.

Tommy was shaking when he left his brother-in-law's office. He felt like a child who'd been chastised for his behavior, but he also was grateful that Bob had been nothing but professional during their conversation. Bob only knew half the story, and Tommy really didn't want to go there.

⋅→▰◉ ◉▰←⋅

Sarah was a hard worker and was well-liked by the rest of the office staff. She was humble and eager to help and learn the business. But Sarah was intimidated by Tommy taking such an avid interest in the work she was doing. Bob had given her free reign and was more interested in the results; Bob was not an overly controlling boss who got involved in the details. Up until now, she had spent the day in the storage room going through files and boxes, unnoticed by everyone.

When he found her working on the floor of the storeroom with production records piled around her, Tommy asked what she was doing. Sarah sheepishly explained her duties. He listened and then enthusiastically started discussing how best to plot the trends into graphs and statistics to give them the most useful information. Tommy liked how his forward-thinking brother-in-law was looking ahead. Nevertheless, Tommy intimidated Sarah; after all, he was the boss's son.

"I'm scared that my efforts will fall short of the expectations," she confessed to Angelica after Tommy left.

"Don't be intimidated by Tommy," Angelica told the young woman. "He's just eager to see the production information computerized."

Sarah hadn't wanted to go to graduate school but felt she didn't have any other choice because unemployment was high due to the oil bust of the mid-1980s. Oil prices had dropped to a fifty-year low, and all the major oil companies were laying people off instead of hiring. She'd spent several months looking for a full-time job before she applied to the engineering program. When a friend of her grandmother referred her to Bob, she was ever so grateful that he gave her a part-time position.

Though Tommy had only come into the office a handful of times since she'd started work, the people in the office had told her all about him—especially Shawn, the computer operator. She could tell that Shawn admired Tommy greatly because he talked about him constantly.

Minerva didn't trust Sarah because Bob had hired her, and she believed that Sarah's work compiling production histories and information was so that Bob could use it against the Colonel someday. Sarah tried to reassure Minerva that she was just a college student and this was her first real job in the oil business. "I'm just trying to get experience that I can put on my résumé."

Most of the time, Sarah hung out in the file room or in Shawn's office. She tried not to make a mess or get in anyone's way and worked quietly on the floor sorting through files.

When Tommy had stepped into the room and introduced himself, Sarah was startled, thinking, *He's pleasant enough. Tommy isn't anything like what I envisioned.* Tommy was wearing blue jeans, black cowboy boots, and a plaid cowboy shirt with short sleeves and pearl snap buttons. He was a tall, heavyset man with a thick black mustache and salt-and-pepper hair, which made him look much older than his age.

After he left, Sarah went into Shawn office to tell him about their meeting. Shawn looked at Sarah and said, "See? I told you that Tommy was the man!"

"He seemed nice enough," she replied. "But he certainly isn't the demigod you and the others make him out to be." She taunted Shawn, who rolled his eyes as he smirked uncomfortably.

⊷⊶

Immediately after Marie caught her husband with Steve's dick in his mouth, she put their house up for sale and filed for divorce. She also had every intention to make good on her threats to move back to Canada, taking Ricky with her.

At first Marie was out for blood and hired the meanest divorce lawyer in town, but her lawyer quickly realized that the bills Marie had run up supporting her counseling business had all but bankrupted their community property.

"You really need to find another attorney to represent you, one you can afford," he'd advised Marie. He also told her that she couldn't claim that her husband was at fault because of infidelity because she had known for several years that he was having sex with men. "You stayed married to the man, tolerating your husband's trysts for years. Marie, this makes you look like you were only staying married to Tommy for the money." Referring Marie to another lawyer, he said, "You really need to work this out without spending what's left of your community property on attorney fees."

After Marie heard the news that their community property was bankrupt, she tried to make up with Tommy. But Tommy was done and wouldn't take her back. He agreed to buy her a house anywhere she wanted to live and gave her all the money that was left in the community property, as well as a quarter million dollars and three thousand dollars a month in child support.

All that Tommy asked was that she give him joint custody of Ricky and visitation rights. Marie's new lawyer explained to her that this was a very generous offer and that she should take the deal and be grateful.

Finding out that Marie had agreed to his terms, Tommy's heart sank; the realization that his marriage to Marie was actually over made him sad and happy at the same time. Tommy leaned back in his chair, shook his head, and sighed. The financing was already set up at the bank for his divorce settlement. But still, he was terribly sad that he wasn't going to see much of Ricky over the next few years until he grew up. Even though he shared joint custody of his son with Marie, he knew that it would be practically unenforceable if she made good on her treats to move back to Canada. At the same time, he was relieved and ecstatic that his marriage to that crazy woman would soon be dissolved.

Before the ink was dry on their divorce papers, Marie had already visited Victoria, British Columbia, and picked out the house that she wanted. All that was left was to go to court and get the judge to bless it. Their court date was scheduled for the upcoming Monday morning, and then his divorce from Marie would be done and dusted.

Undeniably, he'd gotten off easy. His wife had left him before his father died. Tommy had lost custody of his son in the divorce but had protected his elderly father from a greedy woman.

I am amazed at how something I've dreaded for so long turned out to be so easy.

Chapter 29

SARAH WAS TWENTY-FIVE and lived in an efficiency apartment in a sketchy neighborhood between downtown and the campus of U of H in Houston. The that she made part-time wasn't that much, but since she was a poor graduate student, every little bit helped. Still, Sarah's diet consisted mostly of ramen noodles, fried Spam, and tuna salad on white bread.

At the time, Sarah had a boyfriend named Todd that she'd met in the engineering department at U of H. Her boyfriend was having fun instead of studying and, as a result, was taking longer to graduate from college than Sarah.

Being the jealous type, Todd was forever accusing Sarah of cheating on him. When Sarah started working for Bob part-time, Todd became convinced that Shawn was putting the moves on her. Sarah tried her best to reassure her insecure boyfriend. "Shawn is really nice and helpful, and I am glad that he's a work friend, but I have absolutely no romantic interest in him at all."

But Todd wasn't having it. His jealousy got infinitely worse once Tommy started paying attention to her. Sarah admitted, "He's my boss, and I admire the man."

She'd never met anyone like Tommy before, and Todd was suspicious and jealous of everyone. When Sarah had car trouble one day and Tommy not only gave her a ride home after work but paid to have her car towed to a mechanic, Todd blew a gasket.

"You're an idiot! He may be your boss, but he is a married man who's in the middle of a divorce. Don't ever get a ride home from a married man!"

Sarah argued, "He was just being nice. Not all men are nice to women because they are trying to get in their pants. You're overreacting again!"

Todd broke up with her shortly after, saying that he couldn't take all the guys who were always hitting on her. But Sarah thought it sounded a little too convenient and thought that he probably had a new girlfriend.

One evening, not long after her argument and subsequent breakup with Todd, Sarah stopped off at the bathroom before she left at quitting time. Most of her coworkers had already left for the day, and when she came out she found Tommy standing outside the bathroom waiting for her. He offered to walk her to her car in the parking garage, and as Sarah was digging through her purse for her car keys when they got to her car, Tommy kissed her. Sarah was caught off guard. She pulled away, and dropping her keys, she hurriedly picked them up. Saying good-bye, she unlocked her car and drove away, leaving Tommy standing in the garage feeling like a jerk.

It was an awkward situation. Tommy was her boss. And worst of all was that Sarah really liked Tommy; when she and Tommy kissed, her knees had gotten weak.

"I have to get away from these people before something bad happens to me," she told herself on the way home that night. It was like in the movies when fireworks went off. Sarah could see the train wreck coming.

Later, Tommy tried to apologize, but Sarah really didn't know if he was all that sincere. She didn't know if he was sorry he'd kissed her or if he was sorry that he'd put her in such a clumsy place.

At the end of the semester, Sarah decided that the best thing for everyone was to get some distance between her and Houston. She transferred to a new graduate school and moved back home to Corpus Christi.

Todd had been her first real boyfriend; she'd met him in her second year of college. They hadn't lived together officially, but Todd was at her house most of the time. He didn't help with the rent or the bills and would always manage to disappear anytime there was any handyman work to be done. But Sarah loved him, even though he was lazy and jealous and argumentative. They'd been together for so long that she'd naturally assumed they would get married someday, and when they eventually broke up, she was a little lost without him. Surprisingly, Todd had become a big part of her life, and she missed him.

When she moved back to the Corpus Christi area, her parents graciously offered her old room back. Sarah's father had never cared for Todd and had been trying to get her to move home for the last year. But Sarah had been away from home for five years and didn't want to live with her parents. "I appreciate the offer, but I am going to find something closer to campus," she told them, hoping they wouldn't get their feelings hurt.

Instead, Sarah rented a six-hundred-square-foot apartment in Flour Bluff, which was a lot closer to Corpus Christi State University. It was an older apartment on the second floor. It was pretty dirty when she moved in, but with a good cleaning and a little imagination, it was just like home soon enough.

Jobs were scarce, and she was happy that she'd gotten a job at CCSU as a graduate assistant, even if it was just a teaching job. Even though the money wasn't all that great, she was just grateful to be out of the drama. And it was good to be around the friends she'd grown up with.

A few weeks into the spring, Sarah realized that she needed to give the accounting department at her old job her new address so they could send her W-2 form so that she could prepare her tax return. When she called, the receptionist put her through to Tommy immediately. "I didn't mean to interrupt you," Sarah said in surprise. "I was calling Cecil so that he could forward my W-2 to my new address." She stammered like a little girl.

The conversation was clumsy. They hadn't talked much after Tommy had kissed her in the parking garage. After a few minutes of uneasy chitchat, Sarah admitted, "I heard that your ex-wife moved to Canada with your son. I'm very sorry for your troubles. It must be awful not to be able to see your son when you want to."

"Thank you. I sure miss the little guy," Tommy replied as he wrote down her address.

"I really do hope that things work out for the best for you and Ricky," she said consolingly.

After she hung up, Sarah noticed that she was shaking and her hands were all sweaty. She went to the restroom to freshen up and regain her composure before she had to face any of her coworkers.

After teaching a lab the next day, she headed back to her office, which was just a hole in the wall with a desk. When she unlocked her office door, she found a note from Becky, the secretary of the math department, asking her to come by her office when she got in.

Even though Becky had a key to Sarah's office, she never came in and left her notes; she'd always call and leave a voice mail. Sarah thought the whole thing it odd. When Sarah got to Becky's office, Becky was smiling and a vase of a dozen beautiful long-stemmed red roses sat on the corner of her desk.

Sarah asked, "Becky, what's the occasion? Is it your anniversary or something," thinking her husband, Jeff, had sent them to her.

"I don't know. You tell me. These flowers are for you." Becky laughed and poked her in the shoulder with her finger.

Dumbfounded, Sarah pulled the card out of the flowers, and sure enough, it was addressed to her. When she opened the card, it simply read: "Thinking of you, T."

Becky was about to pop. "Who's 'T'?" she asked Sarah coyly.

"I don't know," Sarah replied. But Becky knew she was lying.

The only "T" Sarah knew was Tommy, and surely it wasn't him. And she wasn't going to tell Becky who he was—not yet anyway. Sarah took the roses back to her office. She was excited and nervous because this was the first time anyone had ever sent her roses and it was totally unexpected. But surely the "T" on the card wasn't Tommy. "Tommy couldn't be that interested in me," Sarah told herself.

But when she got back to her office, there was a message from Tommy, asking her if she'd received the flowers he'd sent. Sarah sat there quietly in utter disbelief. She tried to focus on the weekly lab reports that she needed to check. Midterms were coming up, and she didn't want to be one of those lab teachers who waited until the last minute to turn in their midterm grades. She took an interest in her students and wanted to help the ones who needed a little extra attention. After all, there was nothing more discouraging to a college student than flunking a lab.

Sarah was almost done grading her lab reports when the office phone rang. She froze. She wondered why she felt that way about *him* of all people.

She let it ring a couple more times, just in case it was Tommy calling back so that she wouldn't seem so anxious. She shut the door to her office before she answered so that her nosy coworkers couldn't eavesdrop. When she did answer, it was Tommy.

"Did you get my flowers?" he asked almost immediately. The rest of the conversion was light. Toward the end, Tommy asked her if he could come to Corpus to visit her. "I need to get away, and Corpus Christi sounds like the perfect place."

Not knowing what to say, she managed to blurt out, "If you're coming to Corpus, I'd love to see you again." Sarah immediately cringed.

LOVE? Oh crap! Why in the world did I just say LOVE?

"You need to get a hotel room because my apartment is just big enough for me," she informed him.

Tommy laughed and asked if she had a home phone number so that he didn't have to go through her department secretary. "She was being a little nosy after she found out my name was Tommy," he explained. Sarah must have gasped because she heard him laugh. "I'm looking forward to seeing you again," he said as he said good-bye.

At the end of the day, Sarah tried to sneak out the back way with her flowers, but she bumped into her friend Debbie on the way out.

Debbie asked, "Who sent the flowers? They're lovely."

"A friend of mine," Sarah answered sheepishly.

Debbie was a frumpy girl who looked like she'd read too many books. "Just be careful what you wish for because sometimes things don't work out the way you plan," Debbie said as she opened the back door to the parking lot.

That thought stuck in Sarah's head. She decided to listen to her head, not her heart, and that she should be weary of being swept off her feet by Tommy's charismatic, larger-than-life persona.

⇥▰◉ ◉▰⇤

Indeed, Tommy was extremely charming when he wanted to be, and he was pulling out all the stops to sweep Sarah off her feet. Tommy liked Sarah because she was sweet and kind and real. She was the first woman since Nana Harris that he felt wasn't just looking for a meal ticket.

But that was the way he'd felt about Marie at first—till she showed her true colors. Of course, he hadn't known that much about Marie before he knocked her up. If he had, his whole life would now be different.

He planned on taking it slowly this time. There was no doubt that Sarah was on a different level than Marie. Sarah was a really great person and between boyfriends, and he was impatient because a girl like Sarah wouldn't be single for much longer. So he asked her out. He wanted to see what would happen.

After flying into Corpus Christi on a Friday afternoon, Tommy rented a car. He was staying at the Corpus Christi Omni Bay Front Hotel by the marina and yacht club on Ocean Drive.

Sarah got off work as early as she could to get fixed up for her dinner date. She put on the new dress and shoes she'd bought for the occasion—a light-blue dress that was very flattering. She'd never in her life spent so much on clothing, but she wanted to look special, so she'd splurged. They had a reservation for dinner at the yacht club; Sarah had lived in the Corpus Christi area most of her life, and she had never been to the yacht club.

"Dinner at the yacht club. He really is pulling out all the stops." Sarah was so nervous that she was talking to her cat, Molly McKitty, while she got ready.

Sarah was meeting him at seven o'clock for drinks at the hotel lobby bar. She parked her junky old car in the back of the parking lot—she wouldn't dare valet park—and went inside. She found Tommy right where he said he would be: having a drink at the bar. He stood and gave her a kiss on the check when she walked up. She ordered a glass of wine, and when they were done with their drinks, they walked across the street to the yacht club holding hands like they'd been together for a long time.

At dinner, they were seated by the window overlooking the bay. The sun had just set below the western horizon, and the last rays of sunlight colored the sky with purples, reds, oranges, and blues as it bounced off the puffy clouds still visible. The piano man in the corner softly played songs as Tommy ordered a bottle of wine. The food was excellent and the conversation light, as Tommy amused Sarah with stories of his younger days before he was married. Sarah tried not to be obvious, but she hung on his every word.

After dinner, the couple walked back to the hotel arm in arm; outside the hotel's front door, they stopped, and Tommy kissed Sarah. Again, the kiss was powerful, and Sarah's resolve wavered when he asked her to come upstairs and spend the night.

"If I had a dollar for every guy who tried to get in my pants after the first date, I'd be rich." She smiled.

Tommy roared with laughter. "But I'm different," he retorted. "And if you only give me a chance, I'll be happy to show you."

His charms were working. Sarah's resistance was down, and the physical attraction she felt for him was overwhelming.

The next morning, Tommy ordered breakfast from room service, and Sarah wore a hotel robe that had been hanging in the closet while the two ate on the balcony overlooking the bay. The smell of the salt air was strong on the morning mist, and seagulls squawked as they flew by. Tommy read the newspaper while he drank his hot tea and ate eggs Benedict.

Sarah sat quietly thinking how much different he was from Todd. The only time she'd seen Todd read a newspaper was when he was looking through the want ads for a job or checking the scores in the sports sections while he was on the toilet. Most of the guys she'd dated were grown men who wanted to act like teenagers; they wanted to have sex but weren't ready to settle down and get married, much less have children. She didn't know yet what Tommy wanted but was certain that she wanted to see where things were going.

They talked about news events, politics, and world history over breakfast. Tommy's opinions were the polar opposite of her father's. Her father was a retired schoolteacher and a staunch Republican, and would have called Tommy a limousine liberal.

Tommy had arranged a tour by boat around the Corpus Christi harbor at one o'clock, but first Sarah needed to go home and change. She borrowed Tommy's hairbrush to make her hair presentable as she put on the dress she'd worn last night. It was wrinkled, as it had been tossed on the floor in the heat of passion the night before.

Sarah didn't much look forward to the walk of shame through the lobby, so she took the back stairs down and out to her car. Tommy followed her to her house in his rental car so that she could change into more casual clothes for their Saturday outing. After Sarah had changed into shorts and a cotton shirt, Tommy insisted, "You should pack a bag with a change of clothes for dinner and tomorrow." Sarah blushed as she packed her bag, and Tommy teased her for blushing.

Realizing how smitten he was with her, he stared out the window on his flight home the next day like a lovesick puppy. Sarah was nothing like the other women in his life; she was modest, kind, giving, fun, and truly interested in him instead of his money. She also liked sex almost as much as he did. He'd never been with a woman who had actually had an orgasm.

Without knowing why, he was attracted to Sarah. He hadn't been attracted to a woman since college. The best he could figure was that even though Marie had been just awful, he missed being married. And maybe, just maybe, Sarah might be the one he could grow old with.

Chapter 30

AFTER THE DIVORCE was final, Marie wasted no time returning to Canada. Late that summer, Marie and Ricky headed to Canada with the six-month-old German shepherd puppy that Ricky had named Taco. She'd sold the Chevrolet station wagon she'd been driving for the past five years and bought a Toyota SUV for the long drive to British Columbia. Marie took almost the same route she'd driven ten years before when she left Canada—what now seemed like a lifetime ago.

She'd flown up to BC a few weeks earlier to close on her new house, and while there she visited her family, including her mother, who she hadn't seen since before she moved to Tuktoyaktuk. Marie was amazed at how much older her mother looked, and for the first time in her life, her mother was nice to her.

Either the years had mellowed her mother, or Marie was more empathetic toward her now that she had a child of her own. Or maybe it was because she'd been through a bad marriage and rough divorce, and she felt she'd been cheated out of everything. Whatever the reason, she was glad there was someone who was on her side.

After buying a house in the Oak Bay area of Victoria, just off Cobdoro Bay Road, Marie was optimistic about the future. Her new house was quaint and located on a large two-acre lot on a hillside with a view of the Pacific Ocean, about halfway between the University of Victoria and the downtown area. Ricky was beginning fourth grade, and Marie had enrolled him in the local elementary school.

Once again, Marie needed a new start. She wanted to forget the nightmare she'd endured being married to that jerk, Tommy. In the months since her divorce, she'd had to take care of her own bills out of the money she received in her divorce settlement. She was shocked at the amount of money her family counseling practice had eaten up. She was losing between five and ten thousand a month on her business, and as soon as she figured this out, she closed her practice, knowing that otherwise she wouldn't survive very long. Planning to reopen her practice in Victoria once they were settled, Marie had registered with the Canadian Health Care System. She would just have to get her office reestablished.

As Marie and Ricky took the ferry across into Canada and left the United States, she was enormously relieved. They stood on the deck of the ferry watching the seagulls flying alongside the ferry. Ricky's German shepherd barked at the birds. In a short hour and forty-five minutes, Marie and Ricky would be home.

⊸▭ ▭◂⊶

Tommy started going to see Sarah on the weekends. He would drive down to Corpus just to spend time with her, so he wouldn't feel so alone. He missed his family, and she was the closest thing to family that he had at the moment. He'd tried to shake off all the gossip from Minerva, telling himself that she was just a bitter and twisted old woman, but getting away from prying eyes seemed so much easier. Sarah was the first woman since Nana Harris who loved him unconditionally and really understood how he felt. Tommy felt like he'd finally met a woman who got him, and now he need that more than anything.

The next time Tommy went to see Dr. Barrett for his regular three-month checkup, he got the news he'd been fearing: Tommy was HIV positive. And worse, the doctor had called his ex-wife and advised her to get herself and Ricky tested, too.

"For the love of God, why did you tell Marie? I haven't had sex with her for years," Tommy yelled at the doctor.

But Dr. Barrett felt obligated to tell her because no one could say how long the virus had been in Tommy's body before he tested positive. Besides, Tommy had lied to him so times over the years. "I have to follow my conscience. AIDS is a deadly disease, and it is my duty as a physician to notify anyone and everyone who could possibly be at risk for contracting it."

He didn't like what he heard, but Tommy wasn't going argue.

Staring at his shoes for what seemed to be an eternity, Tommy finally looked up. He wiped tears from his eyes and said, "There is someone else. And she is at more of a risk than Marie."

"She? Who is she?" Dr. Barrett was a little shocked that Tommy was in another relationship with a girl.

Insisting he'd take care of it, Tommy refused to tell the doctor who she was. "I will tell her in my own time and in my own way." Tommy needed time to process his test results and figure out what to say.

He continued to visit Sarah in Corpus Christi and tried to tell her, but every time he tried to find the words, she would say something like, "Sweetheart, I would never hurt anyone intentionally." After hearing her say something like that, Tommy just couldn't find the words to tell her the truth.

She knew something was wrong, but Sarah couldn't figure out what the problem was and didn't ask, because she thought it probably had something to do with Marie.

Tommy finally invited Sarah to San Antonio for the weekend thinking that a change of scenery might make things easier. He reserved a suite at La Mansion on the river walk, imagining that the more romantic setting would soften the blow.

No matter what happens, I'll take care of her as long as I can, and maybe if I'm lucky, she won't hate me.

He was resolved to tell her this time no matter what.

It was fall, and there was a chill in the air. The summer crowds along the river walk had thinned, but there were still plenty of tourists walking up and down the cobblestone walkways along the river. Tommy sat at the outdoor bar underneath one of the old-growth cypress trees that lined the river, watching boats full of tourists pass by. Tommy ordered a drink and read a local newspaper to pass the time. He was nervous and terrified. He'd rehearsed what he was going to say to the point where he knew it by heart.

Sarah is a nice girl and the best thing that's happened to me in a long time. When I was in college, a girl like Sarah wouldn't even have held my attention. I wish more than anything I had just married one of those nice girls. Maybe I shouldn't have treated all those townies like crap.

Later on that afternoon, Tommy picked Sarah up from the airport. They had dinner and drinks that evening at a sidewalk café along the river. Tommy noticed that Sarah wasn't her usually bubbly self.

Oh shit, someone has already broken the bad news to her before I could.

Tommy asked her, "What's wrong, sugar?"

Sarah looked at him with tears in her eyes and responded, "I'm pregnant."

Hanging his head, he fought back the tears. Tommy needed a drink in a bad way.

Dear God! How could this have happened? It's bad enough that I might have given her HIV, but now she is pregnant!

Standing up from the table, Tommy started to pace back and forth. He led Sarah by the arm up the path to their hotel room. He opened the hotel room door and led Sarah inside. He turned to her, holding her by her arms, and with tears in his eyes, his voice cracked as he confessed, "Sarah, I don't know how to tell you this…so I'm just going to say it…I am HIV positive."

He paced back and forth for the next hour as he spilled his guts to Sarah. He came clean about how he had been with men and how he had been diagnosed with hepatitis B. Then he laid out what his prognosis was and the doctor's plan for treatment.

Sarah sat quietly on the end of the bed, as if she were watching this nightmare happening to someone else. After what seemed like forever, Tommy finally stopped pacing frantically and sat down beside her on the bed. He put his arm around her, and they sat in silence without looking at each other.

Eventually Tommy broke the silence, asking, "What are you going to do?"

Sarah answered without looking at him, "Live as long as I can, what else can I do?"

"I want you to go to my doctor as soon as you can. I think that you should talk to a specialist before you make a decision that will affect the rest of your life."

Tommy then offered to pay for medical care for her and the baby if she wanted to keep it. "This isn't a decision you should make so rashly."

Sarah just stared at him. This was the first time she'd even looked at him since he broke the news.

⇥ ⇤

For the rest of the weekend, Tommy talked about his life, his secret life, while Sarah quietly tried to process what he was saying.

Sarah was dazed, and she wondered how she could have misjudged someone so terribly. She knew he had cheated on his first wife, but she had written that off as a result of being married to the wrong person. Now that Tommy was spilling his guts, she realized how very little she knew about him. She wanted to go home and get away from this man. She needed to think. She wanted to process everything without Tommy's constant chatter.

The man just won't shut up, and I need time to think!

Nevertheless, Tommy talked on and on as if he were afraid that if he let her out of his sight, she would disappear and he'd never see her again. Tommy's greatest fear was that he would be alone, especially now. Tommy had watched so many of his friends die from AIDS, and most of them were alone at the end. That terrified him more than anything, and he was going to do what he could to make sure that Sarah stayed with him till the end.

"Dr. Barrett is one of the best doctors in the world, and he's in Houston. He's on the cutting edge of all the AIDS studies and research, and he is our best hope of surviving."

He sat beside her, holding her hand gently.

Before he dropped Sarah off at the airport at the end of the weekend, Tommy said. "Promise that you won't do anything without talking to me first."

Tommy was worried about her. He'd witnessed too many of his friends committing suicide after they found out they were HIV positive, and he didn't want anything to happen to her.

As soon as Sarah got on the plane, she finally felt like she could breathe for the first time in days. Sarah hadn't been trying to trap Tommy into marriage; she'd gotten pregnant by accident. Whatever she decided to do, she was going to do what was best for her. Tommy had lobbied pretty strongly, but nothing he'd said had persuaded her one way or the other. She stared out the window at the tarmac as the plane pushed away from the gate and thought about how the only thing she really wanted to do was go home.

Within the week, Tommy made an appointment with Dr. Barrett for Sarah during the Thanksgiving break and called her to let her know. Sarah still hadn't been tested for HIV, admitting that she was terrified to do it, and Tommy was determined to make sure she was OK. "Getting test for HIV is scary, but not knowing is even scarier," Tommy argued when he called.

Reluctantly, she agreed to go to Houston. Once she met with the doctor, Sarah realized that Dr. Barrett was everything Tommy had said he was. He was a brilliant doctor who laid it all out for Sarah. He talked about mortality rate and research and drug therapies that increased the odds of survival. He spent a lot of time with her and made her feel hopeful. After her initial visit, Dr. Barrett sent her down the hall to a lab to have her blood drawn, telling her that he would call her with the results in two weeks.

Those were the longest two weeks of her life. She tried to throw herself into her work and getting ready for finals. She studied and took practice tests and graded lab reports. And she prayed more than she'd ever prayed in her whole life. The only thing she thought about was her test results. She suffered from morning sickness but reckoned that the nerves from waiting for her test results had made her symptoms worse.

On her visit to the doctor, she'd told Dr. Barrett that she was pregnant, and he'd asked her if she'd been to an OB-GYN yet.

"No, not yet." Sarah admitted sheepishly. "I was waiting to see what my test results were before I make a decision. I'm considering having an abortion if I'm HIV positive," she admitted.

"Well, we'll cross that bridge when we get your test results back." Dr. Barrett patted her hand sympathetically. "Being pregnant is scary enough without worrying about AIDS."

By the time Dr. Barrett finally called with the results, Sarah was exhausted. "Your test results are negative," he said, sounding relieved. "You're lucky, but I want you…no, I *need* you to come back in a month to make sure you are still HIV negative," he told her emphatically.

"If I decide to keep my baby, what are the odds the baby will be healthy?" she pressed the doctor.

"Well, there isn't enough data to know for sure, but I will tell you that there have been documented cases where mothers carry babies to term after being exposed to HIV by the baby's father, and mother and child never convert to HIV positive. But conversely, there are cases where mother starts off HIV negative only to become HIV positive later on." Sarah listened intently, as there was a long pause before the doctor continued. "I cannot tell you what to do. If you are going to have an abortion, you need to make that decision soon before you reach the point of no return and the decision is made for you. And if you decide to keep your child, I will do everything in my power to keep you both healthy."

Sarah was in shock. For the last month, she had been preparing for the worst possible outcome. She'd gotten a life insurance policy for a quarter million dollars and made her sister, Marianne, the beneficiary. She'd rehearsed in her head what she would say to her parents—her poor parents. Sarah wasn't religious, but she was very spiritual. She'd been raised in the Methodist Church and believed in a higher power, and so she prayed reciting the twenty-third psalm over and over in her head.

The sense of relief that she felt brought her to tears. As soon she got off the phone, she bowed her head and said a silent prayer of thanksgiving.

If you keep us safe, I will do whatever I can, to help all the innocent people who suffer from AIDS and I will work with Dr. Barrett to end the spread of AIDS.

She made a promised to God and had every intention of keeping her promise.

⋅→▬◉ ◉▬←⋅

It wasn't long before the doctor started Tommy on a regiment of AZT as soon as it was approved by the FDA. AZT wasn't as effective as doctors had hoped, but it was a way to extend a person's life until researchers could come up with a better treatment for AIDS.

To say that Tommy was relieved when Sarah called him at home with the news was an understatement; he'd been having a crisis of conscience. The thought of losing another child sickened him after she'd announced her pregnancy, and the guilt was almost unbearable. He didn't want to think about losing Sarah, too.

As soon as she found out she was HIV negative, Sarah pulled away from Tommy. He was scared he would never hear from her again once the dust settled. But once the sense of relief subsided, he felt an overwhelming sense of envy and jealousy. He didn't want to tell her, but it was hard for Tommy to push those "Why me and not her?" feelings out of his head. Tommy was starting to think that his life was jinxed and resented the hell out of all the people who were telling him how lucky he was to be alive.

Sarah was so grateful and ecstatic that she and her baby were safe; all she could think about was keeping her baby healthy. She felt the life growing inside of her and she soon decided that she would keep her baby.

"I'm keeping the baby," Sarah told him one evening when Tommy called to check on her.

Tommy was stunned when he heard the news. "Are you sure that this is what you want to do? I mean, don't I have a say in the decision?"

Sarah was quiet, searching for the right words. "In a perfect world, I would consider what you want, but this far from a perfect situation. Don't you think?"

Tommy didn't respond. He didn't know what to say or think. Tommy had mixed emotions. He'd given her space, even though everything inside of him missed her terribly. He figured that it was only a matter of time before she left him, and then he wouldn't have anyone to help him through the hard times, especially now that she had no reason to stay.

Marie would have stuck around, thinking that she would be a rich widow once I died. Sarah isn't like that; she isn't motivated by money. She's one of those people who wants to believe the best in everyone,

After their conversation, he decided that the only hope he had of getting her to stay with him was to play on her sympathies.

I need to ask her to marry me before she comes to her senses.

Chapter 31

AT THE END of the semester, Sarah gave her notice at Corpus Christi State University. Her job felt insignificant after what she had been through over the past few months. She also dropped out of graduate school with only a few more credit hours to go.

Tommy had asked her to marry him, and she had agreed to give the relationship a trial run, partly because she felt obligated to help him and partly because she felt like she couldn't be with anyone else. She couldn't dupe some unsuspecting guy the way Tommy had duped her. And if she were honest with anyone about what Tommy had done to her, they'd drop her like a rock.

But mostly it was because she was pregnant, and Tommy was going to take care of them both.

In early January 1989, with Tommy's help, Sarah moved out of her little apartment in Corpus and moved back to Houston. Tommy was overjoyed that he'd convinced Sarah this was the best thing for her, telling her, "I want you to continue going to Dr. Barrett, and this is the easiest way."

Sarah was doing everything she could to stay calm for the sake of the baby. Unfortunately, it was difficult. And Tommy tried not to show it, but he was petrified.

"Do you kill your baby through an abortion, or do you give birth and watch the child you love die from a horrible disease?" he asked the doctor, who shook his head, saying only, "It's in God's hands now."

We're damned if we do and damned if we don't.

Tommy struggled with his moral dilemma, trying not to show how angry he was at himself once again for getting another woman pregnant by accident.

⤛⬤ ⬤⤜

After Dr. Barrett called her to inform her of Tommy's tests results, Marie and Ricky went to the University Of Victoria Medical Center to be tested for HIV, and fortunately both of their test results were negative. However, instead of feeling blessed that she and her son had dodged a bullet Marie became angry and incensed. Once again, Tommy had screwed with her life and walked away without even a second thought.

Marie went on the war path when she found out that Sarah had moved into Tommy's house. In fact, when she found out about Sarah in mid-February, Marie and Ricky flew to Texas for the Canadian equivalent of Sherman's March to the Sea. Ricky was in school, but Marie pulled him out for their two-week visit to Texas.

Marie invited herself to stay with the Colonel, and while she was there she made sure that Tommy's elderly father know that his son was gay and had AIDS, and that he was probably going to outlive his own son. She also convinced him that his son's new girlfriend was only with him to get her hands on the Colonel's money, saying, "Why else would she move in with your son—especially now?"

The Colonel had heard of AIDS because he watched the nightly news religiously. But he didn't know what the ramifications were for Tommy. And much to Marie's dismay, the Colonel was genuinely concerned for his son's well-being.

"I guess she thought that Colonel Ellison didn't have any more use for Tommy now that he has a grandson." Etta was listening at the door and didn't like the crap Marie was pulling. She called Tommy and said, "The Colonel is in his nineties, and he doesn't fully understand what is going on. That witch is a spiteful woman because the Colonel just getting frail and forgetful. What she is doing to your daddy is just plain wrong!"

Tommy wasn't surprised that Marie had sunk so low as to confront his elderly father about his condition. Even though he'd hopeful that somehow, she cared enough about his father as to spare him.

However, the Colonel understood more than anyone gave him credit for. He wasn't so old that he didn't know what a homosexual was. Marie had finally gotten her pound of flesh.

During her two weeks in Texas, Marie told anyone who would listen that Tommy was gay, that he had AIDS, and that Sarah was probably infected with HIV, too. Sarah was humiliated and horrified. "Things are bad enough without that horrible woman sticking her nose in our private and personal lives. She has no compassion for what we are going through. I can't believe she claims to be a family therapist!" Sarah yelled at Tommy as she ran upstairs and slammed the door to their bedroom.

Sarah wanted to crawl in a hole, and she was pissed off at Tommy because he didn't even say anything to the woman about her horrible behavior.

Sarah wasn't showing yet, and the only people she'd told about her pregnancy were Tommy and her doctors. Tommy hadn't talked to anyone about it, either. He wasn't as confident as Sarah was that things would turn out for the best, and he'd found that it was easier to not deal with his inner demons and the guilt he was feeling by avoiding the subject of Sarah's pregnancy altogether.

But through all of Marie's craziness, Tommy got to see his son for the first time in months. And that meant the world to him. Tommy's future was uncertain to say the least, and he'd take any and all the time with his son he could get.

"I don't give a shit what she does or what she says. All I care about is getting to spend time with my son, Ricky," Tommy explained to Sarah when she complained. "I haven't seen my son in six months, and I couldn't care less about what trouble his mother is causing. No one likes her or believes a word out of her mouth anyway."

Sarah didn't know who to trust. The man she thought loved her was not really acting like her feelings mattered at all. He'd already moved beyond "sorry" and was now acting like a pig. Again, Sarah confronted Tommy about the damage that his ex-wife had done and what she'd had to endure. The conversation started out as a lively discussion but soon turned into a terrific fight, fueled by Tommy's heavy drinking.

"I couldn't care less if I've hurt your sensitive sensibilities. I'm the one who has a disease, and I have every intention of doing what I have to do to keep seeing my son," Tommy sneered.

Sarah was getting her first glimpse of Tommy's self-absorbed, deceitful alcoholic side.

Tommy didn't really see it the same way; he was just surviving the only way he knew how under extraordinary circumstances.

At least I'm staying of the coke, for the love of God!

Before long, Tommy had had enough of both women and arranged a business trip to New York. Tommy had found one of his old lovers who had moved to New York and planned to go to visit him. He was tired of hearing that HIV was a death sentence, and wanted just feel normal again. Tommy had disappeared hundreds of time when he was married to Marie, but this was the first time he'd disappeared on a fake business trip since he started dating Sarah. Sarah wasn't invited on the "business trip," so she stayed home alone in his house for the first time since she moved in.

⋯▬◉ ◉▬⋯

Spring break coincided with Easter that year, and Tommy arranged to go to pick up Ricky for the week. He bought plane tickets for he and Sarah to fly up to Seattle and planned to drive over to Victoria by ferry to stay at a resort on Salt Spring Island. Tommy and Sarah flew into Seattle, where they rented a car, spent the night at the Marriott Hotel downtown, and ate at the restaurant at the top of the Space Needle. It was wonderful to be alone with each other without any distractions; it was almost as it had been when they'd first started dating the year before. Almost, except for the ever-present elephant in the room.

Sarah was now six-months pregnant and could no longer hide the fact that she was carrying a baby. They had found out that the baby was going to be a girl, and best of all, both mother and child continued to test negative for HIV. Tommy had been on his medication for long enough that he was getting encouraging test results back from the doctor, and he'd begun feeling a lot more positive about the future.

The day before they went to pick up Ricky, Tommy turned to Sarah and said, "Before we get on the ferry, we need to get married." Tommy's comment took Sarah by surprise.

She looked at him with a shocked expression on her face, saying, "Really? Today?"

"Yes. Today," he replied. "It's time we make you a respectable woman again. You don't really want our little girl to be illegitimate, do you?" Tommy smiled and kissed his soon-to-be wife on the forehead.

"I know it would sure make my parents happy if we got married," Sarah replied.

She'd told her parents about the baby, and though they were happy they were going to be grandparents, she could tell they were pissed off at Tommy for not putting a wedding ring on their daughter's finger. "My daddy is certainly not happy that we put the cart before the horse."

Tommy took Sarah shopping at a jewelry store a few blocks from their hotel, and they picked out a beautiful set of matching wedding rings, which the jeweler sized for them immediately when he found out about their impending marriage. Sarah was euphoric and giggled as she tried on the different rings. She finally picked out a ring that had a half-carat diamond silhouette surrounded by two diamond begets on each side of the gold band.

"That should make your father happy," Tommy joked to Sarah as he paid the jeweler for the rings. "And I hope that someday I can make you happy, too."

"I am happy," she said as she admired her new wedding ring.

That afternoon, Sarah and Tommy got married in a civil ceremony at the Seattle courthouse.

The next day, Tommy and Sarah set off after breakfast, driving north to Anacortes, Washington, where they would take the car ferry up the Puget Sound and weave in and out of the islands scattered along the southern end of the Northwest Passage to the port of Sidney, British Columbia. The only time Sarah had been out of Texas was when she and her then boyfriend, Todd, would go on trips to Mexico, and she sat and listened quietly as Tommy told her stories of the time he spent in Canada before he'd met Marie.

"I really don't want to hear anything else about your life with Marie," she told him. "What you really should be thinking about is Ricky. You haven't told him that he is going to have a little sister, much less that we got married this afternoon." Sarah cocked her head to the side as she waited for his reaction.

"I'll tell him as soon as I can," Tommy responded anxiously.

Tommy called Marie from a pay phone at a Rite Aid pharmacy on the Pat Bay Highway as soon as they disembarked from the ferry. No one answered. "Marie knew we were coming because I called and confirmed yesterday," Tommy said to Sarah.

He was livid; the divorce wars had started again. "More drama!" he said as he slammed the car door.

Sarah watched as Tommy whipped himself into a frenzy. "Marie is just being passive-aggressive because she knows it will rattle your cage," she said, trying to calm him down.

Driving around Victoria, Tommy called a few more times over several hours until Marie finally answered about seven thirty in the evening. By that time, Tommy's head was about to explode. "Ricky had a birthday party to go to that she'd forgotten to tell me about," he fumed after he hung up. What Tommy didn't know was that Ricky knew they were coming and had started making his mother's life miserable until she finally took him home from the party.

Sarah decided to wait in the car when they got there; she wasn't used to being the center of drama and didn't like it one bit. She was apprehensive about being nice to the woman who had wreaked so much havoc on their lives and didn't know how Tommy's ex-wife would react when she realized that Sarah was pregnant.

Sarah was still wearing baggy clothes to conceal the baby she was carrying, but it only camouflaged her pregnancy enough that it wasn't blatantly obvious. "It's probably a good idea for you to stay in the car while I go get Ricky," Tommy whispered as he got out of the car. "It's just that Marie is unpredictable, and I want to be the one to tell Ricky...before she finds out."

→⊫◎ ◎⊨←

Ricky was so excited to see his daddy that he was running around, jumping on the furniture. He showed his father everything, including his new room and the tree fort that he'd built in the yard.

Weirdly enough, Marie was happy they were there until she realized that Tommy had brought Sarah along—at which point Marie disappeared into her bedroom the way she had the first time she'd met Tommy's sister. When Tommy noticed that Marie was gone, he asked Ricky to take his stuff out to the rental while he searched for his ex-wife to say good-bye.

When Sarah saw Ricky coming out to the car, she got out and gave him a hug. "Are you excited to spend the week with us?" she asked. She could tell that Ricky was thrilled. "Where's your father?" she asked as she opened the trunk for Ricky.

A moment later Tommy came out, shaking his head. He walked to the car and put his son in the back seat. "God, that woman is odd," he said, closing the car door so that Ricky wouldn't hear.

The three of them made it back to the Sidney Ferry Terminal just in time to make the last ferry to Salt Spring Island. By the time they checked into their lodge, it was late. Sarah was happy to see father and son so excited to see each other.

Their week with Ricky couldn't have gone better. The family hiked and biked. They explore the primeval forests of the island and dug for clams on the beach nearby. Ricky behaved well until the last day.

The threesome had checked out of their lodge on Salt Spring Island and headed back to Victoria via the short ferry ride. Tommy had been waiting until the end of the trip to break the news of his new wife and baby to Ricky. Once on the ferry, they parked their car on the deck below and climbed up one flight of stairs to the passenger lounge and sun deck. Tommy gave Ricky some money to buy some food at the snack bar, and as soon as he ran off, Sarah turned to her husband and said, "It's now or never."

"I know, honey. I just wanted him to have a little bit more time before I tell him." Tommy sat in the chair across the table from his new wife. Ricky came back to the table with an armload of cookies, candies, and chips, and a soft drink.

As Ricky sat down, Tommy said, "Son, I have some news for you. Sarah and I got married."

Ricky's wasn't paying much attention to Sarah or his father until that moment. He turned to his father with a blank stare. "My mom told me that it's all Sarah's fault we had to move away. She told me that I can't live with you anymore because of her."

"No, Rick, that wasn't the reason. Your mother and I just had too many fights, and that is why we're not married anymore. It had nothing to do with Sarah. I didn't even know Sarah before your mom and I divorced."

Ricky was eleven years old and in the fifth grade, and Tommy was amazed that his ex-wife would say something so misleading to their son. Ricky stuck out his lip, making an unhappy face, and said, "OK. Is that all, because I want to go out on deck."

"No, there's more. Sarah and I are going to have a baby, and it's a little girl. You're going to have a little sister," Tommy continued.

Jumping to his feet, Ricky yelled at Sarah, "I hate you! You ruined my life! I am going to kill myself!"

Suddenly, Ricky became violent, and he physically attacked Sarah, hitting her and pulling her hair. Sarah had to fight off her stepson's attack on her own. Tommy watched, thunderstruck, not knowing what to do. She was shocked that her husband didn't restrain his son. Ricky was much bigger than Sarah was, even at eleven. She was flabbergasted.

Sarah didn't say a word to Tommy until after they'd dropped Ricky off. "You sat and watched while Ricky physically attached me just for being pregnant! I had to fight back to defend myself! And you did nothing."

"What was I supposed to do?" Tommy simply replied. "It looked like you were taking care of yourself." As the words came out of his mouth, he realized that he'd said the wrong thing.

He'd never seen his son become violent like that toward anyone before, and he was at a loss. "Look, I'm really sorry about what happened on the ferry with Ricky. I expected that he'd act out, but I had no idea he'd become violent," Tommy said apologetically. "Are you hungry? Let's stop and feed you and the baby."

Sarah sat quietly during dinner, playing with her food with her fork, while Tommy sulked about the scene on the ferry. By the time they finished their meal, it was getting late.

"We can make the last ferry to Seattle, but by the time we get there it will be awfully late. We're both tired, so let's stay here tonight and get a fresh start in the morning." Tommy hugged his bride in the parking lot, kissing her gently, and said jokingly as they stood by the car, "You didn't know what you were getting into when you got involved with me."

"No, I didn't." Sarah smiled a little and started to let her guard down once again. "I don't think that it's too much to ask for normal every once in a while."

Chapter 32

Victoria Grace Ellison made her entrance into the world on Monday, July 11, 1987. She was a healthy six pounds, eight ounces, and was born HIV negative. She was a beautiful baby, and all the nurses in the nursery announced that she was the most beautiful baby ever born at that hospital. Shortly before the arrival of his new daughter, Tommy had flown up to Victoria to pick up Ricky and bring him to Texas for the summer.

It had taken blood, hair, and eyeballs to get Marie to allow Ricky to come down for the summer. Tommy had flown up to Victoria five times to visit his son in the year and a half since they'd made the move to Vancouver Island. He finally had to hire an attorney in Canada to renegotiate his visitation. Canada and the United States had a treaty enforcing child support agreements in divorce but didn't have a treaty enforcing the visitation rights of the father.

Marie was a Canadian, and the Canadian courts were definitely more favorable to the complaints of one of their own citizens. "She's accused you of unsubstantiated issues that might muddy the waters," the attorney told Tommy when he called for an update. "Marie is trying to make all your visitations moving forward contingent on an assessment by an officer of the court of your home environment," his attorney continued.

Incensed because Marie had unjustly accused him of being an unfit parent, Tommy took it out on his new wife, putting an undue strain on their relationship. He obsessed over his ex-wife's accusations, totally ignoring his wife. Tommy spent a night at a hotel after Sarah kicked him to the curb for acting like a jerk and drinking way too much. A year before, he would've called one of his boyfriends to wallow in a night of sex and drugs, but this time he didn't. The next day he called his pregnant wife to apologize.

When Ricky got to Texas, Sarah saw that he'd grown like a weed. But Ricky seemed different somehow, and Sarah noticed it right away. His parents had stopped fighting with each other after their divorce but were now fighting over him. Ricky didn't know who to believe when his parents would tell him the terrible things the other one had done; however, neither of them seem overly concerned about the effects it had on Ricky.

Tommy decided to take Ricky to the ranch for the summer to give his wife and newborn daughter some peace and quiet. Tommy and Ricky stayed in the same house he'd lived in with Nana when he was a boy. And while they lived at the ranch, Tommy let Ricky ran wild. Tommy's cousin, Tobin, even taught Ricky how to shoot a gun.

"There's a certain responsibility to teach him how to use it safely, and he's at the age where he needs to learn how to shoot one."

Tommy agreed, telling Ricky, "If your mother finds out that Tobin taught you to shoot, this will be your last visit to Texas until you grow up."

The three agreed to keep it among themselves. Ricky liked killing things and blowing things up with fireworks.

When she heard that a boy so young was running wild with a gun, Sarah was appalled. Still stinging from her stepson's attack on the ferry, she thought that giving Ricky a gun wasn't the best idea. But when she tried to talk to Tommy about it, he dismissed her, saying, "You're overreacting."

Tommy defended his son's wild behavior. "Ricky is just blowing off steam. I've been spending summers at the ranch since I was his age."

That was code for "mind your own business," and Sarah realized that this was a fight she couldn't win. She was happy to be in Houston with baby Vicky, leaving Tommy and Ricky to their male bonding.

Sarah was sad to see the disturbing changes in the boy's personality. When he had been in Texas, he was tough, and would be defiant, saying to her, "My mother says that I don't have to listen to you."

Complaining to Tommy was useless, as it fell on deaf ears. "I'm concerned that Tommy has stopped acting like a parent and is trying to be the boy's best friend," she told Ricky's child psychologist on one of their visits. "I understand Tommy's point of view—he has so little time with the boy that he wants to make long-lasting memories to make up for the fact that Ricky was whisked away from his father to Canada. But I believe the boy needs a certain amount of discipline or he'll never learn right from wrong."

On the other hand, Sarah felt immensely blessed that she and the baby were healthy. "I just wish Tommy could see how lucky he is to have a healthy wife and child, instead of battling his ex-wife all the time." Sarah was tired of the drama that Marie created, and worse, she was tired of her husband's reaction to that drama.

"It's the dance of anger," the therapist replied. "The dance will continue until one of them decides to stop."

While they spent most of their summer at Peach Tree Ranch and at the Colonel's house in Black Rock, Tommy periodically returned to Houston to check on his wife and newborn, bringing Ricky with him. Sarah was apprehensive about Ricky being around his baby sister, especially after the initial aggression he'd showed when he found out she was pregnant. However, much to her surprise, Ricky was loving and gentle with his little sister.

At the end of the summer Ricky and Tommy went to child psychiatrist, this time in the Houston area, for Ricky's debriefing. This child psychiatrist was a jovial lady. She said, "It's better for Ricky in the long run to defuse the difference between his parents and deescalate the war so that he won't be caught in the middle." But even though she was supposed to be impartial, it was obvious that she'd been won over by Tommy's charms, and she wrote a glowing report on his behalf.

→═◉ ◉═←

After having the time of his life, Ricky went home at the end of the summer with a huge chip on his shoulder. He resented his mother's interference and started acting out more and more. Marie's relationship with Ricky had always been like a tempest; huge fights would break out, and sometimes Marie would spank the boy. But as he'd gotten older and bigger, Ricky had become a force to be reckoned with.

It was a blessing that Ricky got to spend so much time with his grandfather, because the Colonel's health was declining. He'd just turned ninety-six. If he hung on for four more years, he'd make it to the century mark, but honestly no one thought that was really going to happen.

The death watch had begun, and it was Etta Mae's job to keep the buzzards at bay so they wouldn't pick the old man's bones clean before he passed. Tommy was particularly worried about unscrupulous charlatans who wouldn't think twice about talking a feeble old man into signing over the deed to his land or something worse.

Etta helped out in any way she could, arranging to have someone at the house with the Colonel 24-7 and taking note of his vital signs every few hours. Tommy kept a close watch on Minerva, who'd been given strict orders not to allow his father to sign anything without Tommy's approval.

One week after Ricky went home to Canada, Tommy got a panicked call from Etta. "The sheriff and someone from adult protective services stopped by to check on the Colonel." Her voice cracked when she spoke. "Someone's reported elder abuse at your daddy's home, and they're here to do a welfare check."

They spent about thirty minutes to an hour checking on the Colonel, but after the inspection they left, finding that the complaint was unfounded. "I know that you're taking perfectly good care of the Colonel," the sheriff told Etta Mae apologetically. "But we received an anonymous complaint, and we are required by law to check it out."

After packing his bag, Tommy drove to Black Rock to make sure his father was safe. "I've been so obsessed with my son that I feel like I've neglected the other people in my life," he told Sarah as he packed. "I know I haven't given you and Vicky as much of my time as I should have, and I'm sorry." He kissed his wife good-bye.

"I have to admit, I thought things would be different when Vicky was born," she confessed as he opened the car door. "And I'd be lying if I told you the crap from Marie didn't play on my last nerve."

Tommy closed the door and rolled down the window. "We are at her mercy until Ricky grows up, and there's nothing I can do about it," Tommy said gently as he stroked her cheek. "I just hope you don't give up on me."

Etta was sitting in her chair by the kitchen door as if she were guarding it. She stood up and walked up to the car when Tommy pulled up. He asked Etta to tell him what had happened.

"Well, the sheriff and some caseworker knocked on the door and asked to see the Colonel because somebody had called them and told them we were mistreating your daddy." She had calmed down considerably since she'd first called Tommy. "They went through the house and checked the records the nurses had been taking every day. Then they sat in the living room and talked to the Colonel. After talking to your daddy for about fifteen minutes, they left."

Etta was a proud woman, and it rubbed her the wrong way for anyone to imply that she wasn't taking good care of Colonel Ellison. "I followed them outside, and they told me they couldn't find any evidence of abuse. Hmph! I told them so when they got here, but they had to see for themselves."

"I appreciate what you've done for my daddy," Tommy said as he opened the kitchen door. "You didn't hear if they said anything to daddy about why they were here?" He spoke quietly now that he was in the house.

"Not to my knowledge." That meant no for Etta, because Tommy knew darn good and well that she hadn't let the sheriff and the caseworker out of her sight.

"Thank God! He's a helpless old man, and he deserves to die quietly in his own home," he whispered as he pushed opened the door to the dining room.

Etta heaved a sigh as she heard Tommy's booming voice in the living room. "Hello, daddy. What are you reading?"

Chapter 33

TOMMY WAS WOKEN up by the unnatural howling of Toby, the neighbor's dog. It wasn't the dog's normal bay or bark; it was a mournful kind of cry. Tommy rolled over and checked the clock. It was 3:30 a.m. He got up and went to the bathroom. As he was crawling back in bed, the phone rang. It was Willie, the Colonel's night nurse. "I'm sorry to be calling at this hour, but I need to let you know that the Colonel passed away just a few minutes ago."

Tommy sprang out of bed in disbelief. "I had almost started to believe he was immortal." He sat quietly for a minute and then asked Willie to call Etta. "Could you please ask her to call the funeral home to take care of daddy? I'll get dressed, and be there as soon as I can." He hung up with Willie.

Sarah was up and standing behind him; she'd overheard most of the conversation. Shaking his head, Tommy still couldn't believe that his father was gone. "Will you get Vicky up and pack our bags for the funeral? We need to leave as quickly as we can."

Putting on a pair of pants, Tommy went downstairs and called his attorney, Randolph Meyers. "Sorry for waking you, but daddy just passed away. Sarah and I will be heading to Black Rock within the hour."

The Colonel's had usually been kept in the safe at the office, but after the sheriff and caseworker showed up at his father's house, Tommy had put in his briefcase and brought it home with him. Unless there was a newer version floating around somewhere, Tommy was going to be sure his daddy's will didn't disappear.

When the county clerk showed up for work, she was surprised to find Tommy sitting on steps in front of the courthouse. "What the hell are you doing here at this ungodly hour?"

Getting up slowly after sitting on the cold concrete steps, Tommy stretched as he replied, "I'm here to probate my father's will and file the paperwork for a temporary administrator."

She patted Tommy on the hand, saying, "I'm sorry for your loss. I was beginning to think your daddy was bulletproof."

Tommy laughed. "So did everybody else."

→▶◎ ◎◀←

The Colonel Richard Ellison passed away four years short of his one hundredth birthday, and his funeral was held three days after he died at the Methodist Church, as the Episcopal Church was too small to handle the overflowing crowd of people from all over the world who had come to pay their respects. The Episcopal Archbishop of Texas presided over the funeral, as well as three other Episcopal priests.

Tommy called Marie and asked her to allow Ricky to come to Texas for his grandfather's funeral. Tommy was sick of having to choke back his words and be nice to the woman, especially now that he suspected that Marie and Minerva were behind the complaint with adult protectives services. Much to his surprise, Marie said yes and had the gall to ask Tommy if he would buy her a plane ticket to come to the Colonel's funeral with Ricky. "No," Tommy emphatically replied.

"Man, that woman has some nerve! Now I know she's truly insane," he angrily told his wife when he hung up the phone. Minerva was Marie's only ally, and he suspected that Minerva was sending her money out of one of the Colonel's checking account against, not only his wishes, but also the Colonel's wishes. Over the past few years, the Colonel only barely tolerated her because she had taken his grandson to Canada. It never occurred to her that taking Ricky to Canada would destroy any respect he had for that woman.

Tommy had taken care of this before he'd even called Marie. He'd filed the paperwork as soon as the courthouse opened, and now no one could touch any of the Colonel's property without coming through him. When he called Angelica from his cell phone on the way to Black Rock, one of his instructions was to give Minerva her walking papers as soon as she got to work.

Ricky flew by himself for the funeral; he'd just turned thirteen and was old enough cross the Canadian border by himself. Tommy believed that Marie was finding it harder and harder to cause trouble in his life, mostly because he was always on the lookout for any treachery.

The Colonel was buried in the family plot next to his wife, Babe, who had died almost twenty years before. Tommy hadn't even been to see his mother since her funeral.

Now they can fight in eternity.

After the graveside service ended, several people came over to the Colonel's house for lunch. Some stayed just for an hour or so, and others stayed for several hours to help clean up. Etta Mae and two of her daughters helped to feed the crowd. It was late afternoon before the crowd thinned out and Tommy and Sarah could sit down to ponder the somber events of the day and what their next move would be.

"I guess we watch and wait," Tommy said as he kicked off his cowboy boots and put his feet up on the coffee table next to the Colonel's empty rocking chair.

⇥▬◉ ◉▬⇤

It wasn't long after the funeral when the shit hit the fan. Within a week of the Colonel's funeral, several multimillion-dollar lawsuits were filed against Tommy and father's estate.

The first one Marie filed on behalf of their son to remove Tommy as the executor and trustee of any money that that the Colonel had given to Ricky. Amazingly, her suit was withdrawn within a week.

"She probably withdrew it as soon as her attorney asked her who was going to pay his legal fees," Tommy told Randolph Meyers as they sat in his office on the twenty-third floor of the Texas Commerce Tower in downtown Houston, where the two men were discussing legal strategies and circling the wagons.

He'd seen Minerva at the funeral, glaring at him the whole time. "I should have known she was up to something." He told his attorney. "She had to move in with her son after I fired her, and I'm sure she blames it all on me."

"Now that she and Minerva don't have access to the Colonel's accounts, Marie'd have to pay for it herself," Tommy continued, rubbing his forehead because he was starting to get a headache.

Another lawsuit was filed against the Colonel's estate by Tommy's cousin, Ernie, the grandson of Aunt Mildred, who claimed that an oil-and-gas lease on Aunt Mildred's land outside of Black Rock was invalid. The Colonel had drilled several successful oil wells, and Ernie and his family wanted Tommy off their land.

This was a real problem, because the shallow wells on Aunt Mildred's property made a lot of money for the whole family, not just Tommy. "I can't just walk away from millions of dollars' worth of oil and gas just because Ernie never worked out his childhood inadequacies," Tommy declared as he frantically paced around Mr. Meyers office.

His sister, Beverly, filed the last lawsuit, claiming that Tommy and the Colonel had mismanaged their trusts established when their mother passed away twenty years earlier. Tommy couldn't believe his eyes when he read their petition.

"I hate to believe that Minerva was right all those years about Bob, but damn it, she was!" Tommy gritted his teeth, slamming his desk drawer. This latest lawsuit had stunned Tommy. "He was using his position as my business partner to find my Achilles' heel so that they could go in for the kill after my dad died," he said in disbelief.

But Bob had sorely underestimated Tommy. Five years earlier, Tommy had been a mess, but with Sarah's patience, love, and unwavering support, he'd cleaned his life up and wasn't about to let his chickenshit relatives destroy his father's legacy.

As soon as he found out about the lawsuit, Tommy kicked Bob out of his office and canceled the gas contracts the oil company had with the pipeline company, telling Bob that he was going to shove the pipeline debt down his throat. Although he'd been expecting people to file claims against his father's estate—they always did—he felt blindsided and betrayed. The lawsuits by his greedy relatives were particularly nasty and frankly were hitting below the belt. Tommy was particularly incensed that his own family couldn't wait till his father was cold in the ground before they started grabbing for the money.

"Every single one of those people who are claiming my daddy was a crook came to his funeral and cried," he told Sarah as he mixed himself a stiff drink coming home late in the evening after spending the day with lawyers.

The stress Tommy was under was beginning to show. Although he had cleaned up his life after he married Sarah, he had started drinking heavier than ever before, as the betrayal he felt from his sister and her husband and the rest of his family was more than he could bear. Eventually, the stress from constantly battling family took a heavy toll on Tommy's health, and eventually, he was forced to file for bankruptcy. The claims against his father's estate far exceeded the net worth of that estate. Sickened by circumstances beyond his control, Tommy watched in shame as his father's dynasty crumbled.

All my life I'd expected to step into my father's shoes, and in a matter of just a few months, it's all gone!

Book Four

We are all in the gutter, but some of us are looking at the stars.

—Oscar Wilde

Chapter 34

WHEN TOMMY WENT in for his next checkup, Dr. Barrett told him that his count was spiraling downward at a rapid pace. "Your T-cell count has dipped down below one hundred," Dr. Barrett said calmly as he broke the bad news.

Tommy's T-cell count had been stable for several years. This was the news Tommy had always dreaded, and it couldn't have come at a worse time. He'd survived longer than most, but AIDS was always in the back of his mind.

"I'm putting you on a new experimental antiviral drug that's just been approved by the FDA," the doctor continued. "It has shown promising results in keeping the virus from replicating. I'm very hopeful this will help you." He wrote out the prescription, handing it to Tommy as he left his office. "Don't give up hope, Tommy; you still have a fighting chance."

Almost immediately, Tommy became withdrawn and even more depressed. He was in a dark, dark place since he'd gotten the bad news from the doctor. Sarah tried to be as compassionate as possible, but Tommy didn't want to hear about Sarah's happy little life or experience her sunny disposition. Tommy started eating a lot, gaining several pounds in a matter of weeks and telling Sarah when she complained, "If I get full-blown AIDS, I want to have plenty of weight on me so it will take me longer to wither away."

However, it wasn't just eating that had caused his weight gain. Tommy had started drinking heavily again, polishing off a fifth of whiskey each and every night, on top of being already drunk when he came home from work.

After a few months on his new medication, Tommy started showing signs of improvement, but even though his HIV viral load was back under control, he'd started having problems with his gallbladder. Tommy was in constant pain, and he went to the doctor, who ran a battery of tests on him. "Your blood work shows that your liver enzymes are out of kilter, and it is my opinion that you need to have your gallbladder removed," Doctor Barrett informed him after his examination.

The doctor scheduled the surgery, thinking it would be routine, but there were serious complications. Tommy was put into the intensive care unit after surgery because his gallbladder had grown between the lobes of his liver. The surgeon had to take out part of his liver as well in order to remove gallbladder.

In the waiting room, Sarah became concerned when the surgery took longer than expected. When the surgeon finally came in to talk to her, he said, "Tommy has the worst case of cirrhosis of liver that I have ever seen in the thirty-nine-years I've been a surgeon."

Sarah gasped and began to tremble. She fought back tears as the surgeon continued.

"If your husband makes it through the night, it will be a miracle. He's in ICU. I did what I could. If he makes it out of the hospital, he has to stop drinking and take care of what's left of his liver. He'll never be eligible for a transplant because of his autoimmune disease."

Falling back into her chair as her knees buckled, Sarah was in shock. The doctor had just told her that there was a distinct possibility she was about to be a widow. Sarah always worried about her husband's health and often thought that he'd stopped trying because his life was too overwhelming; Every time he caught a break, life kicked him in the teeth again.

When Sarah went into the ICU and saw her husband hooked up to the machine with a plastic drain bag taped to his side, it finally hit her. "I really could lose him," she said under her breath. Sarah sat down beside his bed, holding his hand. Not knowing what else she could do, she began to pray.

<hr/>

After four long days in ICU, Tommy woke up and his status was upgraded from critical to stable. Soon he was moved to a regular hospital room, where he spent another week before being sent home. "My gallbladder surgery was supposed to be a simple procedure," he whispered faintly to Sarah, recalling that the surgeon had planned to remove it laparoscopically.

"It was supposed to be simple," Sarah explained. "But as soon as the surgeon realized how serious your condition was, he cut a gash in the middle of your stomach. You lost a lot of blood during the procedure because it wasn't clotting, and they removed your gallbladder and part of your liver—and your belly button when he sewed you back up."

Sarah didn't want to be so brutally honest, but she couldn't lie to him. She defended the surgical team because she knew how low Tommy had sunk. "The doctors did what they had to do to save your life."

The drain tube was still protruding out of the side of his stomach; it was a nasty, smelly mess, and the stuff coming out of the tube looked like week-old chili-mac.

Tommy was forever changed that day. He could no longer deny the inevitability of death, and he'd sell his soul to the devil if he could go back to his childhood and start over. He'd always feared dying from AIDS, but he never feared the hepatitis the same way. But between the hepatitis, his alcoholism, and the cocktail of drugs he took daily to combat the HIV, his liver was shot. He'd always made fun of Dr. Barrett when he nagged him to stop drinking and to take care of his liver.

Now I wish I'd listened to the old coot.

However, he'd never listened to the man, thinking all doctors were alarmist and yelling, "The sky is falling," whenever he went to an appointment. After surviving a near-death experience, Tommy now looked back at his life and he didn't like what he saw. Instead of counting his blessings and being thankful for the second chance, Tommy looked in the mirror and asked "why me?" After all, he'd withstood so much adversity in his lifetime that he was slowly but surely becoming jaded, refusing to accept any responsibility for the path he'd chosen to follow in life.

Sarah watched the man she'd fallen in love with change into someone she didn't even recognize. She'd always been naïve and had a very simplistic view of people, but she watched in disbelief as her husband turned into a hateful monster who lashed out vengefully at anyone who dared challenge him.

"I've been hoping for the best for him way too long," she said to the nurse as they put him in the car to take him home from the hospital. "I don't know what else I can do to help him."

The nurse looked at her sternly as she shut the car door, saying. "You can't do anything to save him if he doesn't want to be saved."

⊷⊷◉ ◉⊷⊷

The first thing Tommy wanted when they got home was to take a shower. Sarah went down to the kitchen to get the Saran Wrap so they could protect his abdomen as he bathed. She froze in the doorway of the bathroom, finding Tommy naked in front of the bathroom mirror looking at his image for the first time since his surgery.

The tortured look on his face told the whole story. The once-handsome man was staring at his stiches. His wound was at least twelve-inches long, going from one side of his stomach to the other; his belly button was gone, and a plastic tube protruded from a gaping hole in his side, oozing a reddish-brown puss from his abdominal cavity.

Without a word, Sarah put the on latex gloves on and wrapped Tommy's body like the nurses in the hospital had shown her with the plastic wrap so that he could take his first shower in almost three weeks. After she'd finished, she turned on the water and, without saying a word, left Tommy to his shower.

Tommy was still shaky as he balanced on the bathroom counter with his right hand and slowly limped to the shower. Holding onto the wall, he opened the shower door, turned the water on, and let it run until it got hot. Tommy let the hot water roll down his back. Taking the bar of soap from the soap dish, he rubbed it until a lather foamed up between his hands.

I've never felt as filthy as I do at this moment.

Scrubbing his armpits with a soapy washcloth, he wanted nothing more than to get rid of the stench.

As he opened the shower door and reached for a towel, Tommy wondered why his life was cursed.

I was supposed to the king of the world. Why has God punished me? I didn't ask to be born into this life! What did I do to deserve the suffering I've had to live with?

The scars from the surgery weren't his only wounds He was bitter, twisted, and mad as hell that his life had not turned out the way he'd envisioned. His entire life he'd done everything that he was expected to do, only to end up living a disappointing and unfulfilled existence. Tommy had given up on pretending that he still had any hope and had decided that he was going to punish everyone who had defied him.

Tommy recuperated for just a few weeks, and a month after his surgery he went back to work to rebuild his companies with new determination and resolve to crush his greedy relatives and put an end to their defiance once and for all.

I'm not going to be that stupid patsy that lets his greedy relatives sue their way into the family fortune. This crap stops now!

⋯▸▪◉ ◉▪◂⋯

In the fall of 1995, with help from a team of lawyers, Tommy finally resolved the lawsuits against his late father's estate. It had taken four and a half years and three and a half million dollars in legal fees, but Tommy managed to negotiate an end to all the legal claims against the Colonel's estate.

A few months later, he received a call from one of Etta Mae's daughter, "my mother passed away yesterday."

"I'm very sorry for your loss." He said sympathetically. Etta was getting old, and he'd been expecting to hear news like this sooner or later.

"Her service is tomorrow, and we were wondering if you would speak at her service?" Her voice cracked as she spoke.

"Of course," he replied. "I loved Etta very much."

The next morning Tommy, Sarah, and Victoria drove to the Mount Bethel Baptist Church in Black Rock, and as they parked in the back of the parking lot, saw Beverly, William and Candice out in front of the church with a group of Etta's family.

"I thought she'd move to Mexico already." Tommy bristled as he opened the car door.

After their lawsuit was settled, he'd heard his sister, and her husband sold their river oaks mansion, and moved to a hacienda in San Miguel de Allende, buying a beautiful old house she'd redecorated, and had been featured in a design magazine.

"Please, just try to be nice." Sarah told him before that got out of the car. "We're here to pay our respects to Etta, not fight with your sister."

The small wood frame church was overflowing with well-wisher, and Sarah, and Victoria stood outside with Beverly, and her grown children, while he gave Etta's eulogy on the pitfalls of vanity and riches.

"When Jesus returns from glory, he's not going to be driving a Cadillac with golf clubs in the back," he railed.

Ironically, Tommy was finally rich, but the cost to his personal life, his family, and the people around him was catastrophic. The sweet, considerate, romantic man Sarah had loved deeply was gone. Now he was sick and bitter. "Your father is not the man I married," she told her daughter as she tried to protect her from her father's insults, thinking that she could somehow understand. However, her mother gave her credit, and the child understood more than one might think.

Victoria was almost nine years old and was in the fourth grade. Tommy had been so focused on defeating the greedy relatives who'd stabbed him in the back after his father died that he wasn't around to be a real father to Victoria. He'd missed most of her young childhood. Tommy wasn't physically gone; he was present most every night. But he was so fixated on his problems that he wasn't emotionally present. Victoria had been invisible to her father most of her life.

In addition, more and more red flags were going up about Ricky all the time, and Tommy was so obsessed with his legal problems that he didn't even notice. Ricky was a latchkey kid and had started doing whatever he wanted without any supervision. By the time he turned fourteen, Ricky was out of control, and now that he was seventeen, he getting in trouble at school and rebelling against his mother. He was drinking and doing drugs, and starting to get in trouble with the law. Marie was helpless to control her son and at her wit's end, and so began calling the police and having her own son hauled off to jail.

Marie called Tommy on several occasions asking for help, but Tommy's only answer was, "If you don't want Ricky, I will be glad to take him." Tommy had been encouraging Ricky's bad behavior for years, telling the boy, "You can come live with me if things get too bad between you and your mother."

Nevertheless, Marie would rather die than let her son move to Texas. She didn't want to face the fact that she was a failure as a mother. Besides, her family therapy practice was barely breaking even and the child support was the only thing keeping her head above water. So Marie decided to put Ricky in a boarding school north of Victoria called Schengen Lake School. In the fall, Ricky was shipped off to school, saying, "Maybe they can do something with him.

Secretly, Sarah was relieved that Ricky wouldn't be coming to Texas to live with them. She felt guilty about it, but life with Tommy was incredibly complicated, and she was pretty much raising Vicky by herself. She was panic-stricken anytime Ricky was around, especially after he attacked her years before. Ricky was bigger than she was now, and Sarah had begun to speculate that there was something more wrong with him than bad parenting.

"He's a powder keg waiting to explode, and Tommy doesn't want to hear anything about my concerns," Sarah told her parents when they came to visit.

Things had changed for Tommy. He looked at Sarah differently now; he was no longer attracted to his wife. They'd been married for over nine years, and they'd never even had time to take a honeymoon because of crisis after crisis after crisis. He had lost interest in even trying to fix things, and their marriage was strained to the breaking point. The two of them drifted apart more and more each day, and frankly, Tommy couldn't care less. All he wanted was to repair the damage inflicted on his businesses.

After his business failed, Tommy started taking long business trips staying gone for weeks at a time, and when he got home Sarah would confront him, accusing him of cheating on her with men. Tommy always denied it. "It was just a fantasy, and that part of my life is over." He'd laugh and say, "You're the only one I love."

Frustrated, Sarah knew in her heart of hearts that his denial was a lie. Nevertheless, she had no proof, and being the experienced attorney that he was, she knew he'd never admit to cheating, even if she caught him red-handed. Finding herself hurt and angry all the time, Sarah decided that she had to do something or her life would implode. "If I don't do something to save myself, I will wind up just like Tommy's mother, a lonely old drunk whose only friend was the housekeeper."

Vicky was already in school, and so when Sarah's friend, Glenda, referred her to a job opening at an environmental engineering firm, Sarah jumped at the opportunity.

"You need to get a job and save up money if you are even thinking about leaving your husband," Glenda told Sarah when she gave her the number to call. "If you leave him now the way things are, he'll put you and your daughter out on the street with nothing."

Tommy flipped out when Sarah told him that she'd gotten a job. It had been so long since she had worked that he'd forgotten she had an engineering degree. Worried and jealous, he was not happy about it. From his perspective, she was trying to escape the gravitational pull of their marriage right when he'd finally gotten his life back and things were going his way. Seeing this as a sign that a divorce was imminent, Tommy went to work making sure that she'd take nothing with her. He controlled the family finances, and he wasn't about to go through another nasty divorce. He'd neglected to ask Sarah to sign a prenuptial agreement before they married, and after what he'd been through since the Colonel passed away, he didn't trust anyone, not even Sarah. Tommy had long seen Sarah as a dog with no teeth, and he was going to keep it that way.

The moment Sarah got a job, it upset the equilibrium. Sarah started to get her confidence back, and now she was receiving a paycheck from people who respected her, Sarah's world no longer revolved around Tommy. She made friends at work, and eventually she really opened up to them about what was going on in her marriage. For the first time since she'd been married, her friends weren't beholden to her husband, and as she began to open up to them, they started giving her their advice as well as their support.

"I am the only one who is trying to fix our marriage. I can't make him try. He has to want to try," she told her new girlfriends.

"If you think the man is cheating on you, why don't you hire a private investigator and get proof," Angie, the bookkeeper, suggested one day when they were eating lunch in the office.

Sarah sat thoughtfully for a moment and then said, "Those guys are expensive. I don't have any money to pay for a PI."

"You're getting a paycheck! I know, because I'm the one who writes them. Save up until you have enough to pay for a PI to have your husband followed," Angie said as she got up to throw away her trash. "Who knows if the PI will catch him cheating or not. Either way, you'll know for sure, and then you can decide what to do next."

Sarah opened up a new savings account at a separate bank and saved her paychecks until she had enough to have her husband followed. Unfortunately, it didn't take long before the PI confirmed her suspicions. When she read the report, she began to cry, and that night she started sleeping in the guest room, crying herself to sleep each night.

Sarah continued to have Tommy followed by her PI off and on over the course of a year. She eventually handed over the evidence to a divorce attorney named Eric Schuff, who'd been highly recommended.

"I don't want to destroy the man, but I've seen what he does to people who defy him, and I don't really want to be his next victim," Sarah told the lawyer as she handed him the videotape.

"The video is pretty graphic," Eric told her after he watched it. "I'll put it in our office safe until you decide what you're going to do."

He continued. "The one thing that concerns me the most is the age of the prostitutes your husband is picking up. They are young, and it will get ugly if you ever have to go to court. You really need to be prepared mentally and emotionally to do battle with this man."

Before she left, Mr. Schuff gave her the number of an excellent therapist who could help her. She really didn't want a divorce, but she couldn't live that way anymore. And she knew without a doubt that Tommy was an excellent attorney who considered any kind of betrayal an act of war.

The next day at work, Angie asked her how it went with the lawyer.

"When your husband is cheating on you with a woman, the ground rules are understood and a person can fight fire with fire. When your husband is cheating on you with a man, your ego is crushed on an order of magnitude that cannot be explained unless you experience it firsthand," she explained to Angie on their lunch break.

"If you're not going to leave him, at least get him back by taking a lover. It is an eye for an eye," Angie encouraged, looking around to see if anyone was listening.

"Nope," Sarah replied while laughing at her friend. "I think I'll go to the shrink instead. It's a lot less messy!"

Before long, Sarah made an appointment with the psychologist Mr. Scuff had referred to her. Her name was Millie Barns. Millie was an older woman in her sixties with salt-and-pepper hair cut short off her collar. Millie wore glasses that hung from a chain around her neck. Sarah started going to therapy once a week on her lunch break.

After a couple of months, Millie leaned forward in her chair and looked Sarah in the eye. "Look, Sarah, I do not understand why you are still married to this man. Are you more afraid of a divorce than staying married to him?"

Sarah shrank down in her chair and shook her head. "I don't know," she replied timidly.

"You really don't need therapy. What you need is to go to your divorce attorney and be done with it. I was hoping you'd come to this conclusion on your own, and I really believe that deep down in your heart you know you've done the best you can. I'm not saying that Tommy is a bad person—I don't make those kinds of judgments. But what I'm telling you is that it's my belief that too much has happened between you two, and unless both of you are willing to do the work to fix your marriage, then it will be impossible to save."

Sarah didn't reply. She sat emotionless in the chair across from her therapist, her hands folded in her lap, staring out the window with a blank look on her face.

After a brief pause that seem like forever, Millie asked, "Do you think both of you are willing to put in the time to fix your marriage?"

Sarah turned to her and said, "No, I don't."

"Then I think you have your answer," the therapist replied.

Sarah was distracted on the drive back to her office, hardly noticing anything until she found herself pulling into the parking garage. Parking her car in the usual spot, Sarah sat there for a few moments. Then taking a deep breath, she took her cell phone out of her purse, called Eric Schuff, and told him that she wanted to file for divorce.

"I'll have the paperwork ready to sign tomorrow," he replied.

Chapter 35

TOTALLY CAUGHT OFF guard when Sarah asked him to leave because she'd filed for divorce, Tommy stormed upstairs, packed a suitcase, and slammed the front door behind him. Unlike his first wife who'd caught him with a dick in his mouth, he never saw it coming. He knew Sarah was unhappy because she'd been sleeping in the guest room for almost a year and sometimes he found her crying for no reason. He never could figure out why, Sarah and Tommy had been married almost ten years, and it never occurred to him that she would actually leave him, no matter how unhappy she was.

She's kicked me out before and always let me come home.

Tommy got a hotel room the Hyatt Regency downtown for the night. She had met him in the driveway when he came home from work and told him that she changed the locks on the door. Sarah had let him in the house to get a toothbrush and a change of clothes, but that was it.

"You have plenty of that stuff at the ranch," Sarah yelled up the stairs while he was packing. Tommy wanted to say good-bye to Vicky, but Sarah had made sure their daughter wasn't around when she asked him to leave.

Tommy didn't want to go to the ranch; he just wanted to get drunk at the hotel bar. So he checked in and headed for the bar, and by chance, he bumped into his old friend Lucas Damon in the hotel lobby. Lucas shook his Tommy's hand, asking him how he was.

"Why, pretty good for a man whose wife just kicked him out of his own house," Tommy joked.

"Maybe if you were more honest about being gay you wouldn't keep getting divorced," Lucas replied smugly.

Heading to the bar for a drink, Tommy invited Lucas to come along. As the two sat down at a table in the middle of the room, Tommy asked him for his advice. Lucas was getting older. It had been almost thirty-five years since Tommy had first met him at Ziggy's in Austin the night after the house fire.

Finally, Tommy asked, "Could you represent me in my divorce? Sarah's already got an attorney, and this one means business."

Lucas thought for a moment and then agreed to help him. He asked, "Have you been served yet?"

Tommy answered, "No." He froze, suddenly realizing how easy it would be for the wife he'd taken for granted to mess up everything.

"You need to disappear in the morning and stay gone until we come up with a game plan," Lucas advised Tommy. "You need make sure that all your separate property is neatly buttoned up and that the community property is broke so that your wife will get nothing."

The next day, Tommy stopped by his office to let Angelica know that he was leaving. He instructed Angelica what to do. "If Sarah calls looking for me, tell her that you don't know where I am."

Tommy was going to Hot Springs, Arkansas. He'd met a young handsome man named Eddie who was from there several years back, and he would often stop by to spend time with Eddie while on business trips. Tommy was sure his wife hadn't a clue about his Arkansas boyfriend, and he knew that if he needed to disappear, Arkansas was the place to go.

When he'd first met Eddie, Tommy liked him instantly, mostly because he was different. Eddie was unpretentious, and Tommy thought he was a lot of fun. Sarah had started off being supportive and understanding about his HIV, but over time he realized that she really didn't comprehend what he was facing. "There's a lot of difference in the way she and I view things," he'd told his new friend Eddie. "She's compassionate, but her expectations are unrealistic."

"It sounds like she wanted you to turn your back on your attractions to men and pretend that you don't feel that way anymore." Eddie had perceived his problem without further explanation. "You're a leopard, and how can a leopard change his spots?"

Tommy had never stopped enjoying having sex with men—he'd just had to work harder to hide it from Sarah than he did when he was married to Marie. Tommy visited his new friend as much as he could, and Eddie allowed Tommy a kind of sexual freedom he hadn't had in a long time. His sexual preferences were more on the dark side; Eddie enjoyed multiple partners and exposed Tommy to bondage and sadomasochistic games. They often went to the seedy sex clubs around Houston. Tommy had been spending a lot of time with his new boyfriend, exploring a more exciting side of his sexuality.

Tommy was bored with monogamy, and he was finding himself attracted to younger men. He'd picked up a handsome young thing on a street corner in Montrose, only to find out later that he was a fifteen-year-old runaway. Nevertheless, Tommy didn't care, and he didn't think anyone would ever find out. Tommy justified his behavior by telling himself that he was helping the kid out. He picked up the boy a few more times, but one day the kid disappeared. Tommy convinced himself, "If they're selling it on the street, they're fair game."

Eddie didn't judge him. That's what Tommy liked about him.

"I'm sure she's doesn't know about any of my lovers; Sarah is just a paper tiger," he told Eddie. "I think Lucas will help me get a quick divorce, and after that, I'll be free and able to live the way I've always wanted to."

⇥▅ ▅⇤

After a couple of weeks in Arkansas with his lover, Tommy got a call from Lucas telling him that it was time to come home. "Your wife's attorney served divorce papers to Angelica since she refused to give out the location of her boss in hiding."

Fortunately, the two weeks he'd spent in Hot Springs had given his staff enough time to tidy up the paper trail.

Tragically, the whole time he was hiding out in Arkansas, Tommy never once thought about how his actions were affecting his daughter, Victoria. Vicky had a part in the school play, and her father had promised that he'd come. On her big night, Vicky searched the audience for her dad, realizing that he wasn't coming.

On the way home, Sarah saw how upset Vicky was. Once again, Tommy had selfishly broken his daughter's heart.

The day her mother asked her father to leave, Victoria wasn't surprised. When her mother told her she was getting a divorce, she'd said, "What took you so long?"

Before he agreed to leave, Tommy had demanded to talk to Victoria. "Your mother has asked me to leave," he told her. "You have a school play tomorrow night, and I will be there. I have every intention of still being a good father, even though your mother doesn't want me around."

At the school play the following evening, Victoria looked for her father in the audience, and on her way home she told her mother, "He lied to me again."

"I am so sorry, sweetheart." Sarah patted her on the hand.

"You shouldn't be sorry. You didn't make him lie. He lies a lot." Sarah was shocked and saddened. She'd always done what she could to protect her daughter from her father's lack of empathy for others. "You should've divorced him sooner."

→══ ══←

Tommy leased an expensive high-rise apartment close to downtown in the hip, up-and-coming part of Houston, with plenty of nightlife in the neighborhood. But it wasn't long after he moved in that Tommy realized he was the oldest one in the building. Felling lonely and out of place in his expensive apartment, Tommy sorely missed Sarah and Victoria. His apartment was trendy, and Eddie had helped to pick it out. Nonetheless, it lacked a homey feel. They were the family he'd always longed for, and he knew they were gone. Secretly, Tommy started to see that life without Sarah wasn't everything he'd fantasized it would be.

This wasn't his first divorce, but this time was different. Tommy was older than he'd been when he divorced Marie. Tommy would meet with Lucas to discuss their strategies, and he always left feeling betrayed, the same way he'd felt when his sister sued him when the Colonel passed away. Lucas talked as if he wanted to punish Sarah for her betrayal. Tommy had mixed feelings. He agreed with Lucas that winning was the ultimate goal and that the money was the most important thing, but the level of intensity his lawyer had in his desire to win at all costs was starting to scare Tommy.

"Sarah is still the mother of my daughter, even though she's divorcing me." Tommy tried to get Lucas to tone it down as they sat together in his office. "She's not asking for a lot of money."

But that all changed when it eventually came out that a private investigator had followed Tommy for months and there was a video, proof of his infidelity beyond any doubt. When Tommy found out what she had done, it was like being stabbed in the heart. His sexuality had always been off limits, and Tommy was horrified that she'd hired an attorney who was willing to use his most intimate secret as a weapon against him in their divorce. She'd violated his protective shell and destroyed his illusion that he could cheat on his wife and no one would never find out.

The morning before the court hearing to finalize their divorce, the couple met one last time at Lucas's office. Tommy had been there several times since Sarah filed for divorce, and Tommy and Sarah and the two lawyers met in the conference room sitting at an ornate oak table with paintings of western land-scapes on the walls. Tommy arrived before Sarah and her attorney; as soon as she arrived, Sarah started to cry. The two attorneys went through their divorce decree line by line for hours until the all the details were hammered out. By the time they were done, Sarah was sobbing deep mournful tears.

When it was time to sign and initial every page, Sarah was crying so hard she could barely see to write. She'd come from a different background than Tommy.

"You set our whole marriage up to protect yourself financially. If you'd only acted like a decent husband, we wouldn't be here signing our divorce papers." Sarah sniffed as they were leaving. "Our marriage was doomed to fail from the start."

Tommy and Lucas were totally disarmed. All either of them had cared about was winning. They never expected that Sarah was grieving over the end of her family.

After the last details were hammered out and the paperwork was signed, they all met at the courthouse. They stood before the judge to dissolve their mar-riage, and Sarah sobbed throughout the proceedings.

The whole thing took about ten minutes, and then their marriage was over. Sarah left the courtroom as soon as she was able to. Tommy tried to comfort her, holding her by the elbow as she left, but there was nothing he could do to stem the tide of tears flowing down her cheeks.

"What's done is done, and there's no going back." Lucas stopped Tommy in the hall outside the courtroom to congratulate him on his victory, saying, "You finally got what you wanted your whole life. You now have complete control of all the family assets."

Tommy turned away from Sarah to talk to Lucas for a moment, and when he looked back, Sarah was gone. The cost Tommy had paid to win control of all the money after his father died was that loss of the only woman who had ever loved him unconditionally, except for Nana Harris.

He started to walk toward the elevator when he felt a hand grab his arm. "Let her go," Lucas said gently. "It's over."

Chapter 36

TOMMY WALKED OUT of the Harris County Family Law Center for the second time in twenty years. His attorney, Lucas Damon, had called him back to the courtroom after the divorce proceedings. "The bailiff forgot to enroll you in a state-mandated educational program required for parents of all children of new divorces. Both you and Sarah are required to enroll in these classes before your divorce can be final."

It had been a very long day, and it was only noon; the reality of their divorce was starting to sink in. Stepping outside the Family Law Center with Lucas into the sunlight on that warm November afternoon, the sounds of the downtown Houston traffic in the background, Tommy looked around to see if Sarah was still outside.

Lucas extended his hand to Tommy and cattily remarked, "I hope this will be the last time I have to help you with a divorce."

Tommy just smiled as he shook his attorney's hand and said, "I don't think I have another marriage in me."

He stood on the sidewalk for a few moments trying to decide what to do next. Tommy wanted to be certain he was allowed to see Victoria whenever he wanted. Their divorce decree had set up his visitation rights, but so did his divorce decree with Marie. He didn't intend to go months at a time without seeing his daughter the way he went months at a time without seeing Ricky.

Once Marie had taken Ricky over the Canadian border and Tommy became a part-time father, the whole dynamic of the father/son relationship changed. What little time he had to spend with Ricky he didn't want to waste on discipline.

Tommy never intended to be the ultimate Disneyland Dad, but that's what he'd become.

As he walked into the parking garage, Tommy wondered where he was going to go next. He didn't want to go to his apartment downtown. He'd decorated the place as if it were an apartment in a magazine, using his mother's antiques, but it was still cold and lonely and certainly not the place to go after a depressing event like divorce court. Tommy just couldn't bring himself to go there. Initially, he'd rented the apartment to impress people; he wanted to show Sarah that even if she tossed him out like the trash, he'd still be OK.

Nonetheless, the echo of his footsteps on the stark wood floors only served as a constant reminder that he'd screwed up his only chance for happiness and unconditional love.

I need to go into the office and stay busy.

The people in the office had been supportive after Sarah kicked him to the curb. They'd worked long hours to make sure that Tommy and the company were protected. They'd become more than employees to him; they were like his extended family. The oil company was just recovering from the turmoil of the destructive lawsuits after his father passed away.

On his drive to the office, Tommy tried not to think and, God forbid, to feel. All he wanted was to bury all the awful feelings of loneliness and failure as deep as he could.

Stopping at a Kwik Mart, Tommy bought himself a coke, and when he got back into his car, he mixed himself a stout drink with the bottle of Jack Daniels that he'd started keeping in the console. Tommy didn't like to drink before he went into the office, but today he just didn't care.

Surely, they have the sense not to say anything today of all days.

Once he got to the office, Tommy's mood lightened a little. For the first time all day, he stopped feeling sorry for himself. On the drive to the office, Tommy had been pensive, thinking, *What if I'd done this?* or *What if I did that?* repeatedly.

He decided to spend the night up at the ranch in the same ratty little shack he'd spent his summers in as a boy, Tommy left his office about three o'clock, before rush hour hit the freeway. He'd sold the Colonel's house shortly after he'd passed away to raise money to live off while he'd battled demons. Never once had he regretted selling the Colonel's house…at least until now.

The ranch was his. He'd fought hard for it and fended off the greedy hordes, and once his divorce become imminent, the dream of building a house on Peach Tree Ranch had become his focus. He'd picked out a hilltop where he was going to build his new home and started planning to build the ranch house soon after Sarah kicked him out. There would be a room for Vicky and one for Ricky. Someday they'd all be together like one big, happy family, sharing Christmas and Thanksgiving together.

Who needs a wife? I have my children.

⊷▣ ▣⊶

As soon as the construction his new dream house was completed and Tommy was ready to move in, he received the call from Marie that he'd been waiting for since their divorce. Marie was fed up and agreed to send Ricky to live with his father if Tommy would agree to continue to pay his child support until Ricky turned eighteen. Ricky hadn't been kicked out of his British Columbia boarding school, but he'd been politely asked not to come back for his senior year.

"Done." He agreed to her demands immediately. "That is a small price to pay to have my son back." It was his dream that together Tommy and Ricky would rebuild the oil company back to its former glory—the same kind of glory it had before the Colonel passed away. Tommy was the king, and his son, the prince, would soon be home.

When his son moved back to Texas, Tommy was incensed at how very few possessions he brought with him. Ricky came with everything he wanted, or so he said, and it all fit into two suitcases. "Are you sure this is everything?" Tommy asked him at the baggage carrousel at the airport.

"Yep," he said. "This is all I need." In fact, he'd been in such a hurry to leave that he'd left a lot of his stuff behind, thinking he'd go back and get the rest of it another time.

⊷▣ ▣⊶

Only eleven years old, Vicky wanted to be with her mother, but Tommy hoped that if her brother moved back to Texas, she'd be more likely to want to stay with him more often.

Tommy didn't like the way Sarah was raising his daughter. He believed Vicky was turning into an insolent, spoiled little girl who talked back. Tommy blamed this on her mother and regularly voiced his opinion that if he could just get Victoria away from her mother, her bad attitude would change.

Vicky has been poisoned against me by her mother.

Feeling betrayed that his daughter had taken her mother's side in the divorce instead of showing loyalty to him, he tried to blame Sarah. In reality, Tommy hadn't been much of a father, before the divorce or since, and though Vicky loved to go to the ranch to visit her brother, she couldn't care less if she spent time with her dad.

For the near future, it would be Tommy and Ricky. They were two bachelors living together at the ranch house, and that suited Tommy just fine. He was looking forward to being best friends the way it had been when he was little, before his first ex-wife had taken him away to Canada and messed with his head.

Before moving back to Texas, Ricky had shown symptoms of the early stages of bipolar disorder, which he most likely inherited from his mother. Ricky had started drinking and doing drugs as a means to self-medicate. This was alarming, as he was too young to be using them as a crutch and it only contributed further to his lack of impulse control and mood swings. But Tommy wouldn't admit the boy needed help and wrote it off as a young man sowing his wild oats.

In the years since his father's death, Tommy had rewritten history as best he could. He told his versions of his stories repeatedly to anyone who would listen: Tommy had destroyed the evil family members who waited until his father's funeral to pounce; Tommy had saved his father's honor and protected his children's interest; Tommy had banished all the evil monsters from the kingdom like Beowulf and now was the hero of the land; Tommy had protected the kingdom, and soon it would be prosperous again.

"It will all be theirs someday," he often said, referring to the money his father had left to his grandchildren. It was his way of justifying using their money the same way he had used Beverly's when he managed his sister's trust. "My money went to pay lawyers and taxes. It's only fair that my children's trusts pay their share."

Their trusts were paying for half of everything, from the coffee in the coffee machine to half the working interests in all the dry holes that Tommy drilled. The lines started to blur between his personal property and his children's property and he did with it what he pleased. Tommy was in control of all of the money and the land, and now that his divorce with Sarah was over, any threat of him losing control of the money was gone.

⇥▬◉ ◉▬⇤

The news of Tommy's divorce had spread like wildfire across the small towns and counties in eastern Texas. Soon he had become quite popular and was invited to poker games on Friday nights. They would drink whiskey and scotch while talking about politics and bashing their ex-wives in the most civilized manner.

In his younger days, Tommy had had little problem getting a lover when he wanted, whether it was a girl or a boy. But he was older now and HIV positive. Though he tried his hand at dating, he very rarely got a second date, and if he did, it was even rarer to get a third date, much less sex. Lamentably, Tommy had been through hell over the past twenty years, and it was beginning to show. He was in his late fifties and a hundred pounds heavier; he was so barrel-chested that his arms protruded at an angle when they hung by his side. For the time being, Tommy's friend, Eddie, was the perfect lover.

After his divorce, Tommy often went to Arkansas. He and Eddie talked about taking a vacation to tropical island in the Caribbean. Eddie starting pressing Tommy for a commitment, asking Tommy for dates for their vacation. But Tommy made excuses not to go when Ricky moved in with him. He had no idea how Ricky would react if he ever met Eddie and didn't want to cause problems. Over the years, Marie had blurted out stories to Ricky about his deviant behavior and homosexual affairs, but Tommy had always managed to convince his son that his mother was simply making up vindictive lies about him. Tommy had no intention of opening up to his son about his secret life.

"I don't know how Ricky would take it. I just got him back in my life, and I don't want to jeopardize my relationship with him," he would tell Eddie when he called. Eddie was pushing for a deeper relationship with Tommy and didn't understand why Tommy didn't feel the same way. Eddie claimed that he accepted and appreciated Tommy's position, but really, he didn't, and Tommy was getting pissed off about it.

"I just got out of a divorce and things are going good for the first time in years. You don't have children; if you had children, you'd understand," Tommy said during one of Eddie's calls.

God, he's acting worse than a woman!

⇥⊨◎ ◎⊨⇤

Before Ricky moved to Texas, Marie had become more and more concerned about her son's mental health and well-being. Marie had seen the symptoms in herself and also in her mother, and now her son was starting to show signs of bipolar disorder. When Ricky was thirteen, Marie took him to one of her colleagues to have him tested, which confirmed her worst fears. Ricky was pre-scribed medication to help, but he wouldn't take it, and Marie wasn't big enough to force him.

Afterward, Ricky had called up his father and told him that Marie was try-ing to force him to be medicated. "Let me talk to her," Tommy answered. Marie tried to explain their son's diagnosis, but he'd cut her off; he'd adamantly refused to listen to Marie.

"I don't believe that your quack friend knows enough to diagnose anything. I've already had to put up with your psychobabble, and I don't have to listen to your crap now." Tommy was angry and felt his blood pressure go up as his face flushed red. "Ricky is a teenager; all teenagers are rebellious," Tommy had ar-rogantly argued, asking to speak to Ricky again.

"Don't listen to your mother," Tommy told his son. "She's just trying to drug you so that her life will be easier!"

That was all Ricky needed to hear. He started skipping school and coming and going whenever he pleased. Soon he began to self-medicate with drugs and alcohol.

Ricky was a such lovable kid, but he'd always had poor impulse control and problems developing a moral compass, resulting in difficulty understanding the difference between right and wrong. He'd developed a fascination with anything dangerous, especially guns and fireworks. Ricky couldn't wait to move back home to Texas.

Upon Ricky's arrival in Texas, they scrambled to find a school that would take him on short notice, finding a private academy in Bellaire called the Learning Center that specialized in educating rich kids with issues. Ricky wanted to finish school in Black Rock while living at the ranch, but Tommy put his foot down, saying, "It would be too much temptation for you to drop out and party."

Even if Ricky didn't graduate from high school, as a product of the Canadian school system he was much better educated than the average kid in Texas. The only advantage of allowing Ricky to grow up in Canada was that its educational system offered a superior curriculum compared to the average Texas school. Ricky only needed a few credits to graduate and so only had to attend classes half of the day.

"My son is finally under my roof for good." Tommy was elated! Even if they were living in his high-rise apartment temporarily until Ricky graduated, he was back in Texas and all was right in the world. As in the epic poem *Beowulf*, he'd finally defeated Grendel's mother.

Immediately, Tommy bought Ricky a truck to Texas to drive back and forth to school, but it wasn't long before Ricky was up to his old tricks and had started skipping classes at his new school. Ricky would ditch school and drive up to Black Rock for the day. Tommy had no idea Ricky was ditching classes until the school called to ask where he was.

Soon Tommy figured out that Ricky was getting into his booze. He thought nothing of it at first—boys will be boys, after all. That is, until he discovered that Ricky had had drank a whole gallon of vodka one night when he was out, Tommy became extremely concerned, "If I drank that much vodka in one night, I'd be dead," Tommy told his cousin, Tobin, the next time he saw him on the ranch.

After a couple of months, Ricky dropped out of school. Tommy never knew where he was. Tommy didn't know what to do with Ricky's bad behavior, and before long, he gave Ricky the keys to the old ranch house where he and Nana Harris used to spend the summers.

"The only way you can stay here is if you get a GED," he told Ricky. "If you go to college, I'll pay for it, but if you don't go to college, you need to get a job."

Ricky had finally gotten what he wanted. He was living on the ranch without any adult supervision and had free rein to do whatever he wanted whenever he wanted to do it. He was underage, but before long he'd be turning eighteen. The first thing Ricky figured out was how to buy beer and booze, and it wasn't long before he found out who the drug dealers were. He came and went as he pleased, and had a whole bevy of girlfriends who were willing to do anything to be his one and only.

After passing his GED with flying colors, Ricky soon enrolled in Sam Houston State University in Huntsville, Texas. He moved into an apartment, living part-time in Huntsville and part-time on the ranch. Ricky was extremely grateful to get away from his father. "My dad is as messed up as my mother," Ricky would tell his new college friends.

Ricky had grown up resenting his father and believing that he should have fought harder to keep his mother from taking him away. Ricky had been lost when he went to Canada—losing the stability that not just Tommy but the Colonel had provided was rough on the kid. And at first his mother was so busy trying to make a name for herself as a family therapist that she'd neglected him. She'd clearly underestimated the difficulties faced by a single mother living in a different country from the child's father.

"My dad always said that he wanted me to live with him, but if he'd really meant it, he would have made it happen," Ricky told his little sister one time when she came to visit. He'd lost respect for his father a long time ago because his dad had abandoned him, and now that he was back in Texas, his feelings of resentment were growing stronger. He saw how their dad was treating his sister and knew exactly how she felt.

"He goes months at a time without even calling, and he lives in the same city as my mother," Vicky complained to her brother. "I guess he thinks I'm supposed to pretend that it doesn't hurt my feelings that he always has something more important to do on the weekends he's supposed to pick me up."

⤞▧ ▧⤝

The first thing Ricky did when he turned eighteen was buy a gun. He spent endless hours hunting on the ranch and soon became a proficient marksman. It wasn't long before Ricky began collecting guns, starting out with a few hunting rifles. Between classes Ricky would hang out around a gun range in Huntsville, and before long he'd applied for a Federal Firearms License. Within a year, Ricky was buying and selling heavy-duty artillery. Ricky and his friends would go up to the ranch, usually when his dad wasn't around, to hunt and blow things up.

It wasn't long before his antics put Ricky on the radar of the local law enforcement and sheriff's department. The sheriff called Tommy to complain. "This is more than a boy with a gun. We're afraid that he's going to hurt himself or somebody else."

"Aren't you overreacting?" It was obvious that Tommy was a little more than miffed. "Whatever he's doing, he's on our land, and it's is not your concern."

Eventually, Ricky got in more trouble with the law. Late one night he wrapped his truck around a tree because he was driving too fast on a backwoods road. Ricky called his dad, and Tommy sent someone to get him before the highway patrol got there and saw how drunk he was. In due time, a DPS officer showed up at the ranch looking for Ricky, but not before Tommy had him safely tucked away at someone's house to sober up.

Then Ricky did something really stupid shortly after that Tommy couldn't ignore. Ricky had been drinking and stopped at a gas station that was closed but had a coke machine out front. Ricky put his change in, but the machine ate his money. Ricky became enraged. He backed his truck up to the coke machine, wrapped a chain from the bed of his truck around it, and drug it twenty miles to his father's house on the ranch. The next morning, the sheriff's department followed the trail of coke machine pieces to Tommy's house to find what was left.

That afternoon, Tommy got a phone call that his son had been arrested and was charged with felony theft and felony destruction of property. When he arrived at the county jail, Tommy promptly started lecturing his rebellious young son. "How can I protect you if you have no respect for other people's property? Didn't your mother teach you about honor?" he asked.

Ricky thought it was funny. "You wouldn't know what she taught me. You weren't around." He mocked his father with a smug smirk as he sat on the bed in his cell. "Just hurry up and make bail so I can get out of jail."

His son's disrespect enraged Tommy. No one had ever talked to him that way, especially someone who was staring at him from behind the bars of a jail cell. For the first time, he realized that his son had issues. "You're right. I wasn't around. This is your mother's fault because of the way she raised you." Tommy turned around and left, telling the deputy at the desk that this time his son could get himself out of jail.

Tommy was disappointed in his son and had enough of his antics. He started spending more and more time with Eddie in Arkansas. "For the life of me I cannot figure out what went wrong with the boy," Tommy complained to Eddie. "He's out of control, and I don't know what to do."

"I don't understand why he's acting that way. You are a wonderful father." Eddie didn't have any children and really didn't understand what Tommy was going through with Ricky, but he thought he did.

Eddie Giles still made Tommy feel sexy. They had fun together, and Eddie was playful. He was twenty-five years younger than Tommy; tall, dark, and handsome; and owned a gift shop and antique emporium down the street from Hot Springs Hotels and Bathhouses.

Tommy had fallen in love with the town of Hot Springs nestled in the Ouachita Mountains, a rock's throw from the national park. It was a peaceful little town, and the people there were friendly; Eddie had lots of friends, and Tommy felt comfortable enough to let down his guard. "I'm starting to consider Hot Springs my home away from home," Tommy announced at a dinner party at one of Eddie's friend's house. Most of all, Tommy enjoyed his life in Arkansas because he could get away from all the stress.

Eddie and Tommy had started to traveled together and spent weeks at a time together as companions. Everything was going great between them until Eddie suggested they live together, "Someday when they legalize gay marriage, we can get married." Tommy was caught off guard and didn't know what to say.

"I am recovering from my ten-year marriage to Sarah," he managed to blurt out. Tommy enjoyed Eddie, and he didn't want to hurt his feelings, but any marriage, especially to a man, was not in the cards. "I have two children, and I have their feelings to consider." Tommy was still struggling with the same dilemma he'd faced all his life: Tommy didn't know if he had the courage to come out of the closet in Texas where his persona was larger than life.

"And I have my reputation to consider," Tommy muttered seeing immediately that he'd hurt his lover's feelings.

"Well, if that's the way you feel, then my feelings don't matter. "Tommy and Eddie got into an argument, and Tommy packed up to leave that evening. He'd hoped that his lover would understand how he felt and drop it. But Eddie wasn't having it; the more Tommy avoided the subject, the more Eddie pushed it.

In the year since his divorce, Tommy hadn't spent as much quality time as he could with his daughter, Victoria. When they divorced, he'd insisted on joint custody and weekend visitations. Yet Tommy had been avoiding Vicky because every time he went to pick her up, he had to deal with his feeling of grief and loss.

He'd never admit it to anyone, but he was still in love with Sarah and missed his family terribly. The sadness he felt when he went over to Sarah's house to pick up his daughter for visits was overwhelming and only made him want a drink. As of late, he'd become aware that Victoria was always apprehensive about spending time with him and wasn't very enthusiastic about coming with him for a weekend visit. In fact, it was getting to the point where Vicky didn't want to go with him when he showed up. "He never asks me what I want to do," she'd complain to her mother. "And everything he wants to do is dumb or boring or educational."

Vicky was in middle school now, and if her father had asked her what she wanted to do, she would have told him that she wanted to go to the movies with her friends like any other kid her age. "I was supposed to go to the new Harry Potter movie with Emma Rose." Vicky was fighting back the tears. "Daddy hasn't even called in over a month, and now he wants to see me."

"Maybe your father will take you to see Harry Potter with Emma Rose," Sarah said, trying to smooth things out. But at Vicky's age, the only thing worse than missing the premier of the third Harry Potter movie was to show up at the premier with your dad. Middle school was hard enough without something like that to live down. When Tommy picked Vicky up on Friday evening, Sarah felt sorry for her; she could see in her daughter's eyes that she was fighting back tears.

Vicky hugged her mother good-bye, "The world revolves around him," she said as she begrudgingly picked up her bags and closed the door behind her.

As she crawled into the back seat of her father's car and buckled up, Vicky found a gay porn magazine on the floor that her father had failed to throw away before he picked her up. Vicky rolled her eyes, throwing the magazine into the front seat and saying, "Seriously?"

Chapter 37

TOMMY MOSTLY HUNG around Houston for the next six months, and he was driving his daughter crazy. He still didn't stick to his every-other-weekend visitation schedule, but he did make an effort to see his daughter more often and settle into a semiroutine visitation schedule. Tommy even learned to ask his daughter what her plans were before making plans of his own.

Soon Sarah felt comfortable enough to take a vacation. She left her daughter with her father while she flew down to Belize for a weekend with a girlfriend. The first night there, Sarah got a frantic call from Victoria on her cell. "Mommy!"

Sarah could tell by her voice that something had upset her daughter terribly. "What's wrong, sweetie?" she asked, hoping she could calm her down.

"Dad's got a creepy boyfriend. He's here right now, and when Dad went to bed, he went to bed with him." Victoria was hysterical. "They're sleeping together."

Sarah was dumbfounded. She'd never thought that Tommy would open up and shine a light on his secret life, especially to his daughter.

"Dad told me that he loved him and kissed him right in front of me. I want to go home! Please come home!"

Something else must be going on with this guy, Eddie, that's disturbed Vicky terribly.

"Dad's new boyfriend told me that had been raped by a man when he was a teenager! He started telling me the graphic details! *Yuck! No* boundaries!" Vicky was hysterical. "I locked myself in my bedroom. I don't want to be here anymore!"

Sarah took a deep breath and told Vicky to call her one of her friend's parents. "Ask them if you can stay with them until I get home." Sarah was on the verge of tears. The sensation of helplessness sapped her sensibilities as she nervously strode around her hotel room.

If he'd just told her about Eddie in the first place, Sarah could have helped prepare Vicky for the news and ease her daughter into the idea of her dad's alternative lifestyle. In addition, she would have made other overnight arrangements until Vicky was used her father's new boyfriend.

To drop this on his junior high–aged daughter without any warning or preparation is just irresponsible parenting.

Once she was calmer, Vicky was able to better explain to her mother what was going on. Eddie was there staying with her father; he was recuperating from a motorcycle wreck. Vicky was upset and on the verge of tears.

Sarah knew her daughter wasn't a homophobe; Vicky was actually very mature and insightful for a girl her age. "Baby, I don't know what else to do...I can't get home to help until morning, but for now you need to take care of yourself as best you can." Sarah was out of the country and helpless.

"OK." She heard the relief in Vicky's voice.

Vicky immediately called Emma's mother and asked her to come and get her. After Vicky left, Eddie got upset and insulted. However, Tommy knew it was probably for the best; Eddie had behaved too intensely for his first meeting with Vicky.

⇥◉ ◉⇤

Not long afterward, Ricky was introduced to Eddie. Actually, Ricky was caught completely off guard when went to the ranch one evening unannounced without realizing his dad had a houseguest. There was Eddie, who was obviously gay. At first, Ricky didn't think anything about it until Eddie began hanging all over his father.

The sight of his dad's boyfriend with his hands all over his dad hit Ricky hard like a bus. His mother had bad-mouthed his dad for years, claiming she'd divorced him because he was gay but Ricky had never given it a second thought.

Ricky felt betrayed, not so much because his dad was gay but because he'd lied about it. His father had made fun of his mother, insinuating that she was crazy and vindictive for cooking up such preposterous claims. It seemed so strange to see some guy pawing at his dad. Ricky's stomach was in a knot.

On the drive back to Huntsville, Ricky started thinking about his childhood and all the times his father had called his mother a liar. Suddenly, many emotions overwhelmed him—sadness, confusion, anger, guilt, and shame.

"Dad has been the liar all along," he confessed to his little sister when they opened up to each other at the Alligator Lake camp house about their experiences with Eddie. Suddenly, it hit Ricky that their dad had used Ricky's resentment toward his mother's problems to his advantage. "Dad manipulated me into believing his version of the truth," he said as he slammed his hand on the table where they sat talking unobserved.

Over the next few months, Tommy halfheartedly tried to integrate Eddie into his children's lives, but neither Ricky nor Vicky wanted much to do with Eddie. Ricky stopped answering his father's calls, and after a few weird weekends around Eddie, Victoria refused to go as well.

Soon Tommy lost patience with his children's refusal to have anything to do with Eddie. Eddie would buy her presents, but Victoria refused to accept them. Tommy would get pissed off and force her to accept Eddie's gifts. So when she got home, she'd ask her mother her to give them away to some needy child, saying, "I'm not being selfish or spoiled. Eddie keeps giving me stupid stuff that I don't like or that is for kids a lot younger than me. Eddie is trying to use presents to buy my affection."

Sarah found herself in a very sticky place. She knew just how intolerant Tommy was when it came to his daughter's disobedience. He'd barely come around for almost a year, and now that he was back, he was making unreasonable demands and threatening Sarah. "I've paid a lot of money in child support, health care, private schooling, and alimony, and now I expect my daughter to show some appreciation and to behave accordingly."

"That almost sounds like a threat!" She tried to hold her tongue. Sarah was angry at her ex-husband and didn't want him to make her sound like a homophobe. "All I've ever hoped for was for you and Vicky to have a loving relationship. If you're having issues with Vicky, you need to take a long hard look at yourself and quit blaming me for all your problems."

Sarah was watching and waiting patiently, knowing that eventually Tommy would lose interest in his boyfriend. Soon enough, Eddie would be just another ex in a long line of Tommy's exes. In the meantime, she encouraged her daughter to be patient too and go through the motions until he dumped the guy.

"Your father will lose interest in his boyfriend soon or later. Just try and get through it as best as you can until he does," she told her daughter. She felt uncomfortable giving this kind of advice to her young daughter but knew that if she wasn't honest, her daughter would see through it and resent her, too.

⋅→▶═◉ ◉═◀←⋅

As Sarah predicted, Tommy was losing interest in Eddie anyway. Eddie whined continually about the way Tommy's children treated him. Tommy wasn't going to push too hard for Ricky to accept Eddie, hoping this all be forgotten soon. And despite Eddie's opinion that his daughter was insolent and defiant, Tommy had an underlying fear of losing her, too.

Eddie was just his lover; Ricky and Vicky where his kids, his flesh and blood. Eddie was pushing him to choose between the two, and that wasn't an option. Even though he didn't like his children's treatment of Eddie, they were still his children, and his lover's constant clinginess was beginning to piss him off. Tommy was considering dumping his lover when one day he received the phone call. It was the kind that Tommy had dreaded in the back of his mind for the past two decades.

Calling Tommy crying, Eddie revealed that he had just tested HIV positive, and to make matters worse, he was accusing Tommy of infecting him. Tommy's viral load had been next to nothing for nearly five years, and he'd become complacent about using protection during sex. This was the first time that Tommy knew of that he might have infected any of his lovers.

Tommy was devastated, "Are you sure?" he asked as he fumbled for the words. They weren't in a monogamous relationship; Eddie could have very easily gotten infected by one of his other partners.

Becoming aggressive and belligerent, Eddie yelled, "Of course I'm sure."

"I have never lied to you," Tommy said calmly. "I told you straight up from the beginning of their relationship what the risks were."

But Eddie blamed everything on him, saying that Tommy had all the responsibility for keeping his lover safe. Eddie was a drama queen, but the things he was saying to Tommy were out of line.

"I know what you're going through, but there really isn't any need for you to get ugly about it!"

Tommy had watched a lot of his friends die from AIDS over the years, and it was hard watching someone you cared about in the end stages of AIDS without thinking of your own mortality. Tommy eventually had stopped visiting his dying friends because he just couldn't handle it. Now Eddie was asking him to hold his hand and prop him up, and Tommy just couldn't do it.

Sarah did it for me, and I will always be grateful to her for that, but I'm not Sarah and Eddie needs to get a grip!

Finally, Tommy made up an excuse to hang up on Eddie after what seemed like hours. Tommy sat quietly on his couch in his apartment downtown, thinking that he needed a drink. It wasn't long before Eddie called back, but Tommy didn't answer.

Eddie continued calling every ten to fifteen minutes for three hours straight, leaving messages that were more and more belligerent each time. Eventually, Tommy had to turn off his cell phone and delete the messages without even listening to them. In time, Tommy started avoiding Eddie's calls all together. Eddie was being needy and was really starting to get on his nerves.

A week afterward, Tommy received a call from one of Eddie's friends, Paul, in Arkansas. Tommy was at his office and, recognizing the number on his cell phone's caller ID, and decided to answer. Paul was a reasonable man who'd known Eddie long enough to understand his flair for the dramatic and his propensity to blow things way out of proportion.

"I'm calling to let you know that Eddie is in the hospital," Paul said when Tommy finally answered. "He overdosed on pills when you wouldn't answer his calls." Apparently, Paul had gone by Eddie's house to check on him because he had been saying things like if Tommy didn't want him there was no point in living.

"Thank you for taking such good care of Eddie," Tommy said in a low monotone. "I'll fly there this evening and work things out with him."

Hanging up, Tommy asked Angelica to make a reservation to Hot Springs. "This is getting old," he said quietly after Angelica left.

Tommy flew up to Hot Springs that evening as he promised, but he wasn't happy when he got there. Eddie was already out of the hospital and immediately started in on him about getting married as soon he arrived.

Tommy did everything he could to get through the next few days. He sat on the couch reading a book while Eddie flittered around all happy, thinking that he had Tommy right where he wanted him. When it was time for Tommy to head home, Eddie insisted that he pack his things and go back to Houston with Tommy for an extended stay. Tommy emphatically replied, "No."

While waiting for the cab to take him to the airport, Tommy realized that they needed to have a serious talk. "AIDS is not a death sentence, and life can go on normally," Tommy said as he sat his bag down in front of the door. "People who are HIV positive are able to live long and productive lives just like I have. You need to stay in Hot Springs where your support system is and take care of your gift shop and your employees."

Eddie sat silently with a forlorn look on his face; this was not what he wanted to hear.

"You need to go to counseling like the doctors who treated you at the hospital recommended," Tommy continued. "Once you adjust, then they can help you to see what the future holds."

Eddie was about to throw another tantrum when Tommy's taxi pulled up out front and honked. Tommy turned to say good-bye, but Eddie had already stormed off to his bedroom, slamming the door behind him.

"Your timing couldn't have been better," he said to the taxi driver as he loaded his bag into the trunk.

⤞▧ ▧⤝

Tommy regretted ever bringing Eddie around his family. He was now trying to distance himself from Eddie. He decided that he needed to repair the damage to his relationships with his children. Things had been good at first, but Tommy wished he had seen how needy and attached Eddie was to him sooner. Eddie had pushed him to come out of the closet to his children and his friends in Black Rock, and now he worried that he'd lost respect from the people he loved. He felt like the butt of a joke; He could see people whispering when he went to the grocery store.

Victoria spotted it as soon as she met him. I should have trusted her instincts.

Instead, he'd accused his daughter of just being sassy and spoiled, and rebelling against his wishes, and then he'd tried to force her to conform.

At first, Tommy had loved that Eddie was honest about who he was and made no apologies for his behavior. He was a free spirit. Tommy was even envious that Eddie did what he wanted and didn't care who he offended. Eddie had come out when he was in high school, and his parents and family had turned their backs on him. Being ultrareligious, as far as they were concerned, a gay son was doomed to the fires of hell. His parents' rejection had only made Eddie clingy, anxious, and emotionally needy.

Tommy decided that he was going to give up on new relationships for a while and work on the relationships he'd neglected over the past couple of years. Tommy was trying to see Victoria off and on for visits, but he hadn't seen much of his son, Ricky, lately. Tommy and Ricky talked on the phone regularly, but Ricky always seemed to have something else to do when Tommy would invite him home.

⊷⊷

Ricky was a junior at Sam Houston State University and having the time of his life. While his dad was preoccupied with his lover, Eddie, Ricky had started hanging around Benny's Cabaret, a strip club, with some of his college buddies. At first, being twenty-one, it was simply a cool thing to go hang out a strip club. But then a pretty little dancer named Kellie Long caught his eye. She was a bleached-blond bombshell with an expensive boob job, and Ricky was smitten.

Benny's was a hole in the wall on the outskirts of town. All kinds of men hung out at Benny's, everyone from businessmen to the worst kind of reprobates imaginable. In time, Ricky started going alone to Benny's to impress his favorite dancer because his college friends were on college budgets. He soon got to know all the usuals and became the life of the party.

Impressively, some of the heavy-hitting high rollers that frequented Benny's shoveled big wads of money into the G-strings of the dancers. Eagerly, Ricky struck up conversations with them, hoping to find out their secrets to making money. One day Ricky struck up a conversation with a particularly badass reprobate name Oscar De La Garza.

He'd seen Oscar slip hundred dollar bills in some of the dancer's G-strings, including his favorite, Kellie, and Ricky wanted to know how he did it and if he could get in on the action. Oscar De La Garza was an ex-con and a bad dude, with dark expressionless eyes. Oscar had prison tattoos and was a gangbanger who had business associates in the Mexican Mafia, as well as the Sinaloa Cartel. Ricky frequently started up conversations with Oscar, who was entertained by the cocky kid but didn't really take the boy seriously.

In a bid to attract Oscar's attention, Ricky talked way too much about his life and family. "I have a Federal Firearms License that I got last year," Ricky bragged to Oscar one afternoon when he was cutting classes. This information piqued his interest, and Oscar saw a business opportunity for Ricky.

Up until then, Oscar hadn't paid much attention to Ricky. "Well, gringo, if you sell guns, I'll pay you more money than you've ever seen in your life for some guns," he said while sipping a beer. "More than enough to impress your favorite little dancer."

A few weeks later, Ricky went to Benny's and found Oscar. Oscar and a friend were sitting at a table in front of the stage. Ricky got a beer at the bar and sat down at Oscar's table. "What's going on, gringo?" Oscar greeted Ricky.

"Not much," he said as he took a sip of beer. "Were you serious about wanting to buy some guns?"

Oscar leaned back in his chair, looking Ricky in the eye, said, "Sure, gringo, what you got?"

"Well, I've got a dozen Sarsilmaz 9mm semiautomatic pistols in my truck. Are you interested?" Ricky asked quietly, trying his best to look cool.

"How much?" Oscar asked.

Ricky smiled and decided to go big. "$750 apiece."

Oscar laughed, "You are crazy, gringo!" And he went back to watching the dancer.

"OK. I thought I'd offer." Ricky stood up to leave. "There's a gun show in Dallas next week; I'll take them up there and flip them. Too bad. I thought we could do some business."

As he turned to go, Oscar said, "OK, gringo, let's go out to your truck and see what you've got."

Ricky, Oscar and Oscar's friend went out to his truck, which he'd parked behind the building. Oscar instructed his friend to stand guard while Ricky unlocked his truck. Reaching into the back seat, he pulled out a rectangular, gray metal gun case; he set it on the hood and unlocked it. Inside were twelve black handguns laid out side by side in foam cut out to the shape of the gun.

Oscar picked up one of the handguns and aimed it at a tree. Ricky could tell by the way he handled the pistol that he'd held a gun before. Oscar inspected the rest of the 9 mm handguns, saying, "I'll give you $500 apiece."

"$650 and no paperwork, and they're yours." Ricky was standing behind Oscar watching him as he held each gun, checking its quality.

Oscar signaled to his friend, and the two men walked over to a black Cadillac Escalade and came back with and envelope with $7,800 in it. Handing the money to Ricky, Oscar said, "Good doing business with you, Ricky." Oscar and his friend put the guns into the Escalade and said, "You bring me more, and we'll see what we can do." Oscar started to get into the SUV and then turned back to Ricky, smiling. "And since you got all my money, you can pay my bar bill."

Ricky watched the men drive away, thinking that he'd just made easy money—he'd paid $175 per gun. After they pulled out of the parking lot, Ricky went back inside to drink another beer to celebrate.

Occasionally, Ricky bought guns online and sold them to Oscar at an enormous profit. Oscar would tell Ricky the kind of guns he wanted, and Ricky would buy them and deliver them to him. Ricky was making more money than he ever could have working for his dad, and soon he'd dropped out of college just a few credit hours before he would graduate.

Within a few months, Ricky was living large. That is, until one day he messed up and got greedy. Ricky met one of Oscar's associates drinking beer at Benny's. Diego Villarreal was a well-dressed man, and it seemed odd that he hung out with the likes of Oscar. Knowing that Ricky was doing some shady stuff online, he told him, "I'll pay you big bucks if you'll agree to route an Internet server through your computer."

"What's the catch?" he quizzed Diego. "It sounds too good to be true."

"No catch. I just need some help, and I thought you'd help me out since you're a computer genius." Diego paused as he watched one of the dancers on stage. "It ain't no big thing if you're not interested."

Then Diego flashed $10,000 in cash; Ricky didn't ask questions. It was easy money, and he was in on the deal hooking up the router to his computer.

"Come on," Ricky pressed him. "What's so important that you'd give me 10K for practically nothing."

"It's a website—that's all you need to know." Diego smiled suspiciously and left.

⟶● ●⟵

One week later, Ricky was getting dressed after a shower when he heard someone banging loudly on his door. As soon as he opened the door, a group of FBI agents rushed in, handcuffed Ricky, and began searching his home. It was only a few minutes before the agents found his computer; the IP address for the server that Ricky was routing led them straight to him.

After reading him his rights, the agents questioned him. Ricky only replied, "It's not mine. A guy named Diego paid me to set up the router for his website. He paid in cash and never asked any questions. I figured the website on the router was for a porn site or an illegal gambling site."

Tragically, the website Ricky was routing through his home computer was an Internet child pornography site. The FBI also found a large cache of automatic weapons that Ricky was planning to sell to Oscar.

After his arrest, Oscar and Diego disappeared into Mexico to lay low while Ricky was booked on federal charges.

⇥▣ ▣⇤

Tommy was in the car driving home from the airport when he got a call on his cell from Angelica that Ricky was in jail. "Ricky was arrested in Walker County but has been transferred to the federal holding facility in Montgomery County for arraignment."

Tommy couldn't believe his ears. At first, he'd assumed that Ricky had gotten drunk and stupid again. But the federal holding facility was serious. Tommy got off the freeway and turned around, heading north to Montgomery County to find out what the hell happened.

By the time he got there, Ricky's arraignment was about to start. Tommy decided he would act as Ricky's attorney until they got things sorted out. He didn't get to speak to his son before the arraignment and was horrified when the guards brought Ricky into the courtroom in handcuffs and leg irons. Ricky looked at his father like a bewildered little boy. Tommy stood beside his son as the bailiff read the charges against him: he was facing several counts of federal weapons charges and federal charges for the distribution of child pornography over the Internet.

This is either a really bad joke or a really bad dream. My *son would never, ever get mixed up with this kind of crap.*

Tommy, who was sitting in the back of the courtroom, stood up and stated loudly, "Your Honor, my name is Thomas Ellison, and I'm the defendant's attorney. I have not yet had the chance to speak to my client. Is it possible for me to take a moment to speak to him?"

The judge motioned to Tommy to come forward, asking, "Ellison? That's the same name as the defendant. Any chance there's a relation?"

"Yes, your Honor. The defendant is my son." Tommy choked the words out as pulled his bar card out of his wallet and handed it to the bailiff.

The judge examined the card and handed it back, saying, "OK, Mr. Ellison. Make it quick. This is an arraignment, not a hearing."

Tommy sat down in the empty chair beside his son. He didn't ask him what happened; there'd be enough time to figure that out later.

"Just keep your mouth shut and don't say anything to anyone," Tommy instructed. "Listen to me and do exactly what I tell you. The charges against you are serious. You need to enter a plea of not guilty, and I'll arrange bail and get you a real defense attorney to fight the charges."

Tommy stood up and motioned to Ricky to stand next to him, saying, "Your Honor, we're ready to proceed."

The judge reviewed the file that the bailiff had handed him, and the prosecutor asked that the judge set bail at half a million dollars. Tommy was mortified, and he felt his anger start to well up. "Your Honor, half a million dollars is excessive," Tommy argued. "I'm an attorney and his father. I ask that you release him into my custody. My son is just a stupid kid, but I'm an officer of the court and I will guarantee that he appears at his criminal hearing."

"Your Honor, the evidence show that the defendant has an extensive history of criminal behavior, and the federal authorities have extensive evidence showing not only that Richard Ellison has absolutely no regard for the law but has both a US passport and Canadian passport and is a flight risk," the prosecutor droned.

Tommy started to argue, but the judge cut him off. "I agree with the learned prosecutor. Bail is set at half a million dollars," he said as he slammed his gavel against the block on the bench.

Tommy watch helplessly as the guards led Ricky back out of the courtroom still shackled in chains. The arraignment had taken less than twenty minutes, but Tommy knew in his heart that Ricky's life was ruined.

Tommy went outside feeling as though he'd just lived through a really bad nightmare. His mind was racing, and he began to panic. It was three o'clock in the afternoon, and the banks would be closing soon. Tommy had to find a bail bondsman and get ahold of his banker. He had made bail over the years for some of his friends, but mostly for drunk and disorderly conduct. Tommy knew that if he wanted to make bail, he'd have to come up with 10 percent, which was fifty thousand dollars. And he didn't have that kind of money just lying around.

Tommy made his way to the parking lot where he'd parked his car. He realized that Ricky would have to spend another night in jail, maybe more, until Tommy raised his bail money.

Serves him right! The smug little bastard didn't seem even a little remorseful for whatever he's done.

Tommy unlocked his car and sat in the front seat, fighting back tears. He pulled out his cell phone and dialed Angelica. "I need you to find a bail bondsman and to find Lucas Damon's number."

Book Five

Denial is a river in Egypt.

—*Judge Judith Sheindlin,* Beauty Fades, Dumb Is Forever

Chapter 38

IT TOOK A year and almost a million dollars, but in early 2001, Ricky accepted a plea bargain. He had pleaded guilty to federal weapons charges and to distribution of Internet porn; in exchange, he received five years' probation. Also, his Federal Firearms License was revoked, and he had to register as a sex offender. It had taken almost a week for Ricky to be released from the Montgomery County Federal Detention Center after his arraignment. During his stay, Ricky went through a mental health evaluation and was diagnosed once again with bipolar disorder.

As a condition of his probation, Ricky had to visit his probation officer once a month and was tested for drugs and alcohol during each visit. Ricky also had to prove he was taking the medication prescribed to treat his bipolar disorder. He had to surrender all his firearms and wasn't allowed to possess any guns during his probation.

Tommy had hired his old friend Lucas Damon to defend his son and was very disappointed and upset that they couldn't get a better deal for the money they paid him. Mr. Damon had made no promises when he took Ricky's case, telling Tommy, "They've got him dead to rights, and the only chance he's got is to appeal to the mercy of the courts that the boy was a dumbass young redneck who didn't know that he was bipolar and was self-medicating."

When Lucas saw the evidence the FBI had against Ricky, he said, "I'll plead to the court that he was too young and mentally ill to understand the consequences of his actions, but you really shouldn't expect too much."

Tommy didn't like it, not one bit, but he went along with Mr. Damon's strategy, believing they had no other choice. Even though Ricky was now twenty-one years old, Tommy was making all the decision for his defense, only discussing their legal strategy with him after the deal was done. Ricky smoldered and his resentment grew as his father became more and more controlling and smug.

During the time that he was out on bail, Ricky and Kellie got married, much to the dismay of Tommy. Tommy scoffed at his son's marriage. "What the hell are you thinking. That girl is a gold digger. She doesn't love you," Tommy yelled at his son. "You are still out on bail. Marrying a former stripper who worked at the club where you met the gangbangers who got you into trouble isn't going endear you to the judge!"

Ricky looked coldly at his father, saying, "You can control my money, and you can control my lawyer, but you can't tell me who I can or cannot marry."

Ricky then stood up and turned to his new wife, Kellie, who was wearing cropped blue jeans and a T-shirt and standing sheepishly by the back door. Taking her by the hand, he pulled her out the back door while his ranting father continued to lecture his son as they walked away. Having heard enough, Ricky looked at his father and said, "Who the hell are you to judge me about my choice of life partner. Your track record is nothing to brag about."

Speechless, Tommy stopped in his tracks. He'd never dreamed of talking that way to his father.

⊷━▶ ◀━⊷

Having grown up in less than perfect circumstances, Kellie had a baby when she was sixteen and started dancing in topless bars when she was seventeen in order to support herself and her son, Justin. When she met Ricky, she thought he was just another horny guy who wanted to pay money to manhandle. But Ricky was nice to her and treated her like she was a human being with real feelings instead of just pawing at her like she was some animal in heat—like the other patrons at the club.

When Ricky was arrested, she didn't care—she knew what had happened because she'd witnessed it unfold. He was the best thing that had happened to her and Justin, and she wasn't going anywhere, and when Kellie found out, she'd quit her job that day and moved with him as soon as he made bail. Before long, they moved out of Ricky's apartment in Huntsville into a vacant house on Peach Tree Ranch. His father and Lucas Damon had managed to convince him that it would be in his best interests to live close to his father.

Living on the ranch worked very well for a couple of years. Tommy helped Ricky set up a land title office in the Woodlands, just north of Houston. Ricky's job was to research deeds and titles for oil-and-gas leases and right of ways. At first, Tommy was his only client, but Ricky was a natural at leases and title work, and his business started to grow as he took on new clients.

In time, Ricky's business became profitable, and he started hiring new employees to help with the work. Ricky's confidence and his faith in the future grew as his family grew when Kellie became pregnant with Ricky's first son, Cody Kyle, just a year after they married. Ricky had joined AA and was going to meetings regularly, as well as to a psychiatrist every couple of weeks, and so was coping with his condition in a very positive way.

When Ricky's first son was born, life was normal, considering the circumstances. Doing the work to stay clean and sober, Ricky struggled every day to keep his demons at bay. The medication prescribed for his bipolar disorder helped; however, it only worked for his depression and did nothing for him he when he was in a manic state. Since he had more issues with mania than depression, Ricky began asked his psychiatrist to change his prescriptions.

As long as his parents weren't around, Ricky did all right, but when they were, he would become extremely stressed out, which would usually push him over the edge into a manic state. Ricky stayed away from his father as much as he could, even though they lived only a half mile from each other and Tommy tried to interfere constantly.

It wasn't until Cody was born that Ricky had to deal with his mother. Marie still lived in Canada, but she started coming to Texas for extended stays with Ricky and his family after her first grandchild was born. Kellie and Marie got along fine, which bothered Ricky immensely. "Her friendship with my mother is an unholy union," Ricky complained to his sister, Vicky, when she was at the ranch visiting.

Ricky's parents started their dance of anger as soon as Marie arrived in Texas. Ricky was once again stuck in the middle, having to hear the constant sniping as he did when he was a little boy.

It all came to a head when Kellie was in the hospital after Cody was born. Ricky had to physically remove his mother from his wife's hospital room because she got into an argument with Kellie over the type of care their son was receiving. Ricky became so stressed out by his mother's inappropriate behavior, complicated by his father's constant attempts to control his life, that he had a severe manic episode.

"I am worried about Ricky," Kellie said to Vicky when she came to the hospital to meet her nephew. "It alarms me when he acts like this. It's like a person could almost look into his eyes and watch the circuit breakers start tripping."

They both could see the look in Ricky's eyes and the mannerisms that indicated mania. They worried that he might lose his sense of reality and spiral out of control. Ricky had been off drugs and alcohol for over a year and a half and was attending AA meetings regularly, but all that was at risk as soon as they took the baby home from the hospital. Marie showed up at their house to help; Ricky let her stay for a couple of days, and then he asked her to leave.

Soon after Marie went back to Canada, Tommy's interference in Ricky's life only intensified. He'd never cared much for Ricky's new wife, and now Tommy became paranoid that she'd developed a bond with Marie. Referring to Kellie as Ricky's "starter wife," he told his son, "Kellie's relationship with your mother is an act of disloyalty and treason." He continued to rant to Ricky as he drank whiskey and coke before dinner at his house. "Not only is she beneath us, but your mother is coaching your wife on how to divorce you and take your son away."

Ricky dismissed his father, saying, "You're being paranoid! Kellie loves me and is nothing like my mother."

"When you divorce, you'll never get custody of your son because you're a registered sex offender. You have got to keep her away from your mother," Tommy blustered as he started to get drunk in front of Ricky.

"We're not getting a divorce." His father's irrational response to his wife's friendship with his mother had taken Ricky by surprise, and he attributed it to the alcohol. "The only thing wrong with our marriage is that my interfering father won't leave us alone and stay out of our business," he responded tersely. Shaking his head, Ricky left.

--->+===0 0==+<---

Cody was born the summer before Vicky's freshman year of high school, and on the day she held her nephew for the first time, Victoria fell in love. "I'm going to be the best aunt in the world," she told Cody.

She'd never held a baby that small before and was smitten with the sweet little boy as he slept in her arms. It wasn't until Ricky had moved to Texas from Canada that Vicky had grown close to her brother, and as soon as Cody was born, she started spending more time at her father's house so that she could get to know her nephew. Vicky liked her new sister-in-law and tried not to judge her for her past.

Yet her father's distrust of his son's wife only grew when he realized how much time Vicky was spending over at his son's house. Tommy didn't like his daughter hanging around Kellie. "Kellie used to be a stripper and still dresses like one. I don't want you to start dressing that way," he'd tell his daughter when she'd ask if she could go to her brother's house.

"You don't know what you're talking about. Kellie talks to me like I'm a real human being instead of just a pet," Vicky defended her sister-in-law.

"Kellie only married your brother for the money and is using you to cement her position in the family." Vicky stood shocked with her mouth gaping open as her father railed against Kellie. "Why else would anyone marry Ricky, knowing that he was a convicted felon and a registered sex offender?" he told his daughter, insisting she stay away from Kellie. "She's a bad influence on you."

"You've lost it, Dad! It couldn't possibly be because she loves him?" Vicky sniped back at her father. She then stormed out and walked over to her brother's house.

Kellie did love Ricky. Ricky had always been good to her. It seemed as though Kellie was a stabilizing influence for Ricky, but Tommy didn't care. He only saw her as a threat to the empire. "I have spent my whole life building something, and I'm not about to let some pole dancer walk away with any of Ricky's money," he repeatedly told his daughter. Vicky was incensed that her father was so ugly to Kellie. Yet Tommy continued to rant. "I have to keep a close eye on Ricky to make sure he doesn't screw up again. And you're going to stay away from Kellie because you're an impressionable young girl and I don't like her influence over you."

⊷⊷⊷ ⊶⊶⊶

Before long Tommy turned his focus on his daughter and decided that he was not about to let Vicky follow her brother's footsteps. He spent too much time dealing with his own issues and was determined to send her away to boarding school at St. Martin's. Vicky wanted to stay in Houston with her mother, but Tommy paid the bills and didn't really care what she wanted. So, Tommy strong-armed Sarah into sending Vicky to St. Martin's.

"I don't want to go St. Martin's," Vicky complained to her mother when she found out about her father's plans. "I like going to school in Houston."

They'd applied to several prominent Episcopal high schools in the Houston area, but by the time the school year started in August, St. Martin's was the only option available.

"I don't know what else to do," Sarah told Vicky as she tried to comfort her daughter. "I've tried, but all the schools you applied put you on the waiting list."

Both suspected that Tommy had worked his magic behind the scenes to make sure she didn't get into school in Houston.

Adjusting to boarding school was hard at first, but as soon as Vicky started to make new friends, things got better. Once his daughter was at St. Martin's school, Tommy started going to visit her at school regularly. Meanwhile, Sarah, who still worked, was soon out of the loop. Sarah had never missed a single class party, school play, or basketball game. Yet Vicky was at Tommy's alma mater, and so it was all about him.

Tommy showing up at St. Martin's to visit his daughter any time he wanted to soon started to make Vick uncomfortable. Vicky didn't always want her father around. "He's always reminiscing about the good old days at St. Martin's," she objected to her mother when she came for a visit one weekend. "My friends make fun of him, and it's embarrassing."

Once during her sophomore year, Tommy took Vicky and three of her friends to dinner at Barton Spring's BBQ. As soon as Vicky and her friends got in the car, they smelled the alcohol on his breath. The girls whispered among themselves, wondering what to do. As they ate their dinner, he ordered several more drinks, and the girls wondered if they should even get in the car to go back to school with him.

When it was time to leave, Vicky confronted her father, telling him that he was too drunk to drive. Tommy got belligerent, insisting they get in the car. "I am fine to drive home. Now get in the car so I can get you back to school."

"Maybe we'll be all right," one of the friends, Katelyn, said sheepishly.

The restaurant was on the feeder road of Loop 360 and was only a few miles from school, but Tommy got on the freeway going the wrong direction, only realizing what he'd done when he saw the headlights of oncoming traffic. The girls started screaming and crying, Tommy pulled off on the shoulder of an overpass to turn around and barely missed driving off a bridge.

When they got back to school, the girls got out of the car and ran to their dorm. In Katelyn's room, Vicky sat on the end of her bed shaking and began to cry. "I'm so sorry he did that. My father is a hopeless alcoholic. But I never thought he would put us in danger like that." Mortified by her father's actions, Vicky apologized for her father.

Her friends tried to be supportive and sympathetic, but soon Katelyn spoke up, saying, "You have to do something about his drinking before he hurts someone."

The next week, Tommy once again showed up at school and invited his daughter and her friends to dinner. Vicky confronted her father about his alcoholism for the first time. "Look, my friends don't really want to go to dinner with you anymore. You almost killed us last time."

"You're overreacting!" Tommy retorted. "It didn't happen like that at all. It was dark, and I didn't see the signs. It could have happened to anyone." Tommy lost his temper and yelled in his daughter's face. "It didn't have anything to do with how much I drank, and you were never in any kind of danger! You and your friends are just being stupid."

Vicky was incensed that he would insult her and friends like that. She turned, looking her father in the eye. "I'm not overreacting. You have no idea how many problems your drinking has caused this family. You're an alcoholic, and you cannot drink around Ricky." She continued emphatically. "If Ricky is going to have any chance at staying sober, you're going to have to go to rehab."

Tommy bristled and only said, "I am not an alcoholic; my mother was the alcoholic."

"Then the only hope my brother has to stay sober is with my help." She turned and ran back to her dorm.

Her father's drinking was a real problem. Vicky felt he was selfish down to the core and in denial about his alcoholism. Vicky's dad had never really been a big part of her life, and now that he was, his larger-than-life persona overshadowed her wherever she went.

"He is everywhere!" she told her brother one weekend when she came home to visit. "I can't get away from him."

"I'm glad he's obsessing over you and leaving me alone." Ricky laughed. He acted like it was a joke, but both of them knew it wasn't really all that funny.

"No one sees his flaws; they just see the big wad of money in his pocket," she fumed. "He is an alcoholic who cheated on both our mothers. He paid no attention to me until I started going to St. Martin's. Now he's trying to rewrite history again, pretending that he's an involved, doting father."

Ricky just laughed.

"It's not funny. It's bad enough that he's around all the time," Vicky protested. She paused for a second and swallowed hard. "Something else happened when dad was visiting me at school last week."

Ricky could see that this was something that shook Vicky to her core. "I caught him checking out one of my friends, one of my young male friends. I was at cheerleading practice." Vicky looked around to see if anyone else was listening. "My friends, Brock and Eric, were there watching us practice. When dad walked up, I saw him looking at them like they were fresh meat or something." Vicky was horrified. "Nobody saw it but me! It made my skin crawl, and I wanted to throw up."

Taking a deep breath, Ricky leaned back in his chair. "Are you sure?" Ricky asked. "I'm not questioning your judgment. It's just this is so sick, no one would believe us."

"Sure, I'm sure. I've seen dad doing stuff like that when Eddie was around. It was the exact same thing!" She raised her voice, becoming overwrought.

"He needs to stop hanging around your friends and start acting his age," Ricky said sternly. He suddenly remembered all the times their dad had hung out with him and his friends when he was in high school, and it made him sick to his stomach.

"What am I supposed to do?" she whimpered. "No one at St. Martin's would ever believe me if I said anything."

Chapter 39

IN THE FALL of her junior year, Victoria was growing into womanhood. She was a beautiful girl who'd inherited the best qualities from both parents. She had big blue eyes like her mother, and long light-brown hair that she wore in a topknot most of the time. Vicky missed her mother and the simple life she'd had when she went to school in Houston. She had lots of friends at St. Martin's, but her real friends lived in Houston. At this point, she was making every effort to distance herself from her father.

"Things are so complicated at St. Martin's. Dad is around so much, and he doesn't realize what a drag he is. Things would be a lot easier if he weren't hanging around embarrassing me all the time," she complained to her mother. Nevertheless, she knew there was nothing she could do about her father.

Ecstatic that his father was out of his hair, Ricky was over two years sober, and his wife was pregnant with their second son and due any day. Ricky had found his niche and was doing so well as a leasing agent that he'd opened his own title company. He'd had grown his business so successfully that he had ten employees and was making enough money to support his family without depending on his father for anything.

Ricky's life was going well, but try as he may, he still felt like he was a disappointment to his father. Ricky could see the disapproving looks Tommy would give his son whenever Ricky brought paperwork over for him to sign. He'd question Ricky, "Did you go to the courthouse to research this deed, or did you just look this up on the county's website?"

Ricky was trying to get along with his father, but it was hard to do when he talked to him like a child. "I know I messed up when I was younger, but I'm really trying to straighten out my life and be a husband and father."

Having a little less than three years on his probation, Ricky'd stopped taking his medication, saying, "I don't feel like it was working anymore." He'd also stopped going to his AA meetings and didn't call his sponsor back when he tried to check up on him. He'd almost made it to three years sober when he had his first beer, hiding it from everyone. It wasn't long after that that Ricky stopped checking in with his probation officer altogether.

While off his meds when his second son, Caleb Brian, was born, Ricky became so stressed out by idea of his mother coming to town for a visit that he had another manic episode. Recognizing the signs, Kellie did what she could to help her husband, but between the new baby and taking care of a toddler, she was overwhelmed. Kellie called his AA sponsor, Taylor, begging him for help. "I don't know what to do. I have a newborn and a two-year-old to tend to, and there's only so much I can do."

"All you can do is be there for him. I think Ricky is trying but is having a crisis in faith because it's harder to stay sober than he'd hoped. Sobriety is a daily effort, so you need to be understanding and supportive." Taylor knew Ricky's wife had been before she'd gotten pregnant drinking in front of him but tried not to judge her. "Remember, you have to practice what you preach if you really want to help your husband."

Desperately, she asked Ricky's little sister for help, knowing her heart was in the right place especially when it came to her brother. Kellie confided her concerns to Vicky, adding. "Could you please help me? I don't want anything bad to happen to Ricky, and I am worried."

Deciding she needed to have the same talk with Kellie that Ricky's sponsor had just had with her, Vicky said, "If you truly love my brother, you have to stop drinking and smoking pot." She gave her a stern warning. "You cannot continue to party around him and expect him not to give up."

"I hear what you're saying," Kellie said complacently, and she gave her sister-in-law a hug. Both of them had the same goal in mind and hoped that Ricky hadn't fallen so far off the wagon that he couldn't get back on it.

⤖ ⬿

Meanwhile, Tommy was so wrapped up in his daughter's life that Ricky falling off the wagon went unnoticed. Vicky's father had bought his daughter a car when she turned sixteen, but still she continued to dodge him whenever possible.

"What high school junior wants their dad around all the time? It's starting to get on my nerves," she would gripe to her brother and Kellie when she came to visit. Vicky would never forget the way her father had blown her off most every weekend until she went to St. Martin's.

She started going to the ranch to stay with her brother and his family when Tommy wasn't around. In due time, she became friends with a young man named Grady while she was at her brother's house. Vicky had fun spending time with him. "He's not a boyfriend," she giggled when Kellie asked. "He's nice to me, and we're just hanging out and having fun. But please don't tell my father. He'll overact and act like a jerk if he thinks we're more than friends."

She was afraid her father would interfere the way he'd done with Kellie and Ricky, and she didn't want to hear it.

Lucky for Vicky, her father went to a class reunion in the spring of that year at St. Martin's and met someone who caught his attention. The St. Martin's community was quite small; therefore, all the classes that had graduated went to one weekend-long celebration. At dinner on the first night, Tommy received special recognition and thanks for his fund-raising efforts at the school over the past year. While he glad-handed everyone at the reunion, a brown-eyed beauty came up and reintroduced herself.

"I'm Caroline Carter." She sat down beside Tommy and asked, "Do you remember me? I was four years younger than you. I was in the class of 1971, and everyone called me Charlie when I was here."

Tommy had been a senior when Caroline was a freshman. Usually, Tommy knew most everyone at the reunion, and he apologized when admitting that really didn't remember her. They hit it off right away and spent hours reminiscing over their high school memories. Tommy had dated a few times since Eddie, but nothing had seemed to work out. Since his divorce, Tommy hadn't been attracted to a woman, but quite surprisingly, he was smitten with the pretty woman who laughed at all his jokes and made him feel special. Lonesome since his breakup with Eddie, he'd thrown himself into his daughter and his fund-raising efforts at St. Martin's to distract himself from his disappointment in Ricky and his family.

At the end of the evening, Tommy made sure he got Charlie's phone number, and the next day he'd called her and asked her out on a date.

Caroline was a divorcée with a PhD in sociology. She taught at the University of Texas at El Paso and, like Tommy, had come to Austin for the St. Martin's class reunion. Caroline had two grown children; her daughter was married and lived with her husband and children in Austin, and she also had a son.

They shared many of the same points of view about politics, life, and family. Caroline was perfect for Tommy. She was educated, sophisticated, and articulate, and she seemed to do all the right things to make Tommy feel important and worthwhile.

Tommy and Caroline had a whirlwind romance, and in due time they were traveling together and Caroline had moved into Tommy's townhouse in Houston. Tommy introduced his new girlfriend to his friends almost immediately. Most of them were grateful he was dating again, and it was obvious by the way she looked at him that she truly cared.

Soon the couple was inseparable, and Caroline's constant presence only added to the tensions between Tommy and his daughter. Tommy did like the fact that Victoria spent most of the summer driving back and forth between her mother's house and her brother's house at the ranch, spending most of her time with her brother and his family. She'd heard that her dad was dating but didn't think too much about it. Vicky was just glad that he'd found someone else to bother. "Maybe he'll stay out of my life if he has someone else to obsess about," she exclaimed at the dinner table at Ricky's house.

It was the summer before her senior year Tommy heard rumors that his daughter had made friends with an unsavory local boy. Even though things, her friendship between Vicky and her friend Grady were innocent, all he could think about was his sister and how she'd married someone beneath her because she'd gotten pregnant in high school. Soon, he decided he needed to do something about it.

"The thought of my daughter being deflowered by some shady cowboy makes me want to shoot that punk!" he told Caroline. Tommy could help but think about all the unplanned pregnancies in his family, and the thought of his daughter getting knocked up so young made him crazy.

Tommy couldn't help but think about how easy his life would be right now if he'd never been married. He probably never would have been married if he hadn't gotten Marie in the first place. Tommy would never know if it would have been easier to be openly gay if he'd never been married. All he knew was that he was still conflicted about his sexuality and his children only complicated things.

"It would ruin her life if he gets her pregnant," Caroline replied as they sat on the porch of Tommy's house, holding hands and watching the sun set over the farmland. She'd only known Tommy for a short time, she felt as if she were already part of his family. "I hope I'm not overstepping my bounds by interjecting my opinions about your daughter."

Before long, Vicky started staying with her father mostly to keep the peace in the family. And because change in her brother's demeanor. Kellie and Ricky were fighting a lot, and knew that here presence at his house might add to the stress between her brother and his wife. Besides, now that Caroline was on the scene, her father wasn't around as much as he usually was.

One summer afternoon, Vicky and her friends were off riding four-wheelers when she had a flat tire. It was getting dark, and Vicky called Grady, who gave her a ride to her father's house where she kept some clean clothes. Muddy and exhausted, Vicky went upstairs to her room to clean up and change. Grady was waiting downstairs while she got ready for the party that they'd been invited to that evening. Just as Vicky put on a clean pair of jeans and a shirt, she heard her father shouting. She ran downstairs to see what the commotion was, only to find that her father had kicked her friend, Grady, out of his house.

Tommy's face was twisted with anger, and he whirled around to Vicky as he slammed the front door. "Why was he here?" Tommy inquired. "Were you having sex with that boy?"

Vicky was horrified and tried to explain. "Oh my God! We weren't having sex! Grady's my friend, and I called him to give me a ride home because I had a flat on the four-wheeler. I went upstairs to change clothes because I was muddy." She was horrified at her father's accusations and was trying not to cry.

"I didn't do anything wrong, and neither did Grady!" she declared, realizing instantly that he was determined to think the worst of her. She picked up a pillow off the couch and threw it at her father, shouting, "You're a hypocrite! You think you know everything, but you don't know anything about me!"

As she started to run up the stairs, Caroline caught her by the arm, saying, "You should show more respect for your father! He knows what is best for you, and you should listen to him and stop being so disrespectful."

Vicky jerked her arm away from Caroline, saying, "How dare you stick your nose in my business. Just because you're dating my father doesn't make you my mother. I have a mother." Flabbergasted, Vicky went upstairs and packed up her things to go back to her mother's house in Houston.

Vicky was in tears when she left, and when she got home to Houston, she went straight to her room and cried all night long.

"Dad had it all wrong!" she told her mother. "I'm not sleeping with anyone, and he accused me of having sex with Grady when he only gave me a ride home." Vicky sobbed into her pillow. "The way he talked to Grady was awful. I'll probably never see him again!" Vicky was crying so hard she could barely talk.

"Caroline is complicating things by encouraging Dad to overreact," Vicky added. She sniffed and blew her nose.

After that incident, Vicky tried her best to get along with her father and his new girlfriend, Caroline. Unfortunately, Caroline was around all the time, and Vicky's already strained relationship with her father went from bad to worse.

At first Vicky blamed it all on Caroline. "She thinks she's so superior just because she has a PhD!" Vicky complained to Ricky and Kellie, who were experiencing the same bad attitude from Tommy. In time, though, they concluded that their dad had told Caroline his version of reality, and even though Caroline was still being obnoxious, Tommy hadn't been completely honest about his life with his new girlfriend.

Vicky started to hate Caroline almost as much as she'd hated Eddi, and in the fall after Vicky went back to school for her senior year, she did everything she could to avoid both of them. "They're always together like Mutt and Jeff," she told her friend Katelyn. Vicky was a cheerleader, and they would come to all the games together to watch her cheer. Vicky played basketball and soccer, and would look up into the stands to see her father and Caroline holding hands.

By the time Victoria graduated in the spring of 2005, she was sick of St. Martin's. Her high school experience had been overshadowed by her father's overpowering presence. She was more than ready to go to college and get away from her crazy, control-freak father and his shadow, Caroline. On the day of her graduation. Vicky wore a simple white dress as she graduated from the same chapel on the hill that her father had graduated from almost four decades earlier.

"I can't believe my dad couldn't let me have a good high school experience," she said to her mother after graduation.

"I know, honey. Someday you'll be able to look past your issues with your father and remember what was good about this place." Vicky hugged her mom and went off to the dreaded family lunch.

Chapter 40

MEETING CAROLINE HAD taken Tommy's by surprise. Tommy thought that he'd never find another woman who would want him. His health was a big issue, even though with the advances in medicine his HIV was under control. His children thought he was being overly critical of them, and maybe he was. He saw it as being protective, shielding his children from the mistakes that he'd made that had forever changed his life. Sometimes there are no do-overs, and he was only beginning to figure that out.

Tommy was as healthy as could be expected, and his viral load was virtually undetectable. However, the stigma that went with HIV still scared people. Tommy had other health issues—the biggest and the scariest issue was his liver. Between the hepatitis B, the AZT in the early days of AIDS treatment, and his drinking, Tommy's liver was enlarged and inflamed. With only about 15 percent of his liver function, he'd gained at least fifty pounds since his divorce and was on powerful pain medication due to his constant pain from severe gout.

Tommy had stop drinking so many times he'd lost count, always finding an excuse to go back to the bottle. When he was younger, he could lose twenty pounds by cutting out alcohol, but now that he was old and fat, it really didn't make that big a difference in his weight, and that was even more discouraging. "If I knew I was going to live this long, I would've taken better care of myself when I was younger," he joked to his new girlfriend.

When Caroline came along, Tommy saw her as his last chance at happiness. The only thing that scared him more than dying was dying alone. And now that he had Caroline in his life, he didn't have to think about that anymore.

Pulling out all the stops, Tommy wined and dined her. They vacationed in exotic places, and in short order Tommy bought her a house in Houston Heights, just north of downtown. It was an older craftsman-style bungalow on Harvard Street, and Tommy gave her all the money she needed to remodel it the way she wanted. For the first time in a very long while, Tommy felt safe again. Finally, he wasn't alone and he wasn't overly concerned about whether or not his daughter and son would like his new girlfriend.

Shortly after they started dating, Tommy felt obligated to confess to Caroline that he had very strong feelings for men and that he was HIV positive. "One of the biggest problems I had in my marriage to Sarah was being a monogamist," he told Caroline. "I tried and just couldn't do it."

Much to Tommy's surprise, Caroline didn't balk.

"I can't guarantee I will be monogamous, but I can promise that you'll come first and will be the only one I love." Tommy revealed his soul to Caroline, and she didn't jump and run.

Tommy was in love! He'd finally found the woman of his dreams!

Caroline had found the man of her dreams, too. She was in her sixties and wanted to retire and travel, and Tommy was the perfect companion. Caroline had been married once before to a man name Robert Carter. Robert had been a commercial builder in the Austin housing boom of the 1970s and 1980s, and had talked some wealthy friends in to investing in his business. And when the housing bubble popped, his partners had discovered that he was robbing Peter to pay Paul.

Unbeknown to his wife, their family was living far beyond their means. When Robert's business partners found out that he was using their money to support his lavish lifestyle, they brought in auditors and filed a suit.

Robert and Caroline were several million dollars in debt, and it wasn't long before the couple divorced. Caroline had to get a job. She'd gotten a degree in sociology before they married, and the only job she was able to get to support herself and her children was as a social worker for Travis County.

Following their divorce, Caroline filed for bankruptcy because she couldn't pay her half of the debt. Caroline had always blamed her husband and his desire to live large for most of the couple's financial woes.

Caroline had now been divorced for almost fifteen years, and during that time, she'd gone back to college, eventually earning a PhD in sociology. When she'd met Tommy, she was teaching sociology classes at UTEP. She had dated several men over the years, but nothing had ever worked out for her, and she'd heard Tommy was between marriages before the class reunion and made it a point to bump into him again. When Caroline reintroduced herself to Tommy, she saw not just a chance for love but a chance to retire to a gentile life and the end of the financial problems that had plagued her for so long. She was as surprised as he was when she fell for him, too.

When Tommy confessed to her about his life and health issues, Caroline had to think hard before looking past them. But she soon decided that he was a great guy and that a life with Tommy was worth the risk.

"I have to admit; I'm impressed with your honesty. It took a lot of strength to tell me about this," she replied, taking Tommy by the hand. "Honesty is probably the most important quality a man can possess, and I've never been the jealous type, so I guess as long as you're honest about it and as long as it's only happening every once in a while, I can live with it."

"All men have problems," she told her friends at UTEP before resigning her position. "But it's a lot easier to put up with a rich man's problems than a poor man's," she joked. She knew that even though she had a PhD, she was never going to make the kind of money that would allow her retire comfortably. Tommy was her chance to retire and live in style.

"I'm not being greedy," she continued. "I'm just being practical. I'm not getting any younger, and Tommy's good qualities outweigh the bad."

Just as Caroline had taken an interest in helping Tommy with his misguided daughter, she soon took it upon herself to help Tommy to fix Ricky's white-trash family. Ricky was almost thirty years old when Caroline came on the scene, and she listened intently as Tommy filled her in the long sordid history behind his relationship with his son, Ricky.

"It's Marie's fault that Ricky has behavior problems," he confided in his new girlfriend one evening while enjoying dinner at a local Italian restaurant. "I'm concerned that Ricky and his wife are going to get ahold of his trust someday and rip through the money on cars, booze, and drugs."

Tommy was worried and was glad to have someone he could confide in about his concerns. "Ricky's trust is about to mature and revert to him at age thirty, and if he gets a divorce after that, then that woman he's married to might just wind up with everything, especially if he keeps screwing up and goes back to jail."

Even though he'd only known Caroline for a short time, he trusted her completely and confided some of the details of the trust to his new girlfriend while they ate and drank wine. But what he didn't tell her was that Ricky owned half of everything.

By the time Victoria went to college in the fall after her graduation, Ricky was in real trouble. He'd been off his meds for months, and the stress from the constant bickering with his father and his wife had pushed him to self-medicate again. Ricky's personality had changed, and the person he was when he was sober and on his meds, was 180 degrees different than the person on drugs and alcohol. Ricky had become aggressive, moody, and impulsive, making rash, irrational decisions about even the simplest things.

Aware that his son was screwing up once again, Tommy presented him with divorce papers and begged him to move forward with a divorce from Kellie. When Ricky refused to sign the papers, Tommy closed down Ricky's title company and laid off all his staff.

"You did the right thing," Caroline once again encouraged him. "You have to show him who's in charge."

When he found out his father had shut his business down without even discussing it with him, Ricky was pissed off. Ricky burst into Tommy's office, yelling, "You didn't have any right to close down MY company."

But Tommy was still the trustee of Ricky's accounts. "I did it for your own good. And until you can prove to me that you're behaving rationally, I am going to do what it takes to protect your trust" he told his son. "You're out of control. When you sober up, you can come to work for me."

"You can't judge my life, you old lush." Ricky charged out of the office and went straight to his drug dealer.

When Ricky called him an old lush, it hit Tommy hard. Tommy would rather blame everyone else than ever admit he was an alcoholic. "Vicky said that I had to stop drinking to save my son's life," he confided to Caroline.

"She is just a child," she explained. "What does she know? I don't believe you're an alcoholic, and I'm a trained professional."

However, Caroline had only been around for a short time, and being on his best behavior to impress his new girlfriend, Tommy hadn't yet shown her his dark side.

Now that he had a new enabler in his life, Tommy wasn't about to admit he had a problem with alcohol. It appeared that maybe Caroline was an alcoholic, too, and the two of them drank almost every night.

A few weeks later Tommy and Caroline were married in a small ceremony. They only invited a few of their friends, and the couple intentionally excluded Ricky and Victoria from the ceremony, knowing that they probably wouldn't come anyway. However, before they got married, Tommy asked Caroline to sign a prenuptial agreement.

"It's nothing against you, per se. I just haven't had much luck with woman," Tommy said jokingly as he gave it to Caroline. Lamentably, Caroline wasn't happy about it at all, but she signed it against her better judgment.

⊷⊨● ●⊨⊶

After his father closed the doors on his title company, Ricky got a job driving a truck and separated from his wife. Moving into a trailer house thirty miles from the ranch on a muddy backwoods road, he continued to use drugs. But at least Ricky felt that he was only hurting himself. Occasionally, he'd have to go see his probation officer whenever he failed a drug test.

Emphatically, his PO told him to straighten up. Ricky had already flunked more than one, and the PO was trying to show him some leniency but knew he couldn't continue to protect Ricky if he continued to fail his drug tests.

The probation officer called Tommy. "Look, I like Ricky. He's a good kid. But if he flunks another drug test, Ricky is going to jail."

Finally, Tommy had to open his eyes to the serious problem of his son's drug abuse.

"If you'd been sincere about helping Ricky, you would've gone to his AA meetings and worked with his sponsor to save him. Then maybe he wouldn't be in this mess," the probation officer said, chastising Tommy. "Instead you waited until I called and threatened to put Ricky back in jail to do something to help him. Now it may be too late."

Seeing how upset her husband was after he got off the phone with Ricky's PO, Caroline tried to console her husband. Caroline was getting pretty sick of Ricky and his drama, and she suggested that they stage an intervention. Ricky was unpredictable and violent, and that scared her. Now that she and Tommy were married, she believed that she had a voice in how things should be handled, and so she contacted one of her friends who had a PhD in psychology to arrange an intervention.

"My friend is a professional and knows what she's doing," Caroline assured her husband. "We have to do what we can to save him before he hurts himself or somebody else."

In due time, Caroline's friend, Dr. Martha Bond, set up an intervention for Ricky. Dr. Bond wasn't a medical doctor; however, she was a PhD. Dr. Bond and Caroline taught in the same department at UTEP, and she also had a family counseling service in El Paso.

Dr. Bond contacted Vicky at college to tell her how the intervention was supposed to work and what was expected of her. "I'm worried about my brother, but I don't think this is going to work the way you are anticipating," Vicky informed her. "My dad is an alcoholic, too, and he needs to go to rebab along with Ricky."

"Oh, really," Dr. Bond responded. This was the first she'd heard that Tommy had a problem with alcohol, too. "Well, maybe this is an opportunity for you to express those concerns, and over time and with a lot of therapy, maybe we'll be able to fix the whole family dynamic."

Vicky shook her head, thinking that she'd heard enough. "I've been telling my father that he's an alcoholic for years. He doesn't want to hear it, and it's not going to be any different just because you're there."

Vicky sighed as she continued to map out her concerns about the intervention. "I know my brother. He's going to walk into a room full of drunks telling him how his alcoholism has adversely affected their lives, and he's going to feel betrayed," Vicky declared losing her patience, thinking how naïve and ill-informed this woman was.

"That is certainly one possible outcome," Dr. Bond retorted. "But it is my professional opinion that his response is more likely to be a positive one."

Again, Vicky shook her head. "I will think about it, but I am not going to make any promises." She hung up, telling the therapist that she had to go to class.

Later that afternoon Vicky called Kellie to relay her concerns about the way Ricky's intervention was being handled. "Look, I really don't trust this woman, and it has nothing to do with her being Caroline's friend. Something has to be done, but this isn't it."

"Things have gotten so bad since you went off to college," Kellie informed her. "I love your brother with all my heart, and I can't sit back and do nothing while he kills himself."

Concerned about her brother's reaction and about the odds of the intervention working, Vicky again tried to reiterate her concerns. "I'm worried that this will push him over the edge."

"I don't know what else to do. Your father has frozen us out of all of Ricky's money, and I can't afford the treatment he needs." Vicky could hear the desperation in Kellie's voice. "I don't think it will work either, but I don't have any choice. I have to do something."

"Well, I can't go. I think it's a really bad idea." Vicky paused. "I am concerned that even though your intentions are good and right, he's going to be so pissed off because you ambushed him that nothing you say is going to matter." Vicky paused and took a deep breath. "Dad is turning this into a circus. He's inviting his employees and people outside of our family who have no business coming. Ricky is way too paranoid to not be mad as hell—he's going not trust anyone involved." Vicky spoke thoughtfully. She continued. "I may have to be the one to save him if this pushes him over the edge." Vicky was terrified. "So many things can go wrong on so many levels. I need to be there for him so that he won't eat a bullet when things go badly."

After she hung up with her brother's wife, Vicky called her father to tell him that she wasn't coming to her brother's intervention. It was the first time she had spoken to her father in over six months, and Tommy reacted badly. He yelled at his daughter and demanded she come.

"You are a sick puppy. Did you tell the therapist about your alcoholism, or did you leave that part out?"

Tommy didn't respond to his daughter's question.

Vicky yelled back. "I hope you are getting a group discount, because you need to be in rehab next to your son!" Then she hung up on him.

⊷▬◖ ◗▬⊷

One the day of the intervention, Tommy called Ricky up and asked him to come to the ranch house to discuss some business. Ricky was still estranged from his wife and soon showed up, knowing nothing of the intervention. It was a windy fall day, and rain clouds were building in the heat of the afternoon. As Ricky drove up, he noticed three cars in the driveway. He parked behind his dad's white SUV.

He stepped out of his truck and slapped the dirt off his blue jeans with his baseball cap. He'd just come from feeding his horses, and he was covered in sweat and dust from the horse barn. He used the bottom of his T-shirt to wipe the sweat of his face as he climbed the stairs to the front porch.

Walking inside his father's house, he found everyone sitting in the living room. "What's going on?" he asked.

Dr. Bond spoke first. "Ricky, my name is Dr. Martha Bond, and we are staging an intervention. Everyone in this room loves you and wants to help you. Could you please sit down for a moment and listen?" she said as she motioned for Ricky to sit in a chair she'd put at the front of the room.

She had asked everyone to write letters to Ricky that they would read out loud, describing how Ricky's drug and alcohol abuse had adversely affected each of their lives. Ricky warily sat down in the chair that they had set up for him. He looked around the room seeing the ranch manager, three of the oil field hands, and both field office secretaries, as well as some friends and family, he wondered what in the world was going on. Starting with Kellie, they went around the room reading the letters they'd written.

Angrily, Ricky sat fidgeting while he listened to the letter after letter. About halfway through Ricky became extremely agitated, and when he couldn't take anymore, he yelled, "This is bullshit," and got up and charged out the door, yelling from the driveway, "If anybody wants me, I'll be at my drug dealer's house!"

Ricky got in his truck, peeling out as he drove away.

Chapter 41

FOLLOWING RICKY OUT on to the front porch, Tommy watched helplessly as his son sped down the white-rock road toward the highway, kicking up a cloud of dust behind him. As his son's truck disappeared out of sight, Tommy felt his rage boil up. Turning, he exploded back into the house, shouting at the top of his lungs, "Get out! Everyone! Leave! Now!" He flailed his arms as he tossed everyone out.

Tommy then sat down in the chair that Ricky had been in just moments before and put his head in his hands. Trying to comfort her husband, Caroline rubbed his shoulders.

"Stop it! Just stop it!" he shouted as he pushed her hand away.

Shaking, Tommy fought back the tears. This was probably the only chance they were going to have to get Ricky to go to rehab, and they'd blown it. He was pissed off at everyone. He was mad at Dr. Bond because she'd obviously lied when she said she knew what she was doing. He was pissed off at his wife, not just for letting that unprofessional woman handle his son's intervention, but for turning it into such a fiasco by inviting everybody and his brother to participate. Most of all, he was pissed off at Vicky for being right. Everything that she'd told him was going to happened had happened, and he wished more than anything he'd taken her more seriously.

If she hadn't called me an alcoholic, I might have listened to her.

⋄►▬ ◖▬◗ ◄▬⋄

When he left, Ricky felt as though he had been stabbed in the heart. He'd been ambushed by a room full of people, most of whom he'd personally witnessed falling down drunk themselves. Not one of the people in that room, except maybe his wife, had attempted to help him stay sober.

It all been staged not to help him but to show the world that they cared so their conscience would be clear if he killed himself. The farther away he drove from his father's house, the madder he got. Ricky wasn't too young to remember his dad strung out on cocaine when he was a kid, but somehow now that his dad was the patriarch of the family, everyone pretended like that never happened.

The whole ordeal had pushed Ricky into a manic state. It had only taken about fifteen minutes before he'd snapped. His mind was reeling at a hundred miles an hour. Ricky felt abandoned and alone. When he was in one of his manic states, it felt like no one understood him or showed him any compassion for what he was going. At that moment, Ricky didn't care if he lived or died. He just wanted to stop feeling for a little while.

As he drove down the dirt road that led to his drug dealer's trailer, Ricky mind spun in all directions. Thinking what a hypocrite his father had become, he couldn't believe he'd just waylaid him with a sneak attack.

When Ricky got to the trailer, he saw his dealer, Boo, looking out of the curtains, watching him drive up. Boo was a tall, skinny man covered with tattoos and piercings. Ricky knew that Boo probably wasn't his real name, but he didn't care. He understood why Boo didn't tell his customers his real name; it was just part of the business. Ricky didn't stay long, buying some cocaine, ecstasy, and oxy.

Driving straight to the ratty little trailer he was renting, he felt safe because no one knew where his trailer was, not even Kellie. It was his secret little piece of heaven where he could go when he was manic and ride it out while he self-medicated. After the intervention from hell, Ricky locked the doors and turned off his phone. Pulling a mirror out from under his brown plaid couch, he poured a pile of coke onto it and began chopping up lines.

As soon as he started doing lines, Vicky called her brother, but he didn't answer, she left him a message. The message was simply, "I love you. Call me when you get a chance. I know what they did to you, and it was terrible. I need to talk to you about it."

After he listened to the message, he turned his phone off, only turning it on to check his messages. Lots of people had called, and periodically he would turn on his phone to delete the messages that they had left without listening to them. He didn't delete the message his little sister had left him; he played it back over and over again.

His little sister loved him and didn't judge him. They shared a father, and she was the only one who really understood what he was going through. He was in the middle of a tempest, and his little sister was his anchor.

After a couple of days, he called her back.

"I've been really worried about you." She tried not to cry. "Kellie is afraid that you don't care whether or not you live or die."

"I know she's worried," he replied. "But I really don't want to talk about Kellie."

"Kellie only went along with dad and Caroline because she didn't know what else to do," Vicky said calmly. "You know that she loves you and wants the best for you. She doesn't know how manipulative Dad is. She was genuinely trying to do the right thing."

Ricky didn't respond.

"You and I are in this together," she continued. "My life would be empty without you in it."

After some talking, Vicky managed to convince him to check into rehab and save himself, not just for her sake or the sake of his children, but because he was worthwhile and his life was worth living.

"You sound like my sponsor." Ricky laughed.

"Call your sponsor," Vicky said, and in that moment, she knew that her brother was going to be all right.

After a week, Ricky went home to his wife. The day after he got home, he contacted his sponsor, who helped him get checked into rehab to undergo drug and alcohol treatment.

The next day, Ricky's sponsor drove him to the Pine Grove Recovery Center in Tom Ball, Texas. It was located just north of Houston on ten acres. It was a tranquil environment with walking trails and duck ponds scatter among a well-manicured forest locale. Kellie kissed him good-bye as they dropped him off, and as he turned to wave good-bye, he told his sponsor, "Well it doesn't look like a nuthouse."

⊶ ⊷

After his son's failed intervention blew up in their faces, Tommy was a mess and Caroline wasn't much help, either. It seemed to him that Caroline bitched non-stop for days. Tommy was genuinely afraid for his son, and couldn't think. The first he heard about Ricky was almost ten days later when he got a phone call from the director of the Pine Grove Recovery Center.

Thank God Ricky's OK! How did it get this bad?

Grateful to hear that Ricky hadn't killed himself, Tommy called the director back immediately. Dr. Marvin Lewis answered and informed Tommy that his son Ricky was a patient at his facility. Elated, Tommy started asking questions about Ricky's condition and treatment, and became testy when the man avoided answering his questions.

"I don't mean to seem like I'm dodging your questions, but Ricky's treatment is confidential, and as he's a patient in my facility, I'm obligated to respect his privacy. I only called because Ricky gave me permission to call you to set up payment for his treatment."

Tommy flew off the handle, saying, "I'm not paying for anything unless Ricky signs over his power of attorney."

"Ricky seems to think that he has plenty of money to pay for his treatment and that you'd be the one to authorize imbursement." Tommy's response had taken Dr. Lewis by surprise. "What is your issue with arranging payment for the expense of his treatment?"

"As you well know, rehab is the same as a civil commitment, and as my son's attorney and trustee, I have to insist that he sign over power of attorney, as there is no guarantee that he won't be in your facility for an extended stay," Tommy replied matter-of-factly. "I'll have the papers drawn up and bring them over for his signature."

"It is a matter of policy that the patient not have contact with the immediate family for the first several weeks of treatment," the doctor insisted. "I don't think this is the sort of thing Ricky needs to deal with right now."

"Fine," Tommy replied, and he hung up well aware what the doctor must think of him. Tommy'd been dealing with alcoholism for so long that he'd lost any compassion for anyone with a substance abuse problem, including his son.

⇥▶ ◀⇤

Contact with anyone outside of rehab wasn't allowed for good reason, and so Ricky couldn't just call his father to straighten this mess out. It was quite obvious that Ricky's family were the triggers that caused stress, and after Dr. Lewis's first conversation with the man, he could understand why. Dr. Lewis was perturbed that his patient's father was more concerned about money than his own son's health and well-being.

A few weeks after Ricky checked into rehab, a girlfriend invited her over for dinner and drinks where she met another one the guests named Boyd. After dinner, they talked and Kellie had a couple more glasses of wine. He listened and seemed supportive, telling her it wasn't her fault and that she deserved to be treated with more respect. She'd been blamed for Ricky's problems for so long that it was a relief that someone cared. At the end of the night of drinking, Kellie was a little tipsy, so he volunteered to give her a ride home.

The morning after, Kellie woke up to the sound of the shower running. She immediately became alarmed. Her two youngest sons had spent the night at her grandmother's house, and Justin was over at a friend's house. Walking into the hall, she found Boyd coming out of the bathroom wrapped in a bath towel. "Good morning, babe," he said as he kissed her.

Startled, Kellie pushed him away.

"What's wrong, sweetheart. I haven't shaved yet, but I didn't think my morning stubble was that bad." Boyd grabbed Kellie around her waist and tried to pull her in for a kiss.

Kellie pushed him away again. "Oh my God! I was drunk, and you took advantage of me," Kellie screamed.

"That's not what happened at all, sugar. You kissed me first," he said.

Either Boyd was lying or Kellie was a lot drunker when she left her friend's house than she'd thought. Boyd was only supposed to give her a ride home. Instead, he'd seduced her, and she was too drunk to stop him. Kellie had screwed up. "Look, Boyd, you are going to have to leave. This shouldn't have happened. I'm a married woman." Hurriedly, she made Boyd get dressed and shoved him out the door before anyone could see his truck in the driveway.

"When am I going to see you again?" Boyd asked as she slammed the door in his face. Instantly, she became physically ill, and she threw up all morning.

In the weeks that followed, Boyd started showing up places where she was. She told him to leave her alone, but Boyd wasn't having any of it.

In the meantime, Ricky's doctor had arranged for Kellie to visit her husband. Ricky had been in treatment for a month before Kellie was allowed to visit her husband and participate in his recovery. Everything started out well as they walked hand in hand around the grounds, with Kellie telling Ricky stories about his children, However, shortly after their joint session with the therapist began, Kellie's conscience got the best of her and she confessed her stupid mistake to her husband and his therapist, and begged for forgiveness.

Ricky sat stoically staring out the window when he heard that his wife had been unfaithful.

The therapist knew by the angry look on his face that this was a problem and asked him, "How do you feel about your wife's indiscretions?"

Ricky didn't know what to say. He stared at the floor for a minute and asked, "How am I supposed to feel?"

The therapist was getting frustrated with Ricky answering his questions with questions.

The therapist then asked Kellie how she felt. "Well, I made a big mistake while I was drinking, and I am sorry. He took advantage of me when my defenses were down, and I'm terrified of this guy. Boyd has become obsessed with me and is convinced that I am going to leave my husband for him."

The therapist once again asked Ricky how he felt about his wife. Ricky had been in treatment for a month and had been asked at least twenty times a day how he felt. He finally looked the therapist in the eye, saying, "I feel like I am ready to go home."

Chapter 42

AFTER ONLY A month in rehab, Ricky checked out and went home, against the recommendations of Dr. Lewis. News of his wife's affair while he was in rehab spread through the East Texas gossip grape like wildfire. Shortly after Ricky's release, Tommy and Caroline heard the gossip around town regarding Kellie's infidelity, and once again, Tommy presented his son with divorce papers that he'd gotten an attorney to draw up.

"You need to sign these divorce papers and get that woman out of your life," Tommy huffed, throwing the document down on the table in front of his son, believing with all his heart that his son would be better off without Kellie in his life.

"I really don't think that this is any of your business," Ricky said, pushing the divorce decree back at his father. "You don't know the whole story, and you are the last person who should judge people about being unfaithful."

Incensed, Tommy pointed his finger at his son and said "You are going to regret this decision someday."

"Maybe I will, or maybe I won't—but this is my decision to make. Not yours," Ricky added calmly.

Only Kellie and Ricky knew what really had happened.

"The one thing I learned at rehab is that I can't control other people. I can only control my reaction to other people," Ricky asserted calmly. "I'm doing my best and taking it day by day."

⊷⊨● ●⊨⊶

Ricky was doing what he could to stay clean and sober after checking himself out of rehab early, but bad luck just followed him around like a dark rain cloud. Ricky had only been home for a few days when Kellie's "lover," Boyd, showed up at their house and picked a fight with Ricky in his driveway. Ricky was so angry at what Boyd had done to his wife and to his family that he took a baseball bat and broke every window out of Boyd's truck. After Boyd filed charges against Ricky, a sheriff sent a deputy to Ricky's house to investigate.

"Just between me and you, that guy probably had it coming," the deputy disclosed. "But he filed a report, and I have to take you in." The deputy handcuffed him, took him to jail, and released him the next day, telling Ricky they would leave him alone if he kept his nose clean.

Boyd didn't like that the sheriff's department had let Ricky go and complained. It wasn't long before the police were harassing him. Once when Ricky was shopping at Walmart, the police were waiting for him by his truck when he came out. They put him in handcuffs in the back of the police car while searching his truck.

"We received an anonymous call from a concerned citizen that you're in violation of your probation and carrying firearms," the deputy responded when Ricky asked what the charges were. Ricky spent the night in jail, and when he got out the next morning, the sheriff told him not to leave town.

Afterward, Ricky went to see an attorney recommended to him by his AA sponsor, John Walsh, hoping there was something he could do. John Walsh was a fair-complexed older man with white hair and a receding hairline. He wore a bow tie with a navy blue blazer and gray polyester pants. Mr. Walsh sat behind his beat-up old office desk, pondering Ricky's plight for a moment. He too was a recovering alcoholic and understood all too well the difficulties Ricky was facing.

After a minute of silence, he said, "I wish I had better news for you, but it looks like because of the charges brought against by Mr. Boyd Taylor, your probation will be revoked. You should consider turning yourself into the sheriff's department," Mr. Walsh said in a low calm tone.

Ricky sat in the chair across from his new attorney, shaking his head.

"You only have a year and a half more left on your probation, and once you get it over with, then it'll be done and the police will have nothing left to hang over your head except the trumped-up charges that Boyd filed against you, and I believe that we can beat those charges. He came on your property and provoked a fight. It's a stretch, but you could claim that it was self-defense."

Ricky sat quietly for a moment, staring out the window of Mr. Walsh's office. He wanted control of his life back, and this was the only logical way of getting it.

On Monday morning of the following week, Ricky surrendered himself to the detention office in the sheriff's department. A few days later, Ricky was transferred to the Montgomery County detention facility, where he was to serve out the remainder of his probation.

A week later, Kellie was having breakfast with her children when she heard a knock at the door. Upon answering it, she found a dozen FBI agents who served a search warrant to search the house. After asking Kellie and her children to step outside, she watched helplessly as the FBI stormed her house, dressed in body armor and with weapons drawn.

Tearing her house apart, they immediately found Ricky's stash of guns hidden behind the false wall in the guest room. But the way they tore up the house made it clear to Kellie that they were looking for much more than just guns.

After speaking to the prosecutor, his lawyer found out that the authorities had not only charged Ricky with violation of his probation, but more charges were pending. "They are about to move you to a federal holding facility while you are awaiting sentencing."

"What in the world had just happened?" Ricky asked Mr. Walsh. He didn't have any outstanding warrants, and except for getting into a fight with his wife's stalker in his own driveway, he hadn't been in trouble for years.

"Why is the FBI involved?" Ricky had guns, but they were nothing like the stash he'd had when he was buying guns and selling them to Oscar in shady deals. "Why in the world would the FBI raid the house over fewer than a dozen guns?" Ricky repeated. He was stunned and confused.

Mr. Walsh was just as perplexed as Ricky was. "I don't know what is going on, but I intend to get to the bottom of this. This is a gross miscarriage of justice!"

The answer came three months later. At first, the FBI refused to let Ricky or Mr. Walsh see the allegations against him or release the name of his accuser. Mr. Walsh finally forced the FBI to release a copy affidavit of the allegations made against him using the Freedom of Information Act. In the ten-page affidavit, it was alleged that Ricky was a homegrown terrorist who was building bombs and weapons of mass destruction. It included ten pages of very detailed unsubstantiated accusations against Ricky. None other than his dad's wife number three, Caroline Ellison, had signed it.

Despite reading the document repeatedly, Ricky was in shock and couldn't believe his eyes. In three short years, Caroline had managed to marry his father, alienate his little sister, and get him thrown in prison on some trumped-up terrorism charge.

Ricky froze in that moment. "This can't be happening," he said to his attorney as he moaned in disbelief. "What the hell?"

Ricky began to pace around the interview room. He was dressed in a prison-issue jumpsuit and wore prison-issue sandals. "You can't tell me that my dad didn't know anything about this. He had to have known!"

―――――――――

On the day of his sentencing hearing, Tommy sat in the courtroom anxiously. He intended to speak on his son's behalf, and the magnitude of Ricky's problems were beginning to sink in. Tommy felt like a failure as a father. He wasn't there for the boy when he grew up and he knew it. He'd just found out that he was HIV positive when the boy moved to Canada with his mother, and every day was a struggle when a death sentence loamed over your head. He'd not been the kind of father that Ricky deserved and now he was facing prison time.

In the courtroom, Tommy spoke up, addressing the judge. "Your Honor, it was all a big misunderstanding. We were afraid that Ricky would get into more trouble if he had guns in his house, so we hired a man to go through my son's house and see if he had guns hidden somewhere. When he found the false wall, he tried to open it and found an electric wire attached to it. He reported it to my wife, who filed the affidavit with the FBI. She mistakenly thought that Ricky had wired it with explosives."

After defending his wife's affidavit for several minutes, Tommy tried to convince the judge that his wife had filed the affidavit based on a misunderstanding cause by a not-so-bright private investigator who had mislead her about the potential danger.

"Mr. Ellison, that is probably the most farfetched story ever concocted by anyone in my courtroom." The judge learned forward, looked Tommy square in the eye, and said, "I don't believe anything you just told me."

A few minutes later, the judge threw out Ricky's probation and sentenced him to a minimum of five years, and then he scheduled another hearing to determine if the year Ricky had already spent in jail would apply to his sentence.

After Ricky's sentence was handed down, he was escorted back to the detention facility and Tommy stayed behind to discuss Ricky's finances with his attorney. He'd tried several times to visit his son in jail to take care of the details, but found that Ricky had taken him off the visitation list.

"Ricky will be turning thirty while he's in custody, and I've been taking care of finances so far," he said to Mr. Walsh. "But now that it's clear Ricky isn't getting out anytime soon, I thought it best if I were given power of attorney over his assets so that I can manage the until the end of his sentence."

The attorney cleared his throat, obviously uncomfortable about being the barer of bad news. "Ricky has already made arrangements for his property to be managed while he's incarcerated," Mr. Walsh informed him.

"Why am I just now hearing about this?" Tommy jumped to his feet and shouted. Darkness came over Tommy. "Ricky's been in and out of trouble since he was young. I've been taking care of business, and I think it's best that I continue to do so."

"After what just transpired, Ricky has a problem believing that you have his best interests at heart," Ricky's attorney said in a calm voice.

Tommy was incensed that anyone would question his intentions towards his son.

"Ricky's been in and out of trouble so much that I thought it best not to tell him where all his assets are until he needed to know," Tommy yelled as he paced at the back of the courtroom, flailing his arms as he spoke. "I didn't want him to blow it up his nose."

"I don't really know what you expected to happen, because like the judge, I felt as though your explanation was simplistic and rehearsed. Hiding the truth from someone doesn't protect them," Mr. Walsh continued. "Ricky has instructed me that under no circumstance am I to give you power of attorney."

Tommy became enraged and started yelling so loud and demonstratively that the bailiff and a guard promptly asked him to leave the courtroom. He'd controlled Ricky's money for almost fifteen years since the death of his father, and he never imagined that his son would remove him as his trustee. He'd built an empire, and now a big part of that empire was no longer in his control.

→▷■◁ ▷■◁←

Sitting in the Colonel's rocking chair on the front porch at the ranch, Tommy pretended to read his book. He stared at the same page for over an hour. He'd just gotten home from his son's sentencing hearing, was in a bad mood, and didn't really want to talk to Caroline about what had transpired.

His ranch house sat on a sand ridge deposited there by ancient floods from glacial runoff after the last ice age. He'd always loved that hill ever since he was a boy. Overlooking the Brazos River bottom where the farmers were busy plowing the fields getting ready to plant cotton in the spring, Tommy would glance up and sip his drink every once and a while. It was late February, and it was the first warm day of the winter. All it would take for the trees to burst out in bloom would be a few more beautiful days like this one.

The childhood jubilation and excitement Tommy used to have when he watched the farmers ready their fields had waned. Tommy was numb. Two months ago was Christmas, and if it hadn't been for Caroline and her family, he'd have been alone during the holidays.

Caroline joined her husband on the porch, and with a gin and tonic in hand, she sat down in the chair next to Tommy. She took a sip of her drink as she watched a dozen robins hopping around the yard. "Robins are here; spring must be just around the corner." She glanced at her husband, hoping he'd talk to her.

"It's a shame the judge threw the book at Ricky," she said as she went back to watching the robins. "It seems harsh, but it's probably for the best. Maybe he'll dry out...and besides, they'll make him stay on his medication."

Tommy looked up from his book and glared at Caroline. "You didn't have to go to the FBI. That was overkill. I know you were concerned that he was out of control. We both were. But I asked you to talk to the sheriff, not throw him in prison."

Caroline got up and leaned on the porch railing. "Oh no! You're not changing your story just because Ricky got a harsher punishment than we expected." She shook her hand in the air. "We discussed this extensively. Ricky wasn't just out of control. He was violent. It was only a matter of time before someone got hurt, and you know it."

Caroline finished her drink. "I'm going to mix another drink. Do you want one, too?" she asked as he reached out and grabbed her hand.

"I'd do it myself, but my gout is bothering me tonight and I can hardly walk." Tommy handed Caroline his glass, and she went back inside.

⇥⇥▐ ▐⇤⇤

After Ricky went to jail, Tommy began drinking again in earnest. For the second time in his life, Tommy had lost the will to live. He had just quit caring. After gaining almost a hundred pounds, he now weighed almost four hundred pounds and took Hydrocodone because he was in constant pain from gout. He called his pills "blue bombers" and ate them like candy.

Tommy would get drunk with his wife and whine about how crappy his life was and the troubles that Ricky and his family were causing. That's what they had been doing when the two of them cooked up the scheme to have Ricky arrested. It sounded good at the time; however, their plans went south as soon as the FBI got involved. Once Caroline told the sheriff that she suspected Ricky built bombs and he'd wired his house with explosives, things just escalated beyond their control.

To complicate matters, neither of them had suspected that Ricky's lawyer was smart enough to get ahold of Caroline's affidavit. As farfetched as it sounded, the story Tommy had told the judge about the private investigator had been partly true. At first, Tommy claimed that he didn't know about the affidavit, until Mr. Walsh sent him a copy at which time he changed his story, and it was all Caroline's idea. Apparently, Ricky just couldn't imagine that Caroline would do something like that without the full support of his father. Even Tommy had a hard time believing the story that he made up, but he wasn't about to come clean to anyone about what had really transpired.

However, Tommy never expected that his son wouldn't let him take care of the finances once Ricky turned thirty and control of his trust reverted to him. Ricky had assigned his sister power of attorney over his property and finances, and that had blindsided Tommy.

Tommy went to visit Ricky a few times in prison, but Ricky refused to see his father and had him removed from his visitors list. "I may not have much freedom in here," he told the prison guard who came to his cell to tell him he had a visitor. "But I do get to choose who I get visits from, and frankly, I really don't want to see that man." As he spoke, he sat on the bed in his eight-by-ten-foot cell, staring at a picture of his wife and kids that he'd taped to the wall.

On the other hand, Caroline was glad that Ricky was in jail. The truth was that she was afraid of Ricky, and now that Ricky and Vicky were out of the way, she had her husband and the ranch all to herself. Neither Caroline nor Tommy had expected the judge to throw the book at Ricky or for Tommy to take it so hard when Ricky went to prison.

⤞▬◉ ◉▬⤝

For the next five years, Ricky was incarcerated, and only he allowed a handful of people to visit. A few members of his father's inner circle tried to get Ricky to put them on the visitors list, but he wouldn't see them. He lived in a tiny cell for most of the day and worked in the prison laundry. It was an adjustment for Ricky to live in such a confined space, but he had to get used to it or at least accept it, and after a while, he found the minimalist mentality comforting. Ricky would spend time in the prison library. He was interested in sailing, and so he researched online how to get a captain's license. He spent hours lying in his bunk at night, dreaming of sailing the open seas.

Ricky was clean and sober for the first time since childhood. The prison infirmary dispensed his meds every day, and those were the only drugs he was taking. The prison guards controlled and regulated his time and his daily routine, and his movements were deliberate and monitored. Vicky sent money to his prison account to spend at the commissary, and he had lots of time to think.

Mostly he thought about what he would do when he got out. He planned to move his family to Florida and live by the water, and maybe buy a sailboat and live on it. However, as always, his dreams would go up in smoke with something as simple as a letter from his wife.

Not long after Ricky's sentencing, Kellie moved in with her mother in Baytown and enrolled in nursing school. Once she received her LVN license, Kellie got a job at one of the area hospitals and started making enough money to pay for childcare. Eventually, between taking care of her two sons and her new job, Kellie had less and less time to visit her husband.

It wasn't long before Ricky started getting anonymous letters from someone claiming his wife was having an affair while he was in prison. This news upset Ricky to no end. Vicky would tell her brother when he called her from the prison pay phone, "It's probably some crackpot. You can't let this upset you. You've only got a couple of years left on your sentence, so just ignore those people. If you don't, you won't ever find any peace."

One day during mail call, Ricky got a letter from his wife Kellie. As he eagerly opened it, Ricky hoped to find news about his family or pictures of his sons. Instead, his heart felt like she'd suddenly ripped out of his chest.

After receiving a "Dear John" letter from Kellie, Ricky fell limp on the end of his cot. Tears welled up in his eyes as he read the letter; he choked back the tears before anyone saw them. Kellie confessed that she'd that she couldn't take the stress anymore and that she'd filed for divorce to be with her new boyfriend.

He wiped the tears from his eyes and lay down on his bed. He crumpled up the letter and threw it across his cell, saying to his cellmate, "I guess my father finally got his way. My wife is divorcing me."

Ricky lay on his back, staring at the dingy ceiling. "I hope dad's happy," he said glumly.

Chapter 43

THE RAIN CAME down in sheets as Vicky sat in the parking lot of the Federal Detention Center north of Dallas. She had been sitting in the parking lot in the car she'd rented at the airport for almost an hour as they impatiently waited for her brother's release. "It's taking an awful long time," she said, as she stared out of the car window watching for the gate to swing open and her brother to walk through a free man.

It was October of 2012, and after five long years, Ricky had served the full term of his sentence as a guest at the Federal Correction Agency. Ricky was free. Since he served out the full sentence, Ricky wouldn't have to deal with parole officers. Once he walked out the gates and drove off, it would all be over.

The rain finally let up as he walked through the gate to freedom. Vicky saw her brother and gasped.

Ricky looked as though he were ten years older. He had gained twenty-five pounds, and his hairline had receded, with streaks of gray mixed with his light brown hair. As he got closer to the car, Vicky could see the deep creases in his face and the dark circles below his eyes that showed the years that he'd spent behind bars. Ricky wore prison-issue kakis and a plaid shirt that didn't fit. "It is good to have this nightmare behind us," Vicky said as she hugged her brother, noticing how much he had aged.

Ricky was carrying a box of stuff that he had collected as a guest there, mostly pictures of his children and books that he had read. Ricky realized during the first year of his sentence that the stuff he'd managed to collect in life didn't really matter as much as it once had when he was younger. He had lost so much. No one could ever put a value on the things that he had lost.

He couldn't wait to see his sons. Ricky had not seen his children since he'd first gone into prison. Kellie had stopped bringing them to visit him after a couple of visits, saying, "Prison is no place for children. I don't want my sons remembering their father in jail."

He'd lost five Christmases with his sons. He'd lost birthdays and school projects, report cards and Little League games. Now his kids were living with some guy he'd never met and calling him dad. Ricky was trying so hard not to be bitter; he was trying to be grateful that he could walk in the sun again without the shadow of the ever-present razor wire following him around the recreation field.

Vicky was now twenty-five years old. During her brother's stay as a guest of the federal government, she had graduated from college. "I'm working at a law firm in Richmond, Virginia as a paralegal. I love my job and I'm thinking of going to law school," she told her brother when he asked her how she was. "You wouldn't believe how little drama and stress I have in my life since I moved away from Texas." She laughed.

Taking some much-needed time off from work to help her brother get reacclimated to the outside world, Vicky had flown into Dallas the night before renting a car at the airport.

They didn't dawdle long in the parking lot of the prison. There would be plenty of time to celebrate, and the sooner they got that place behind them the better. Vicky apologized for not visiting her brother for a while. "I couldn't risk coming back to Texas because dad is still married to Caroline and neither one of them have changed," she explained. Ricky nodded as he got into the car.

Vicky turned on the engine and as she backed out of her parking spot. He turned to look at the prison that had been his home for the past few years. "I'm glad that I will never set foot in that place ever again," he commented as the pulled out of the parking lot and onto the muddy highway leading south to Dallas.

Stopping at a Whataburger on the edge of the first town they come to, they ordered food and Ricky went into the bathroom to change into the new clothes his sister had brought with her. Putting the prison clothes in the shopping bag that his new clothes were in, Ricky tossed them into the trash as soon he came out of the bathroom. The simple joy that Ricky felt in a new pair of Levis and tennis shoes was almost overwhelming.

His little sister fought back tears knowing that her brother's ordeal was finally over. They ordered some food and talked while they ate. "I have been dreaming of a Whataburger for years!" He smiled and gave Vicky a nudge the way he had when they were children.

"Let's not talk about that now," Vicky told him. "Let's just enjoy the day."

After eating, they got on the road again, heading south for Houston. Vicky had rented her brother a hotel room until they worked out the things that would make his life normal again. She'd scheduled a meeting with Ricky's attorney for the next day to transfer her brother's assets back over to him, and the paperwork was all ready for him to sign. "Normal life." Ricky had spent countless nights wondering if there would ever be such a thing again. Everything he had taken for granted before his time in prison seemed intimidating and overpowering but also insignificant.

The rest of the ride to Houston was quiet; most of the chatter came from Vicky, while Ricky watched out the window in the front seat. This was the first time in years he'd been in a car. Ricky had ridden in prison transports in leg irons and handcuffs any time the authorities transported him from one facility to another, and he counted only seven times that he'd left the confines of the prison.

The car ride got quieter still when they passed by the exit they would've taken to go the ranch. There was a big pink elephant in the car that no one wanted to talk about, but Ricky finally broke the silence and asked, "How is Dad doing?"

"I hear that our father is not doing well, but I can't bring myself to go see him." Vicky mood clouded over as she drove, glancing to the right at her brother. "People are telling me these things trying to make me feel guilty so I'll go see him. But it's not working. I couldn't care less."

"I bet Caroline is taking good care of him." Ricky smirked.

"I really don't care anymore. They deserve each other." Darkness came over the car as she turned and faced the front again.

"It's a miracle he can look himself in the eye in the mirror." Ricky laughed. It was obvious to everyone that he was starting to let his guard down and relax. The once joyous gleam in his eye had become a dull glare. His defiant posture was now sullen and demure. It would be a long time before he could truly be himself again.

"Time to change the subject! I called Kellie to let her know that you're being released," Vicky said, going back to her mindless chatter. "Remind me tomorrow that we need to get you a new cell phone."

"I have a lot to take care of—a new phone is the least of it." Ricky laughed a more normal laugh. He hadn't been allowed to have a cell phone in prison and was looking forward to talking on the phone without having his conversations monitored.

It was late evening when they arrived at the downtown Marriot. "I've already checked us in—you just need to rest and enjoy your first night out," Vicky said as they got out of the car.

They dropped the car off in front of the hotel with the valet. Vicky could see that her brother was finally starting to relax. She hugged him and said, "I'm glad this is all over with. There is no place for you to go from here but up."

⇥▦ ▦⇤

The first thing Ricky did when he got to his room was take a shower. This was the first time in five years that he had been able to take a shower alone. At last, all the tension seemed to wash away with every drop of hot water that rolled down the drain.

Suddenly, Ricky found himself crying. He stayed in the shower for what seemed like an hour, just feeling the clean, fresh hot water. He wanted to be clean again. He'd never seemed to feel clean the whole time he was in jail. That was probably the hardest thing to get used to in prison—bathing with other men. Being stripped of his basic right to privacy as he showered or sat on the toilet was degrading, and Ricky felt violated on so many levels, but there was no complaining, no whining or crying.

"The person who said 'What doesn't kill you makes you stronger' never used a prison bathroom," Ricky said to himself as he dried off, wiping the steam from the bathroom mirror.

He wanted to forget the past five years and just sleep.

He hadn't slept in a king-size bed or on anything but prison-issue sheets for years. It was weird at first, but once he got past the weirdness, the simple luxury of being in the hotel was both relaxing and enjoyable.

Ricky lay down and turned on the TV, remembering what his lawyer said. "It will take some time, but soon you'll be able to let your guard down." His attorney told him this when they were arranging his release.

Ricky was free, and he was safe there in that moment. It was finally sinking in that it was over. When he lay in bed on those clean sheets watching TV from his bed with a remote control, he could watch whatever he wanted to without getting a consensus from the others in the room or asking permission from the guards. Once again, the tears of joy and relief started to flow.

For five long years, Ricky had wanted to cry but couldn't. He had seen what had happened to the weak ones in prison. Even in federal prison, the stronger inmates chewed up the weaker ones like helpless baby animals on the Serengeti. He'd had to be tough or he wouldn't survive. And now he was finally free.

Ricky couldn't just pick up where he'd left off because he wasn't that person anymore, but at least he didn't have to start over from scratch. Vicky gave Ricky his ex-wife's phone number in Galveston, but Ricky wasn't ready to see his children yet. He wanted to get his life back in order first. He needed a place to live, and he needed to prove that he was responsible so she would let him be a part of their lives again. He'd always been glad to see his sons when they came to visit him in prison, but deep down he was worried that they would grow up ashamed of him.

After buying a used truck with cash, Ricky found a used sailboat advertised for sale on the Internet at the Kemah Yacht Club. In prison, Ricky had dreamed about buying a boat, and he decided to check it out.

It was a forty-two-foot sailboat for just a little more than what he had paid for his new truck. So, Ricky drove to Kemah and looked it over on a Wednesday afternoon, taking his friend, Red, with him. They'd met in AA before Ricky went to jail. Red had a captain's license, and knew about boats. Red was a gentle giant, an older man with bright red hair that was turning white. His deep-blue eyes were the same color as the sky, and he wore brown shorts, a T-shirt, and a neckless with a shark tooth on it around his neck.

They found the boat in the slip with a "For Sale" sign hanging on the side, and the two men stood on the dock for a couple of minutes before they boarded her. Ricky had only been out of jail for a couple of weeks; however, he needed a place to call his own, and he needed it right away.

"Buying a house seems too permanent for a man still adjusting to life on the outside," he told Red. The next day, Ricky went to the bank and got a cashier's check for the full amount, and then took it to the seller, who signed over the title and gave him the keys.

The cabin's living space was small, but his prison cell had been a lot smaller. Ricky immediately moved onto his sailboat and spent the night on the water with nothing but the stars over his head and the sound of the waves lapping on the sides of the boat.

Ricky slept soundly for the first time in years. The gentle rocking of the boat—his boat—on the water was soothing. In the morning, Ricky decided that he would call his ex-wife and ask to see his sons. There were three people he'd been avoiding since he got out: his mom, his dad, and his ex-wife.

Knowing that Ricky would need some support, Mr. Walsh had given him the number of an AA sponsor in the Clear Lake area, saying, "It might be time for you to reach out to him and get back into the program. Just take one day at a time."

Ricky took the number. He figured that if he was going to face his family, then he was going to need all the help he could get. He knew there wasn't any hope for his mom and dad, but maybe there was for his ex-wife. She could have gouged him in their divorce, but she didn't. Still, he was anxious to call her because he still loved her. He'd learned coping exercises in prison therapy, but he was still worried that even while on his medication he'd be pushed into a manic state of depression.

"I'll do it tomorrow," he said to himself as he sat on the deck of his new boat and stared at the stars in the night sky. "I just want one more night of peace."

⊷⊷≣◯ ◯≣⊶⊶

The next day, Ricky got up and made breakfast in his galley kitchen and ate it out on the deck. The morning was still and tranquil, and he could smell the salt in the humid air. The only sound he could hear was the clanging of a metal hook as it rhythmically swung against the mast as the boat slowly rocked in the boat slip. He piddled around as much as he could until lunchtime, when he finally decided he could no longer put it off. He dialed the number to his ex-wife and took a few deep breaths to calm himself before he hit send.

Kellie answered after three rings. "I heard you were out and was wondering when you were going to call," she admitted. "How have you been?"

"I'm good," Ricky stammered. "I'm living on a sailboat that I bought in Kemah."

"That's wonderful." She giggled, saying, "I was really hoping that you wouldn't move back to the ranch."

Ricky paused, then said, "I was hoping I could see the boys soon. Is that OK?"

"Of course it is," Kellie replied kindly. "Cody has a Little League game this evening in League City, and you're welcome to come."

"I would like that," Ricky said, trying hard not to sound nervous or overly excited. "But only if it isn't a problem. I don't want to cause any problems."

Ricky hung up; he exhaled and was relieved that he had gotten it over with. Taking a deep breath, he closed his eyes, feeling the warmth of the Texas sun on his face. He wondered what his sons look like now. Kellie had stopped sending pictures of them shortly after their divorce.

About eleven o'clock Red came over, and they filled up the boat with diesel and cruised around the marina and Clear Lake. Red was a salty old dog who was a Vietnam vet and had spent most of his life fishing the inland bays along the upper Texas Gulf Coast. He knew the waters of Clear Lake and Galveston Bay like the back of his hand and was able to teach Ricky how to rig his sails and read the channel markers.

Most of the stuff Red was teaching him Ricky had already read in the books in the prison library. Ricky was beyond excited to actually be doing it.

"Reading and doing are two completely different things," Red told him as he guided the sailboat out into the channel.

Ricky picked things up fast, and they sailed around the bay until about three thirty. When they returned to the slip, he barely had enough time to get cleaned up and on the road to make it in time for the game, and by the time he got there, it had already started. Ricky parked in the gravel lot at the Little League field and calmly walked over to the stands where the parents were sitting.

Ricky surveyed the stands, looking for Cody on the field and his ex-wife in the stands. Kellie saw Ricky before he saw her. She was sitting about four rows up with her oldest son, Justin, who was now a grown man, and their youngest son, Caleb.

It shocked Ricky how much Caleb had changed. He was even more shocked to see that Kellie was about six months pregnant. Kellie had stopped dyeing her hair blond and had let it go back to its natural color. She looked much more mature and respectable than the bleached-blond stripper he'd met at Benny's Cabaret all those years before. Even though, Ricky never regretted marrying Kellie, he'd also spent many long nights in his cell wondering how his life would have turned out if he'd never set foot in that place.

When he got there, Cody's team was at bat and Cody was on second base. Ricky watched the game for a minute before looking up into the stands. Cody was taller than Ricky had expected.

Kellie waved to Ricky, motioning him to come up into the stands and sit. As soon as Caleb saw his dad, he stood up and waved. Ricky slowly climbed up the bleachers. Caleb and Justin hugged him before he sat down. which Ricky hadn't expected. Secretly, he was surprised and relieved that they were happy to see him.

As Ricky sat down, the batter hit the ball into right field, Cody ran around third and, with everyone cheering, ran home. The game was in the third inning, and Cody's team was winning by four runs. At the end, Cody's team won by a score of seven-to-three, and Ricky beamed with pride as he watched his son's Little League game for the first time.

As soon as it was over, Ricky walked out on to the field and hugged Cody. It was a manlier, more standoffish hug than the one he'd gotten from Caleb, but it was a hug, and Ricky would take what he could get.

"That was a great game, Cody," he said as he patted him on the back. "I'm proud of you."

Before long, Kellie walked up with Cody's coach and introduced him as her new husband. He knew his ex-wife had remarried, but it was a hard pill to swallow seeing Kellie's new husband taking his place as a father figure.

A shudder went through him as he shook the man's hand. Feeling the signs of stress coming over him, Ricky made a hasty good-bye and left. He was shaking when he got to the parking lot, feeling like he was about to throw up.

He'd lost more than five years of his children's live because of his own stupidity. And for the first time since he'd gotten out, he wanted a drink really badly. His hands shook as he reached in his pocket and dialed the AA sponsor. "Hello, Casey, I'm Ricky. I really hope this is a good time to talk."

⇥⊟ ⊟⇤

The morning mist was hovering on top of the water when Red showed, expecting to find Ricky up and enthusiastic. Instead, he found Ricky still in bed. The morning was cool, the wind was still, and the only sound was the squawk of seagulls looking for breakfast as Red stepped off the dock onto the sailboat.

Ricky hadn't fallen asleep until the wee hours of the morning, as Casey, his new sponsor, had come over and they had talked for a long time. Clean and sober since jail, Ricky was still on his daily meds and determined to stay that way no matter what.

"I thought I was ready to see my ex-wife and kids again," he told Red as he rolled out of bed. "Life was easier on the inside. You knew who the bad guys were, and life was structured. Most of all, I was safe from the temptations of drugs and alcohol." He talked while Red made coffee in the galley.

"I guess I was holding on to the hope that I would be one of the lucky ones whose wife stayed with me while I served out my sentence." Ricky sighed, drinking from the coffee cup that Red handed him.

Red stirred his coffee after dumping sugar into his cup and said, "It takes a real man to face down his demons like you've done." They both walked out on to the deck to drink their coffee in the warm morning sun.

⇥⊟ ⊟⇤

The rest of the afternoon, he sat in his lawn chair on the deck of his sailboat thinking about all the times in prison he'd been angry with his wife for not bringing his children to visit him—now he knew why she didn't. He'd dreamed of seeing his children again, but now that was something else that had been robbed from him—his sons. Ricky was fight back what Red so aptly labeled his demons, but the old anger and bitterness welled up, and he knew the only hope he had was to call his new sponsor and get back into AA.

His father was another demon he needed to face down if he ever wanted to be whole. Sadly, Ricky's father was toxic, and he had to keep him at arm's length for his own sanity and protection until he was strong enough.

If only for a short time, Ricky wanted to go away.

Ricky couldn't get on a plane and go on vacation if he wanted to, and he really wanted nothing more than to just sit on a beach somewhere and watch the waves roll in. Ricky knew that ultimately, he couldn't blame anyone but himself for going to jail. He wasn't more than a dumb kid when he got tied up with Oscar De La Garza and his bunch of thugs. He'd accepted that he should have known better and that being young and stupid was no excuse. AA preached acceptance.

Changing the past was impossible; however, learning to forgive himself for the past was the key to happiness. Once Ricky's children got used to him being around, he'd work on making amends. But when Ricky saw his ex-wife pregnant and met her new husband, who was his son's Little League coach, it was hard to reconcile his feelings of regret. They were having the normal childhood—the kind of childhood he could never have given them, and it was a hard pill to swallow.

Lamentably, forgiving his dad was his biggest obstacle to making amends and moving on. Maybe something had happened to his dad when he was growing up that affected him. After all, being raised by an alcoholic mother couldn't have been easy. Seeing how things turned out in his own life certainly made him rethink his relationship with his dad. He'd acted like a jerk when his dad came out of the closet, even though, he'd never really admitted that he was HIV positive; it couldn't have been an easy for his dad.

But Ricky would probably never know and as long as his dad was married, he didn't know if forgiveness was possible. From the moment Caroline walked in the door, she'd alienated Ricky's and Victoria's relationships with their father; whether she did it intentionally, that was anyone's guess. Ricky had really worked with the prison psychiatrist to come to terms with his rough childhood and believed he was strong enough emotionally to take anything. For now, a vacation and a change of scenery was just what the doctor ordered.

→═ ═←

The next day Red came over to cheer his friend up. "I was married to the same woman for forty years when we divorced." Red laughed at Ricky. "In my experience, the best cure for any kind of woman trouble is to go fishing."

Ricky poured coffee down his throat, and Red cast the boat off and headed out of the marina. They left Clear Lake and Galveston Bay behind and headed south down the intercostal waterway to Matagorda Bay and Red's favorite fishing hole. Red and Ricky fished all afternoon; they caught plenty, keeping enough for supper and letting the rest of them go. It was almost dark when the two fishermen made their way back up the intercostal waterway toward Galveston Bay. It was then that Red opened up to Ricky.

"The biggest regret I had was killing people in Vietnam," he told Ricky as they made their way north. "I did it because I was a soldier and it was my duty to defend and protect our country, but it's taken me most of my life to come to terms with killing people. I drank heavily after I came home, but I came a point in my life where I just had to let it go."

The sun was setting, and the high wispy clouds glowed red, orange, and purple as they navigated across the choppy waterway. "And I figure that it's time now for you just to let it go." Red and Ricky quietly stared at the magical sunset as though the final rays bouncing off the billowing clouds had a special healing power that only the both of them could understand.

The twilight had turned to dusk, and Red turned on their running lights as they entered the channel to the Kemah Yacht Club.

"I know I have to let it go if I ever want to be happy again. That's why I bought this sailboat. I needed to get away for a little while until I can figure things out," Ricky said after a long silence. "My kids are probably better off without me around. I'd like to think that they love me and I love them, but they are better off with a dad who's a Little League coach with a steady job."

Ricky watched the reflection of the running lights on the water. "How long will it be before this boat's ready to go at it alone?" Ricky asked Red as they pulled up to his boat slip.

"I think you are ready to go now," Red answered as he lit a cigarette.

Chapter 44

As HE OPENED the back door to their house in the Houston Heights neighborhood, the strong fragrance of the roses wafted through air. Tommy had never been a fan of roses until Caroline talked him into planting a rose garden in the backyard of the restored craftsman bungalow. Now that Tommy was spending a lot of time at the doctor's office, they were spending much more time in Houston than he wanted.

After carefully limping down the steps, Tommy hobbled to his favorite chair using a cane that had once belonged to the Colonel. He sat down heavily, putting his foot up on a nearby stool. "Caroline, would you bring my book out to me?" he yelled over his shoulder.

Tommy's gout was acting up again, and his left foot was swollen so badly that he could barely walk. After breakfast, he'd taken a couple of pain pills and decided to sit outside in the crisp morning air until they started working. It was about 10:00 a.m. on a cool November day. Winter had not yet set in, and so the cool morning would probably warm up to a seasonably nice afternoon.

Caroline was in the kitchen washing dishes after cooking her husband's breakfast, and she heard him yell through the open window over the sink. She didn't like the way he yelled at her sometimes. Be that as it may, she swallowed back her retort because she knew he was in constant pain and sometimes forgot his manners.

Tommy had heard rumors that his son had recently been released from prison, and he half expected, half hoped that Ricky would come to see him. Nonetheless, he hadn't heard from his son. Both of his children were so ungrateful; Tommy would never have treated the Colonel the way his children were treating him. Of course, he'd treated his mother badly, but she was a drunk and deserved it.

"I've been the best father I could be under the circumstance." Tommy complained to Caroline, trying to hide his feelings of regret. He'd always conveniently blamed all the problems he was having with his children on his ex-wives. Tommy's children had cut him out of their lives shortly after Ricky went to prison, and now he truly missed them. "They're overreacting and refusing to give me a chance to explain what happened."

After his children found out about Caroline's affidavit with the FBI, they had naturally assumed he'd masterminded the whole thing. Even though he and Caroline had come up with the plan together, their intentions had been good. Tommy had been just as surprised as everyone that the feds and the judge threw the book at Ricky. He and Caroline were really only trying to protect Ricky from his cheating wife and his drug and alcohol problems. After all, no one really understood what Tommy went through when his mother passed away and the Colonel had to give half of what was supposed to be his birthright to his half sister and her family.

"Greed is an ugly thing," he'd told his newest wife when they were cooking up their harebrained scheme over scotch. "I don't want Ricky to have to fight for his inheritance the way I had to." Yes, their intentions had been good, but the whole thing had gone terribly, terribly wrong.

Tommy had been suspicious of Kellie from the start and was incensed after he found out she'd moved in with Ricky, saying, "It's better to rent a stripper; you don't have to buy one."

He had always insisted that Kellie was a Pandora's box who would bring nothing but woes to their family, and so Tommy had felt righteously justified when Kellie divorced Ricky in jail, as he'd always blamed Kellie for getting his son into trouble in the first place.

"Ricky was young and sowing his wild oats. Admittedly, he was getting into trouble with the law, but it never was that serious until he met Kellie," he'd explained to Caroline. "The only reason he got involved with that thug from the Mexican Mafia in the first place was to impress that tart," he said in a misogynistic way.

"Ricky wasn't strung out on drugs until they got married, either," he'd ranted.

Tommy didn't believe for a moment that his son's drug abuse was because he was trying to numb himself, much less that his son was bipolar. "Ricky's mother still claims he's bipolar and that he wasn't that bad when he lived with her. But she medicated him needlessly with prescription drugs meant to control his behavior. He's not crazy! She's the crazy one."

Caroline had let her husband rant. She'd heard this story so many times that she could almost recite it by heart. She was tired of Tommy obsessing about his son. The two of them had spent more time than she wanted discussing Ricky and Kellie, and it was starting to get on her nerves. Her husband would never admit that his son had mental health problems. But Caroline believed Ricky was bipolar with all her heart, and she was scared of him, especially now that he was out of prison. Caroline really didn't want him around in case he hadn't been rehabilitated.

When Tommy heard that his son was out of jail, he was relieved and hopeful that the nightmare for Ricky was finally over. Tommy wanted to reach out to Ricky and try to explain why he did what he did, but he didn't know how to even start. He'd written him letters in prison only to have them sent back unopened. Tommy wanted to start over with his son. He'd even reaching out to Ricky's attorney, Mr. Walsh, asking him to let Ricky know that he wanted to work things out. It broke his heart that his son had been out of prison for almost a month, and Tommy hadn't heard so much as a word out of him.

He was getting old, and the years of abusing drugs and alcohol had taken its toll on his health. He'd lived longer than anyone ever expected, but now that he was old, his quality of life was pretty dismal. The once attractive and charismatic man was in pain and wore his pain all over his face. He was jaundiced and gaunt.

Tommy's liver was enlarged and protruded from the side of his abdominal in a noticeable way. He was covered with bruises and was fatigued and in pain all the time. His urine was dark and had a strong odor. He spent an awful lot of time in the bathroom because his stool was loose and he was flatulent, sometimes soiling himself when he passed gas.

Tommy took pill after pill after pill every day. He had pills to control his HIV and pills to boost the liver enzymes that his own liver was no longer making. But most of all, he took pills to manage the pain. Tommy's gout was so bad that his ankles, hands, and feet swelled, and there were days he could hardly walk. He mostly used a cane to help him get around, using a wheelchair only if he needed to go long distances.

Now that Tommy's health was at issue, he depended on his wife more and more to care for him. At first Caroline took care of him by herself, but lately she had a nurse named Lucy coming in to help her during the day. She tried to elicit sympathy from Lucy any chance she could, but even the nurse was suspicious of her sincerity.

Like the Colonel when he was older, Tommy had a parade of friends who came in and out to visit. In spite of the years they'd spent together, Caroline felt completely alone. Tommy's friends tolerated his wife, but Caroline had become a pariah after Ricky went to prison.

It took a while for people to find out the reason Ricky got sent to prison. Deflecting the rumors, Tommy defended and protected his wife as best he could, but slowly the truth came out about how Ricky's sentence was unjustly harsh. Caroline could tell by the looks people gave her that everyone blamed her. Even though Tommy had had a hand in the debacle, he wasn't going to admit that he'd been the one who instigated the plan to put his son in prison for his own good. It was easier for him to blame Caroline when their plan blew up in their faces.

Although she resented her husband, Caroline stuck it out. Fortunately, the end was near. She had stuck it out for eight long years, and once her husband was dead, she could tell all the small-minded people who had judged her to shove it up their asses. After all, she still loved her husband, even though nothing had worked out like she'd imagined.

However, Caroline had underestimated how difficult it was to take care of a sick husband. She was frazzled. She was in her late sixties, and it was getting harder and harder to attend to Tommy's needs.

Needless to say, Caroline didn't share her husband's joy and enthusiasm when she found out that Ricky was out of prison. "I wouldn't get my hopes up that Ricky will come see you now that he's out of jail," Caroline told her husband when she brought out his book to the garden. She sat down in the chair next to him on the brick patio surrounded by rosebushes.

"Ricky has been through a lot, but he probably should blames us. We tried to help him the best we could." Caroline's hair was rumpled, and she was wearing a robe. The stress of the years showed on her face; dark circles hung below her eyes, and the sparkle had long left them. She poured her ailing husband a glass of orange juice and set it down on the table next to him along with his pills.

"I know you've never liked Ricky and you don't trust him with good reason. But I want nothing more than to see both of my children one more time before I die."

Caroline could see the heartache in his eyes, and she reached over and squeezed his hand.

"You'll see him again. You just have to be patient and give him time." She smiled gently.

Tommy read his book while the sunshine filtered through the branches of the neighbors' oak tree. After a few minutes, he lowered his book and said, "I reached out to Ricky's lawyer." Caroline froze turning to her husband with a shocked look. "I asked him if he would ask Ricky to come by to see me." Looking at his wife, Tommy half expected her to protest.

"Whatever you want, dear. I just hope that he calls before he comes." Caroline swallowed hard, forcing the words out.

Just then, Lucy came out through the back door. Caroline stood up, talked to Lucy briefly, and excused herself to shower and dress. She calmly went to her room and shut the door behind her. Caroline had long moved into her own room, claiming that she wanted Tommy to get the best rest he could. In reality, she couldn't sleep beside him anymore. Tommy smelled sick, and she couldn't sleep because of the sickly odor of his illness.

As soon as she closed the door behind her, Caroline began to shake. She was panicked.

Ricky coming here?

Just the thought of Ricky knowing where they lived terrified her. After she showered and dressed, Caroline found her husband asleep in his chair, with his book in his lap open to the page he'd been reading. She kissed him on the forehead and went back inside, where Lucy was sitting on the couch watching a game show. She said casually, "I have to go out and run some errands. I won't be gone long."

Caroline left and drove straight to a pawn shop she'd found online on her smartphone and bought a gun. As she filled out the paperwork, the store owner asked her if she knew how to use it. "No, could you show me?" she replied.

He showed her a few things about the gun and gave her a brochure for a gun range where she could go to get an open-carry license. As they headed to the register, he asked Caroline, "Why are you buying a gun today?"

"I'm buying it for protection," she said as she handed him her credit card.

Chapter 45

ON THE WAY home from a doctor's appointment, Tommy sat quietly in the front seat of their Cadillac SUV, gazing out of the window. Caroline glanced over at her husband, as she turned on her blinker for the exit off Interstate 10 onto Yale street. She'd given up on small talk since her husband was in a particularly gloomy mood.

When they arrived hone, Caroline parked in the driveway, and helped her husband out of the car, holding his arm, they climbed the front porch stairs, and went into the house. It was the first week of December, and Caroline knew that her husband's bad mood hadn't been caused by anything his doctor had said. On the contrary, Dr. Willis had told him that he was doing fairly well for a man with a bum liver. Tommy had been going to Dr. Willis, ever since Dr. Barrett died from pancreatic cancer a few years earlier.

Finally, he'd quite drinking. The Christmas season was coming, and Tommy was once again dreading it. Christmas had once been his favorite time of the year, but now it only depressed him. Neither of his children called or came to visit during the holidays. Ricky had had an excuse because he'd been incarcerated. However, Vicky did not. His daughter had willfully chosen to turn her back on her father.

Sadly, the only communication Tommy had these days with his daughter went through Ricky's attorney regarding his finances. He'd tried to dangle money and financial support out like a carrot, to lure his children back into the fold, but it hadn't worked. In fact, it backfired on him. His daughter only found it appalling. "Money isn't everything," she'd say in response to her father's efforts. "Money is supposed to make life easier. It's not supposed to be a weapon used to hurt someone, or a tool to control people."

⋯⊨⊙ ⊙⊨⋯

Once inside the house, Caroline set her purse down on the coffee table next to the couch, and helped her husband into his recliner, kissing Tommy on the forehead. "Would you like a glass of water, or maybe iced tea?" she asked him, walking toward the kitchen.

"Iced tea would be nice," he replied, looking up, and smiling.

"Thank goodness he is starting to relax," she muttered to Lucy who was in the kitchen cooking dinner, closing the kitchen door behind her. "The closer we get to Christmas, the grouchier he gets."

After asking Lucy to get the iced tea for her husband, she opened a drawer next to the back door, pulling out a pair of gardening shears and her gloves, she went outside. The day was cooling off rapidly, and some of her rosebushes were still blooming. She wanted to pick the last of her roses for an arrangement for the dinner table before the first winter frost nipped the bushes back into dormancy.

When she came back inside, Lucy commented on how pretty the flowers were as Caroline laid them on the counter, and searched for a vase. The fragrance of the roses filed the air, mingling with the savory smells of the meatloaf baking in the oven. She was putting the finishing touches on the salad, chopping carrots and tomatoes, as Caroline finished putting the flowers into the vase.

Tommy appetite wasn't as hardy as it once was, but his wife still made every effort to make each, and every dinner into a special event. Helping to set the table before leaving for the evening, Lucy cleaned up the pots and pans. "I'll see you in the morning. Call me if you need anything," She said as she left through the back door.

"Don't worry about us; we'll be fine," Caroline replied as she opened a bottle of wine, and poured herself a glass before sitting down at the table. The two ate quietly, only a bit of small talk broke the silence.

"I don't think the heater has cut off even once today," Tommy said as Caroline filled her wine glass again. Caroline was drinking a lot lately—or that was what Tommy thought. Actually, she wasn't drinking any more than she usually did; he simply noticed her habits more now that he was clean and sober. He wanted to say something to her, but kept his comments to himself, remembering how biting his daughter's remarks about his drinking.

No sense in starting a war tonight.

In due time, they finished dinner, and Tommy went to the bathroom. Caroline was clearing the table, and washing dishes when she heard a knock on the door. Without thinking, she answered it to find Ricky at the threshold holding a bottle of wine in a brown paper bag. At first, Caroline was stunned, and caught off guard by her stepson's visit.

"What are you doing here? I'd heard that you'd sailed away into the sunset," she said coldly. Caroline was obviously uncomfortable, "It would have been nice if you'd given us a little bit of a warning that you were coming over."

"Hello to you, too." Ricky replied, smugly glancing over her shoulder to see if his father was around. "Why would I give you a warning? So you could make up some lame excuse that would keep me away?"

Caroline stiffened. "I see that prison has done nothing about your attitude," she declared looking over her shoulder to see if Tommy was still in the bathroom, making sure he hadn't heard what she'd just said.

Luckily, he hadn't come out yet. Caroline decided to try to get rid of her ex-con stepson before her husband found out he was there, and invited him into their home for the evening. She turned back to Ricky, softening her voice, she asked, "Why are you here?"

"I came to see to my dad. Is he here?" Ricky asked smugly.

As Ricky leaned against the open door, she found herself becoming noticeably anxious. Her eyes darted around the room, looking for her purse where she kept the handgun that she'd just purchased. It sat on the coffee table just a few feet away. Caroline had not yet gotten her concealed handgun license, but she kept it in her purse anyway. Knowing her purse was just a few feet away suddenly gave her a burst of courage.

"Your father isn't well, and I was about to put him to bed. Come back tomorrow." Caroline tried to shut the door, but Ricky had put his foot against it.

"I'm leaving for a vacation and I don't know how long I'll be gone. I want to say good-bye to my dad before I leave. I hear he isn't doing well." Ricky glared at his father's wife. "After I'm gone, he'll be all yours and you can do whatever you want. But I'm not leaving until I see my dad."

Ricky had been going through his twelve steps at AA, and with the encouragement and support of his sponsor, he wanted to put this chapter of his life to rest and move on. He didn't feel compelled to explain anything to the woman who had helped send him to prison.

"I brought dad a bottle of wine as a going-away present," he said, holding up the wine bottle.

"You're an ass," she said as Ricky pushed past her. "You know good and well your father can't drink anymore."

"Yeah, I hear that he doesn't drink anymore, but I see that you still drink," he said, pointing to the half-empty wine glass she was holding.

Realizing that Ricky wasn't leaving until he saw his father, Caroline closed the front door. "Your father is in the bathroom; he may be in there awhile," she said as she walked over to the dining room table, and filled her wine glass again. "I'd appreciate it if you didn't stay too long. I'm about to put him to bed, and I don't want you to cause any problems."

From the dining room, she could keep an eye on Ricky while she watched the bathroom door for her husband to emerge. She still hoped that she could get rid of Ricky before her husband realized he was there.

"What about you? Are you still sober?" she asked snidely, hoping that if she poked at his weak spot he'd leave sooner. "It must have been difficult walking into a liquor store to buy that bottle of wine without wanting some booze for yourself. I bet your children are proud of their jailbird father. Have you seen them since you got out?" Walking back into the living room, she set her wine glass down on a coaster on the coffee table. She looked at Ricky, who was glaring spitefully at her.

"You leave my children out of this, you psycho," he growled intensely, finding himself getting angry. "Your lies took five years of my life, and five years of my children's lives were taken away from me because of you." It had taken every ounce of strength he had to come to his father's house, and he didn't want to give her the satisfaction of leaving without seeing his father.

Caroline smiled a wicked smile. She could see that her words had hit their mark. "Your children are certainly a lot better off without you for a father!" she taunted, thinking that maybe if she continued to goad him he'd leave.

Ricky couldn't take anymore. Instinctively, he stomped over to Caroline and grabbed her by the arm. He got in her face menacingly and said, "You're a gold digger who weaseled her way into my dad's life. My life was just fine before you came along. I had a wife and kids who loved me. Dad really didn't like my wife, but he didn't start acting like jerk toward me and my family until you came along, and started spewing your venom in his ear."

Abruptly, Ricky pushed her away. Caroline stumbled back, knocking her wine glass off the coffee table which shattered onto the floor. Suddenly, she was terrified, grabbing her purse as she gained her footing, and immediately, pulled out her gun.

She whirled around. Hands shaking, Caroline pointed the gun at Ricky. "I didn't ruin your life. You ruined your own life!" she shouted. "You're a junky and a thug who was on probation for kiddie porn, and running guns for the Mexican Mafia!" Ricky stopped in his track and stood stiff with his hands in the air, not saying a word. "If it hadn't been for your father, you'd have gone to prison a long time ago," Caroline screamed.

"What the hell is going on?"

Caroline nearly jumped out of her skin as all at once she saw Tommy upon her, grabbing for the gun in her trembling hands.

Tommy had heard the commotion between his wife and son as it rapidly escalated. As he came out of the bathroom, he witnessed his wife pointing a gun at Ricky. Impulsively, he ran as fast as he could in his condition and, without thinking, lunged at his wife to disarm her.

Seeing his chance to escape, Ricky whirled around and ran outside. As he reached the front porch, Ricky stopped in his tracks as a gunshot rang out.

"Holy crap!" Ricky yelled, not knowing whether to go back inside in case someone was hurt or to just get in his truck and drive away.

All at once, Ricky became aware that his brown T-shirt was dripping with sweat. He took his baseball cap off to wipe the sweat from his forehead. Suddenly, Ricky realized that he'd set the bottle of wine down onto the coffee table when he went inside. His fingerprints were all over that wine bottle, and if, God forbid, someone had gotten shot, he'd be the first one the police would look for.

It was eerily silent. Taking a deep breath, Ricky decided to go back inside. He pulled his phone out of the pocket of his blue jeans and called 911.

"This is 911. What's your emergency?" Ricky heard the operator say.

"My stepmother pulled a gun on me, and my dad tried to take it away from her. I ran outside. I don't know if anyone got hurt, but maybe you should send an ambulance." Ricky shook uncontrollably as he talked.

"Stay on the line, sir. I'm sending an ambulance and a patrol car. They'll be there momentarily."

Ricky gave the operator the address and slowly opened the door, hoping that his father had disarmed his crazy wife and everything was all right—he'd say his good-byes and be on his way.

Instead, Ricky saw both his father and Caroline lying on the floor. "What the hell?" he said as he saw his father in a puddle of blood. Walking over to his father, he realized Tommy was still alive.

"Caroline must have hit her head on the coffee table," Tommy said as Ricky kneeled down beside him. Ricky looked over and saw that Caroline was on the floor between the coffee table and the couch. She was bleeding as a result of falling on the wine glass she'd knocked over earlier.

Ricky was still on the phone with the 911 operator, trying his best to describe what had happened, when he realized that his father had been shot in the chest. "Send an ambulance! My father's been shot!" he yelled frantically over the phone.

Ricky laid his phone on the table, saying to his father, "It's all right. The ambulance is coming."

Tommy was in distress. His breathing was labored. He looked up at his son, seeing him for the first time since that day in the courtroom. "I'm so sorry I wasn't a better parent to you and Vicky."

Ricky had tears in his eyes as he shushed his father. "Save your strength." His voice cracked as he spoke. "The ambulance will be here soon."

"I don't think it will be here in time to save me. I'm so sorry. I haven't been a good father." Tommy struggled to speak and coughed as he took a breath. "I was so wrapped up in my own life and the money.... My life just didn't happen the way it was supposed to, and I took it out on you and Vicky... I'm for all the terrible things that I've caused you and everyone."

A grayish pawl was coming over his yellow face. "I probably never would have gotten married it your mother hadn't gotten pregnant."

Tommy tried to take a breath but it was agonizing; he just couldn't. He closed his eyes for a moment and continued. "The day you were born was the best day of my life. But it was too easy to let the drugs and alcohol take over my life. I used your mother as an excuse for my bad behavior. I used your mother as an excuse to cheat on her."

Tommy groaned as he tried to get comfortable. "When your mother took you to Canada, I found out I had HIV... I gave up all hope... I was so scared... I felt like I'd lost everything... I should have been there for you, but I just couldn't... I should have been stronger, but I just couldn't."

"You made some mistakes, but I know that your intentions were good." Ricky held his father's hand as he talked, and realized how cold his hand was. "You never did anything out of malice or meant anyone any harm."

Tommy was in pain, and blood bubbled in his mouth as he spoke. "No, you're wrong. I poisoned my mother. I killed her because she burned the house down when she was drunk. I hated my mother... She was a drunk who let me get molested by one of the neighbors when I was a boy... I wanted her dead."

Ricky was stunned and sat silently as his father whispered. "She was taking Antabuse to stop drinking. She used to play cards at Mrs. Harper's house every Tuesday afternoon, and one day when she was at her card game, I snuck into the guesthouse and put rat poison in her Antabuse."

Ricky recoiled as his father confessed. In the distance, he heard the sound of sirens, and beside the couch he heard Caroline starting to stir. Ricky hadn't even thought to check on Caroline and at that moment couldn't care less if she was hurt.

Tommy took one last breath and said, "God, forgive me my sins." With that, Tommy's life slipped away.

Tommy Ellison was gone. He'd confessed to his son as if he'd be cleansed of all the burdens he'd carried all his life. The pain he saw in his father's eyes wasn't just from his wounds from the gunshot, but from the path he'd taken in life, the sins of his youth and the unforeseen consequences of his choices made throughout his life.

Most of all, the man who'd desperately wanted to be loved as a boy, who'd struggled his whole life to come to terms with his own sexuality and the sexual abuse of his childhood, died without loving himself.

As if he were in a bad dream, Ricky stood up, walked out onto the front porch, and sat down on the front steps. Nothing seemed real at that moment.

The ambulance and police arrived within minutes of the 911 call Ricky had made, but they didn't get there in time. Ricky sat on the stoop just watching as people scurried in and out, as if he were in a trance. He watched as the ambulance attendant carried Caroline out of the house on a stretcher, and was jarred out of his daze as a Houston police officer put his hand on Ricky's shoulder

"Is this your cell phone?" He was holding the phone that Ricky had left on the table. Apparently, Ricky had not hung up with the 911 operator. "Sir, do you mind answering a few questions?"

Ricky looked up at the officer saying, "No. I'll tell you anything you want to know."

Spending over six hours being questioned by police before he was released into the custody of his attorney, he was elated when they finally let him go home. "That's the quickest I've ever been able to get out of a police station in my whole life," he joked to Mr. Walsh when they got outside. "I was beginning to think that Caroline was going to set me up again."

"Well, Caroline's hands tested positive for gunshot residue and yours didn't. I'm sure she would have if she could have."

He put his hand on Ricky's shoulder as they walked outside. "Even a blind hog finds an acorn every once in a while." His attorney reminded him as the two men walked toward the parking garage and the rest of his life.

"Come on, let me give you a ride." Mr. Walsh asked.

Ricky looked around and sighed in the early morning air. It was after 3:00 a.m. when they'd finally let him go, but he didn't care.

"Well, I hope this is the last time I'll ever meet you at the police station!" Mr. Walsh laughed as he pulled his keys out of his pants pocket. "Have you decided what you're going to do with the rest of your life?" the lawyer asked as he opened his car door.

"I really don't know," Ricky answered thoughtfully as he stood outside his attorney's car. "But one thing I learned when Red was showing me how to sail was that you can't control the wind; you can only control the direction the wind takes you."

The End